The Critics Love

JOHN GRISHAM

"With every new book I appreciate John Grisham a little more, for his feisty critiques of the legal system, his compassion for the underdog, and his willingness to strike out in new directions."
—*Entertainment Weekly*

"John Grisham is exceptionally good at what he does. . . . Grisham's books are also smart, imaginative, and funny, populated by complex, interesting people, written by a man who is driven not merely by the desire to entertain but also by genuine (if under-stated) outrages at human cupidity and venality."
—*The Washington Post*

"John Grisham is about as good a storyteller as we've got in the United States these days." —*The New York Times Book Review*

"John Grisham owns the legal thriller." —*The Denver Post*

"John Grisham is not just popular, he is one of the most popular novelists of our time. He is a craftsman and he writes good stories, engaging characters, and clever plots." —*The Seattle Times*

"A mighty narrative talent and an unerring eye for hot-button issues." —*Chicago Sun-Times*

"A legal literary legend." —*USA Today*

BY JOHN GRISHAM

ROGUE LAWYER

A NOVEL

JOHN GRISHAM

BANTAM BOOKS
NEW YORK

2016 Bantam Books Trade Paperback Edition

Copyright © 2015 by Belfry Holdings, Inc.
Reading group guide copyright © 2016 by Penguin Random House LLC

Published in the United States by Bantam Books, an imprint of Random House, a division of Penguin Random House LLC, New York.

BANTAM BOOKS and the HOUSE colophon are registered trademarks of Penguin Random House LLC.

Originally published in hardcover in the United States by Doubleday, a division of Penguin Random House LLC, in 2015.

ISBN 978-1-101-96766-9
ebook ISBN 978-0-385-53944-9

randomhousebooks.com

2 4 6 8 9 7 5 3 1

Book design by Maria Carella

ROGUE
LAWYER

PART ONE

CONTEMPT

1.

My name is Sebastian Rudd, and though I am a well-known street lawyer, you will not see my name on billboards, on bus benches, or screaming at you from the yellow pages. I don't pay to be seen on television, though I am often there. My name is not listed in any phone book. I do not maintain a traditional office. I carry a gun, legally, because my name and face tend to attract attention from the type of people who also carry guns and don't mind using them. I live alone, usually sleep alone, and do not possess the patience and understanding necessary to maintain friendships. The law is my life, always consuming and occasionally fulfilling. I wouldn't call it a "jealous mistress" as some forgotten person once so famously did. It's more like an overbearing wife who controls the checkbook. There's no way out.

These nights I find myself sleeping in cheap motel rooms that change each week. I'm not trying to save money; rather, I'm just trying to stay alive. There are plenty of people who'd like to kill me right now, and a few of them have been quite vocal. They don't tell you in law school that one day you may find yourself defending a person charged with a crime so heinous that otherwise peaceful citizens feel driven to take up arms and threaten to kill the accused, his lawyer, and even the judge.

But I've been threatened before. It's part of being a rogue lawyer, a subspecialty of the profession that I more or less fell into ten years ago. When I finished law school, jobs were scarce. I reluctantly took a part-time position in the City's public defend-

er's office. From there I landed in a small, unprofitable firm that
handled only criminal defense. After a few years, that firm blew
up and I was on my own, out on the street with plenty of others,
scrambling to make a buck.

One case put me on the map. I can't say it made me famous
because, seriously, how can you say a lawyer is famous in a city of
a million people? Plenty of local hacks think they're famous. They
smile from billboards as they beg for your bankruptcy and swagger in television ads as they seem deeply concerned about your
personal injuries, but they're forced to pay for their own publicity.
Not me.

The cheap motels change each week. I'm in the middle of a
trial in a dismal, backwater, redneck town called Milo, two hours
from where I live in the City. I am defending a brain-damaged
eighteen-year-old dropout who's charged with killing two little
girls in one of the most evil crimes I've ever seen, and I've seen
plenty. My clients are almost always guilty, so I don't waste a lot
of time wringing my hands about whether they get what they
deserve. In this case, though, Gardy is not guilty, not that it matters. It does not. What's important in Milo these days is that Gardy
gets convicted and sentenced to death and executed as soon as
possible so that the town can feel better about itself and move on.
Move on to where, exactly? Hell if I know, nor do I care. This
place has been moving backward for fifty years, and one lousy verdict will not change its course. I've read and heard it said that Milo
needs "closure," whatever that means. You'd have to be an idiot
to believe this town will somehow grow and prosper and become
more tolerant as soon as Gardy gets the needle.

My job is layered and complicated, and at the same time it's
quite simple. I'm being paid by the State to provide a first-class
defense to a defendant charged with capital murder, and this
requires me to fight and claw and raise hell in a courtroom where

no one is listening. Gardy was essentially convicted the day he was arrested, and his trial is only a formality. The dumb and desperate cops trumped up the charges and fabricated the evidence. The prosecutor knows this but has no spine and is up for reelection next year. The judge is asleep. The jurors are basically nice, simple people, wide-eyed at the process and ever so anxious to believe the lies their proud authorities are producing on the witness stand.

Milo has its share of cheap motels but I can't stay there. I would be lynched or flayed or burned at the stake, or if I'm lucky a sniper would hit me between the eyes and it would be over in a flash. The state police are providing protection during the trial, but I get the clear impression these guys are just not into it. They view me the same way most people do. I'm a long-haired roguish zealot sick enough to fight for the rights of child killers and the like.

My current motel is a Hampton Inn located twenty-five minutes from Milo. It costs $60 a night and the State will reimburse me. Next door is Partner, a hulking, heavily armed guy who wears black suits and takes me everywhere. Partner is my driver, bodyguard, confidant, paralegal, caddie, and only friend. I earned his loyalty when a jury found him not guilty of killing an undercover narcotics officer. We walked out of the courtroom arm in arm and have been inseparable ever since. On at least two occasions, off-duty cops have tried to kill him. On one occasion, they came after me.

We're still standing. Or perhaps I should say we're still ducking.

2.

At 8:00 a.m. Partner knocks on my door. It's time to go. We say our good mornings and climb into my vehicle, which is a large black Ford cargo van, heavily customized for my needs. Since it doubles as an office, the rear seats have been rearranged around a small table that folds into a wall. There is a sofa where I often spend the night. All windows are shaded and bulletproof. It has a television, stereo system, Internet, refrigerator, bar, a couple of guns, and a change of clothes. I sit in the front with Partner and we unwrap fast-food sausage biscuits as we leave the parking lot. An unmarked state police car moves in front of us for the escort to Milo. There is another one behind us. The last death threat was two days ago and came by e-mail.

Partner does not speak unless spoken to. I didn't make this rule but I adore it. He is not the least bit bothered by long gaps in the conversation, nor am I. After years of saying next to nothing, we have learned to communicate with nods and winks and silence. Halfway to Milo I open a file and start taking notes.

The double murder was so gruesome no local lawyer would touch it. Then Gardy was arrested, and one look at Gardy and you know he's guilty. Long hair dyed jet-black, an astonishing collection of piercings above the neck and tattoos below, matching steel earrings, cold pale eyes, and a smirk that says, "Okay, I did it, now what?" In its very first story, the Milo newspaper described him as "a member of a satanic cult who has a record of molesting children."

How's that for honest and unbiased reporting? He was never a member of a satanic cult and the child molestation thing is not what it seems. But from that moment Gardy was guilty, and I still marvel at the fact that we've made it this far. They wanted to string him up months ago.

Needless to say, every lawyer in Milo locked his door and unplugged her phone. There is no public defender system in the town—it's too small—and the indigent cases are doled out by the judge. There is an unwritten rule that the younger lawyers in town take these low-paying cases because (1) someone has to and

(2) the older lawyers did so when they were younger. But no one would agree to defend Gardy, and, to be honest, I can't really blame them. It's their town and their lives, and to rub shoulders with such a twisted murderer could do real damage to a career.

As a society, we adhere to the belief in a fair trial for a person accused of a serious crime, but some of us struggle when it comes to the business of providing a competent lawyer to guarantee said fair trial. Lawyers like me live with the question "But how do you represent such scum?"

I offer a quick "Someone has to" as I walk away.

Do we really want fair trials? No, we do not. We want justice, and quickly. And justice is whatever we deem it to be on a case-by-case basis.

It's just as well that we don't believe in fair trials because we damned sure don't have them. The presumption of innocence is now the presumption of guilt. The burden of proof is a travesty because the proof is often lies. Guilt beyond a reasonable doubt means if he probably did it, then let's get him off the streets.

At any rate, the lawyers ran for the hills and Gardy had no one. It's a commentary, sad or otherwise, on my reputation that I soon got the phone call. In this end of the state, it is now well known in legal circles that if you can't find anybody else, call Sebastian Rudd. He'll defend anybody!

When Gardy was arrested, a mob showed up outside the jail and screamed for justice. When the police perp-walked him to a van for the ride to the courthouse, the mob cursed him and threw tomatoes and rocks. This was thoroughly reported by the local newspaper and even made the City's evening news (there is no network station based in Milo, only a low-end cable outfit). I howled for a change of venue, pleaded with the judge to move the trial at least a hundred miles away so we could hopefully find some jurors who hadn't thrown stuff at the kid, or at the least cursed him over dinner. But we were denied. All of my pretrial motions were denied.

Again, the town wants justice. The town wants closure.

There is no mob to greet me and my van as we pull in to a short driveway behind the courthouse, but some of the usual actors are here. They huddle behind a police barricade not far away and hold their sad signs that say such clever things as "Hang the Baby Killer," and "Satan Is Waiting," and "Crud Rudd out of Milo!" There are about a dozen of these pathetic souls, just waiting to jeer at me and, more important, to show their hatred to Gardy, who will arrive at the same place in about five minutes. During the early days of the trial, this little crowd attracted cameras and a few of these people made it into the newspapers, along with their signs. This, of course, encouraged them and they've been here every morning since. Fat Susie holds the "Crud Rudd" sign and looks like she wants to shoot me. Bullet Bob claims to be a relative of one of the dead girls and was quoted as saying something to the effect that a trial was a waste of time.

He was right about that, I'm afraid.

When the van stops, Partner hurries around to my door, where he's met by three young deputies about his size. I step out and am properly shielded, then I'm whisked into the rear door of the courthouse as Bullet Bob calls me a whore. Another safe entry. I'm not aware of any case in modern times in which a criminal defense attorney was gunned down while entering a courthouse in the middle of a trial. Nevertheless, I have resigned myself to the likelihood that I could well be the first.

We climb a narrow rear staircase that's off-limits to everyone else, and I'm led to a small windowless room where they once held prisoners waiting to see the judge. A few minutes later, Gardy arrives in one piece. Partner steps outside and closes the door.

"How ya doing?" I ask when we are alone.

He smiles and rubs his wrists, unshackled for a few hours. "Okay, I guess. Didn't sleep much." He didn't shower either because he's afraid to shower. He tries it occasionally but they won't turn on the hot water. So Gardy reeks of stale sweat and dirty sheets, and I'm thankful he's far enough away from the jury. The black dye is slowly leaving his hair and each day it gets lighter, and his skin gets paler. He's changing colors in front of the jury, another clear sign of his animalistic capabilities and satanic bent.

"What's gonna happen today?" he asks, with an almost child-like curiosity. He has an IQ of 70, just barely enough to be prosecuted and put to death.

"More of the same, Gardy, I'm afraid. Just more of the same."

"Can't you make them stop lying?"

"No, I cannot."

The State has no physical evidence linking Gardy to the murders. Zero. So, instead of evaluating its lack of evidence and reconsidering its case, the State is doing what it often does. It's plowing ahead with lies and fabricated testimony.

Gardy has spent two weeks in the courtroom, listening to the lies, closing his eyes while slowly shaking his head. He's able to shake his head for hours at a time, and the jurors must think he's crazy. I've told him to stop, to sit up, to take a pen and scribble something on a legal pad as if he has a brain and wants to fight back, to win. But he simply cannot do this and I cannot argue with my client in the courtroom. I've also told him to cover his arms and neck to hide the tattoos, but he's proud of them. I've told him to lose the piercings, but he insists on being who he is. The bright folks who run the Milo jail forbid piercings of all types, unless, of course, you're Gardy and you're headed back to the courtroom. In that case, stick 'em all over your face. Look as sick and creepy and satanic as possible, Gardy, so that your peers will have no trouble with your guilt.

On a nail is a hanger with the same white shirt and khaki
pants he's worn every day. I paid for this cheap ensemble. He
slowly unzips the orange jail jumpsuit and steps out of it. He does
not wear underwear, something I noticed the first day of the trial
and have tried to ignore since. He slowly gets dressed. "So much
lying," he says.

And he's right. The State has called nineteen witnesses so far
and not a single one resisted the temptation to embellish a bit,
or to lie outright. The pathologist who did the autopsies at the
state crime lab told the jury the two little victims had drowned,
but he also added that "blunt force trauma" to their heads was a
contributing factor. It's a better story for the prosecution if the
jury believes the girls were raped and beaten senseless before being
tossed into the pond. There's no physical proof they were in any
way sexually molested, but that hasn't stopped the prosecution
from making this a part of its case. I haggled with the pathologist
for three hours, but it's tough arguing with an expert, even an
incompetent one.

Since the State has no evidence, it is forced to manufacture
some. The most outrageous testimony came from a jailhouse snitch
they call Smut, an appropriate nickname. Smut is an accomplished
courtroom liar who testifies all the time and will say whatever
the prosecutors want him to say. In Gardy's case, Smut was back
in jail on a drug charge and looking at ten years in prison. The
cops needed some testimony, and, not surprisingly, Smut was at
their disposal. They fed him details of the crimes, then transferred
Gardy from a regional jail to a county jail where Smut was locked
up. Gardy had no idea why he was being transferred and had no
clue that he was walking into a trap. (This happened before I got
involved.) They threw Gardy into a small cell with Smut, who
was anxious to talk and wanted to help in any way. He claimed

to hate the cops and know some good lawyers. He'd also read about the murders of the two girls and had a hunch he knew who really killed them. Since Gardy knew nothing about the murders, he had nothing to add to the conversation. Nonetheless, within twenty-four hours Smut claimed he'd heard a full confession. The cops yanked him out of the cell and Gardy never saw him again, until trial. As a witness, Smut cleaned up nicely, wore a shirt and tie and short hair, and hid his tattoos from the jury. In amazing detail, he replayed Gardy's account of how he stalked the two girls into the woods, knocked them off their bikes, gagged and bound them, then tortured, molested, and beat them before tossing them into the pond. In Smut's version, Gardy was high on drugs and had been listening to heavy metal.

It was quite a performance. I knew it was all a lie, as did Gardy and Smut, along with the cops and prosecutors, and I suspect the judge had his doubts too. Nevertheless, the jurors swallowed it in disgust and glared with hatred at my client, who absorbed it with his eyes closed and his head shaking, no, no, no. Smut's testimony was so breathtakingly gruesome and rich with details that it was hard to believe, at times, that he was really fabricating it. No one can lie like that!

I hammered at Smut for eight full hours, one long exhausting day. The judge was cranky and the jurors were bleary-eyed, but I could have kept going for a week. I asked Smut how many times he'd testified in criminal trials. He said maybe twice. I pulled out the records, refreshed his memory, and went through the nine other trials in which he'd performed the same miracle for our honest and fair-minded prosecutors. With his muddled memory somewhat restored, I asked him how many times he'd had his sentence reduced by the prosecutors after lying for them in court. He said never, so I went through each of the nine cases again. I produced the paperwork. I made it perfectly clear to everyone, especially the jurors, that Smut was a lying, serial snitch who swapped bogus testimony for leniency.

I confess—I get angry in court, and this is often detrimental. I blew my cool with Smut and hammered him so relentlessly that some of the jurors became sympathetic. The judge finally told me to move on, but I didn't. I hate liars, especially those who swear to tell the truth and then fabricate testimony to convict my client. I yelled at Smut and the judge yelled at me, and at times it seemed as though everyone was yelling. This did not help Gardy's cause.

You would think the prosecutor might break up his parade of liars with a credible witness, but this would require some intelligence. His next witness was another inmate, another druggie who testified he was in the hallway near Gardy's cell and heard him confess to Smut.

Lies on top of lies.

"Please make them stop," Gardy says.

"I'm trying, Gardy. I'm doing the best I can. We need to go."

3.

A deputy leads us into the courtroom, which is again packed with people and heavy with a layer of tense apprehension. This is the tenth day of testimony, and I now believe there is absolutely nothing else happening in this backwater town. We are the entertainment! The courtroom is packed from gavel to gavel and they're lined up against the walls. Thank God the weather is cool or we'd all be soaked with sweat.

Every capital murder trial requires the presence of at least two lawyers for the defense. My co-counsel, or "second chair," is Trots, a thick, dull boy who ought to burn his law license and curse the day he ever dreamed of showing his face in a courtroom. He's from a small town twenty miles away, far enough, he thought, to shield him from the unpleasantness of getting caught up in Gardy's nightmare. Trots volunteered to handle the preliminary matters, intending to jump ship if a trial became a reality. His plans have not worked out to suit him. He screwed up the preliminaries as only a rookie can, then tried to extricate himself. No go, said the judge. Trots then thought it might be an acceptable idea to sit in the second chair, gain some experience, feel the pressure of a real trial, and so on, but after several death threats he stopped trying. Death threats are just part of the daily grind for me, like the morning coffee and lying cops.

I've filed three motions to remove Trots from the second chair. All denied, of course, so Gardy and I are stuck with a moron at our table who's more of a hindrance than an assistant. Trots sits as far away as possible, though given Gardy's current state of hygiene I can't really blame him.

Gardy told me months ago that when he was first interviewed by Trots at the county jail the lawyer was shocked when Gardy claimed he was innocent. They even argued about it. How's that for a vigorous defender?

So Trots sits at the end of the table, his head buried in useless note taking, his eyes seeing nothing, his ears hearing nothing, but he feels the stares of all those sitting behind us who hate us and want to string us up with our client. Trots figures this too shall pass and he'll get on with his life and career the moment the trial is over. He is wrong. As soon as possible, I'll file an ethics complaint with the state bar association alleging Trots provided "ineffective assistance of counsel" before and during the trial. I've done this before and I know how to make it stick. I'm fighting my own battles with the bar and I understand the game. After I get finished with Trots, he'll want to surrender his license and get a job at a used-car lot.

Gardy takes his seat in the middle of our table. Trots does not look at his client, nor does he speak.

Huver, the prosecutor, walks over and hands me a sheet of paper. There are no good mornings or hellos. We are so far beyond even the most benign pleasantries that a civilized grunt from either of us would be a surprise. I loathe this man the way he loathes me, but I have an advantage in the hating game. Almost monthly I deal with self-righteous prosecutors who lie, cheat, stonewall, cover up, ignore ethics, and do whatever it takes to get a conviction, even when they know the truth and the truth tells them they are wrong. So I know the breed, the ilk, the subclass of lawyer who's above the law because he is the law. Huver, on the other hand, rarely deals with a rogue like me because, sadly for him, he doesn't see many sensational cases, and almost none in which a defendant shows up with a pit bull for a protector. If he dealt with rabid defense lawyers more regularly, he might be more adept at hating us. For me, it's a way of life.

I take the sheet of paper and say, "So who's your liar of the day?"

He says nothing and walks a few feet back to his table, where his little gang of assistants huddle importantly in their dark suits and ham it up for the home crowd. They are on display in this, the biggest show of their miserable backwater careers, and I often get the impression that everyone from the DA's office who can walk, talk, wear a cheap suit, and carry a new briefcase is packed around the table to insure justice.

The bailiff barks, I stand, Judge Kaufman enters, then we sit. Gardy refuses to stand in homage to the great man. Initially, this really pissed off His Honor. On the first day of trial—it now seems like months ago—he snapped at me, "Mr. Rudd, would you please ask your client to stand?"

I did, and he refused. This embarrassed the judge and we discussed it later in his chambers. He threatened to hold my client in contempt and keep him in jail all day long during the trial. I tried to encourage this but let it slip that such an overreaction would be mentioned repeatedly on appeal.

Gardy wisely observed, "What can they do to me that they haven't already done?" So each morning Judge Kaufman begins the ceremonies with a long, nasty scowl at my client, who's usually slouched in his chair either picking at his nose ring or nodding with his eyes closed. It's impossible to tell which one of us, lawyer or client, Kaufman despises the most. Like the rest of Milo, he's been convinced for a long time that Gardy is guilty. And, like everybody else in the courtroom, he has loathed me from day one.

Doesn't matter. In this line of work you rarely have allies and you quickly make enemies.

Since he's up for reelection next year, as is Huver, Kaufman slaps on his phony politician's smile and welcomes everyone to his courtroom for another interesting day in the pursuit of the truth. Based on the calculations I made one day during lunch when the courtroom was empty, there are about 310 people sitting behind me. Except for Gardy's mother and sister, everyone is fervently praying for a conviction, with a quick execution to follow. It's up to Judge Kaufman to deliver. This is the judge who has so far allowed every word of bogus testimony offered by the State. At times it seems as though he's afraid he might lose a vote or two if he sustains one of my objections.

When everyone is in place, they bring in the jury. There are fourteen people crammed in the box—the chosen twelve plus a couple of alternates in case someone gets sick or does something wrong. They are not sequestered (though I requested this), so they are free to go home at night and trash Gardy and me over dinner. Late each afternoon, they are warned by His Honor not to utter a single word about the case, but you can almost hear them yakking as they drive away. Their decision has been made. If they voted right now, before we offer a single witness in defense, they would find him guilty and demand his execution. Then they would return home as heroes and talk about this trial for the rest of their lives. When Gardy gets the needle, they will take special pride in their crucial role in finding justice. They will be elevated in Milo. They will be congratulated, stopped on the streets, recognized at church.

Still sappy, Kaufman welcomes them back, thanks them for their civic service, asks gravely whether anyone tried to contact them in an effort to gain influence. This usually prompts a few looks in my direction, as if I have the time, energy, and stupidity to slink around the streets of Milo at night stalking these same jurors so I can (1) bribe them, (2) intimidate them, or (3) plead with them. It's now gospel that I'm the only crook in the room, in spite of the torrent of sins committed by the other side.

The truth is, if I had the money, the time, and the personnel, I *would* bribe and/or intimidate every juror. When the State, with its limitless resources, commences a fraudulent case and cheats at every turn, then cheating is legitimized. There is no level playing field. There is no fairness. The only honorable alternative for a lawyer fighting to save an innocent client is to cheat in defense.

However, if a defense lawyer is caught cheating, he or she gets nailed with sanctions by the court, reprimanded by the state bar association, maybe even indicted. If a prosecutor gets caught cheating, he either gets reelected or elevated to the bench. Our system never holds a bad prosecutor accountable.

The jurors assure His Honor that all is well. "Mr. Huver," he announces with great solemnity, "please call your next witness." Next up for the State is a fundamentalist preacher who converted the old Chrysler dealership into the World Harvest Temple and is drawing crowds to his daily prayer-a-thons. I watched him once on local cable; once is enough. His claim to fame here is that he says he confronted Gardy in the middle of a late-night youth service. According to his version, Gardy was wearing a T-shirt advertising a heavy metal rock group and conveying some vague satanic message, and this T-shirt was allowing the devil to infiltrate the service. Spiritual warfare was in the air, and God was unhappy with things. With divine direction, the preacher finally located the source of evil in the crowd, stopped the music, stormed back to where Gardy was sitting, and kicked him out of the building.

Gardy says he's never been near the church. Further, Gardy claims he's never seen the inside of *any* church in all of his eighteen years. His mother confirms this. As they say out here in the country, Gardy's family is severely "unchurched."

Why this is allowed as testimony in a capital murder case is thoroughly inconceivable. It is ridiculous and borders on stupidity. Assuming there is a conviction, all of this crap will be reviewed in about two years by a dispassionate appellate court two hundred miles away. Those judges, only slightly more intelligent than Kaufman but anything is an improvement, will take a dim view of this redneck preacher telling his trumped-up story about an altercation that supposedly took place some thirteen months before the murders.

I object. Overruled. I object, angrily. I'm overruled, angrily.

Huver, though, is desperate to keep Satan involved in his theory of the case. Judge Kaufman opened the gates days ago and anything is welcome. However, he'll slam them as soon as I start calling witnesses. We'll be lucky to get a hundred words into the record.

The preacher has an unpaid tax bill in another state. He doesn't know I've found it, and thus we'll have some fun on cross-examination. Not that it will matter; it will not. This jury is done. Gardy is a monster who deserves to go to hell. Their job is to speed him along.

He leans over long enough to whisper, "Mr. Rudd, I swear I've never been to church."

I nod and smile because this is all I can do. A defense lawyer cannot always believe his clients, but when Gardy says he's never been to church, I believe him.

The preacher has a temper and I soon stoke it. I use the unpaid tax bill to really irritate him, and once he's pissed he stays that way. I lead him into arguments over the inerrancy of scripture, the Trinity, the apocalypse, speaking in tongues, playing with snakes, drinking poison, and the pervasiveness of satanic cults in the Milo area. Huver yells objections and Kaufman sustains them. At one point the preacher, pious and red-faced, closes his eyes and raises both hands as high as possible. Instinctively, I freeze and cower and look at the ceiling as if a lightning bolt is coming. Later, he calls me an atheist and says I'm going to hell.

"So you have the authority to send folks to hell?" I fire back.

"God tells me you're going to hell."

"Then put Him on the loudspeaker so we can all hear."

Two jurors actually chuckle at this. Kaufman has had enough. He raps the gavel and calls for lunch. We've wasted the morning with this sanctimonious little prick and his bogus testimony, but he's not the first local to wedge himself into the trial. The town is filled with wannabe heroes.

4.

Lunch is always a treat. Since it's not safe to leave the court-house, actually the courtroom itself, Gardy and I eat a sandwich by ourselves at the defense table. It's the same box lunch fed to the jurors. They bring in sixteen of them, mix them up, draw ours at random, and take the rest to the jury room. This was my idea because I prefer not to be poisoned. Gardy has no clue; he's just hungry. He says the food at the jail is what you'd expect and he doesn't trust the guards. He eats nothing there, and since he's surviving only on lunch, I asked Judge Kaufman if the county could perhaps double up and give the boy two rubber chicken sandwiches, with extra chips and another pickle. In other words, two box lunches instead of one. Denied.

So Gardy gets half of my sandwich and all of my kosher dill. If I weren't starving, he could have the entire box of crap.

Partner comes and goes throughout the day. He's afraid to leave our van in one spot due to the high probability of slashed tires and cracked windows. He also has a few responsibilities, one of which is to meet occasionally with the Bishop.

In these cases where I'm called into a combat zone, into a small town that has already closed ranks and is ready to kill one of its own for some heinous crime, it takes a while to find a contact. This contact is always another lawyer, a local who also defends criminals and butts heads weekly with the police and prosecutors. This contact reaches out eventually, quietly, afraid of being exposed as a traitor. He knows the truth, or something close to it. He knows the players, the bad actors, and the occasional good one. Since his survival depends on getting along with the cops and court clerks and assistant prosecutors, he knows the system.

In Gardy's case, my deep-throated pal is Jimmy Bressup. We call him the Bishop. I've never met him. He works through Partner and they meet in strange places. Partner says he's about sixty with long, thinning gray hair, bad clothes, a loud, foul mouth, an abrasive nature, and a weakness for the bottle. "An older version of me?" I asked. "Not quite," came the wise reply. For all his bluster and big talk, the Bishop is afraid of getting too close to Gardy's lawyers.

The Bishop says Huver and his gang know by now they've got the wrong guy but have too much invested to stop and admit their mistakes. He says there have been whispers from day one about the real killer.

5.

It's Friday and everyone in the courtroom is exhausted. I spend an hour haranguing a pimply, stupid little brat who claims he was at the same church service when Gardy called forth the demons and disrupted things. Honestly, I've seen the worst of bogus court-room evidence, but I've never seen anything as bad as this. In addition to being false, it is wholly irrelevant. No other prosecutor would bother with it. No other judge would admit it. Kaufman finally announces an adjournment for the weekend.

Gardy and I meet in the holding room, where he changes into his jail uniform while I offer banalities about having a good weekend. I give him ten bucks for the vending machines. He says tomorrow his mother will bring him lemon cookies, his favorite. Sometimes the guards pass them through; sometimes they keep them for their own nourishment. One never knows. The guards average three hundred pounds each, so I guess they need the stolen calories. I tell Gardy to take a shower over the weekend and wash his hair.

He says, "Mr. Rudd, if I find a razor, I'm gone." With an index finger, he does a slashing motion against his wrist.

"Don't say that, Gardy." He's said it before and he means it. The kid has nothing to live for and he's smart enough to see what's coming. Hell, a blind man could see it. We shake hands and I hurry down the back steps. Partner and the deputies meet me at the rear door and shove me into our vehicle. Another safe exit.

Outside Milo, I begin to nod and soon fall asleep. Ten minutes later, my phone vibrates and I answer it. We follow the state trooper back to our motel, where we grab our luggage and check out. Soon we are alone and headed for the City.

"Did you see the Bishop?" I ask Partner.

"Oh yes. It's Friday, and I think he starts drinking around noon on Friday. But beer only, he's quick to point out. So I bought a six-pack and we drove around. The joint is a real dive, out east, just beyond the city limits. He says Peeley is a regular."

"So you've had a few beers already? Should I be driving?"

"Only one, boss. I sipped it until it was warm. The Bishop, on the other hand, took his cold. Three of them."

"And we believe this guy?"

"I'm just doing my job. On the one hand, he has credibility because he's lived here all his life and knows everyone. On the other, he's so full of crap you want to dismiss everything he says."

"We'll see." I close my eyes and try to nap. Sleep is virtually impossible in the midst of a capital murder trial, and I've learned to grab it whenever possible. I've stolen ten minutes on a hard bench in an empty courtroom during lunch, just as I've paced back and forth in a dingy motel room at three in the morning. I often black out in mid-sentence when Partner drives and the van hums along.

At some point, as we head back to our version of civilization, I fade away.

6.

It's the third Friday of the month, and I have a standing date, if you'd call two drinks a real date. It feels more like an appointment for a root canal. The truth is this woman wouldn't date me at gunpoint, and the feelings are so mutual. But we have a history. We meet at the same bar, in the same booth where we had our first meal together, in another lifetime. Nostalgia has nothing to do with it; it's all about convenience. It's a corporate bar downtown, one of a chain, but the ambience is not bad and it's lively on Friday evenings.

Judith Whitly arrives first and gets the booth. I slide in a few minutes later just as she's about to get irritated. She has never been late for anything and views tardiness as a sign of weakness. In her opinion, I possess many of these signs. She, too, is a lawyer—that's how we met.

"You look tired," she says without a trace of compassion. She, too, is showing signs of fatigue, though, at thirty-nine, she is still strikingly beautiful. Every time I see her I'm reminded of why I fell so hard.

"Thank you, and you look great, as always."

"Thanks."

"Ten days and we're all running out of gas."

"Any luck?" she asks.

"Not yet." She knows the basics of Gardy's case and trial and she knows me. If I believe the kid is innocent, that's good enough for her. But she has her own clients to fret and lose sleep over. We order drinks—her standard Friday night glass of chardonnay and my whiskey sour.

We'll have two drinks in less than an hour, then that's it for another month. "How's Starcher?" I ask. I keep hoping that one day I can pronounce my son's name without hating it, but that day has not arrived. My name is on his birth certificate as the father, but I wasn't around when he was born. Therefore, Judith had control over the name. It should be someone's last name, if it has to be used at all.

"He's doing well," she says smugly, because she's thoroughly involved with the kid's life and I am not. "I met with his teacher last week and she's pleased with his progress. She says he's just a normal second grader who's reading at a high level and enjoying life."

"That's good to hear," I say. "Normal" is the key word here because of our history. Starcher is not being raised the normal way. He spends half his time with Judith and her current partner and the other half with her parents. From the hospital, she took Starcher to an apartment she shared with Gwyneth, the woman she left me for. They then spent three years trying to legally adopt Starcher, but I fought them like a rabid animal. I have nothing against gay couples adopting kids. I just couldn't stand Gwyneth. And I was right. They split not long afterward in a nasty fight, one I enjoyed immensely from deep in left field.

It gets more complicated. The drinks arrive and we don't bother with a polite "Cheers." That would only waste time. We need the alcohol ASAP.

I deliver the awful news by saying, "My mother is coming to town next weekend and she'd like to see Starcher. He is, after all, her only grandson."

"I know that," she snaps. "It's your weekend. You can do what you want."

"True, but you have a way of complicating everything. I just don't want any trouble, that's all."

"Your mother is nothing but trouble."

Truer words were never spoken, and I nod in defeat. It would be a dramatic understatement to say that Judith and my mother hated each other from the opening bell. So much so that my mother informed me she would cut me out of her last will and testament if I married Judith. At the time, I was secretly having some serious doubts about our romance and our future, but that threat was the last straw. Though I expect Mom to live to be a hundred, her estate will be a delight. A guy with my income needs a dream. A subplot in this sad story is that my mother often uses her will to bully her children. My sister married a Republican and got herself cut out of the will. Two years later, the Republican, who's really a nice guy, became the father of the most perfect granddaughter in history. Now my sister is back in the will, or so we think.

Anyway, I was preparing to break up with Judith when she gave me the crushing news that she was pregnant. I assumed I was the father, though I didn't ask that loaded question. Later I learned the brutal truth that she was already seeing Gwyneth. Talk about a shot to the gut. I'm sure there were clues that my dearly beloved was actually a lesbian, but I missed every one of them.

We got married. Mom said she changed her will and I would get not a penny. We lived together off and on for five wretched months, were technically married for fifteen more, and split to save our sanity. Starcher arrived in the middle of the war, a casualty from birth, and we've been sniping at each other ever since. This ritual of meeting once a month for drinks is our homage to forced civility.

I think I'm back in my dear mother's will.

"And what does Mummy plan to do with my child?" she asks. It's never "our" child. She has never been able to resist the little digs, the sophomoric cheap shots. She picks at the scabs, but not even in a clever way. It's almost impossible to ignore, but I've learned to bite my tongue. My tongue has scars.

"I think they're going to the zoo."

"She always takes him to the zoo."

"What's the harm in going to the zoo?"

"Well, last time he had nightmares about pythons."

"Okay, I'll ask her to take him somewhere else." She's already causing trouble. What could be wrong with taking a fairly normal seven-year-old boy to the zoo? I don't know why we meet like this.

"How are things around the firm?" I ask, my curiosity similar to that of watching a car wreck. It's irresistible.

"Fine," she says. "The usual turmoil."

"You need some boys in that firm."

"We have enough problems." The waiter notices both glasses are empty and goes for another round. The first drinks always disappear fast.

Judith is one of four partners in a firm of ten women, all militant lesbians. The firm specializes in gay law—discrimination in employment, housing, education, health care, and the latest: gay divorce. They're good lawyers, tough negotiators and litigators, always on the attack and often in the news. The firm projects an image of being at war with society and never backing down. The outside fights, though, are far less colorful than the inside brawls.

"I could join as the senior partner," I say in an effort at levity.

"You wouldn't last ten minutes." No man would last ten minutes in their offices. In fact, men avoid them zealously. Mention the name of her firm and men run for the hills. Fine fellows caught screwing around jump off bridges.

"You're probably right. Do you ever miss sex with the opposite sex?"

"Seriously, Sebastian, you want to talk about straight sex, after a bad marriage and an unwanted child?"

"I like straight sex. Did you ever like it? You seemed to."

"I was faking."

"You were not. You were pretty wonderful, as I recall." I know two guys who slept with her before I came along. Then she ran to Gwyneth. I've often wondered if I was so lousy in bed that I drove her to switch teams. I doubt it. I must say she has a good eye. I loathed Gwyneth, still do, but the woman could stop traffic on any street in town. And her current partner, Ava, once modeled lingerie for a local department store. I remember her ads in the Sunday newspaper.

The second drinks arrive and we grab them.

"If you want to talk about sex, I'm leaving," she says, but she's not angry.

"I'm sorry. Look, Judith, every time I see you I think about sex. My problem, not yours."

"Get help."

"I don't need help. I need sex."

"Are you propositioning me?"

"Would it do any good?"

"No."

"Didn't think so."

"You have fights tonight?" she asks, changing the subject, and I don't resist.

"I do."

"You're sick, you know. That's such a brutal sport."

"Starcher says he wants to go."

"You take Starcher to the cage fights and you'll never see him again."

"Relax. I'm just joking."

"You may be joking, but you're still sick."

"Thank you. Have another drink." A shapely Asian in a short, tight skirt walks by and we both have a look. "Dibs," I say.

The alcohol kicks in—it takes longer for her because she is naturally wound tighter—and Judith manages a grin, the first of the evening. Could be the first of the week. "Are you seeing anyone?" she asks, her tone noticeably softer.

"Not since we last met," I say. "It's been all work." My last girlfriend said good-bye three years ago. I get lucky occasionally, but I'd be lying if I said I was on the prowl for a serious woman. There is a long, heavy gap in the conversation as we get bored. When we're down to the last few drops of our drinks, we go back to Starcher and my mother and the next weekend that we both now dread.

We walk together out of the bar, dutifully peck each other on the cheek, and say good-bye. Another box checked off.

I loved her once, then I truly hated her. Now I almost like Judith, and if we can continue these monthly meetings, we might become friends. That's my goal, because I really need a friend, one who can understand what I do and why I do it.

And it would be much better for our son, too.

7.

I live on the twenty-fifth floor of a downtown apartment building, with a partial view of the river. I like it up here because it's quiet and safe. If someone wanted to bomb or burn my apartment, it would be difficult without taking down the entire building. There is some crime downtown, so we live with plenty of video surveillance and guards with guns. I feel secure.

They fired bullets into my old apartment, a duplex on the ground floor, and they firebombed my old office five years ago. "They" have never been found or identified, and I get the clear impression the cops aren't looking that hard. As I said, my line of work inspires hatred and there are people out there who'd love to see me suffer. Some of these people hide behind badges.

The apartment has a thousand square feet, with two small bedrooms, an even smaller kitchen, seldom used, and a living area that's barely big enough to hold my only substantial piece of furniture. I'm not sure a vintage pool table should be classified as furniture, but it's my apartment and I'll call it what I want. It's nine feet

long, regulation size, and was built in 1884 by the Oliver L. Briggs
company in Boston. I won it in a lawsuit, had it perfectly restored
and then carefully reassembled smack in the middle of my den.
On an average day, or when I'm not away in cheap motels dodg-
ing death threats, I rack 'em up time after time and practice for
hours. Shooting pool against myself is an escape, a stress reliever,
and cheap therapy. It's also a throwback to my high school days
when I hung out at a place called The Rack, a real local dive that's
been around for decades. It's an old-fashioned pool hall with rows
of tables, layers of smoke, spittoons, cheap beer, some petty gambling, and a clientele that acts tough but knows how to behave.
The owner, Curly, is an old friend who's always there and keeps it
running smoothly.

When the insomnia hits and my walls are closing in, I can
often be found at The Rack at two in the morning playing nine
ball alone, in another world and quite happy.

Not tonight, though. I glide into the apartment, floating on
the whiskey, and quickly change into my fight clothes—jeans, a
black T-shirt, and a bright, shiny yellow jacket that snaps at the
waist, practically glows in the dark, and screams "Tadeo Zapate"
across the back. I pull my slightly graying hair into a tight pony-
tail and stuff it under the T-shirt. I change glasses and select a pair
rimmed in light blue. I adjust my cap—also a bright yellow that
matches the jacket, with the name Zapate across the front. I feel
sufficiently disguised and the evening should go well. Where I'm
going the crowd is not interested in misfit lawyers. There will be
a lot of thugs there, a lot of folks with legal troubles past, present,
and future, but they'll never notice me.

It's another sad fact of my life that I often leave the apartment
after dark with some sort of disguise—different cap, glasses, hidden hair, even a fedora.

Partner drives me to the old city auditorium, eight blocks from my apartment, and drops me off in an alley near the building. A crowd is swarming out front. Loud rap booms across the front plaza. Spotlights sweep maniacally from building to building. Bright digital signs advertise the main event and the undercard.

Tadeo fights fourth, the last warm-up before the main event, which tonight is a heavyweight contest that is selling tickets because the favorite is a crazy ex-NFL player who's well known in the area. I own 25 percent of Tadeo's career, an investment that cost me $30,000 a year ago, and he hasn't lost since. I'm also betting on the side and doing quite well. If he wins tonight, his cut will be $6,000. Half of that if he loses.

In a hallway, somewhere deep under the arena, I hear two security guards talking. One is claiming the evening is a sellout. Five thousand fans. I flash my credentials and get waved through another door, then another. I enter the dark locker room and the tension hits like a brick. Tonight we're assigned to one half of a long room. Tadeo is moving up in the world of mixed martial arts, and we're all beginning to sense something big. He's lying on a table, on his stomach, naked except for his boxers, not an ounce of fat on his 130-pound body. His cousin Leo is massaging his shoulder blades. The lotion makes his light brown skin glisten. I ease around the room and speak to Norberto, his manager, Oscar, his trainer, and Miguel, his brother and workout partner. They smile when they speak to me because I, the lone gringo, am viewed as the man with the money. I'm also the agent, the guy with the connections and brains who'll get Tadeo on a UFC card if he keeps winning. There are a couple of other relatives in the background, hangers-on who have no discernible role in Tadeo's life. I don't like these extras because they expect to be paid at some point, but after seven wins in a row Tadeo thinks he needs the entourage. They all do.

With the exception of Oscar, they're all members of the same street gang, a mid-level organization of El Salvadorans who run cocaine. Tadeo has been one of the gang since he was initiated at the age of fifteen but has never aspired to a leadership position. Instead, he found some old boxing gloves, discovered a gym, and then discovered he had freakishly quick hands. His brother Miguel also boxed, but not as well. Miguel runs the gang and has a nasty reputation on the street.

The more Tadeo wins the more he earns, and the more I worry about dealing with his gang.

I lean down and speak softly to him. "How's my man?"

He opens his eyes, looks up, suddenly smiles, and pulls out the earphones. The massage ends abruptly as he sits on the edge of the table. We chat for a few moments and he assures me he's ready to kill someone. Attaboy. His prefight ritual includes avoiding a good shave for a week, and with his scraggly beard and mop of black hair he sort of reminds me of the great Roberto Duran. But Tadeo's roots are in El Salvador, not Panama. He's twenty-two, a U.S. citizen, and his English is almost as good as his Spanish. His mother has documents and works in a cafeteria. She also has an apartment full of kids and relatives and I get the impression that whatever Tadeo earns gets divided many ways.

Every time I talk to Tadeo I'm thankful I'm not forced to face him in the ring. He has fierce black pupils that scream angrily, "Show me the mayhem. Show me the blood." He grew up on the streets, fighting anyone who got too close. An older brother died in a knife fight, and Tadeo is afraid he'll die too. When he steps into the ring, he's convinced someone is about to be killed, and it won't be him. His three losses were on points; nobody's kicked his ass yet. He trains four hours a day and he's close to mastering jujitsu.

His voice is low, his words slow, the usual prefight jitters where fear clouds all thoughts and your stomach churns. I know.

I've been there. A long time ago, I had five Golden Gloves boxing matches. I was 1–4 until my mother found out about my secret career and mercifully brought it to an end. But I did it. I had the guts to step into the ring and get the shit knocked out of me.

However, I cannot imagine the guts it takes to crawl into the cage with another fighter who's superbly conditioned, highly skilled, well trained, hungry, nasty, and terrified and whose only thoughts are how to rip your shoulder out of its socket, mangle your knees, open a gash, or land a knockout punch on the jaw. That's why I love this sport. It takes more courage, more in-your-face raw guts, than any sport since the gladiators battled to the death. Sure, many others are dangerous—downhill skiing, football, hockey, boxing, car racing. More people die on horses each year than in any other sport. But in those you don't willingly enter the game knowing you will get hurt. When you walk into the cage, you will get hurt, and it could be ugly, painful, even deadly. The next round could well be your last.

That's why the countdown is so brutal. The minutes drag by as the fighter fights his nerves, his bowels, his fears. The waiting is the worst part. I leave after a few minutes so Tadeo can go back into his zone. He told me once that he's able to visualize the fight and he sees his opponent on the mat, bleeding and screaming for mercy.

I weave through the maze of corridors in the depths of the arena, and I can hear the crowd roaring in echoes, thirsting for blood. I find the right door and step inside. It's a small administrative office that's been hijacked by my own little street gang. We meet before the fights and place our wagers. There are six of us, and membership is closed because we don't want any leaks. Some use their real names, others do not. Slide dresses like a street pimp and has served time for murder. Nino is a mid-level meth importer who served time for trafficking. Johnny has no criminal record (yet) and owns half of the fighter Tadeo will face tonight. Denardo drops hints of Mafia ties, but I doubt his criminal activity is that well organized. He aspires to promote MMA events and longs to live in Vegas. Frankie is the old guy, a local fixture in the fight scene for decades. He admits he's been seduced by the violence of cage fighting and now is bored with old-fashioned boxing.

So these are my boys. I wouldn't trust any of these clowns in a legitimate business deal, but then we're not doing anything legitimate. We go down the card and start the betting. I know Tadeo is going to kill Johnny's fighter, and evidently Johnny is worried. I offer $5,000 on Tadeo, and no one will take it. Three thousand, and no takers. I chide them, cuss them, ridicule them, but they know Tadeo is on a roll. Johnny has to wager something, and I finally haggle him into a $4,000 bet that his fighter won't make it to the third round. Denardo decides he wants some of this, for another $4,000. We cover the card with all manner of wagers, and Frankie, the scribe, records it all. I leave the room with $12,000 in play, on four different fights. We'll meet in the same room later when the fights are over and settle up, all in cash.

The fights begin and I roam around the arena, killing time. The tension in the locker room is insufferable and I can't stand to be in there as the clock ticks along. I know that by now Tadeo is laid out on a table, motionless, covered by a thick quilt, saying his prayers to the Virgin Mary and listening to filthy Latin rap. There is nothing I can do to help, so I find a spot on an upper level, high above the ring, and take in the show. It is indeed a sellout, and the fans are as loud and crazed as ever. Cage fighting appeals to the savage instinct in some people, including me, and we're all here for the same reason—to see one fighter annihilate another. We want to see bleeding eyes, gashes across the forehead, choke holds, bone-ripping submissions, and brutal knockout punches that send the corners scrambling for the doctor. Mix in a flood of cheap beer, and you have five thousand maniacs begging for blood.

I eventually work my way back to the locker room, where things are coming to life. The first two fights ended with early knockouts, so the evening is moving quickly. Norberto, Oscar, and Miguel put on their glowing yellow jackets, same as mine, and Team Zapate is ready for the long walk to the cage. I'll be in the corner, along with Norberto and Oscar, though my role is not as important. I make sure Tadeo has water while Norberto yells instructions in the fastest Spanish you'll ever hear. Oscar tends to the facial wounds, if any. From the moment we hit the floor, everything becomes a blur. Along the tunnel, drunk fans reach for Tadeo and scream his name. Cops shove people out of our way. The roar is earsplitting, and it's not all for Tadeo. They want more, another fight, preferably one to the death.

Outside the cage, an official checks Tadeo's gloves, applies oil to his face, and gives him the green light. An announcer yells his name over the PA, and our man bounces into the cage in his bright yellow trunks and robe. His opponent tonight goes by "the Jackal," real name unknown and unimportant. He's a sub-mission specialist, a tall white guy without much bulk, but looks are deceiving. I've seen him fight three times and he's guileful and crafty. He plays defense well and looks for a takedown. He wrapped his last opponent into a pretzel and made him scream for mercy. Right now I loathe the Jackal, but deep down I admire the hell out of him. Any man who can climb into the cage has far more spine than the average guy.

The bell rings for round 1, three minutes of fury. Tadeo the boxer bores in straight ahead and immediately has the Jackal backing up. Both jab and spar for the first minute, then tie up but there's no damage. Like the other five thousand fans, I'm yelling

my head off, though I have no idea why. Any advice is useless and
Tadeo isn't listening anyway. They go down, land hard, and the
Jackal has him in a scissors hold. For a long minute, the action
dies as Tadeo squirms and wiggles and we hold our breath. He
finally breaks free and manages a sharp left jab to the Jackal's nose.
Finally, there's blood. There's no question my man is the better
fighter, but it just takes one mistake and you've got an arm twisted
to the breaking point. Between rounds, Norberto unloads a torrent of instructions, but Tadeo isn't listening. He knows much
more about fighting than any of us, and he's got the guy figured
out. When the bell rings for round 2, I grab him by the arm and
yell into his ear, "Take him in this round and there's an extra two
thousand bucks." This, Tadeo hears.

The Jackal lost the first round, so, like many fighters, he starts
pressing in the second round. He wants to get inside, to get his
wiry arms fixed into some manner of vile death grip, but Tadeo
reads him perfectly. Thirty seconds in, Tadeo does a classic left-
right–left combo and knocks his opponent squarely onto his butt.
Tadeo then makes a common mistake as he attempts to launch
himself like an idiot onto the Jackal, much like a manic dive-
bomber lunging for the kill. The Jackal manages to kick with his
right foot, a brutal blow that hits Tadeo just above the crotch. He
stays on his feet as the Jackal scrambles to his, and for a second or
two neither man pushes the action. They finally shake it off and
begin circling. Tadeo finds his boxer's rhythm and begins pep-
pering the Jackal with unanswered jabs. He opens a cut above his
right eye and widens it with a relentless barrage. The Jackal has the
bad habit of throwing a wild fake left hook just before he ducks
and comes in low at the knees, and he tries this one time too often.
Tadeo reads it, times it perfectly, and executes his finest trick, a
blind elbow spin, a move that takes balls because for a split second
his back is turned to his opponent. But the Jackal is too slow and

Tadeo's right elbow crushes into the right jaw. Lights out. The Jackal is out before he lands on the mat. The rules allow Tadeo to pounce on him for a few shots to the face, to properly finish him off, but why bother? Tadeo just stands in the center of the ring, hands raised, staring down, admiring his work as the Jackal lies as still as a corpse. The referee is quick to stop it all.

Somewhat nervously, we wait a few moments as they try and revive him. The crowd wants a stretcher, a casualty, something to talk about at work, but the Jackal eventually comes to life and starts talking. He sits up, and we relax. Or try to. It's not easy staying calm in the aftermath of such furious action, when you have something at stake, and when five thousand maniacs are stomping their feet.

The Jackal gets to his feet and the maniacs boo.

Tadeo walks over to him, says something nice, and they make peace.

As we leave the cage, I follow Tadeo and smile as he slaps hands with his fans and soaks up another win. He made a couple of boneheaded moves that would get him killed against a ranked opponent, but all in all it was another promising fight. I try and savor the moment and think about the future and the potential earnings, maybe some sponsorships. He's the fourth fighter I've invested in and the first one who's paying off.

Just before we leave the floor and enter the tunnel, a female voice yells, "Mr. Rudd! Mr. Rudd!"

It takes a second or two for this to register because no one in this crowd should possibly recognize me. I'm wearing an official Team Zapate trucker-style rap cap, a hideous yellow jacket, and different eyeglasses, and my long hair is tucked away. But by the time I pause and look, she's reaching for me. A heavyset woman of twenty-five with purple hair, piercings, enormous boobs exploding from just under a skintight T-shirt, pretty much the typical classy gal at the cage fights. I give her a curious look and she again says, "Mr. Rudd. Aren't you Mr. Rudd, the lawyer?"

I nod. She takes a step even closer and says, "My mother is on the jury."

"What jury?" I ask, suddenly panicked. There's only one jury at the moment.

"We're from Milo. The Gardy Baker trial. My mom's on the jury."

I jerk my head to the left, as if to say, "That way." Seconds later we're off the floor and walking side by side along a narrow corridor as the walls shake around us. "What's her name?" I ask, watching everyone who passes.

"Glynna Roston, juror number eight."

"Okay." I know every juror's name, age, race, job, education, family, residence, marital history, prior jury service, and criminal record, if any. I helped select them. Some I wanted, most I did not. I have been sitting in a packed courtroom with them five days a week for the past two weeks, and I'm really getting tired of them. I think I know their politics, religions, biases, and feelings about criminal justice. Because I know so damn much, I've been convinced since they were seated that Gardy Baker is headed for death row.

"What's Glynna thinking these days?" I ask cautiously. She could be wearing a mike. Nothing surprises me.

"She thinks they're all a bunch of liars." We're still walking, slowly, going nowhere, each afraid to look the other in the eyes. I am stunned to hear this. Reading her body language and knowing her background, I would bet the farm that Glynna Roston would be the first to yell "Guilty!"

I look behind us to make sure there's no witness, then say, "Well, she's a smart woman because they *are* lying. They have no proof."

"Do you want me to tell her that?"

"I don't care what you tell her," I say, looking around as we stop and wait for one of the heavyweights to pass with his entourage. I have $2,000 on the guy. I'm up $6,000 for the night and I'm feeling pretty good. And to top it off, I'm hearing the shocking news that not all of my Gardy Baker jurors are brain-dead.

I ask, "Is she alone, or does she have buddies?"

"She says they're not discussing the case."

I want to laugh at this. If she's not discussing the case, then how does this cutie know how her mother's leaning? At this precise moment, I am violating the rules of ethics and perhaps a criminal statute as well. This is unauthorized contact with a juror, and though it's not clear-cut, and not instigated by me, there's no doubt it would be interpreted badly by the state bar association. And Judge Kaufman would blow a gasket.

"Tell her to stick to her guns because they've got the wrong guy," I say, and walk away. I don't know what she wants and there is nothing I can give her. I guess I could take ten minutes and point out the glaring deficiencies in the State's evidence, but that would require her to absorb it all correctly and then give an accurate report to her mother. Fat chance. This gal is here for the fights.

I take the nearest stairway to a lower level, and as soon as I'm safely away from her, I duck into a restroom and replay what she said. I still can't believe it. That jury, along with the rest of the town, convicted my client the day he was arrested. Her mother, Glynna Roston, gives every indication of being the model Milo citizen—uneducated, narrow-minded, and determined to be a heroine for her community in its time of need. Monday morning will be interesting. At some point, after we resume testimony, I'll get the chance to glance into the jury box. So far Glynna has not been afraid to return my looks. Her eyes will reveal something, though I'm not sure what.

I shake it off and return to reality. The heavyweight fight lasts for a full forty seconds with my favorite still standing. I can't wait to reconvene with my little gang. We meet in the same dark room with the door locked, and the trash talk is brutal. All six of us pull cash from our pockets. Frankie has the notes and keeps it all straight. For the evening, I've netted $8,000 from my wagers, though $2,000 of this will go to Tadeo for his impromptu bonus. I'll get it back from his cut of the purse. That will go on the books for IRS purposes; this cash will not.

Tadeo earns $8,000 for his efforts, a great night that will allow him to add another gang member to his entourage. He'll pay some bills, keep the family afloat, save nothing. I've tried to offer financial advice, but it's a waste of time.

I stop by the locker room, hand over the $2,000, tell him I love him, and leave the arena. Partner and I go to a quiet bar and have some drinks. It takes a couple to settle me down. When you're that close to the action, and you've got your own hitter in the ring two seconds away from a concussion or a broken bone, and five thousand idiots are screaming into your ears, your heart races wildly as your stomach flips and your nerves tingle. There's a flood of adrenaline like nothing I've ever felt.

8.

Jack Peeley is a former boyfriend of the mother of the two Fentress girls. Their father was long gone when they were murdered, and their mother's apartment was a revolving door for local tomcats and slimeballs. Peeley lasted about a year and got the boot when she met a used-tractor dealer with a little cash and a house without wheels. She moved up and Peeley moved out, with a broken heart. He was the last person seen near the girls when they disappeared. Early on, I asked the police why they did not treat him as a suspect, or at least investigate him, and their lame response was that they already had their man. Gardy was in custody and confessing right and left.

I strongly suspect Jack Peeley killed the girls in some sick act of revenge. And, if the cops had not stumbled onto Gardy, they might have eventually questioned Peeley. Gardy, though, with his frightening appearance, satanic leanings, and history of sexual perversion, became the clear favorite and Milo has never looked back.

According to the Bishop, who is relying on his low-life sources, Peeley hangs out almost every Saturday night at a joint called the Blue & White. It's about a mile east of Milo and was originally a truck stop. Now it's just a redneck dive with cheap beer, pool tables, and live music on the weekends.

On Saturday night, we ease into the gravel parking lot at around ten, and the place is packed, wall-to-wall pickups. We have our own, a rented Dodge club cab with Ram power and big tires, perhaps a bit too shiny for this joint but then it belongs to Hertz, not me. Behind the wheel, Partner is pretending to be a redneck but is a pathetic excuse for one. He's ditched his daily black garb and is wearing jeans and a Cowboys T-shirt, but it's not working.

"Let's do it," I say from the front passenger's seat. Tadeo and Miguel jump from the rear seat and casually walk through the front door. They're met just inside by a bouncer who wants ten bucks each for the cover. He looks them over and does not approve. They are, after all, darker-skinned Hispanics. But at least they're not black. According to the Bishop, the Blue & White will tolerate a few Mexicans but a black face would start a riot. Not that there's anything to worry about. Such a cracker dive has zero appeal to any sensible black guy.

But a riot is what they'll get anyway. Tadeo and Miguel order a beer at the crowded bar and do a passable job blending in. They get some stares but nothing bad. If these fat, drunk rednecks only knew. Tadeo could take out any five with his bare hands in less than a minute. Miguel, his brother and sparring partner, could take out four. After fifteen minutes of surveying the crowd and getting the layout, Tadeo flags a bartender over and says in unaccented English, "Say, I need to get some money to a guy named Jack Peeley, but I'm not sure I can recognize him."

The bartender, a busy man, nods to a row of booths near the pool table and says, "Third booth, the guy with the black cap on."

"Thanks."

"No problem."

They order another beer and kill some time. In Peeley's booth there are two women and one other man. The table is covered with empty beer bottles, and all four are chomping away on roasted peanuts. Part of the ambience of the Blue & White is that you toss your empty shells onto the floor. At the far end a band cranks up and a dozen folks ease that way for a dance. Evidently, Peeley is not a dancer. Tadeo sends me a text: "JP spotted. Waiting."

They kill some more time. Partner and I sit and watch and wait, nervous as hell. Who can predict the outcome of a brawl in a roomful of drunken idiots, half of whom carry NRA membership cards?

Peeley and his buddy head to a pool table and get ready for a game. Their women stay in the booth, eating peanuts, swilling beer. "Here we go," Tadeo says and drifts away from the bar. He walks between two pool tables, times it perfectly, and bumps hard into Peeley, who's minding his own business and chalking up his cue. "What the hell!" Peeley yells angrily, hot-faced and ready to kick a wetback's ass. Before he can swing his cue, Tadeo hits him with three punches that no one can possibly see. Left-right-left, each landing on an eyebrow, where the cuts are always easier, each drawing blood. Peeley goes down hard and it will be a while before he wakes up. The women scream and there's the usual rumble of activity and loud voices as a melee unfolds. Peeley's friend is slow to react but finally pulls back his stick to take off Tadeo's head. Miguel, though, intervenes and lands a hard fist at the base of his skull. Peeley's friend joins Peeley on the floor. Tadeo pounds Peeley's face a few more times for good measure, then ducks low and darts into the men's restroom. A beer bottle cracks and splashes just above his head. Miguel is right behind him, angry voices calling after them. They lock the door, then scramble through a window. They're back in the pickup seconds later, and we casually drive away.

"Got it," Tadeo says eagerly from the backseat. He thrusts his right hand forward and it is indeed covered with blood. Peeley's blood. We stop at a burger place, and I carefully scrape it clean.

It's midnight before we make it back to the City.

9.

The monster who killed the Fentress girls bound their ankles and wrists together with their shoelaces, then threw them in a pond. During Jenna's autopsy, a single strand of long black hair was found wrapped up in the laces around her ankles. Both she and Raley had light blond hair. At the time, Gardy had long black hair—though the color changed monthly—and not surprisingly the State's hair analysis expert testified that there was a "match." For over a century, true experts have known that hair analysis is wildly inaccurate. It is still used by authorities, even the FBI, when there's no better proof and the suspect has to be nailed. I begged Judge Kaufman to order DNA testing with a sample of Gardy's current hair, but he refused. Said it was too expensive. We're talking about a man's life.

When I was finally allowed to view the State's evidence, of

which there was virtually none, I managed to steal about three-quarters of an inch of the black hair. No one missed it.

Early Monday morning, I ship by overnight parcel the hair and the sample of Jack Peeley's blood to a DNA lab in California. It will cost me $6,000 for a rush job. I'll bet the ranch I find the real killer.

10.

Partner and I speed away to Milo for another grueling week of lies. I'm eager to get my first glance at Glynna Roston, juror number eight, and see if there are any telltale signs of backdoor communications. Typically, though, things do not go as planned.

The courtroom is once again packed and I marvel at the crowd. For the eleventh court day in a row, Julie Fentress, the mother of the twins, sits on the front bench, directly behind the prosecutor's table. She's with her support group and they glare at me as if I killed the girls myself.

When Trots finally arrives and opens his briefcase and goes through the motions of pretending to be of some value, I lean down and tell him, "Watch juror number eight, Glynna Roston, but don't get caught." Trots will get caught because Trots is a blockhead. He should be able to covertly glance at the jurors and gauge their reactions, study their body language, see if they're awake or interested or pissed, do all the things you learn to do in a trial when you're curious about your jury, but Trots checked out weeks ago.

Gardy is in relatively good spirits. He's told me he enjoys the trial because it gets him out of his cell. They keep him locked down in solitary, usually with the lights off because *they know* he killed the Fentress twins and the harsh punishment should start now. My spirits are better because Gardy took a shower over the weekend.

We kill some time waiting for Judge Kaufman. Huver, the prosecutor, is not at his table at 9:15. His gang of Hitler Youth assistants have deeper frowns than usual. Something is going on. A bailiff appears and whispers to me, "Judge Kaufman wants to see you in chambers." This happens almost every day, it seems. We run back to chambers to fistfight over something we want to keep away from the public. But why bother? After two weeks, I know that if Huver wants the crowd to see or hear something, it's going to happen.

I walk into an ambush. The court reporter is there, ready to capture it all. Judge Kaufman is pacing, in his shirt and tie, robe and coat hanging on the door. Huver stands smug and grim-faced by a window. The bailiff shuts the door behind me and Kaufman throws some papers on the table. "Read this!" he growls.

"Good morning, Judge," I say, as smart-ass as possible. "Huver."

They do not respond. It's a two-page affidavit in which the deponent, or in this case the liar, claims she bumped into me the previous Friday night at the MMA fights in the City, and that I discussed the case with her and told her to tell her mother, a juror, that the State had no evidence and all their witnesses were lying. She signed it Marlo Wilfang before a notary public.

"Any truth to it, Mr. Rudd?" Kaufman growls, really steamed up.

"Oh, a little, I suppose."

"You wanna tell your side of the story?" he asks, obviously not ready to believe a word I say. Huver mumbles loud enough to be heard, "Clear case of jury tampering."

To which I snap, "You wanna hear my side first or you wanna string me up without all the facts, same as Gardy?"

Judge Kaufman says, "That's enough. Knock it off, Mr. Huver."

I tell my version, accurately, perfectly, without a single word of embellishment. I make the point that I've never met this woman, wouldn't know her from Eve—how could I?—and that she deliberately sought me out, initiated the contact, then couldn't wait to hustle back home to Milo and try to insert herself into this trial.

Often it takes a village to properly convict a killer.

Almost yelling, I say, "She says here I initiated contact? How? I don't know this woman. She knows me because she's been in the courtroom, watching the trial. She can recognize me. How am I supposed to recognize her? Does this make *any* sense?"

It doesn't, of course, but Huver and Kaufman won't budge. They are convinced they have me nailed. Their hatred of me and my client is so intense they can't see the obvious.

I hammer away: "She's lying, okay? She deliberately planned all of this. She bumped into me, had a conversation, then prepared this affidavit, probably in your office, Huver, and she is lying. That's perjury and contempt of court. Do something, Judge."

"I don't need you to tell me—"

"Oh, come on. Get up off your ass and do the right thing for a change."

"Listen, Mr. Rudd," he says, red-faced and ready to take a swing at me. I want a mistrial at this point. I want to provoke these two into doing something really stupid.

Loudly, I say, "I want a hearing. Keep the jury out, call this fine young lady to the witness stand, and let me cross-examine her. She wants to get involved in this trial, bring her on. Her mother is obviously biased and unstable and I want her off the jury."

"What did you say to her?" Kaufman asked.

"I just told you, word for word. I told her the same thing I would say to any other person on the face of this earth—your case is built on nothing but a bunch of lying witnesses and you have no credible proof. Period."

"You've lost your mind," Huver says.

"I want a hearing," I practically yell. "I want this woman off the jury and I will not proceed with the trial until she's gone."

"Are you threatening me?" Kaufman asks as things spin rapidly out of control.

"No, sir. I am promising you. I will not continue."

"Then I'll hold you in contempt and throw you in jail."

"I've been there before. Do it, and we'll have ourselves a mistrial. We can come back in six months and have this party all over again."

They don't know for sure that I've been in jail, but at this moment they figure I'm not lying. A fringe lawyer like me is constantly flirting with ethical boundaries. Jail time is a badge of honor. If I'm forced to anger a judge, or humiliate him, so be it.

We go silent for a few minutes. The court reporter stares at her feet, and if given the chance she would sprint from the room, knocking over chairs in the process. At this point, Huver is terrified of a reversal, of having his great conviction frowned upon by an appellate court that sends it back for another trial. He doesn't want to relive this ordeal. What he wants is that glorious date in the future when he drives, probably with a reporter in the car with him, to a prison called Big Wheeler, where the State keeps its death house. He'll be treated like royalty because he will be the Man—the gunslinger who solved the hideous crime and secured the guilty verdict that sent Gardy Baker to his execution, thus allowing Milo to have its closure. He'll be given a front-row seat behind a curtain that will be dramatically pulled aside to reveal Gardy lying on a gurney with tubes in his arms. Afterward, he, Huver, will find the time to chat somberly with the press and describe the burdens his office places upon him. He has yet to

witness an execution, and in this death-happy state that's worse
than being a thirty-year-old virgin. *State v. Gardy Baker* is Dan
Huver's finest hour. It will make his career. He'll get to speak at
those all-important prosecutors' conferences held in cheap casinos.
He'll get reelected.

At the moment, though, he's sweating because he has over-
played his hand.

They were convinced they had me by the balls. What foolish-
ness. Nailing me with some bogus improper contact charge will
not help their case and cause at this point. It's overkill, and it's not
unusual. They have Gardy all but convicted and sentenced to die,
and for fun they thought it would be cute to take a bite out of me.

"Smells like improper contact to me, Judge," Huver says, trying to be dramatic.

"It would," I say.

"Let's deal with it later," Kaufman says. "The jury is waiting."

I say, "I guess you guys are deaf. I'm not proceeding until I get
a hearing. I insist on getting this into the record."

Kaufman looks at Huver and both seem to lose air. They know
I'm crazy enough to go on strike, refuse to participate in the trial,
and when that happens they are staring at a mistrial. The judge
glares at me and says, "I hold you in contempt."

"Put me in jail," I say, mocking, taunting. The court reporter
is getting every word. "Put me in jail."

But he can't do it right now. He has to make a decision, and
a wrong one could jeopardize everything. If I go to jail over this,
the entire trial is hijacked and there's really no way to save it.
Somewhere down the road, an appellate court, most likely a federal one, will review Kaufman's exact movements right here and
call a foul. Gardy has to have a lawyer, a real one, and they simply
cannot proceed with me in jail. They've handed me a gift.

A few seconds pass and tempers cool. Helpfully, almost sweetly,

I say, "Look, Judge, you can't deny me a hearing on this. To do so is to hand me some heavy ammo for the appeal."

"What kind of hearing?" he says, cracking.

"I want this woman, this Marlo Wilfang, on the witness stand in a closed hearing. You guys are hell-bent on nailing me with improper contact, so let's get to the bottom of it. I have the right to defend myself. Send the jury home for the day and let's have us a brawl."

"I'm not sending the jury home," he says as he falls into his chair, defeated.

"Fine. Keep 'em locked up all day. I don't care. This gal has lied to you, and in doing so she's stuck her nose into the middle of this trial. There's no way her mother can stay on the jury. It's grounds for a mistrial now, and it's damned sure grounds for a reversal five years from now. Pick your poison."

They are listening because they are suddenly frightened and woefully inexperienced. I've gotten the mistrials. I've gotten the reversals. I've been here many times, in the center of the arena where death is on the line and one mistake can ruin a case. They are novices. Kaufman has presided over two capital murder trials in the seven years he's been on the bench. Huver has sent only one man to death row, an embarrassment for any prosecutor around here. Two years ago he bungled a death case so badly the judge (not Kaufman) was forced to declare a mistrial. The charges were later dismissed. They are in over their heads and they have just blundered badly.

"Who prepared the affidavit?" I ask.

No response.

I say, "Look, the language used here definitely came from a lawyer. No layperson speaks like this. Did your office prepare it, Huver?"

Huver, trying to remain cool but now far beyond desperate,

says something that not even Kaufman can believe: "Judge, we can continue with Trots while Mr. Rudd sits over in the jail."

I burst out laughing as Kaufman looks like he's been slapped.

"Oh, go right ahead," I say, taunting. "You've managed to botch this case from the first day, just go ahead and award Gardy with a reversal."

Kaufman says, "No. Mr. Trots has said nothing so far and it would be wise if that boy just continues sitting there with that stupid look on his face." While this is funny, I look hard at His Honor and then hard at the court reporter, who's capturing it all.

"Strike that," Kaufman barks at her as he catches himself. What a moron. A trial often resembles a bad circus as various acts spin out of control. What began as a fun-and-games attempt to humiliate me now looks like a terrible idea, at least for them.

I don't want Huver coming up with any good ideas—not that I have much to worry about—and so to keep him off balance I throw some gas on the fire by saying, "Of all the stupid things you've said so far in this trial, that has got to be the winner. Bennie Trots. What a joke. You would want him in the first chair."

"What's your position, Mr. Rudd?" Kaufman demands.

"I'm not walking back into that courtroom until we have a hearing on improper contact with juror number eight, the lovely Mrs. Glynna Roston. If I'm really in contempt, then throw me in jail. Right now I'd rather have a mistrial than a triple orgasm."

"No need to be crude, Mr. Rudd."

Huver begins fidgeting and stammering. "Well, uh, Judge, uh, I suppose we could deal with the improper contact and the contempt later, you know, after the trial or something. Me, I'd just rather get on with the testimony. This, uh, just seems so unnecessary at this point."

"Then why'd you start it, Huver?" I say. "Why did you clowns get all excited about improper contact when you knew damned well this Wilfang woman is lying?"

"Don't call me a clown," Judge Kaufman sneers.

"Sorry, Judge, I wasn't referring to you. I was referring to all the clowns in the prosecutor's office, including the district attorney himself."

"If we could elevate the level of discourse here," Kaufman says.

"My apologies," I say, about as sarcastically as humanly possible.

Huver retreats to the window, where he stares onto the rows of shabby buildings that comprise the Main Street of Milo. Kaufman retreats to a bookcase behind his desk where he stares at books he's never touched. The air is strained and tense. A weighty decision must be made, and quickly, and if His Honor gets it wrong the aftershocks will ripple for years.

He finally turns around and says, "I guess we'd better question juror number eight, but we're not doing it out there. We'll conduct the inquiry here."

What follows is one of those episodes in a trial that frustrate litigants, jurors, and observers. We spend the rest of the day in Judge Kaufman's less than spacious chambers haggling and often yelling over the ins and outs of my improper contact with a juror. Glynna Roston is dragged in, put under oath, and is almost too terrified to speak. She begins lying immediately when she says she has not discussed this case with her family. On cross-examination, I attack with a vengeance that seems to astonish even Kaufman and Huver. She leaves the room sobbing. Next, they drag in her daffy daughter, Ms. Marlo Wilfang, who repeats her little narrative under the clumsy questioning of Dan Huver, who's really off his game now. When she's handed over to me, I sweetly walk her down the golden path, then slice her throat from ear to ear. Within ten minutes, she's crying, gasping for breath, and wishing a thousand times she'd never called my name at the arena. It becomes painfully obvious she's lying in her affidavit. Even Judge Kaufman asks her, "In a crowd of five thousand people, how did Mr. Rudd find you if he's never met you before?"

Thank you, Judge. That would be the great question.

As her story goes, she came home from the fights late on Friday. When she finally woke up on Saturday, she called her mother, who immediately called Mr. Dan Huver, who knew exactly what to do. They met in his office on Sunday afternoon, worked out the language for the affidavit, and, presto! Huver was in business.

I call Huver as a witness. He objects. We argue, but Kaufman has no choice. I question Huver for an hour, and two bobcats trapped in the same burlap sack would be much more civilized. One of his assistants wrote every word of the affidavit. One of his secretaries typed it. Another secretary notarized it.

He then questions me and the squabbling continues. Throughout this tedious ordeal, the jurors wait in the deliberation room, no doubt briefed by Glynna Roston and no doubt blaming me for another frustrating delay in the trial. As if I care. I keep reminding Kaufman and Huver that they are playing with a cobra here. If Glynna Roston stays on the jury, I'm guaranteed a reversal. I'm not sure of this—on appeal nothing is guaranteed—but I gradually see them wither under the strain and doubt their own judgment. I repeatedly move for a mistrial. The motions are repeatedly denied. I don't care. It's in the record. Late in the afternoon, Kaufman decides to excuse Mrs. Roston and replace her with Ms. Mazy, one of our blue-ribbon alternates.

Ms. Mazy is no replacement to get excited about; in fact, she's no better than the last old gal who occupied her chair. No one in Milo would be better. You could select twelve from a pool of a thousand and every jury would look and vote the same. So why did I burn so much clock today? To hold them accountable. To scare the hell out of them with the scenario that they—prosecutor and judge, duly elected by the locals—could screw up the most sensational case this backwater hick town has ever seen. To collect ammunition for the appeal. And, to make them respect me.

I demand that Marlo Wilfang be prosecuted for perjury, but the prosecutor is tired. I demand she be held in contempt. Instead, Judge Kaufman reminds me that I'm in contempt. He sends for a bailiff, one with handcuffs.

I say, "I'm sorry, Judge, but I've forgotten why you found me in contempt. It was so long ago."

"Because you refused to continue the trial this morning, and because we've wasted an entire day back here fighting over a juror. Plus, you insulted me."

There are so many ways to respond to this nonsense, but I decide to let it pass. Tossing me in jail over a contempt charge will only complicate matters for them, for the authorities, and it will give me even more ammo for Gardy's appeal. A large deputy comes in and Kaufman says, "Take him to jail."

Huver is at the window, his back to it all.

I don't want to go to jail, but I can't wait to get out of this room. It's beginning to reek of stale body odor. The handcuffs are locked around my wrists, hands in front, not back, and as I'm led away I look at Kaufman and say, "I'm assuming I will be allowed to continue as lead counsel in the morning."

"You will."

To frighten them even more, I add, "The last time I was tossed in jail in the middle of a trial the conviction was reversed by the state supreme court. Nine to zero. You clowns should read your cases."

Another large deputy joins our little parade. They take me

through the back doors and down the rear hallway I use every day. For some reason we pause on a landing as the deputies mumble into their radios. When we finally step outside, I get the impression that word was leaked. A cheer goes up by my haters when they see me frog-marched out, handcuffed. For no apparent reason, the cops stall as they try to decide which patrol car to use. I stand by one, exposed, smiling at my little mob. I see Partner and yell that I'll call him later. He is stunned and confused. For sport, they shove me into the same backseat with Gardy; lawyer and client, off to jail. As we pull away, with lights and sirens fully engaged to give this miserable town as much drama as possible, Gardy looks at me and says, "Where you been all day?"

I'm not about to try. I lift my bound hands and say, "Fighting with the judge. Guess who won?"

"How can they throw a lawyer in jail?"

"The judge can do whatever he wants."

"You getting the death penalty too?"

I chuckle for the first time in many hours. "No, not yet anyway."

Gardy is amused by this unexpected change in routine. He says, "You're gonna love the food there."

"I'll bet." The two deputies in the front seat are listening so hard they're barely breathing.

"You ever been in jail before?" my client asks.

"Oh yes, several times. I have a knack for pissing off judges."

"How'd you piss off Judge Kaufman?"

"It's a long story."

"Well, we got all night, don't we?"

I suppose we do, though I doubt they'll throw me in the same cell with my dear client. Minutes later we stop in front of a 1950s-style flat-roofed building with several additions stuck to its sides like malignant tumors. I've been here a few times to meet with Gardy and it's a miserable place. We park; they yank us out of the car and jostle us inside a cramped open room where some cops lounge around pushing paper and acting like badasses. Gardy disappears into the rear, and when an unseen door opens I can hear prisoners yelling in the background.

"Judge Kaufman said I can make two phone calls," I snap at the jailer as he moves toward me. He stops, uncertain as to what exactly a jailer is supposed to do when confronting an angry lawyer sent over for contempt. He backs away.

I call Judith, and after barking at her receptionist, then her secretary, then her paralegal, I get her on the phone, explain I'm in jail again and need help. She curses, reminds me of how busy she is, then says all right. I call Partner and give him the update.

They hand me an orange jumpsuit with "Milo City Jail" stenciled across the back. I change in a filthy bathroom, carefully arranging my shirt, tie, and suit on one hanger. I hand it to the jailer and say, "Please don't wrinkle this. I have to wear it tomorrow."

"You want it pressed?" he says, then roars with laughter. The others break down too at this real knee-slapper, and I smile like a good sport. When the laughing is over I say, "So what's for dinner?"

The jailer says, "It's Monday, Spam day. Always Spam on Monday."

"Can't wait." My cell is a ten-by-ten concrete bunker that reeks of stale urine and body odor. On the bunk beds are two young black men, one reading, the other napping. There is no third bed, so I'll sleep in a plastic chair stained with dark brown splotches. My two new cellies do not appear the least bit friendly. I don't want to fight, but getting beat up in jail, in the middle of a capital murder defense, would cause an automatic mistrial. I'll ponder it.

Because she's done this before, Judith knows exactly what to do. At 5:00 p.m., she files a petition for habeas corpus in federal court in the City, with an urgent demand for an immediate hearing. I love federal court, most of the time.

She also sends a copy of her petition to my favorite reporter at the newspaper. I'll make as much noise as possible. Kaufman and Huver have blundered badly, and they'll pay for it. The reader on the bottom bunk decides he wants to talk, so I explain why I'm here. He thinks it's funny, a lawyer in jail for pissing off the judge. The napper on the top bunk rolls over and joins the fun. Before long, I'm giving legal advice, and these guys need as much as I can dish out.

An hour later, a jailer fetches me with the news that I have a visitor. I follow him through a maze of narrow hallways and find myself in a cramped room with a Breathalyzer. This is where they bring the drunk drivers. The Bishop stands and we shake hands. We've spoken on the phone but never met. I thank him for coming but caution him about doing so. He says screw it—he's not afraid of the locals. Plus, he knows how to lie low and stay under the radar. He also knows the police chief, the cops, the judge— the usual small-town crap. He says he's tried to call Huver and Kaufman to tell them they've made a big mistake, but he can't get through. He's leaning on the police chief to put me in a better cell. The more we talk, the more I like the guy. He's a street fighter, a worn-out, frazzled old goat who's been knocking heads with the cops for decades. He hasn't made a dime and doesn't care. I wonder if I'll be him in twenty years.

"How about the DNA tests?" he asks.

"The lab will get the samples tomorrow and they've promised a quick turnaround."

"And if it's Peeley?"

"All hell breaks loose." This guy is on my side, but I don't know him. We chat for ten minutes and he says good-bye.

When I return to my cell, my two new friends have spread the word that there's a criminal lawyer in here with them. Before long, I'm yelling advice up and down the block.

11.

Common sense is not always my strong suit, but I decide not to start a fight with Fonzo and Frog, my two new partners in crime. Instead I sit in my chair all night and try to nap. It doesn't work. I said no to the Spam for dinner and no to the putrid eggs and cold toast for breakfast. Thankfully, no one mentions a shower. They bring me my suit, shirt, tie, shoes, and socks, and I dress quickly. I say good-bye to my cellies, both of whom will be behind bars for several years, regardless of the brilliant advice I dispensed for hours.

Gardy and I are given separate rides back to the courthouse. A larger crowd of enemies jeer at me as I'm sort of dragged out of the car, still in handcuffs. Once I'm inside and away from any photographers, they remove the handcuffs. Partner is waiting in the hallway. I made the morning edition of the *Chronicle,* the City's daily. Metro section, third page. No big deal—Rudd is thrown in jail again.

As instructed, I follow a bailiff back into the chambers of Judge Kaufman, who's waiting with Huver. Both wear smirks and are curious to see how I survived the night. I do not mention the jail, do not acknowledge the fact that I've not slept, eaten, or showered in a long time. I'm in one piece, raring to go, and this seems to irritate them. It's all fun and games, with Gardy's life on the line.

Seconds after I step into chambers, another bailiff rushes in and says, "Sorry, Judge, but there's a U.S. marshal out here says you gotta be in federal court in the City at eleven this morning. You too, Mr. Huver."

"What the hell?" Kaufman says.

Oh so helpfully, I explain, "It's a habeas corpus hearing, Judge. My lawyers filed it yesterday afternoon. An emergency hearing to get me out of jail. You guys started this crap, now I have to finish it."

"Does he have a subpoena?" Huver asks. The bailiff hands over some paperwork and Huver and Kaufman scan it quickly.

"It's not a subpoena," Kaufman says. "It's sort of a notice from Judge Samson. Thought he was dead. He has no right to notify me to be present for a hearing of any kind."

"He's been off his rocker for twenty years," Huver says, somewhat relieved. "I ain't going. We're in the middle of a trial here."

He's not wrong about Judge Samson. If the lawyers could vote for the craziest federal judge in the land, Arnie Samson would win in a landslide. But he's my crazy friend, and he's freed me from jail before.

Kaufman says to the bailiff, "Tell the marshal to get lost. If he starts trouble, tell the sheriff to arrest him. That'll really piss him off, won't it? The sheriff arresting a marshal. Ha. Bet that's never happened before. Anyway, we're not leaving. We have a trial to resume here."

"Why'd you run to federal court?" Huver asks me in all seriousness.

"Because I don't like being in jail. What kinda stupid question is that?"

The bailiff leaves and Kaufman says, "I'm vacating the contempt order, okay, Mr. Rudd? I figure one night in the slammer is enough for your behavior."

I say, "Well, it's certainly enough for a mistrial or a reversal."

"Let's not argue that," Kaufman says. "Can we proceed?"

"You're the judge."

"What about the hearing in federal court?"

"Are you asking me for legal advice?" I fire back.

"Hell no."

"Ignore the notice at your own risk. Hell, Judge Samson might throw the both of you in jail for a night or two. Wouldn't that be funny?"

12.

We eventually make it back to the courtroom, and it takes some time to get everyone settled. When the jury is brought in, I refuse to look at them. By now they all know I spent the night in jail, and I'm sure they're curious about how I survived. So I give them nothing.

Judge Kaufman apologizes for the delays and says it's time to get to work. He looks at Huver, who stands and says, "Your Honor, the State rests."

This is an amateurish ploy designed to make my life even more miserable. I rise and angrily say, "Your Honor, he could've told me this yesterday or even this morning."

"Call your first witness," Kaufman barks.

"I'm not ready. I have some motions. On the record."

He has no choice but to excuse the jury. We spend the next two hours haggling over whether or not the State has presented enough proof to keep going. I repeat the same arguments. Kaufman makes the same rulings. It's all for the record.

My first witness is a scraggly, troubled kid who looks remarkably similar to my client. His first name is Wilson; he's fifteen years old, a dropout, a druggie, a kid who's basically homeless, though an aunt allows him to sleep in the garage whenever he's sick. And he's our star witness!

The Fentress girls went missing around 4:00 on a Wednesday afternoon. They left school on their bikes but never made it home. A search began around 6:00 and intensified as the hours passed. By midnight, the entire town was in a panic and everyone was outside with a flashlight. Their bodies were found in the polluted pond around noon the following day.

I have six witnesses, Wilson and five others, who will testify that they were with Gardy on that Wednesday afternoon from around 2:00 until dark. They were at a place called the Pit, an abandoned gravel pit in the middle of some dense woods south of town. It's a secluded hideout for truants, runaways, homeless kids, druggies, petty felons, and drunks. It attracts a few older deadbeats, but for the most part it's a haven for the kids nobody wants. They sleep under lean-tos, share their stolen food, drink their stolen booze, take drugs I've never heard of, engage in random sex, and in general waste away the days while sliding closer to either death or incarceration. Gardy was there when someone else abducted and murdered the Fentress girls.

So we have an alibi—my client's whereabouts can be vouched for. Or can it?

By the time Wilson takes the stand and is sworn in, the jurors are suspicious. For the occasion he's wearing what he always wears—grimy jeans with lots of holes, battered combat boots, a green T-shirt proclaiming the greatness of some acid-rock band, and a smart purple bandanna looped around his neck. His scalp is skinned above the ears and yields to a bright orange Mohawk roaring down the center. He's displaying the obligatory collection of tattoos, earrings, and piercings. Because he's just a kid without a clue and is now being dragged into such a formal setting, he instantly retreats behind a smirk that makes you want to slap him.

"Just be normal," I told him. Sadly, he is. I wouldn't believe a word he says, though he's telling the truth. As rehearsed, we walk through that Wednesday afternoon.

Huver annihilates him on cross-examination. You're fifteen years old, son, why were you not in school? Smoking dope, huh, along with your pal here, that's what you're telling these jurors? Drinking, and drugging, just a bunch of deadbeats, right? Wilson does a lousy job of denying this. After fifteen minutes of abuse, Wilson is disoriented, afraid he might be charged with some crime. Huver hammers away, a bully on the playground.

But because Huver is not too bright, he goes too far. He's got Wilson on the ropes and is drawing blood with each question. He's grilling him about dates—how can he be certain it was that Wednesday back in March? You kids keep a calendar out there at the Pit?

Loudly, "You have no idea what Wednesday you're talking about, do you?"

"Yes, sir," Wilson says, politely for the first time.

"How?"

"Because the police came out there, said they were looking for two little girls. That was the day. And Gardy had been there all afternoon." For a kid without a brain, Wilson delivers this perfectly, just like we practiced.

Evidently, when there is a crime in Milo slightly more serious than littering, the police rush out to the Pit and make accusations. Harass the usual suspects. It's about three miles from the pond where the Fentress girls were found. It's blatantly obvious none of the regulars at the Pit have any means of transportation other than their feet, yet the police routinely show up and throw around

their considerable weight. Gardy says he remembers the cops asking about the missing girls. The cops, of course, do not remember
seeing Gardy at the Pit.

None of this matters. This jury is not about to believe a word
Wilson says.

Next, I call a witness with even less credibility. They call her
Lolo, and the poor child has lived under bridges and in box cul-
verts for as long as she can remember. The boys protect her and
in return she keeps them satisfied. She's now nineteen and there's
no way she will see twenty-five, not on this side of the bars. She's
covered in tattoos, and by the time she's sworn in the jurors are
already disgusted. She remembers that particular Wednesday,
remembers the cops coming out to the Pit, remembers Gardy
being there all afternoon.

On cross, Huver can't wait to bring up the fact that she's been
busted twice for shoplifting. For food! What are you supposed to
do when you're hungry? Huver makes this sound like she deserves
the death penalty.

We plow ahead. I call my alibi witnesses, who tell the truth,
and Huver makes them look like criminals. Such is the lunacy and
unfairness of the system. Huver's witnesses, the ones testifying on
behalf of the State, are cloaked with legitimacy, as if they've been
sanctified by the authorities. Cops, experts, even snitches who've
been washed and cleansed and spruced up in nice clothes, all take
the stand and tell lies in a coordinated effort to have my client
executed. But the witnesses who know the truth, and are telling
it, are discounted immediately and made to look like fools.

Like so many, this trial is not about the truth; it's about winning. And to win, with no real evidence, Huver must fabricate
and lie and attack the truth as if he hates it. I have six witnesses
who swear my client was nowhere close to the scene when the
crime was committed, and all six are scoffed at. Huver has pro-

duced almost two dozen witnesses, virtually all known to be liars by the cops, the prosecution, and the judge, yet the jurors lap up their lies as if they're reading Holy Scripture.

13.

I show the jurors a map of their lovely town. The Pit is far away from the pond; there's no possible way Gardy could have been in both places at the approximate time the girls were murdered. The jurors don't believe any of this because they have known for some time that Gardy was a member of a satanic cult with a history of sexual perversion. There is no physical proof that the Fentress girls were sexually assaulted; yet every miserable redneck in this awful place believes Gardy raped them before he killed them.

At midnight, I'm lying across my lumpy motel bed, 9-millimeter by my side, when my cell phone beeps. It's the DNA lab in San Diego. The blood Tadeo brutally extracted from the forehead of Jack Peeley matches the strand of hair the murderer left behind in the shoelaces he tightly bound around the ankles of Jenna Fentress, age eleven.

14.

Sleep is impossible; I can't even close my eyes. Partner and I leave the motel in the dark and are almost to Milo before we see the first hint of light in the east. I meet with the Bishop in his office as the town slowly comes to life. He calls Judge Kaufman at home, gets him up and out of bed, and at 8:00 a.m. I'm in his chambers with Huver and the court reporter. All of what follows will be on the record.

I lay out my options. If they refuse to stop the trial, dismiss the case, and send everybody home—and this is what I expect them to do—then I will either (1) issue a subpoena for Jack Peeley, have him hauled into court, put him on the stand, and expose him as the killer; or (2) go to the press with the details of the DNA testing; or (3) announce to the jury what I know; or (4) do all of the above; or (5) do nothing, let them get their conviction, and slaughter them on appeal.

They demand to know how I obtained a blood sample for Jack Peeley, but I'm not required to tell them. I remind them that for the past ten months I've begged them to investigate Peeley, to get a blood sample, and so on, but they have had no interest. They had Gardy, one of Satan's foot soldiers. For the tenth time I explain that Peeley (1) knew the girls, (2) was seen near the pond when they disappeared, and (3) had just broken up with their mother after a long, violent romance.

They are bewildered, stunned, at times almost incoherent as reality settles in. Their bogus and corrupt prosecution has just unraveled. They have the wrong man!

Virtually all prosecutors have the same genetic flaw; they cannot admit the obvious once it's on the table. They cling to their theories. They know they are right because they've been convinced of it for months, even years. "I believe in my case" is one of their favorite lines, and they'll repeat it mindlessly as the real killer walks forward with blood on his hands and says, "I did it."

Because I've heard so much of their idiotic bullshit before, I have tried to imagine what Huver might say at this point. But when he says, "It's possible Gardy Baker and Jack Peeley were working together," I laugh out loud.

Kaufman blurts, "Are you serious?"

I say, "Brilliant, just brilliant. Two men who've never met, one eighteen years old, the other thirty-five, join up for about half an hour to murder two little girls, then go their separate ways, never to see each other again and both determined to keep their mouths shut forever. You wanna argue that on appeal?"

"It wouldn't surprise me," Huver says, scratching his chin as if his high-powered brain is clicking right along and sifting through new theories of the crime.

Kaufman, whose mouth is still open in disbelief, says, "You can't be serious, Dan."

Dan says, "I want to proceed. I think Gardy Baker was involved in this crime. I can get a conviction." It's pathetic to watch him plunge onward when he knows he's wrong.

"Let me guess," I say. "You believe in your case."

"Damned right I do. I want to go forward. I can get a conviction."

"Of course you can, and getting a conviction is far more important than justice," I say, remarkably under control. "Get your conviction. We'll slog through the appellate courts for the next ten years while Gardy wastes away on death row and the real killer walks the streets, then one day a federal judge somewhere will see the light and we'll have another high-profile exoneration. You, the prosecutor, and you, the judge, will look like idiots because of what's happening right now."

"I want to go forward," Huver says like a defective recording.

I keep going: "I think I'll go to the press, show them the DNA test results. They'll splash it around and you'll look like a couple of clowns still trying the case. Meanwhile, Jack Peeley will disappear."

"How'd you get his DNA?" Judge Kaufman asks me.

"He got in a bar fight last Saturday at the Blue & White, got his face busted, and the guy who did it works for me. I personally scraped Peeley's blood off my guy's fist and sent it to the lab, along with a sample of the hair I collected earlier."

"That's tampering with the evidence," Huver says, predictably.

"Oh, sue me, or throw me in jail again. This little party's over, Dan, give it up!"

Kaufman says, "I want to see the test results."

"I'll have them by tomorrow. The lab's in San Diego."

"We're in recess until then."

15.

At some point during the day, the judge and the prosecutor meet secretly. I'm not invited. The rules of procedure prohibit such clandestine meetings, but they happen. These guys need an exit strategy, and fast. By now they know I'm half-crazy and I will indeed run to the press with my test results. At this desperate hour, they are still more concerned with politics than with the truth. All they care about is saving face.

Partner and I return to the City, where I spend the day working on other cases. I convince the lab to e-mail the test results to Judge Kaufman, and by noon he knows the truth. At 6:00 p.m. I get the phone call. Jack Peeley has just been arrested.

We meet the following morning in Kaufman's chambers, not in open court, where we belong. A dismissal in open court would be far too embarrassing for the system, so the judge and the prosecutor have conspired to do it behind closed doors, and as quickly as possible. I sit at a table with Gardy by my side and listen as Dan Huver limps through a tepid motion to dismiss the charges. I strongly suspect that Huver wants to proceed with his beloved case, the one he believes in so strongly, but Kaufman said no; said this little party is over; said let's cut our losses and get this radical bastard and his brain-damaged client out of here.

When the paperwork is signed, Gardy is a free man. He's spent the last year in a tough jail—I should know. But a year in jail for an innocent man is pure luck in our system. There are thousands locked away for decades, but that's another soapbox.

Gardy is bewildered, not sure where to go or what to do. As they lead us out of Kaufman's chambers, I hand him two $20 bills and tell him good luck. They'll sneak him back to the jail to collect his assets, and from there his mother will take him somewhere safe. I'll never see him again.

He doesn't say thanks because he doesn't know what to say. I don't want to embrace him because he didn't shower last night, but we manage a quick hug in a narrow hallway while two deputies watch us. "It's over, Gardy," I keep saying, but he doesn't believe me.

Word has leaked and there's a mob waiting outside. The town of Milo will never believe anyone but Gardy killed the Fentress girls, regardless of the evidence. This is what happens when the cops act on one of their smart hunches and march off in the wrong direction, controlling the rumors and taking the press along with them. The prosecutor joins the parade early on, and before long it becomes an organized and semi-legitimate lynching.

I slip through a side door to where Partner is waiting. We make our escape, without an escort of any sort, and as we speed away from the courthouse two tomatoes and an egg splash onto our windshield. I can't help but laugh. Once again, I'm leaving town in style.

PART TWO

THE
BOOM BOOM
ROOM

1.

Rich people tend to avoid death row. Link Scanlon has not been so lucky, though you couldn't find three people in this city who care about Link or his luck. There are about a million people here, and when Link was finally convicted and sent away, virtually everyone felt some measure of relief. Drug trafficking was dealt a severe blow, though it soon recovered. Several strip clubs closed, which pleased many young wives. Parents of teenage girls told themselves their daughters were safer. Owners of fancy sports cars relaxed as auto thefts plummeted. Most important, the police and narcotics agents relaxed and waited for the dip in crime. It happened, but didn't last long.

Link was sentenced to death by an untampered jury for killing a judge. Soon after he arrived on death row, his lead defense lawyer was found strangled. So I suppose the City's bar association was also relieved to see Link put away.

On second thought, there must have been several hundred people here who truly missed Link, at first. Morticians, strippers, drug runners, chop shop operators, and crooked cops, to name a few. But it doesn't matter now. That was six years ago, and once in prison Link proved capable of running most of his businesses from behind bars.

All he ever wanted was to be a gangster, an old-style Capone-like character with a lust for blood and violence and unlimited cash. His father had been a bootlegger who died of cirrhosis. His mother had remarried often and badly. Unrestrained by a normal family life, Link hit the streets at the age of twelve and soon mastered petty thievery. By fifteen, he had his own gang and was selling pot and porn in our high schools. He was arrested at sixteen, got a slap on the wrist, and thus began a long and colorful relationship with the criminal justice system.

Until he was twenty, his name was George. It didn't fit, so he adopted and discarded several nicknames, jewels such as Lash and Boss. He finally settled on Link because he, George Scanlon, was so often linked to various crimes. Link fit him nicely and he hired a lawyer to make it legal. Just Link Scanlon, no middle initial, nothing stuck on the end. The new name gave him a new identity. He was a new man with something to prove. He became reckless in his desire to become the toughest mobster in town, and he was quite successful. By the time he was thirty, Link's thugs were killing regularly as he took over the City's skin business and cornered his share of the drug traffic.

He has been on death row for only six years and his execution is scheduled for 10:00 tonight. Six years is not long on death row; on the average, at least in this state, the appeals drag on for fourteen years before an execution. Twenty is not unusual. The shortest was two years, but that guy begged for the needle. It's fair to say Link's case has been rushed along, or expedited. Kill a judge and all the other judges take offense. His appeals were met with surprisingly few delays. His conviction was affirmed, affirmed, and reaffirmed. All rulings were unanimous, not a single dissent anywhere, state or federal. The U.S. Supremes refused to consider his case. Link pissed off those who truly run the system, and tonight the system gets the ultimate revenge.

Judge Nagy was the one Link killed. He, Link, didn't actually pull the trigger; instead he sent word down the line that he wanted Nagy dead. A career hitter called Knuckles got the assignment and carried things out in splendid fashion. They found Judge

Nagy and his wife in bed, in their pajamas, bullet holes in their heads. Knuckles then talked too much and the cops had a wire in the right place. Knuckles was on death row too, for about two years, until they found him with Drano packed in his mouth and throat. The cops quizzed Link but he swore he didn't know a thing about it.

What was Judge Nagy's offense? He was a tough law-and-order type who hated drugs and was famous for throwing the book at traffickers. He was about to sentence two of Link's favorite henchmen—one was his cousin—to a hundred years each, and this upset Link. It was his town, not Nagy's. He, Link, had been wanting to knock off a judge for years; sort of the ultimate take-down. Kill a judge, walk away from it, and the world knows you are indeed above the law.

After his defense lawyer was murdered, folks thought I was a fool to take his case. Another bad outcome for Link, and they might find me at the bottom of a lake. But that was six years ago, and Link and I have gotten along just fine. He knows I've tried to save his life. He'll spare mine. What would he gain by killing his last lawyer?

2.

Partner and I pull in to the main gate at Big Wheeler, the maximum security prison where the State maintains its death row and does its executing. A guard steps to the passenger door and says, "Name?"

"Rudd, Sebastian Rudd. Here to see Link Scanlon."

"Of course." The guard's name is Harvey and we've chatted before, but not tonight. Tonight Big Wheeler is locked down and there is a thrill in the air. It's execution time! Across the road, some protesters with candles sing a solemn hymn while others

chant support for the death penalty. Back and forth. There are TV
news vans lining the highway.

Harvey scribbles something on a clipboard, says, "Unit Nine,"
and as we're about to drive away he leans in and whispers, "What
are your chances?"

"Slim," I say as we begin moving. We follow a prison security
truck with gunmen standing in the back; another one trails us.
Floodlights nearly blind us as we inch along, passing brightly lit
buildings where three thousand men are locked in their cells and
waiting for Link to die so things can return to normal. There is
no sensible reason for a prison to go nuts when there's an execution. Extra security is never needed. No one has ever escaped from
death row. The condemned men there live in isolation, and thus
do not have a gang of friends who might decide to storm the
Bastille and free everyone. But rituals are important to the men
who run prisons, and nothing gets their adrenaline pumping like
an execution. Their little lives are mundane and monotonous, but
occasionally the world tunes in when it's time to kill a killer. No
effort at heightened drama is to be missed.

Unit Nine is far away from the other units, with enough chain
link and razor wire around it to stop Ike on the beaches of Nor-
mandy. We eventually reach a gate where a platoon of jumpy
guards can't wait to search Partner and me and our briefcases.
These boys are far too excited about the evening's festivities. With
escorts we enter the building, and I'm led to a makeshift office
where Warden McDuff is waiting, chewing his fingernails, obviously wired. When we're alone in a room with no windows he
says, "Have you heard?"

"Heard what?"

"Ten minutes ago, a bomb went off in the Old Courthouse,
same courtroom Link got convicted in."

I've been in that courtroom a hundred times, so, yes, I am

shocked to hear it's been bombed. On the other hand, I'm not at all surprised to discover that Link Scanlon does not intend to go quietly.

"Anybody hurt?" I ask.

"Don't think so. The courthouse had just closed."

"Wow."

"Wow's right. You better talk to him, Rudd, and quick."

I shrug and give the warden a hopeless look. Trying to talk sense to a gangster like Link Scanlon is a waste of time. "I'm just his lawyer," I say.

"What if he hurts somebody . . ."

"Come on, Warden. The State's executing him in a few hours. What else can it do to him?"

"I know, I know. Where are the appeals?" he asks, crunching a sliver of a thumbnail between his front teeth. He's about to jump out of his skin.

"Fifteenth Circuit," I say. "A Hail Mary. They're all Hail Marys at this point, Warden. Where's Link?"

"In the holding room. I got to get back to my office and talk to the governor."

"Tell him I said hello. Tell him he still hasn't ruled on my last request for a reprieve."

"I'll do that," the warden says as he's leaving the room.

"Thanks."

Few people in this state love an execution as much as our handsome governor. His routine is to wait until the last possible moment, then appear somberly in front of the cameras and announce to the world that he cannot, in good conscience, grant a reprieve. On the verge of tears, he'll talk about the victim and declare that justice must be done.

I follow two guards dressed in full military gear through a maze and come to the Boom Boom Room. It's nothing more than a large holding cell where the condemned is placed precisely five hours before his big moment. There, he waits with his lawyer, spiritual adviser, and maybe some family. Full contact is allowed, and there can be some pretty sad moments when Momma arrives for the final hug. The last meal is served precisely two hours before the final walk, and after that only the lawyer can hang around.

In decades past, our state used a firing squad. Cuffed and bound, the condemned was strapped to a chair, a black veil was dropped over his head, and a bright red cross was attached to his shirt, over his heart. Fifty feet away, five volunteers waited behind a curtain with high-powered rifles, though only four were loaded. The theory was that none of the five would ever know for sure that he killed a man, and this was somehow supposed to assuage his guilt later in life, in the event that he had a change of heart and became burdened. What a crock! There was a long list of volunteers, all eager to put a bullet dead center in another man's heart.

Anyway, prison lingo is vibrant and creative, and over time the execution room picked up its nickname. Legend has it that an air vent was intentionally left open so the cracking sound of the rifles echoed over the prison. When we adopted the needle, for humane reasons, less space was needed. Death row was reconfigured; walls were added here and there. Supposedly, the current Boom Boom Room includes the very spot where the condemned men sat and waited for the bullets.

They frisk me again and I walk through the door. Link is alone, sitting in a folding chair that is leaning against a cinder-block wall. The lights are low. He's glued to a small muted television screen hanging in a corner, and he does not acknowledge my arrival. His favorite movie is *The Godfather*. He's watched it a hundred times, and years ago began working on his imitation of Marlon Brando. Scratchy, painful voice, one he blames on smoking. Clenched jaw. Slow delivery. Aloof. Completely devoid of emotion.

Our death row has a unique rule that allows the condemned man to die in any clothing he chooses. It's a ridiculous rule because, after living here for ten, fifteen, or twenty years, these guys have nothing in the way of a wardrobe. Standard-issue coveralls; maybe a pair of frayed khakis and a T-shirt to wear during visitation; sandals; thick socks for the winter. Link, though, has money and wants to be buried in solid black. He's wearing a black linen shirt with long sleeves buttoned at the wrists, black denim jeans, black socks, and black running shoes. It's not nearly as stylish as he thinks, but at this point who cares about fashion?

Finally he says, "I thought you were going to save me."

"I never said that, Link. I even put it in writing."

"But I paid you all that money."

"A fat fee is no guarantee of a good outcome. That's in writing too."

"Lawyers," he grunts in disgust, and I don't take this lightly. I have never forgotten what happened to his last one. He slowly leans forward, tipping his chair onto all fours, and stands up. Link is fifty now, and for most of his time on the Row he's managed to maintain his good looks. But he's aging quickly, though I doubt if anyone with a firm execution date worries too much about wrinkles and gray hair. He takes a few steps and turns off the television.

The room is maybe fifteen by fifteen, with a small desk, three folding chairs, and a cheap Army-style cot, just in case the condemned might want to catch a few winks before being sent to his eternal rest. I was here once before, three years ago, when my client came within thirty minutes of getting the needle before we were handed a miracle by the Fifteenth Circuit.

Link will not be so lucky. He sits on a corner of the desk and looks down at me. He grunts and says, "I trusted you."

"And with good reason, Link. I fought like hell for you."

"But I'm insane, legally, and you haven't convinced anyone of it. Crazy as hell. Why can't you make them see this?"

"I have tried and you know it, Link. No one listened because no one wanted to listen. You killed the wrong person, a judge. Kill a judge, and his brethren take offense."

"I didn't kill him."

"Well, the jury said you did. That's all that matters." We've had this conversation a thousand times, and why not have it again? Right now, with less than five hours to go, I'll chat with Link on any subject.

"I'm insane, Sebastian. My mind is gone."

It is often said that everyone goes crazy on death row. Twenty-three hours a day in isolation breaks a man mentally, physically, and emotionally. Link, though, has not exactly suffered like the rest. Years ago I explained to him that the U.S. Supreme Court has ruled that a state cannot execute a person who is either mentally retarded or who becomes mentally unsound. Soon thereafter, Link decided he should go insane and he's been acting so ever since. The warden at that time agreed to move Link to the psych unit, where he enjoyed a much more comfortable lockup. Link lived there for three years before a journalist dug deep enough to discover a money trail between various members of the warden's immediate family and a certain crime syndicate. The warden quickly retired and dodged an indictment. Link got slammed back to death row, where he stayed for about a month before getting moved to PC—protective custody. There, he had a larger cell and more privileges. The guards gave him anything he wanted because Link's boys on the outside were taking care of the guards with cash and drugs. In time, Link manipulated a transfer back to the psych unit.

In his six years at Big Wheeler, he's spent about twelve months locked up with the other killers on death row.

I say, "The warden just told me the courthouse got bombed this afternoon. Same courtroom where you got convicted. What a coincidence, huh?"

He frowns and offers a casual, Brando-like shrug, revealing nothing. "I got an appeal floating somewhere right now?" he says.

"It's at the Fifteenth Circuit, but don't get excited."

"Are you telling me I'm gonna die, Sebastian?"

"I told you that last week, Link. The fix is in. The last-minute appeals are worthless. Everything's been litigated. Every issue covered. There's little we can do right now but wait and hope for a miracle."

"I shoulda hired that radical Jew lawyer, what's his name, Lowenstein?"

"Maybe, but you didn't. He's had three clients executed in the past four years."

Marc Lowenstein is an acquaintance of mine and a fine lawyer. Between the two of us, we handle most of the untouchable cases in our end of the state. My cell phone vibrates. It's a text message—the Fifteenth Circuit has just denied.

I say, "Bad news, Link, the Fifteenth just turned us down."

He says nothing but reaches over and turns on the television. I turn the switch for more lighting and ask, "Is your son stopping by tonight?"

He grunts, "No."

He has one child, a son who just got out of federal prison. Extortion. He grew up in the family business and loves his old man, but no one can blame him for avoiding a prison, if only for a visit. Link says, "We've said good-bye already."

"So no guests tonight?"

He grunts, says nothing. No, no visitors for the last hug. Link was married twice but hates both ex-wives. He hasn't spoken to his mother in twenty years. His only brother mysteriously disappeared after a bad business deal. Link reaches into his pocket, produces a cell phone, and makes a call. Inmate cell phones are violently forbidden, and they've caught Link with a dozen over the years. The guards sneak them in; one who got caught said he was paid $1,000 in cash by a stranger in a Burger King parking lot, after lunch.

It's a quick call—I can't understand a word—and Link returns the phone to his pocket. Using the remote, he changes channels and we watch a local cable news show. There's a lot of interest in his execution. A reporter does a nice job of recapping the Nagy murders. They flash photos of the judge and his wife, a pretty lady.

I knew the judge well and appeared several times in his courtroom. He was a hard-ass but fair and smart. We were shocked when he was murdered, but not too surprised when the trail led to Link Scanlon. They run a clip of Knuckles, the gunman, as he's leaving court in handcuffs. What a nasty one.

I say, "You know you're entitled to the counsel of a spiritual adviser?"

He grunts. No.

"The prison has a chaplain, if you'd like a word with him."

"What's a chaplain?"

"A man of God."

"And what might he say to me?"

"Oh, I don't know, Link. I'm told that some folks, right before they pass, like to get things right with God. Confess their sins, stuff like that."

"That might take some time."

Contrition would be an inexcusable act of weakness for a mobster like Link. He has absolutely no remorse, for the Nagy murders or for all those before them. He glares at me and says, "What are you doing here?"

"I'm your lawyer. It's my job to be here, to make sure the final appeals run their course. To give advice."

"And your advice is to talk to a chaplain?"

We're startled by a loud knock on the door. It opens immediately and a man in a cheap suit strolls in, with two guards as escorts. He says, "Mr. Scanlon, I'm Jess Foreman, assistant warden."

"A real pleasure," Link says without taking his eyes off the television.

Foreman ignores me and says, "I have a list of all those who will witness the execution. There's nobody on your list, right?"

"Right."

"Are you sure?"

Link ignores this. Foreman waits, then says, "What about your lawyer?" He looks at me.

"I'll be there," I say. The lawyer is always invited to watch.

"Anybody from Judge Nagy's family?" I ask.

"Yep, all three of his children." Foreman places the list on the desk and leaves. As the door slams behind him, Link says, "Here it is." He lifts the remote, increases the volume.

It's a breaking story—a bomb just exploded in the stately courthouse where the Fifteenth Circuit does its work. The scene outside is frantic as police and firemen scurry about. Smoke boils from a second-floor window. A breathless reporter is moving along the street with his cameraman in tow, looking for a better angle and gushing on about what's happening.

Link's eyes glow as he watches. I say, "Wow, another coincidence." But Link does not hear me. I try to act cool, calm, as if this is no big deal. A bomb here, a bomb there. Couple of phone calls from death row and the fuses get lit. But I am astonished.

Who might be next? Another judge, perhaps the one who presided over his trial and sentenced him to death? That was Judge

Cone, since retired, and for about two years, during and after the trial, he had armed protection. Perhaps the jurors? They lived cautiously thereafter with the cops close by. No one was hurt or threatened.

Link grunts, "Where does the appeal go now?"

I guess he plans to bomb every courthouse from here to Washington. He knows the answer to his question; we've discussed it enough. I reply, "The Supremes, in D.C. Why do you ask?"

He ignores this. We watch the television for a while. CNN picks up the story and in its usual, hysterical fashion soon has us on red alert, as if jihadists were invading.

Link is smiling.

Half an hour later, the warden is back, fidgeting more than ever. He pulls me out of the room and hisses, "You've heard about the Fifteenth Circuit?"

"We're watching it."

"You gotta stop him."

"Who?"

"Don't 'Who' me, dammit! You know what I'm talking about."

"We're not in control here, Warden. The courts run their own schedules. Link's boys have their orders, evidently. Besides, the bombings might be coincidental."

"Yeah, right. The FBI is on the way here right now."

"Oh, that's real good, real smart. My client gets the needle in exactly three hours and fourteen minutes, yet the FBI wants to grill him about these bombings. He's a seasoned thug, Warden, a gangster from the old school. Battle hardened. He'll spit on any FBI agent within twenty feet."

He looks like he's about to faint. "We gotta do something," he says, wild-eyed. "The governor's yelling at me. Everybody's yelling at me."

"Well, it's up to the gov, if you ask me. He grants the reprieve, and I suppose Link stops the bombing campaign. Not sure, though, because he's not listening to me."

"Can you ask him?"

I laugh out loud. "Sure, Warden, I'll just have a little heart-to-heart with my client, get him to confess, and convince him to stop whatever he'll admit to doing. No problem."

He's too ashen to strike back, so he leaves, shaking his head, chewing his nails, another bureaucrat thoroughly overwhelmed with decision making. I step back into the room and take a chair. Link is glued to the television.

"That was the warden," I say. "And they'd really appreciate it if you'd call off the dogs."

No response. No acknowledgment.

CNN finally connects the dots, and suddenly my client is the hour's hottest story. They flash a mug shot of Link, a much younger version, as they interview the prosecutor who sent him away. From across the desk, Link curses under his breath, though he's still smiling. None of my business, but if I were inclined to plant bombs, this guy's office would be at the top of my list.

His name is Max Mancini, the City's chief prosecutor and a true legend in his own mind. He's been popping off in the press all week as the countdown grew louder. Link will be his first execution, and he wouldn't miss it for anything. Frankly, I've never understood why Link chose to rub out his own defense lawyer instead of going after Mancini. But I won't ask.

Evidently, Link and I are on the same page. Just as the reporter is wrapping up the interview, there is a loud noise somewhere in the background, behind Mancini. The camera pulls back and it's clear to me that they're standing on the sidewalk outside his downtown office.

Another explosion.

3.

The courtroom was bombed at precisely 5:00 p.m.; the Fifteenth Circuit, precisely at 6:00; the prosecutor's office, precisely at 7:00.

As we approach 8:00 p.m., many people who've had the misfortune of crossing paths with my client are nervous. CNN, now in full unbridled frenzy, is reporting that security has been beefed up around the Supreme Court Building in Washington. Their reporter on the scene keeps showing us a few offices with lights on and we're supposed to believe the justices are up there, hard at work, debating the merits of Link's case. They are not. They're all safely at home or at dinner. One of their clerks will deny our petition any minute now.

The Governor's Mansion is crawling with state police, some armed from head to toe in full combat regalia, as if Link might decide to mount a ground assault. With so many cameras around, so much drama everywhere, our handsome governor couldn't help himself. Ten minutes ago he dashed out from his bunker to chat with the reporters, live of course. Said he wasn't frightened, justice must go on, he'd do his job without fear, et cetera, ad nauseam. He tried to act as though he's really wrestling with the reprieve issue, so he's not ready to announce his decision. He'll save it for later, say around 9:55. He hasn't had this much fun in years.

I'm tempted to ask Link, "Who's next?" but let it pass. We're playing gin rummy as the clock ticks and Rome burns. He's told me several times I could leave, but I'm hanging around. I won't admit that I'm keen to watch his execution, but I am fascinated by it.

No one has been hurt. The three bombs were mainly gasoline, according to some so-called expert CNN dragged in for authenticity. Low-tech time bombs, probably in small packages, designed to make a little noise and a lot of smoke.

At 8:00 p.m., everyone takes a deep breath. All's quiet for the moment. They knock on the door and wheel in the last meal. For the occasion, Link has chosen a steak with fries and coconut pie for dessert, but he has no appetite. He takes two bites of the steak and offers me the fries. I say no thanks and shuffle the deck. There's something about eating another man's last meal that doesn't seem right. At 8:15, my cell phone vibrates. Our petition has been denied at the Supreme Court. No surprise there. There's nothing left. All Hail Marys have been thrown and dropped.

We go Live! outside the Supreme Court Building in Washington, where the CNN reporter is practically praying for some type of explosion. Dozens of cops loiter about, their trigger fingers just itching. A small crowd has gathered to watch the carnage, but there's nothing. Link keeps one eye on the television as he deals the cards.

I suspect he's not finished.

4.

The prison has a food storage warehouse on the west side of its vast complex and a vehicle maintenance facility on the east side. The buildings are about three miles apart. At 8:30, both mysteriously catch on fire, and the prison goes berserk. Evidently, there are a couple of news helicopters in the area. They are not allowed to fly over Big Wheeler, so they're hovering above farmland next door, and thanks to their long-range lenses we're able to watch the excitement courtesy of CNN.

As Link toys with his coconut pie and plays gin rummy, the anchor wonders why the State doesn't speed up his execution before he burns down the prison. A stuttering spokesperson with the governor's office tries to explain that the rules and laws do not allow this. It's 10:00 p.m., period, or as soon thereafter as possible. Link watches this as if it's a movie about some other guy on death row.

At 8:45, a bomb goes off in the administration building, not far from the warden's office.

Ten minutes later, the warden bursts into the Boom Boom Room and screams, "You gotta stop this!" Link ignores him as he shuffles the cards.

Two nervous guards grab Link, lift him up, search him, find his cell phone, then throw him back into his chair. His face does not change expression.

"You got a phone, Rudd?" the warden yells at me.

"Yes, but you can't have it. Rule 36, section 2, paragraph 4. Your rule. Sorry."

"You son of a bitch!"

"So you think I'm making phone calls to the bad guys? You think I'm a part of the conspiracy, with all my calls being traced? That right, Warden?"

He is too panic-stricken to respond. From behind the warden, a guard yells into the room, "There's a riot in Unit Six!"

5.

The riot started when an inmate, an old lifer with a history of heart problems, faked cardiac arrest. At first the guards decided to ignore him and let him go, but on second thought they got involved. His cell mate stabbed two guards with a shank, grabbed their Tasers, fried them, then beat them senseless. The inmates quickly put on the guards' uniforms and managed to open the doors to about a hundred cells. With near flawless coordination, the inmates flooded other wings in the unit and soon several hundred extremely dangerous convicts were on the loose. They began burning mattresses, laundry, anything that could possibly be ignited. Eight guards were beaten; two would later die. Three guards with pistols hid in an office and called for help. Before long, the inmates found weapons and gunfire could be heard across the prison. In the melee, four snitches were hanged with electrical extension cords.

We wouldn't know these details until later, so at the time Link and I casually play cards while Big Wheeler explodes around us. It takes CNN less than five minutes to pick up the riot story, and when we hear it we stop and watch the television. After a few minutes I say, "So, Link, are you in charge of prison riots, too?"

To my surprise he says, "Yes, at this moment anyway."

"Oh really? Then tell me how this one started?"

"It all goes back to personnel," he says like a polished CEO. "You gotta have the right people in the right place at the right time. You got three guys in Unit Six doing life with no parole, so they got nothing to lose. You set up an outside contact who promises all sorts of stuff, like a van and a driver waiting in the woods if the guys make it out. And lots of cash. You give them plenty of time to plan it all, and at exactly 9:00 on this night, when the warden and his goons are thinking of only one thing—giving me the needle—you launch your assault. Unit Four should blow up any minute."

"I won't tell a soul. And the bombs? Who rigged the bombs?"

"Can't give you the names. You gotta understand prisons and how stupid the men are who run them. Everything here is designed to keep us in, with little thought to keeping bad stuff out. Those incendiary devices were planted two days ago, well hidden; they've got timers and all, really basic stuff. No one was looking, piece of cake."

It's a relief to hear him talking like this. I suppose his nerves are starting to jump, though he looks as calm as ever.

"What's the endgame tonight, Link? Are these guys gonna attack death row and rescue you?"

"Wouldn't work. Too many guns around here. Just having some fun, that's all. I'm at peace."

As he says this, they flash another image of the prison burning, another camera shot from a helicopter nearby. We're too deep in the building to hear anything, but it looks like total chaos. Buildings on fire, a million red and blue lights flashing, an occasional gunshot. Link can't help but smile. Just fun and games.

"It's the warden's own stupid fault," he says. "Why all the pomp and ceremony, just for an execution? He brings in every available guard, gives them automatic weapons and Kevlar vests as if someone—me, the guy getting the needle—might somehow put together an offensive. Goons everywhere. Then he turns on all the lights and locks down the entire prison. Why exactly? No good reason. Hell, two guards without guns could just as easily walk me down the hall at the appointed hour and strap me onto the table. No big deal. No cause for all this drama. But no, the warden likes his rituals. It's a big moment for law enforcement and, hell, they gotta make the most out of it. What any fool can see, anyone but the warden, is that he's dealing with men who live in cages and who hate anybody in a uniform. They're already looking for trouble, so you crank up the pressure on them and they blow a gasket. Just takes someone like me to facilitate things."

He sips a cherry cola and nibbles a french fry. He's got forty minutes.

The door opens again and Assistant Warden Foreman is back, now with three heavily armed warriors. Foreman says, "How you guys doing in here?"

"Swell," I say.

Nothing from Link.

I say, "Looks like you boys got your hands full out there."

He says, "Things are hopping. Just wanted to check on the prisoner and make sure everything is okay."

Link glares at him and says, "This is my last hour. Why can't I have some peace and quiet? Please, you and your goons just get the hell outta here, okay?"

"We can accommodate you," Foreman says.

"And take him too," Link says, pointing at me. "I need to be alone."

Foreman says, "Well, sorry, Link, but there's no place for Mr. Rudd to go. The roads are blocked right now. We're in super lock-down. It's not safe out there."

"And for some reason I don't feel so safe in here," Link sneers. "Can't imagine why."

"Looks like we should postpone the execution," I say.

"Probably not going to happen," Foreman says, backing away.

They leave, slamming the door and locking it from the outside.

The governor feels the need to address his people. On the screen we see his troubled face. He's at a podium with mikes and cameras before him, a politician's dream. Random questions are hurled at him, and we soon learn that the situation at Big Wheeler is "tense." There are casualties, even deaths. There are about two hundred inmates "out of their cells," though none have yet to penetrate the exterior fences of the prison. Several fires are now under control. Yes, it seems as though some of this activity was coordinated from outside the prison, and, no, there is no evidence that Link Scanlon is behind it, not yet anyway. He, the governor, has called in the National Guard, though the state police have things under control. And, oh, by the way, he is denying the final request for a reprieve.

6.

Protocol requires that the condemned man be handcuffed at 9:45 and escorted for his final walk to the death room. There he is strapped to a gurney with six thick leather bands, from his feet to his forehead. While he is being strapped down, a doctor pokes around his arms looking for a suitable vein while a medic of some variety checks his vital signs. Ten feet away, behind glass windows and black curtains, the witnesses wait in two separate rooms, one for the victim, one for the killer.

An IV is inserted and secured with tape. A large clock on the wall allows the unlucky soul to count down his last minutes. At precisely 10:00 p.m., the prison attorney reads the death warrant, and the warden asks the condemned if he has any last words. He can say whatever he wants. It's recorded and available online. He'll say a few words, maybe proclaim his innocence again, maybe forgive everyone, maybe beg for forgiveness. When he's finished, the warden nods to a guy hidden in a nearby room, and the chemicals are released. The condemned begins to float away and his breathing becomes labored. Some twelve minutes later, the doctor pronounces him dead.

Link knows all this. Evidently, he has other plans. I'm just a guy in the wrong place at the wrong time.

At 9:30, all electricity at Big Wheeler is cut off—a complete blackout. They would later trace the power failure to a utility pole that got chainsawed in two. The backup generator for Unit Nine—death row—failed to start because its fuel injectors had been vandalized.

At 9:30, we don't know this. All we know is that the Boom Boom Room is pitch-black. Link jumps to his feet and says, "Get out of the way." He slides the desk to jam the door. There is a quick flash of light above us, and noise, grunting. A panel in the false ceiling opens up and a voice says, "Link, here." The flashlight sweeps down and through the room. A rope drops and Link grabs it. "Slow, now," the voice says, and Link inches upward, literally hanging on for his life. There are sounds up there, grunting and scuffling, but I can't tell how many men are involved.

Within seconds Link is gone, and if I were not so stunned I would laugh. Then I realize that I'll probably get shot. I take off my coat and tie and stretch out on the Army cot. Guards kick the door open and burst in with guns and a flood of light.

"Where is he?" one guard barks at me.

I point to the ceiling.

They yell and curse as two of them yank me up and drag me into the hall, where dozens of guards and cops and officials are running around in complete panic.

"He's gone! He's gone!" They are yelling. "Check the roof."

In the hall, and in the midst of an incredible racket, I can hear the thumping of a helicopter. They drag me into a room, then another. In the chaos I hear a guard yell that Link Scanlon has vanished. It takes an hour for the lights to come on. I am eventually arrested by the state police and taken to the nearest county jail. Their initial theory is that I am an accomplice.

7.

The pieces soon come together, and because I am being partially blamed for the escape, I have access to the information. I'm not worried about the charges; they can't stick.

At 9:30 that night, there were two news helicopters buzzing around the fringes of Big Wheeler. The prison officials and police had warned them to stay away, but they were close by. In a show of muscle, the state police flew in two of its own helicopters to secure the airspace over the prison, and this proved helpful when the trouble started. It also proved distracting. There was a tremendous amount of smoke hanging over the prison as six different fires were blazing at one time. Witnesses said the noise was deafening—four helicopters in the area, dozens of emergency vehicles with sirens, radios squawking, guards and police yelling, guns being shot, fires roaring. On cue, and with impeccable timing, Link's small black helicopter arrived from nowhere, descended through the clouds of smoke, and snatched him off the roof of Unit Nine. There were witnesses. Several guards and prison employees saw the helicopter as it hovered for a few seconds, dropped a line, then disappeared back into the smoke with two men swinging from the lifeline. A guard in a tower at the unit managed to fire a few shots but hit nothing.

One of the State's choppers gave chase, but was no match for whatever brand and model Link leased for the night. It was never found; no record of it was ever traced. It flew low to avoid radar; air traffic control did not see it. A farmer sixty miles away from Big Wheeler told authorities he saw a small helicopter land on a county road a mile from his front porch. A car met it, then both disappeared.

An investigation dragged on and three officials got fired. It was eventually revealed that (1) the Boom Boom Room is part of an old section of Unit Nine and was built back in the 1940s; (2) its roof is three feet higher than the rest of death row; (3) between the ceiling and the roof there is a crawl space crammed with duct-work, heating vents, and electrical work; (4) the crawl space winds around and branches off, and one section of it leads to an old door that opens onto the flat roof; and (5) the two guards who had roof duty that night had been dispatched to help with the riot, so there was no one on the roof when Link made his dramatic escape.

What if the guards had been there? Given the skill and exper-tise of the operative who fetched Link, it's safe to speculate that the guards would have been shot between the eyes. This Spider-Man, as he was nicknamed by the investigators, is already a legend.

There are a lot of what-ifs but few answers. Faced with certain death, Link Scanlon figured he had nothing to lose by attempting a ridiculous escape. He had the money to hire the right commandos and equipment. He got lucky and it worked.

There was a possible but unconfirmed sighting in Mexico.

I haven't heard from my client and don't really expect to.

8.

In addition to Big Wheeler, there are a dozen or so prisons in this state, each with a different security classification. I have clients in most of them, and they write me letters begging for money and demanding I do something to get them out. For the most part I ignore this correspondence. I have learned that a letter from me only encourages an inmate to write again and demand more. For those of us who defend criminals, there is always the possible scenario in which an ex-client with a grudge shows up after years in the pen and wants to discuss mistakes made at trial. But I don't dwell on this. It's just part of the job and another reason I carry a gun.

To keep me in my place, our esteemed prison officials ban me from visiting any prison for an entire month after the Scanlon escape. However, as it becomes clear that Link outfoxed them with no help from me, they eventually relent.

There are a few clients that I visit occasionally. These little road trips get me out of town for a day. Partner and I are driving to a medium-security facility affectionately called Old Roseburg, named after a governor from the 1930s who himself was later sent to prison. He died there, in a slammer bearing his own name. I've often wondered what that felt like. According to legend, his family tried in vain to get him paroled so he could die at home, but the sitting governor wouldn't allow it. He and Roseburg were blood enemies. The family then tried to change the name of the prison, but that would have ruined a colorful story and the legislature declined. The prison officially remains the Nathan Roseburg Correctional Facility.

We are cleared through the main gate and park in an empty visitors' lot. Two guards with high-powered rifles watch us from the tower, as if we might haul in some weapons or a pound or two of cocaine. At the moment, there's no one else to watch, so we get their full attention.

9.

After Partner was acquitted for killing a narc, he begged me for a job. I wasn't hiring at the time, and I haven't hired since, but I couldn't say no. He was headed back to the streets, and if I didn't help him he would end up either dead or in prison. Unlike most of his friends, he had a high school diploma and had even managed to pick up a few credits at a community college. I paid for more classes, most at night. He blitzed through a paralegal curriculum and got himself certified.

Partner lives with his mother in a subsidized apartment in the City. Most of the units in his building are packed with large families, but none of the traditional variety—mother, father, children. Almost all the fathers are gone, either locked up or living elsewhere and producing more children. The typical apartment belongs to a grandmother, a long-suffering soul who's stuck with a passel of kids who may or may not be blood related. Half the mothers are in prison. The other half work two and three jobs. Young cousins drop in and out; almost every family is in a chaotic state of flux. The primary goal is to keep the kids in school, away from the gangs, alive, and hopefully out of prison. Partner guesses that half of them will drop out anyway and most of the boys will end up in jail.

He says he's lucky because it's just him and his mother in the small apartment. There is a tiny spare bedroom that he uses as an office for his work—our work. Many of my files and records are stored there. I often wonder what my clients would do if they knew their confidential files were actually kept in Army surplus cabinets in a tenth-floor apartment in a government housing project. I don't really care because I trust Partner with my life. He and I have spent hours in the little room digging through police reports and plotting trial strategies.

His mother, Miss Luella, is partially disabled by severe diabetes. She does some sewing for friends, keeps a spotless apartment, and cooks occasionally. Her primary job, as far as I'm concerned, is answering the telephone for the Honorable Sebastian Rudd, Attorney-at-Law. As I said, I'm not listed in any phone book, but my "office" number does get passed around. In fact, people call that number all the time, and they get Miss Luella, who sounds as crisp and efficient as any receptionist sitting at a fine desk in a tall building and directing calls for a firm with hundreds of lawyers.

She'll say, "Sebastian Rudd, Attorney-at-Law. How may I direct your call?" As if the firm has dozens of divisions and specialties. No caller ever gets me the first time because I'm never at the office. What office? She'll say, "He's in a meeting," or "He's in a deposition," or "He's in a trial," or, my favorite, "He's in federal court." Once she has effectively stiff-armed the caller, she zeroes in on his or her legal problem with "And this is regarding what?"

A divorce. The caller will get "I'm sorry, but Mr. Rudd does not handle family matters."

A bankruptcy, real estate closing, will, deed, contract. The same response—Mr. Rudd doesn't do those.

A criminal matter might get her attention but she knows that most lead nowhere. So few of the accused can afford a fee. She'll lead the caller through her standard questions to determine whether or not they can pay.

Someone's been injured? Now we're talking. She'll go into her sympathy mode and extract all manner of information. She won't let them off the phone until she's picked them clean and gained their trust. If the facts fall into place and the case shows real potential, she'll promise to have Mr. Rudd stop by the hospital that very afternoon.

If the caller is a judge or some other important person, she treats them with great respect, ends the call, and immediately sends me a text message. I pay her $500 a month in cash and an occasional bonus when I settle a good car wreck. Partner, too, is paid in cash.

Miss Luella's people were from Alabama and she learned to cook the southern way. At least twice a month she'll fry chicken and boil collards and bake corn bread and I'll eat until I can hardly breathe. She and Partner have managed to transform the small, cheap, mass-produced apartment into a home, a place of warmth. There is a sadness, though, a cloud that hangs like a thick fog and will not go away. Partner is only thirty-eight, but he has a nineteen-year-old son at Old Roseburg. Jameel is serving ten years for gang-related crap, and he's the reason for our visit today.

10.

After we do the paperwork and get patted down, Partner and I walk half a mile along sidewalks lined with chain link and razor wire to Camp D, a tough unit. We go through security again and deal with grim-faced guards who would like nothing better than to turn us away. Because Partner is a certified paralegal and carries the paperwork to prove it, he is allowed into the visiting wing with me. A guard selects a consultation room for attorneys and we take our seats facing a screen.

Attorneys can visit anytime, with notice, while the families are limited to Sunday afternoons only. As we wait, Partner, who says little, now says even less. We check on Jameel at least once a month, and the visits take a toll on my confidant. He carries heavy burdens because he blames himself for many of his son's problems. The kid was headed for trouble, but after Partner's acquittal the cops and prosecutors were out for revenge. Kill a cop, even in self-defense, and you make some nasty enemies. When Jameel was arrested, there was no room for negotiation. The max was ten years and the prosecutors wouldn't budge. I represented him, pro bono of course, but there was nothing I could do. He was caught with a backpack full of pot.

"Only nine years to go," Partner says softly as we stare at the screen. "Man oh man. I lie awake at night and wonder what he'll be like in nine years. Twenty-eight years old and back on the streets. No job, no education, no skills, no hope, no nothing. Just another convict looking for trouble."

"Maybe not," I say cautiously, though I have little to add. Partner knows this world far better than me. "He'll have a father waiting on him, and a grandmother. I'll be around, I hope. Between the three of us we'll think of something."

"Maybe you'll need another paralegal by then," he says with a rare smile, though a brief one.

"Never know."

A door opens on the other side and Jameel walks through it, followed by a guard. The guard slowly unsnaps the handcuffs and looks at us. "Morning, Hank," I say.

"Hello, Rudd," he says. Hank is one of the good guys, according to Jameel. I suppose it's some sort of commentary on my law practice that I'm on such good terms with some of the prison guards. Some, but certainly not all.

"Take your time," he says and disappears. The length of the visit is determined by Hank and Hank alone, and since I'm nice to him he doesn't care how long we stay. I've had hard-asses say things like "You got one hour, max," or "Make it quick," but not Hank.

Jameel smiles at us and says, "Thanks for coming."

"Hello, son," Partner says properly.

"Great to see you, Jameel," I say.

He falls into a plastic chair. The kid is six feet five, skinny, and seemingly made out of rubber. Partner is six two and built like a fireplug. He says the kid's mother is tall and lanky. She's been out of the picture for years, vanished into the black hole of street life. She has a brother who played basketball at a small college, and Partner has always assumed Jameel came from that gene pool. He was six three in the ninth grade and scouts were beginning to notice. At some point, though, he discovered pot and crack and forgot about the game.

"Thanks for the money," he says to me. I send him $100 a month, which he's supposed to use for canteen food and basics such as pencils, paper, stamps, and soft drinks. He bought a fan— Old Roseburg is not air-conditioned. None of our prisons are. Partner sends him money too, though I have no idea how much. Two months after he landed here, they raided his cell and found some pot hidden in his mattress. A snitch had squealed, and Jameel spent two weeks in solitary. Partner would have choked him if he could have penetrated the screen, but the kid swore it would never happen again.

We talk about his classes. He's taking remedial courses in an effort to get his high school equivalent, but Partner is not impressed with his progress. After a few minutes, I excuse myself and leave the room. Father and son need time alone, which is why we're here. According to Partner, the conversations get rough and emotional. He wants his son to know that his father cares deeply and is watching from a distance. Old Roseburg is full of gangs and Jameel is easy prey. He swears he's not involved, but Partner is skeptical. Above all, he wants the kid to be safe, and membership in a gang is often the best protection. It also leads to warfare and revenge and the circle of violence. Seven inmates were killed last year at Old Roseburg. It could be worse. Down the road is a U.S. penitentiary, a federal joint, and they average two murders a month.

I buy a soft drink from a vending machine and find a spot in a row of empty plastic chairs. No other lawyer is visiting today and the place is empty. I open my briefcase and spread papers on a table covered with old magazines. Hank appears and says hello again. We chat for a few minutes. I ask how the kid is doing.

He says, "All right. Nothing great. He's surviving and he hasn't been hurt. He's been here a year and knows his way around. Doesn't want to work, though. I got him a job in the laundry and he lasted a week. Goes to most of his classes, but not all of them."

"A gang?"

"Don't know, but I'm watching."

Another guard enters through a door far away and Hank suddenly has to go. He can't be seen fraternizing with a lowly criminal defense lawyer. I try and read a thick brief, but it's too boring. I walk to a window that looks out upon a vast yard lined with double rows of chain link. Hundreds of inmates, all in prison whites, are killing time as guards look down from a tower.

Young and black, almost all of them. According to the numbers, they're in for nonviolent drug offenses. The average sentence is seven years. Upon release, 60 percent will be back here within three years.

And why not? What's on the outside to prevent their return? They are now convicted felons, a branding they will never be able to shake. The odds were stacked against them to begin with, and now that they're tagged as felons, life in the free world is somehow supposed to improve? These are the real casualties of our wars. The war on drugs. The war on crime. Unintended victims of tough laws passed by tough politicians over the past forty years. One million young black men now warehoused in decaying prisons, idling away the days at taxpayer expense.

Our prisons are packed. Our streets are filled with drugs. Who's winning the war?

We've lost our minds.

11.

After two hours, Hank says it's time to wrap things up. I knock and reenter the room, an unventilated little box that's always stuffy. Jameel sits with his arms crossed, his eyes on the floor. Partner sits with his arms crossed too, staring at the screen, and I get the feeling that, though much has been said, no words have passed in some time. I say, "We gotta go."

This is what both want to hear. They manage to say good-bye with some fondness. Jameel thanks us for coming, passes along greetings and love to Miss Luella, and stands as Hank enters the room from behind him.

Driving away, Partner says nothing for an hour.

12.

Link Scanlon is not my first mobster. That honor goes to a sensational crook named Dewey Knutt, a man I do not visit in prison. While Link relished the blood, broken bones, intimidation, and notoriety, Dewey went about his life of crime as quietly as possible. While Link dreamed of being a Mafia don from childhood, Dewey was actually an honest furniture salesman who didn't break bad until he was in his mid-thirties. While Link's net worth was substantial but largely untraceable, a business magazine claimed Dewey was worth $300 million before his troubles. They sent Link to death row; Dewey got forty years in a federal slammer. Link managed to escape; Dewey has hair down to his waist and grows organic herbs and vegetables in a prison garden.

Dewey Knutt was a fast-talking salesman who moved a ton of cheap furniture, and with his earnings he bought a rental house. Then another, then several more. He learned the trick of using other people's money and acquired a prodigious appetite for risk. He parlayed his properties and loans into shopping centers and subdivisions. During a short recession, a bank said no to a loan, so he bought the bank and fired all the suits who worked there. He memorized banking regulations and found all of the gaping loopholes. During a longer recession, he picked up a few more banks and some regional mortgage companies. Money was cheap and Dewey Knutt proved to be a master at the borrowing game. His downfall, as we later learned, began with his penchant for double- and even triple-collateralizing assets. A visionary in the world of shady profits, he was one of the first to churn the fertile fields of subprime mortgages. He fine-tuned the intricacies of loan-sharking. He became a skilled briber of politicians and regulators. Add tax evasion, money laundering, mail fraud, insider trading, and the outright looting of pension funds, and Dewey richly deserved his forty years.

Those still searching for hidden remnants of his fortune include an entire cast of present and former enemies, some banking regulators, at least two bankruptcy courts, his ex-wife's lawyers, and several branches of the federal government. So far, they've found nothing.

When Dewey was forty-nine, his shiftless son, Alan, was caught with a trunk load of cocaine. Alan was twenty, a real mess of a kid, and was trying to impress his father with his own style of entrepreneurship. Dewey was so incensed and embarrassed that he refused to hire a lawyer for Alan. A friend referred him to me. I took one look at the seizure and realized the cops had blown it. They'd had no warrant and no probable cause to search the car. It was cut-and-dried, black-and-white. I filed the proper motions and briefs and the City halfheartedly contested the issue. The cocaine bust was ruled unconstitutional, the evidence was thrown out, and all charges against Alan were dismissed. It was a big story for a few days and I got my picture in the papers for the first time.

Dewey used his favorite lawyers for his heavy work, but he was so impressed with my slick maneuvers he decided to throw me a few scraps. Most of it was outside the scope of my expertise, but one case intrigued me and I signed on.

Dewey loved golf but had a hard time working it into his frenetic schedule. In addition, he had little patience for the staid traditions of most golf and country clubs, few of which, if any, would consider such an outlaw as a member. He became obsessed with the idea of building his own course and lighting it so he could play at night, either alone or with a few pals. At the time, there were only three other lit courses in the entire country, and none within a thousand miles of here. Eighteen holes, all private, under lights—the ultimate rich boy's toy. To avoid the City's zoning Nazis, he selected two hundred acres a mile from the city limits. The county objected. The neighbors sued. I handled the legal work and eventually won approval. More headlines.

However, the real notoriety was just around the corner. A housing bubble popped. Interest rates spiked. A perfect storm blew in and Dewey couldn't borrow fast enough. His house of cards collapsed in spectacular fashion. With flawless timing, the FBI, IRS, SEC, and a trainload of other tough guys with badges arrived on the scene, all waving warrants. The indictment was an inch thick and loaded with brutal allegations against Dewey, the obvious target. It also alleged grand conspiracies involving his bankers, accountants, partners, lawyers, a stockbroker, and two city councilmen. It detailed, in very convincing narratives, dozens of violations under the Racketeer Influenced and Corrupt Organizations Act. RICO for short, the greatest gift Congress has ever bestowed upon federal prosecutors.

I was investigated and became convinced I would be indicted too, though I had done nothing wrong. Thankfully, I had managed to remain on the fringes. For a while it seemed to be a shoot-now-and-ask-questions-later inquisition. But the Feds backed off and lost interest in me. They had much bigger crooks to nail.

Alan was indicted, basically for being Dewey's son. When the FBI threatened to indict Dewey's daughter, he caved and agreed to a forty-year deal. The bogus charges against his kids were dismissed, and most of his co-indictees pled to light sentences. All avoided serious jail time. In short, Dewey did the honorable thing and took a mighty fall.

He was building his golf course—grandly named the Old Plantation—just as the Feds moved in. All the money vanished in a matter of weeks and construction stopped—after the fourteenth green.

Today, it is the only fourteen-hole course with lights in the entire world, as far as anyone knows. In honor of Dewey, it's called Old Rico. Its membership consists solely of his cronies and conspirators. Alan's job these days is taking care of the course and keeping it playable, which he manages to do. He plays nonstop himself and dreams of becoming a pro. He collects enough in dues to hire a few groundskeepers, all undocumented workers, plus we suspect he knows where some of Dewey's old loot is buried. I pay $5,000 a year and it's worth it just to avoid the crowds. The greens and tee boxes are usually in good shape. The fairways can get rough, but no one cares. If we wanted a manicured course we would join a real club, though none of us at Old Rico could survive the vetting process.

Every Wednesday night at seven o'clock we gather for Dirty Golf, a game that bears little resemblance to what you might see on CBS. Dewey's original plans were to build the course first, so he would have a place to play, and then build the clubhouse, so he would have a place to drink. Absent a proper clubhouse, we meet for pregame drinks and wagering in a converted tractor barn where Dewey once enjoyed cockfighting, perhaps the only crime not covered by his indictment. Alan lives upstairs with two women, neither his wife, and he's the organizer of Dirty Golf. The two gals work the bar, absorb the crudities, and banter with the crowd. The rituals call for the first pint—in fruit jars—to be lifted in a toast to Dewey, who's smiling down from a bad portrait above the bar. Tonight there are eleven of us, a workable number since Old Rico has only twelve golf carts. As we drain the first pints, Alan goes through the rather raucous chore of bracketing the tournament, establishing handicaps, and collecting money. Dirty Golf costs $200 each, winner take all, not a bad pot but I've never won it.

Winning takes skill, of course, but also a higher handicap and the ability to cheat without getting caught. The rules are flexible. For example, a bad shot that goes outside the fairway boundaries is always in play if it can be found. There's really no such thing as out-of-bounds at Old Rico. If you find it, play it. A putt of three feet or less is always conceded, unless an opponent is having a bad night and wants to play hard-ass. Every player has the right to require another player to putt everything. A foursome can agree that each guy can take a mulligan, or a free shot in the aftermath of a bad one. And, if all four are in the right mood, each can take one mullie on the front seven and another on the back. Needless to say, the sponginess of the rules leads to disagreement and conflict. Since not one golfer in ten knows the real rules anyway, each round of Dirty Golf is loaded with incessant carping, bitching, complaining, and even threats.

Partner drives my golf cart and I'm not the only one here with a bodyguard. Since I play alone, tonight I'm paired up with Toby Chalk, a former city councilman who served four months in the wake of Dewey's demise. He drives his own golf cart. Caddies are forbidden at Old Rico.

After an hour of drinking and preliminaries, we head for the course. It's getting dark, the lights are on, and we do indeed feel privileged to be playing golf at night. It's a shotgun start. Toby and I are assigned the fifth tee, and when Alan yells "Go" we race away, carts bouncing, clubs rattling and jangling, grown men half-drunk and puffing on big cigars, whooping and yelling happily into the night.

Partner grins and shakes his head. Crazy white men.

PART THREE

WARRIOR COPS

1.

Here's what happened:

My clients, Mr. and Mrs. Douglas Renfro, Doug and Kitty to everyone, lived for thirty quiet and happy years on a shady street in a nice suburb. They were good neighbors, active in local charities and the church, always ready to lend a hand. They were in their early seventies, retired, with kids and grandkids, a couple of dogs, and a time-share in Florida. They owed no money and paid off their credit cards in full each month. They were comfortable and reasonably healthy, though Doug was dealing with atrial fibrillation and Kitty was rebounding from breast cancer. He had spent fourteen years in the Army, then sold medical devices for the rest of his career. She had adjusted claims for an insurance company. To stay busy, she volunteered at a hospital while he puttered in the flower beds and played tennis at a city park. At the insistence of their children and grandchildren, the Renfros had reluctantly bought his-and-her laptops and joined the digital world, though they spent little time online.

The house next door to them had been bought and sold a dozen times over the years, and the current owners were oddballs who kept to themselves. They had a teenage son, Lance, a misfit who spent most of his time locked in his room playing video games and peddling drugs through the Internet. To hide his habits, he routinely piggybacked on the Renfros' wireless router. They, of course, did not know this. They knew how to turn their laptops on and off, send and receive e-mails, do basic shopping, and check the weather, but beyond that they had no idea how the technology worked and had little interest in it. They did not bother with passwords or security of any kind.

The state police initiated a sting operation to crack down on Internet drug trafficking and tracked an IP address to the Renfros' home. Someone in there was buying and selling a lot of Ecstasy, and the decision was made to launch a full-scale SWAT team assault. Warrants—one to search the house and one to arrest Doug Renfro—were obtained, and at 3:00 on a quiet, starlit night a team of eight city policemen rushed through the darkness and surrounded the Renfro home. Eight officers—all in full combat gear with Kevlar vests, camouflage uniforms, panzer-style helmets, night-vision goggles, tactical radios, semiautomatic pistols, assault rifles, knee pads, some even with face masks, and a few even with black face paint for maximum drama—ducked and squatted and moved fearlessly through the Renfros' flower beds, their itchy fingers eager for combat. Two carried flash-bang stun grenades and two carried battering rams.

Warrior cops. The vast majority, as we would later learn, were woefully untrained, but all were thrilled to be in battle. At least six later admitted to consuming highly caffeinated energy drinks to stay awake at that awful hour.

Instead of simply ringing the doorbell and waking the Renfros and explaining that they, the police, wanted to talk and search the house, the cops launched the assault with a bang by kicking in the front and rear doors simultaneously. They would later lie and claim they had called out to the occupants, but Doug and Kitty were sound asleep, as you would expect. They heard nothing until the invasion began.

What happened in the next sixty seconds took months to unravel and get straight. The first casualty was Spike, the yellow Lab who slept on the kitchen floor. Spike was twelve, old for a

Lab, and hard of hearing. But he certainly heard the door crash just a few feet away. His mistake was to jump up and start barking, at which time he was shot three times by a 9-millimeter semiautomatic pistol. By then Doug Renfro was scrambling out of bed and reaching for his own gun, one properly registered and kept in a drawer for protection. He also owned a Browning 12-gauge shotgun he used twice a year to hunt geese, but it was tucked away in a closet.

In attempting to defend the home invasion, our bumbling chief of police would later claim that the SWAT assault was necessary because they knew Doug Renfro was heavily armed.

Doug had made it to the hallway, when he saw several dark figures swarming up the stairs. An Army veteran, he hit the floor and began firing away. Fire was returned. The gun battle was brief and deadly. Doug was shot twice, in the forearm and shoulder. A cop named Keestler was hit in the neck, presumably by Doug. Kitty, who had rushed in a panic out of the bedroom behind her husband, was shot three times in the face and four times in the chest and died at the scene. Their other dog, a schnauzer who slept with them, was also shot and killed.

Doug Renfro and Keestler were rushed to the hospital. Kitty was taken to the city morgue. Neighbors gawked in disbelief as their street was lit by flashing lights while ambulances rushed away with the casualties.

The police stayed at the home for hours and collected all possible evidence, including the laptops. Within two hours, before sunrise, they knew the Renfros' computers had never been used to peddle drugs. They knew they had made a mistake, but coming clean is simply not in their playbook. The cover-up began immediately when the commander of the SWAT team gravely informed television reporters on the scene that the occupants of the home were suspected of trafficking in drugs and that the man of the house, a Mr. Doug Renfro, had attempted to kill several officers.

After his recovery from surgery, six hours after getting shot, Doug was told of his wife's death. He was also informed that the invaders were actually police officers. He had no idea. He thought they were armed criminals invading his home.

2.

My cell phone rings at 6:45. I'm staring at an impossible bank shot to sink the 9 ball in a corner pocket and run the table. I've been drinking strong coffee and missing too many shots for the past hour. I grab the phone, look at the ID, and say, "Good morning."

"Are you awake?" Partner asks.

"Guess." I haven't been asleep at 6:45 in years. Neither has Partner.

"Might want to flip on the news."

"Okay, what's up?"

"Looks like our toy soldiers just botched another home invasion. Casualties."

"Shit!" I say and grab the remote. "Later." Wedged into one corner of my den is a small sofa and a chair. A wide-screen HD television hangs from the ceiling against a wall. I fall into the chair just as the first image appears.

The sun is barely up but there's enough light to capture the mayhem. The Renfros' front yard is swarming with cops and rescue personnel. Lights flash in the background behind the breathless and stuttering reporter. Neighbors in bathrobes gawk from across the street. Bright yellow police crime scene tape is strung high and low and in all directions. It's a crime scene all right, but I'm already suspicious. Who are the real criminals? I call Partner, tell him to get to the hospital and start snooping.

Sitting in the Renfros' driveway is a tank, with an eight-inch barrel, thick rubber tires instead of treads, a camouflage paint job, and an open turret where, at the moment, a warrior cop is sitting, his face hidden behind biker sunglasses, his expression one of extreme readiness. The City's police department owns only one tank and they're proud of it. They use it whenever possible. I know this tank; I've dealt with it before.

Several years ago, not long after the terror attacks on September 11, our police department managed to bilk Homeland Security out of a few million bucks so it could arm up and join the national craze of ETF—Extreme Terror Fighting. Never mind that our city is far away from the major metropolitan areas, or that there has been absolutely no sign of any jihadists around here, or that our cops already had plenty of guns and ninja gear. Forget all that—we had to be ready! So in the arms race that followed, our cops somehow got a new tank. And once they learned how to drive it, then, hell, it was time to use it.

The first victim was a rather rustic old boy named Sonny Werth who lived at the edge of the city limits in a part of town that realtors tend to avoid. Sonny, his girlfriend, and a couple of her kids were asleep at 2:00 a.m. when the house seemed to explode. It wasn't much of a house, but that really didn't matter. The walls shook, there was a roar, and Sonny at first thought a tornado had hit.

No, only the police. They would later claim that they had knocked on the door and tried the doorbell, but no one inside the house heard anything until the tank plowed through the front window and stopped in the den. A mixed spaniel mutt tried to escape through the gaping hole but was gunned down by a brave warrior. Luckily, there were no other casualties, though Sonny spent two nights in the hospital with chest pain, after which he went to jail for a week before he could post bond. His crimes:

bookmaking, gambling. The cops and prosecutors claimed Sonny was part of a ring, thus a conspirator, thus a member of organized crime, and so on.

On Sonny's behalf, I sued the City for "excessive force" and got a million bucks. Not one dime of which, by the way, came out of the pockets of the cops who planned the raid. As always, it came from the taxpayers. The criminal charges against Sonny were later dismissed, so the raid was a complete waste of time, money, and energy.

As I sip my coffee and watch the scene, I think to myself that the Renfros were lucky in that the tank was not used to bust up their house. For reasons we'll never know, the decision was made to keep it in the driveway, just in case. If the eight soldiers were not enough, if the Renfros had somehow managed a counterattack, then the tank would have been sent in to destroy the den.

The camera closes in on two cops standing beside the tank, each with an assault rifle. Both weigh over three hundred pounds. One is wearing a uniform of green-and-gray camouflage, as if he were hunting deer in the woods. The other is wearing a uniform of brown-and-beige camouflage, as if he were hunting insurgents in the desert. These two clowns are standing in the driveway of a suburban home, about fifteen minutes from downtown, in a well-developed city of a million people, and they're wearing camouflage. The sad and scary thing about this image is that these guys have no idea how stupid they look. Instead, they're proud, arrogant. They're on display, tough guys fighting bad guys. One of their brethren has been hit, wounded, fallen in the line of duty, and they're pissed about it. They scowl at the neighbors across the street. One wrong word, and they might start shooting. Their fingers are on the triggers.

The weather comes on and I go to the shower.

Partner picks me up at eight and we head to the hospital. Doug

Renfro is still in surgery. Officer Keestler's wounds are not life threatening. There are cops everywhere. In a crowded waiting room, Partner points to a huddle of stunned people, all sitting knee to knee and holding hands.

Not for the first time, I ask myself the obvious question: Why didn't the cops simply ring the doorbell at a decent hour and have a chat with Mr. Renfro? Two cops in plain clothes, or maybe just one in a uniform? Why not? The answer is simple: These guys think they're part of an extreme, elite force, and they need their thrills, so here we are in another frantic hospital with casualties.

Thomas Renfro is about forty. According to Partner, he's an optometrist out in the suburbs. His two sisters do not live around here and are not yet at the hospital. I swallow hard and approach him. He wants to wave me off, but I say over and over it's important that we talk. He finally steps away and we find privacy in a corner. The poor guy is waiting on his sisters so they can go to the morgue and start arranging things for their dead mother; meanwhile, their father is in surgery. I apologize for intruding but get his attention when I explain that I've been through this before with these cops.

He wipes his red eyes and says, "I think I've seen you before."

"Probably on the news. I take some crazy cases."

He hesitates, then, "What kinda case is this?"

"Here's what will happen, Mr. Renfro. Your father is not coming home anytime soon. When the doctors are finished with him, the cops will take him to jail. He'll be charged with the attempted murder of a police officer. Carries a max of twenty years. His bond will be set at a million bucks or so, something outrageous, and he won't be able to make it because the prosecutor will freeze his assets. House, bank accounts, whatever. He can't touch anything because this is how they rig prosecutions."

As if this poor guy hasn't been hit with enough crap in the

past five hours. He closes his eyes and shakes his head, but he's listening. I go on: "The reason I'm bothering you with this is that it's important to file a civil lawsuit immediately. Tomorrow if possible. Wrongful death of your mother, assault on your father, excessive force, police incompetence, violation of rights, et cetera. I'll throw everything at them. I've done it before. If we get the right judge, then I'll have access to their internal records right off the bat. They're covering up their mistakes as we speak, and they're very good at it."

He breaks down, fights it, gets some control, and says, "This is too much."

I hand him a card and say, "I understand. Call me as soon as you can. I fight these bastards all the time and I know the game. You're going through hell now, but, unfortunately, it will only get worse."

He manages to say "Thanks."

3.

Later that afternoon, the police stop by and have a chat with Lance, the shiftless kid next door to the Renfros. Just three cops, in plain clothes, bravely approaching the house without assault weapons or bulletproof vests. They didn't even bring their tank. Things go smoothly; no one gets shot.

Lance is nineteen, unemployed, home alone, a real loser, and his world is about to change dramatically. The police have a search warrant. After they grab his laptop and cell phone, Lance starts talking. He's in the den when his mother comes home, and he's admitting everything. He's been piggybacking on the Renfros' Wi-Fi system for about a year. He trades on the Dark Web, on a site called Millie's Market, where he can buy any quantity of any drug, illegal or prescription. He sticks to Ecstasy because it's accessible and the kids, his customers, love it. He does his business in Bitcoin, current balance valued at $60,000. All the details pour out in a torrent, and after an hour he's led away in handcuffs.

So at 5:00 p.m., or about fourteen hours after the raid, the police finally know the truth. But their cover-up is already in play. They leak some lies here and there, and early the next morning I'm reading the *Chronicle* online and see the front-page news. There are photos of Douglas and Katherine Renfro, she now deceased, and Officer Keestler. He sounds like a hero; the Renfros sound like outlaws. Doug is a suspect in an Internet drug-trafficking ring. Shocking, a neighbor says. Had no idea. The nicest people. Kitty just got caught in the cross fire when her husband fired upon peace-loving officers of the law. She'll be buried next week. He'll be indicted shortly. Keestler is expected to survive. There's not one word about Lance.

Two hours later, I meet Nate Spurio at a bagel shop in a strip mall north of town. We can't be seen in public, or at least identified by anyone who might be a cop or know a cop, so we alternate our secret meetings between A, B, C, and D. A is an Arby's roast beef joint in the suburbs. B is one of two bagel shops. C is the dreadful Catfish Cave, six miles east of the City. D is for a donut shop. When we need to talk, we simply choose a letter from our little alphabet game and agree on a time. Spurio is a thirty-year veteran of the police force, a genuine, honest cop who plays by the book and despises almost everyone else in the department. We have a history, which began with me as a twenty-year-old college boy who got too drunk in a beer hall and found myself outside on the sidewalk getting roughed up by the cops, one of whom was Nate Spurio. He said I cursed him and shoved him, and after I woke up in jail he stopped by to check on me. I apologized profusely. He accepted and made sure the charges were dropped. My broken jaw healed nicely, and the cop who punched me was later

dismissed. The incident inspired me to go to law school. Over
the years, Spurio has refused to play the political games necessary
to advance and has gone nowhere. He's usually hanging around
a desk, filing papers, counting the days. But there is a network of
other officers who have been ostracized by the powers that be, and
Spurio spends a lot of time tracking the gossip. He's not a snitch by
any means. He's simply an honest cop who hates what his department has become.

Partner stays in the van, in the parking lot, on guard in case
other cops happen by and want a bagel. We huddle in a corner and
watch the door. He says, "Boy oh boy, it's a big one."

"Let's have it."

He starts with Lance's arrest, the confiscation of his computer,
the clear proof that the boy is a small-time dealer, and his detailed
admission about tagging along on the Renfros' router. Their
computers are squeaky-clean, but Doug will be indicted day after
tomorrow. Keestler will be cleared of all wrongdoing. The typical
cover-up.

"Who was there?" I ask, and he hands me a folded sheet of
paper. "Eight, all from our department. No state boys, no Feds."

If I have my way, they'll be named defendants in a lawsuit
seeking damages of, oh, I don't know, how about $50 million.

"Who led the party?" I ask.

"Who do you think?"

"Sumerall?"

"You got it. We could tell from watching the news. Once
again, Lieutenant Chip Sumerall leads his fearless troops into a
quiet home where everybody's asleep, and he gets his man. You
gonna sue?"

I reply, "I don't have the case yet, but I'm working on it."

"Thought you were the best at chasing ambulances."

"Only the ones I want. I'll catch this one."

Spurio chews on an onion bagel, washes it down with coffee, says, "These guys are outta control, Rudd. You gotta stop them."

"No way, Nate. I can't stop them. Maybe I can embarrass them from time to time, cost the City some money, but what they're doing here is happening everywhere. We live in a police state and everybody supports the cops."

"So you're the last line of defense?"

"Yep."

"God help us."

"Indeed. Thanks for the scoop. I'll be in touch."

"Don't mention it."

4.

Doug Renfro is too physically damaged and emotionally overwhelmed to meet with me, and since a meeting would have to take place in his hospital room, it's a bad idea anyway. The cops have the only door secured as if he were on death row. Privacy would be impossible. So I meet with Thomas Renfro and his two sisters in a coffee shop down the street from the hospital. The three are sleepwalking through their nightmare, exhausted, stunned, angry, grief stricken, and desperate for advice. They ignore their coffee and at first seem content to let me do the talking. Without the least bit of bluster, I explain who I am, what I do, where I come from, and how I protect my clients. I tell them that I'm not a typical lawyer. I don't maintain a pretty office filled with mahogany and leather. I don't belong to a big firm, prestigious or otherwise. I don't do good works through the bar association. I'm a lone gunman, a rogue who fights the system and hates injustice. I'm here right now because I know what's about to happen to their father, and to them.

Fiona, the older sister, says, "But they murdered our mother."

"Indeed they did, but no one will be charged with her murder. They'll investigate, send in the experts, and so on, and in the end they'll all agree that she simply got caught in the cross fire. They'll indict your father and blame him for starting the gun battle."

Susanna, the younger sister, says, "But we've talked to our father, Mr. Rudd. They were sound asleep when something crashed inside the house. He thought they were being robbed. He grabbed his gun, ran into the hallway, then hit the floor when he saw figures in the dark. Someone fired a shot, then he began returning fire. He says he remembers Mom screaming and running into the hall to check on him."

I say, "He's very lucky to be alive. They shot both dogs, didn't they?"

"Who are these goons?" Thomas asks helplessly.

"The police, the good guys." I then tell them the story of my client Sonny Werth, with the tank sitting in his den, and the lawsuit we won. I explain that a civil lawsuit is their only option right now. Their father will be indicted and prosecuted, and once the truth is finally learned—and I promise them that we will expose everything—there will be enormous pressure on the City to settle. Their endgame is to keep their father out of jail. They can forget justice for what happened to their mother. A civil lawsuit, one put together by the right lawyer of course, guarantees a safer flow of information. The cover-up is already under way, I say more than once.

They're trying their best to listen, but they're in another world. Who could blame them? The meeting ends with both women in tears and Thomas unable to speak.

It's time for me to back off.

5.

Uninvited, though it's open to the public, I arrive at the large Methodist church just minutes before the service for Katherine Renfro. I find the stairs, climb up to the balcony, and sit in the semidarkness. I am alone up here, but the rest of the sanctuary is packed. I look down on the crowd: all white, all middle class, all in disbelief that their friend got shot seven times in her pajamas by the police.

Aren't these senseless tragedies supposed to take place in other parts of town? These people are hard-core law-and-order. They vote to the right and want tough laws. If they think about SWAT teams at all, they think they're necessary to fight terror and drugs in other places. How could this happen to them?

Absent from this ceremony is Doug Renfro. According to yesterday's *Chronicle,* he has just been indicted. He's still hospitalized, though recovering slowly. He begged the doctors and the police to allow him to attend his wife's funeral. The doctors said sure; the cops said no way. He's a threat to society. A cruel footnote to this tragedy is that Doug will live the rest of his life under the cloud of somehow being involved with drug trafficking. Most of these people will believe him and his denials, but for some there will be doubts. What was old Doug really up to? Surely he must've been guilty of something or our brave police would not have gone after him.

I suffer through the service, along with everyone else. The air is thick with confusion and anger. The minister is comforting, but at times clearly unsure of what has happened. He tries to make some sense of it, but it's an impossible challenge. As he's wrapping things up, and as the crying gets louder, I ease down the stairs and exit through a side door.

Two hours later my phone rings. It's Doug Renfro.

6.

A lawyer like me is forced to work in the shadows. My opponents are protected by badges, uniforms, and all the myriad trappings of government power. They are sworn and duty-bound to uphold the law, but since they cheat like hell it forces me to cheat even more.

I have a network of contacts and sources. I can't call them friends because friendships require commitments. Nate Spurio is one example, an honest cop who wouldn't take a dime for inside information. I've offered. Another guy is a reporter with the *Chronicle,* and we swap gossip when it's convenient. No cash changes hands. One of my favorites is Okie Schwin, and Okie always takes the money.

Okie is a mid-level paper pusher in the federal court clerk's office in a downtown courthouse. He hates his job, despises his co-workers, and is always looking for an easy way to make a buck. He's also divorced, drinks too much, and constantly tests the boundaries of workplace sexual harassment. Okie's value is his ability to manipulate the court's random assignment of cases. When a civil lawsuit is filed, it is supposedly assigned by chance to one of our six federal judges. A computer does this and the little procedure seems to work fine. There's always a judge you'd prefer, depending on the type of case and perhaps your history in various courtrooms, but who cares when it's completely random? Okie, though, knows how to rig the software and find the judge you really want. He charges for this, handsomely, and he'll probably get caught, though he assures me there's no way. If he's caught, he'll get fired and maybe prosecuted, but Okie seems unconcerned by these possibilities.

At his suggestion, we meet in a seedy strip club far from downtown. The crowd is staunchly blue collar. The strippers are not worth describing. I turn my back to the stage so I don't have to look. Just under the roar, I say, "I'm filing suit tomorrow. Renfro, our SWAT boys' latest home invasion."

He laughs and says, "What a surprise. Let me guess, you think justice will be best served if the Honorable Arnie Samson presides."

"My man."

"He's 110 years old, on senior status, half-dead, and he says he's not taking cases anymore. Why can't we make these guys retire?"

"That's between you and the Constitution. He'll take this one. The standard fee?"

"Yep. But what if he says no and bounces it down the line?"

"I'll have to take that chance." I hand him an envelope with $3,000 in cash. His standard fee. He quickly shoves it into a pocket without even a thank-you, then turns his attention to the girls.

7.

At nine the following morning, I walk into the clerk's office and file a $50 million lawsuit against the City, the police department, the police chief, and the eight SWAT boys who attacked the Renfros' home six days earlier. Somewhere in the murky depths of the office, Okie does his magic and the case is "randomly and automatically" assigned to Judge Arnold Samson. I e-mail a copy of the lawsuit to my friend at the *Chronicle.*

I also file a request for a temporary restraining order to prevent the prosecutor from freezing Doug Renfro's assets. This is a favorite strong-arm tactic used by the government to harass criminal defendants. The original idea was to tie up assets supposedly accumulated in whatever criminal activity the defendant was engaged in, primarily drug trafficking. Seize the ill-gotten gains and make things tough for the cartels. And like so many laws, it didn't take the prosecutors long to get creative and expand its use. In Doug's case, the government was prepared to argue that his assets—home, cars, bank and retirement accounts—were accumulated, in part, with dirty money he earned while peddling Ecstasy.

Say what? By the time we have the emergency hearing on the temporary restraining order, the city prosecutors are backing down and looking for a way out. Judge Samson, as feisty as ever, scolds them and even threatens them with contempt. We win round 1.

Round 2 is a bail hearing in state court, where the attempted murder charge is pending. With his assets free, I'm able to argue that Doug Renfro poses absolutely no flight risk and will show up in court whenever he's supposed to. His home is worth $400,000 with no mortgage, and I offer to post the deed as security. To my surprise, the judge agrees, and I walk my client out of court. We win round 2, but these are the easy ones.

Eight days after getting shot and losing his wife and both dogs, Doug Renfro returns home, where his three children, seven grandchildren, and some friends are waiting. It will be a subdued homecoming. They graciously ask me to join them, but I decline.

I fight tooth and nail for my clients and will break most laws to protect them, but I never get too close.

8.

At ten on a perfect Saturday morning, I'm sitting on a bench at a playground, waiting. It's a few blocks from my apartment, our usual meeting place. On the sidewalk, a beautiful woman approaches with a seven-year-old boy. He is my son. She is my ex-wife. The court order allows me to see him once a month for thirty-six hours. As he gets older, I will be entitled to more lenient visitation, but for now things are restricted. There are reasons for this but I'd rather not discuss them now.

Starcher does not smile when they get to the bench. I stand and peck Judith on the cheek, more for the kid's benefit than hers. She prefers not to touch.

"Hey, buddy," I say, rubbing his head.

"Hey," he says, then walks over to a swing and climbs onto it. Judith sits beside me on the bench and we watch him kick and begin swaying.

"How's he doing?" I ask.

"Fine. His teachers are happy." A long pause. "I see you've been quite busy."

"Indeed. And you?"

"The usual grind."

"How's Ava?" I ask about her partner.

"She's great. What are your plans for the day?"

Judith does not like leaving our son with me. Once again, I've managed to offend the police and this worries her. Worries me too but I would never admit it.

I say, "I figure we'll do lunch. Then there's a soccer game at the university this afternoon."

She thinks a soccer game is safe enough. She says, "I'd like to have him back tonight, if that's okay."

"I get thirty-six hours once a month and that's too much?"

"No, Sebastian, it's not too much. I'm just worried, that's all."

Our fighting days are almost over, I hope. Take two lawyers with sharp elbows and even sharper tongues, give them an unwanted pregnancy, a nasty divorce with brutal aftershocks, and you have two people who can inflict serious damage. We're still scarred, so we don't fight, much.

"Fine," I say, in full retreat. Truthfully, there's nothing appealing about my apartment and Starcher doesn't really like staying there, not yet anyway. He's too short to shoot pool on my vintage table and I don't own any video games. Maybe when he's older.

He is being raised by two women who freak out if another kid shoves him at school. I'm not sure I can toughen him up by popping into his life once a month, but I'm trying. Down the road, I suspect he'll get tired of living with a couple of edgy, intense women and want more time with his old man. My challenge is to remain relevant enough in his life to offer him that option.

"What time shall we meet?" she asks.

"Whenever."

"I'll meet you here at 6:00 p.m.," she says as she gets to her feet and walks away. Starcher, his back to us, soars through the air and does not see her leave. It does not escape me that Judith did not bother to bring an overnight bag for the kid. She had no intention of allowing him to sleep at my place.

I live on the twenty-fifth floor because I feel safer there. I routinely get death threats for a variety of reasons, and I've been honest with Judith about this. She is not wrong for wanting the kid at home, where things are probably calmer. Probably, but I don't know for sure. Just last month Starcher told me his "two mothers" yell at each other all the time.

For lunch we go to my favorite pizza parlor, a place his mothers would never take him. The truth is I don't care what he eats. In many ways I'm more like a grandparent who spoils the kids before sending them back home. If he wants Ben & Jerry's before and after lunch, so be it.

As we eat, he comes to life while I quiz him about school. He's in the second grade in a public school not far from where I grew up. Judith insisted he attend some crunchy little granola academy where all plastic is forbidden and all the teachers wear thick wool socks and old sandals. At $40,000 a year I said hell no. She ran back to court, and for once the judge sided with me. So Starcher is in a normal school with kids of all colors and a seriously cute teacher, recently divorced.

As I've said, Starcher was a mistake. Judith and I were in the process of ending our chaotic relationship when she somehow got pregnant. The split grew even more complicated. I moved out and she assumed total possession of him. I was stiff-armed at every point, though, to be honest, I have never clamored to be a father. He's all hers, at least in her opinion, so it's becoming hilarious to watch him grow into a little boy who looks exactly like me. My mother found my second-grade school photo. At seven, we could pass for identical twins.

We talk about fighting, the school-yard variety. I ask him if he sees fights during recess, and he says, "Occasionally." He tells me the story of the day when kids began yelling, "Fight! Fight!" and everyone ran over to watch. Two third graders, one black and one white, were on the ground kicking and squirming, biting and clawing and swapping punches while the crowd yelled encouragement.

"Was it fun to watch?" I ask.

He smiles and says, "Sure. It was cool."

"What happened?"

"The teachers came and got them and took them into the office. I think they got in trouble."

"I'm sure they did. Has your mother ever talked to you about fighting?"

He shakes his head. No.

"Okay. Here are the rules. Fighting is bad and will only get you in trouble, so don't fight. Never start a fight. But, if someone else hits you, or pushes you, or trips you, or if two guys jump on a friend of yours, then sometimes you have to fight. Never back down when the other guy starts a fight. And when you fight, never, never, never give up."

"Did you get into fights?"

"All the time. I was never a bully and I never started a fight.

And I didn't like to fight, but if the other guy pushed me around, then I hit him back."

"Did you get in trouble?"

"I did. I took my punishment."

"What does that mean?"

"Means the teacher yelled at me and my mother yelled at me and maybe they kicked me out of school for half a day or something like that. Again, bud, fighting is wrong."

"Why do you always call me bud?"

Because I loathe the name your mother chose for you. "Just a nickname, that's all."

"Mom says you don't like my name."

"Not true, bud." Judith will always be at war over the soul of her son. She cannot rise above the temptation of the silliest cheap shot. Why on earth would one parent tell a seven-year-old that the other parent doesn't like his name? I'm sure I'd be shocked at the other crap she's told him.

Partner has the day off, so I drive my van to the soccer stadium on campus. Starcher thinks the van is cool, with its sofa, swivel chairs, small desk, and television. He's not sure why I use it as an office, and I have not gone into details about the bulletproof windows and automatic pistol in the console.

It's a women's soccer game, not that it matters to me. I don't follow the sport, so if I'm forced to watch it I'd rather see girls in shorts than guys with hairy legs. Starcher, though, loves the excitement. His mothers do not believe in team sports, so he's just been signed up for tennis lessons. Nothing wrong with tennis, but if he gets my moves he won't last long. I always liked to hit. In youth basketball I was the kid with four fouls by halftime. Always more fouls than points. In Pop Warner football I played linebacker because I loved the contact.

After an hour someone finally scores, but by then I'm thinking about the Renfro case and any interest I had in the game is gone. Starcher and I share a popcorn and talk about this and that. The truth is, I'm so far detached from his little world that I can't sustain a decent conversation.

I'm such a pathetic father.

9.

Sanity slowly arrives in the Renfro disaster. Under pressure from all sides, but especially from my pal at the *Chronicle,* the City flounders with its response. The chief of police has gone mum, claiming he can't comment because of pending litigation. The mayor is running for cover, obviously trying to create some distance. Hot on his ass are his enemies, some city councilmen who enjoy the grandstanding and would like to have his job. They are in a minority, though, because no one really wants trouble with the police department.

Sadly, dissent nowadays is considered unpatriotic, and in our post-9/11 atmosphere any criticism of those in uniform, any uniform, is stifled. Being labeled soft on crime or soft on terror is a politician's curse.

I'm feeding everything to my pal at the newspaper. Citing unnamed sources, he's having a ball hammering away at the cops and their tactics, screwups, and attempts to cover up. Using materials from my files, he runs a lengthy piece about the history of botched invasions and excessive force.

I'm getting as much press as I can possibly generate. I cannot lie and say I don't love this; indeed, I live for it.

The defendants file a motion with Judge Samson and ask him to, in effect, put a muzzle on "all lawyers involved in the civil lawsuit." Judge Samson denies the motion without even the benefit of a hearing. Right now, the attorneys for the City are terrified of the judge and running for cover. I'm firing as many bullets as possible.

I practice alone, without a real office and certainly without a real staff. It's extremely difficult for a lone gunman like me to engage in high-powered civil and criminal litigation without some support, which is where the two Harrys come in. Harry Gross and Harry Skulnick run a fifteen-lawyer shop in a converted warehouse downtown by the river. They do mostly appellate work and try to avoid jury trials, and thus spend their hours buried in books and pushing legal pads and briefs around their desks. Our arrangement is simple: They do my research and paperwork, and I give them one-third of the fees. This allows them to play it safe, to keep some distance from me, my clients, and the people I tend to irritate. They will prepare a stack of motions an inch thick, hand it to me for my review and signature, and nothing can be traced back to them. They toil away behind locked doors and never worry about the police. In the case of Sonny Werth—the client who woke up with the tank roaring into his den—the City settled for a million bucks. My cut was 25 percent. The two Harrys got a nice check and everybody was happy, except for Sonny.

In this state, all damages in civil cases are capped at $1 million. This is because the wise people who make the laws in our state legislature decided ten years ago that their judgment was far superior to that of the actual jurors who hear the evidence and evaluate the damages. They, the lawmakers, were hoodwinked by the insurance companies who are still funding the national tort reform movement, a political crusade that has been wildly successful. Virtually every state has fallen in line with caps on damages and other laws designed to keep folks away from the courthouse. So far, no one has seen a decline in insurance rates. An investigative report by my pal at the *Chronicle* revealed that 90 percent of our legislators took campaign money from the insurance industry. And this is considered a democracy.

Every street lawyer in this state can tell you a horror story of a badly maimed and permanently injured client who, after medical expenses, got almost nothing.

Not long after slamming the courthouse doors, these same wise and courageous legislators passed another law that prohibits homeowners from firing upon cops who invade their homes, regardless of whether the cops have the right home or not. So when Doug Renfro hit the floor and began firing his pistol, he was violating the law, with no real defense.

What about the real criminals? Well, our legislators passed yet another law that grants criminal immunity to SWAT teams who get a bit carried away and shoot the wrong person. In the Renfro disaster, four cops fired at least thirty-eight rounds. It's not clear who actually shot Doug and his wife, and it doesn't matter. They are all immune from criminal prosecution.

I spend hours with Doug trying to explain these legal principles, none of which make sense. He wants to know why his wife's life is worth only $1 million. I explain that his state senator voted for this cap on damages—and that he also takes money from insurance lobbyists—so perhaps Doug should contact this elected official and bitch about the way he votes.

Doug asks, "Then why did we sue for $50 million when the most we can get is only $1 million?" Another question with a long answer. First, it's called making a statement. We're angry and fighting back, and suing for $50 million sounds much more aggressive than a mere $1 million. Second, a quirk in this already screwed-up law prohibits the jurors from knowing about the $1 million cap. They can sit through a month of testimony, evaluate the evidence, deliberate thoughtfully, and return a proper verdict of, say, $5 to $10 million. Then they go home, and the next day the judge quietly reduces the verdict down to the cap. The newspaper might trumpet another big verdict, but the lawyers and judges (and insurance companies) know the truth.

It makes no sense, but bear in mind this law was written by the same conspirators who insert endless gibberish into your insurance policies.

Doug asks, "But how can a cop kick in my door and shoot me with immunity, but if I return fire I'm a criminal looking at twenty years?" The simple answer is because they are cops. The complicated answer is that our lawmakers often pass laws that are not fair.

My client is still in mourning, but some of the shock and grief are beginning to subside. His thinking is getting clearer; reality is setting in. His wife is gone, murdered by men who will not be held accountable. Her life is worth only $1 million. And he, Mr. Doug Renfro, is in the midst of a criminal prosecution that will one day drag him into a courtroom where his only hope will be a hung jury.

The road to justice is filled with barriers and land mines, most of them created by men and women who claim to be seeking justice.

10.

My little cage fighter, Tadeo Zapate, has won his last four fights, all by brutal knockouts. That's eleven in a row, with only three career losses, all on points. He's now thirty-second in the world bantamweight rankings and moving up nicely. UFC promoters are taking notice. There's talk of a fight in Vegas in six months, if he keeps winning. Oscar, his trainer, and Norberto, his manager, tell me they can't keep the kid out of the gym. He is focused, hungry, almost manic in his quest for a title fight. They work him hard and are convinced he can be a top-five contender.

Tonight he fights a tough black kid with the stage name of Crush. I've seen Crush fight twice and he doesn't worry me. He's just a brawler, a street fighter with limited training in mixed martial arts. In both fights he got knocked out late in the third round because of fatigue. He starts with a bang, cannot pace himself, and pays for it at the end.

I wake up with a bad case of butterflies, thinking of nothing but the fight, and cannot eat breakfast. I'm puttering around the apartment late in the afternoon when Judith calls my cell. There's an emergency—her college roommate has been seriously injured in an auto accident in Chicago. Judith is racing to the airport. Ava, her partner, is out of town, so it's up to me to man up and be a father. I bite my tongue and do not tell her that I have plans. It's fight night!

We meet at the park and she delivers our son, his duffel bag, and a barrage of warnings and instructions. Normally, I'd snap back and we'd argue, but Starcher seems to be in good spirits and eager to get away from her. I've never met her college roommate, so I don't inquire. She storms off, jumps in her car, and disappears. Over pizza, I ask Starcher if he's ever seen a cage fight on television. Of course not! His mothers monitor everything he reads, watches, eats, drinks, and thinks.

Last month, though, he spent the night with a friend, Tony, who has a big brother named Zack, and late that night Zack pulled out a laptop and they watched all manner of evil, including an Ultimate Fight.

I ask, "How was it?"

"Pretty cool," he says with a grin. "You're not mad?"

"Of course not. I love those fights."

I go on to explain how our night will go. The kid's face lights up like I've never seen. I make him swear that he will not, under any circumstances, tell his mothers about going to the fights. I explain that I have no choice; that I have to be there as part of a team; and that under normal circumstances he would not be invited. "Let me handle your mother," I say, without much confidence, but then I realize he will be grilled mercilessly about the evening.

"Let's just say we had pizza and watched TV in my apartment, which will be the truth because we're eating pizza now and we'll turn on the television when we get to my apartment."

For a second he looks confused, then lights up again.

Back at my apartment, he watches a cartoon while I change clothes. He likes my shiny yellow jacket with "Tadeo Zapate" emblazoned across the back, and it takes me a while to explain that I work the corner. Each fighter has a corner team to help him between rounds, and, well, I'm in charge of water and anything else that Tadeo might need. No, I'm not really that necessary, but it sure is a lot of fun.

Partner picks us up in the black van and we ride to the city auditorium. For the next two hours, Partner will do the babysitting, a new role for him. Driver, bodyguard, errand boy, investigator, confidant, strategist, and now this. He doesn't mind. I pull some strings and get them two seats on the floor, six rows back from the cage. Once they are situated with popcorn and sodas, I tell Starcher that I have to go check on my fighter. He's excited, wide-eyed, chattering away to Partner, who's already his best friend. Though I know the kid is safe, I'm still worried. Worried that his mother will find out and sue me again for neglect, corruption of a minor, and anything else she can possibly throw at me. Worried also that with this crowd anything can happen. I watch a lot of fights and have often thought that it's safer inside the ring than out in the crowd. The fans are drinking and rowdy and they want blood.

A city councilwoman in some place like Wichita tried to pass

an ordinance that would prohibit anyone under the age of eighteen from being admitted to a cage fight. It failed, but there is
some wisdom behind it. Since there's no such law in our city,
young Starcher Whitly has a ringside seat.

Zapate versus Crush is the main event, which is fantastic, of
course, right where we want to be, but it requires a long wait
through the undercard. Tonight there are five warm-ups, so the
evening will move painfully slowly.

I check in with Team Zapate and everyone is in good spirits.
Subdued, as always, but quite confident. Tadeo is still in street
clothes, lying on a table with his headphones on. His brother
Miguel says he's ready. Oscar whispers that it will be a first-round
knockout. I hang around for a few minutes but can't stand the
tension. I leave and walk through a tunnel to a lower level where
my little gang of criminals is waiting in a supply room. Slide,
the convicted murderer, has been losing lately and has cut back
on his wagers. Nino, the meth dealer, has, as always, a pocketful
of cash and is splashing it around. Denardo, the Mafia wannabe,
doesn't like any of the fights. Johnny is absent. Frankie, the old
guy and our scorekeeper, is nursing a double scotch, probably not
his first. We work through the undercard and place our bets. As
usual, no one will bet against my man. I chide them, taunt them,
curse them, but they don't budge. I offer $10,000 for a first-round
knockout but get no takers. Frustrated, I leave with only $5,000
on the table, a grand for each bout on the undercard.

I pay eight bucks for a watered-down beer and climb to the
nosebleed section, which is packed. A sellout, standing room only.
Tadeo is becoming a big draw in his hometown, and I hammered
the promoter for a guaranteed purse. Eight thousand dollars—
win, lose, or draw. I lean on a steel beam above the top row and
watch the first fight. I can barely see my kid in the crowd, way
down there.

I lose my bets on the first four fights, win the fifth, then hustle to the dressing room. Team Zapate crowds around its hero, who also wears bright yellow. We look like a sack of organic lemons. We walk him through the tunnel and into the lights, and the crowd goes wild. I wave at Starcher and he waves back with a huge smile on his face.

Round 1. Three minutes of boredom as Crush, to our surprise, does not charge across the ring like a mad dog. Instead, he plays defense and escapes serious damage. Using a left jab that at times is hard to see, Tadeo opens a cut over Crush's right eye. Late in the round, Crush returns the favor with a nasty gash across Tadeo's forehead. Oscar manages to close it between rounds. Cuts are not that critical in cage fighting because the fights are so short. In boxing, a first-round cut is terrifying because it becomes a target for the next half hour.

Round 2. They hit the deck and grapple for the first half of the round. Crush has a strong upper body and Tadeo is unable to pin him. Boos can be heard. Back on their feet, they spar and kick with neither scoring much. Just before the bell, Tadeo lands a hard right to the jaw that would have flattened any of the last dozen or so men he's faced, but Crush stays on his feet. As Tadeo goes in for the kill, Crush manages to grab his waist and hang on until the bell. Suddenly I don't like this fight. Tadeo is clearly ahead on points, but I don't trust judges.

Perhaps it's the nature of my profession.

I like knockouts, not decisions.

Round 3. Having paced himself, Crush figures he's got some gas in the tank. He charges across the ring and surprises everyone with a wild flurry that ignites the crowd. It's certainly exciting, but not damaging. Tadeo covers well, then lands a couple of hard jabs that draw more blood. Crush charges again, and again. Tadeo, the boxer, picks his openings and shoots jabs that land beautifully.

I'm screaming, the crowd is screaming, the floor seems to be shaking. Meanwhile, the clock is ticking and Crush is still out there, charging and charging, his face a bloody mess. He lands a wild right and Tadeo goes down, but only for a second. Crush leaps on top of him and they kick and claw and finally manage to untangle. Tadeo has not gone this late in a fight in a long time, and he begins to press. Crush charges again, and for the final minute they go toe-to-toe in the center of the ring, just two mad dogs beating the crap out of each other.

My heart is pounding, my stomach is rolling, and I'm just the water boy. We assure Tadeo he's won again as we wait and wait. Finally, the referee walks the fighters to the center of the ring. The announcer proclaims a split decision, with Crush winning by a point. A thunderous wave of booing and screaming rocks the auditorium. Tadeo is stunned, shocked, his mouth wide open, his swollen eyes filled with hate. The fans are throwing things at the cage and we're on the verge of a riot.

The next fifteen seconds will change Tadeo's life forever.

He suddenly whirls and throws a hard right into the left side of Crush's face. It's a sucker punch, a vicious one that Crush never saw coming. He crumples to the mat, out cold. Instantly, Tadeo attacks the referee, who's also black, and pummels him with a flurry. The ref stumbles and lands against the cage, half sitting up, and Tadeo pounces on him with a furious barrage of punches. For a few seconds, everyone is too stunned to react. They are, after all, in a cage, and it takes time to mount a rescue. By the time Norberto tackles Tadeo, the poor ref is unconscious.

The auditorium erupts as fights break out everywhere. Tadeo's fans, most of them Hispanic, and Crush's fans, most of whom are black and heavily outnumbered, attack each other like gangs in the street. Cups of beer and cartons of popcorn rain down like confetti. A security guard nearby gets hit over the head with a folding chair. It's total chaos and no one is safe. I forget about the carnage inside the cage and sprint for my son. He's not in his seat, but through the melee I see the hulking figure of Partner as they make their escape. I go after them, and within seconds we are safe. As we duck out of the auditorium, we pass panicked police running toward the action. In the van, I clutch Starcher in the front seat as Partner takes the side streets. I say, "Are you okay, bud?"

He says, "Let's do it again."

Minutes later, we enter my apartment and take a deep breath. I get drinks—beers for Partner and me and a soda for Starcher—and we turn on the local news. The story is still unfolding and the reporters are frantic. The kid is excited and talks enough to let me know he's not traumatized. I try in vain to explain what happened.

Partner sleeps on the sofa. I wake him at 4:00 a.m. to talk strategy. He leaves for the city jail, to try and find Tadeo, and for the hospital, to dig for information about the referee. I can't shake the image of Tadeo pounding the guy's face. He was knocked cold from the first punch and there were dozens afterward, all delivered by a man completely out of his mind. I try not to think about what's next for my fighter.

I grind beans, and while the coffee is brewing I go online to check the news. Fortunately, no one has died yet, but at least twenty people are in the hospital. Rescue personnel are still on the scene. And the blame is being heaped upon one Tadeo Zapate, age twenty-two, an up-and-coming cage fighter who's now locked away in the city jail.

Judith calls at 6:30 to check on her son. She's hours away and knows nothing about the riot we survived. I ask about her college roommate. She is surviving but things look bad. Judith will be home tomorrow, Sunday, and I assure her the kid will be just fine. All is well.

With some luck, she'll never know.

Luck, though, is not going my way. A few minutes after our brief chat, I check the *Chronicle* online. The late edition managed to catch the breaking story down at the old auditorium, and on the front page is a rather large color photo of two people racing toward an exit. One is Partner, and he's holding a kid. Starcher seems to be staring at the photographer, as if posing for the shot. Their names are not given; there was no time to ask. But to those who know him, his identity is indisputable.

How long before one of Judith's friends sees the photo and gives her a call? How long before she opens her laptop and sees for herself? While I wait, I turn on the television and go to *SportsCenter*. The story is irresistible because it's all right there, on video, blow by blow by blow. I get sick watching it again and again.

Partner calls from the hospital with the news that the referee, a guy named Sean King, is still in surgery. It's no surprise that Partner is not the only person sniffing around the corridors waiting for any bit of news. He's heard of "massive head wounds," but has no details. He's already been to the jail, where a contact confirmed that Mr. Zapate is safely locked away and not receiving visitors.

At 8:00 a.m., our blundering chief of police decides the world should hear from him. He arranges a press conference, one of those little muscle pageants in which a thick wall of uniformed white men line up behind the chief and scowl at the reporters while acting as though they really don't want to be seen. For thirty minutes the chief talks and answers questions and reveals not a single fact that wasn't posted online two hours earlier. He's obviously enjoying the moment because nothing can be blamed on him or his men. Just as I'm getting bored, Judith calls.

The conversation is predictable—tense, bitchy, and accusatory. She's seen the front-page photo of her son escaping the melee and she wants answers, and now, dammit. I assure her our son is sleeping soundly and probably dreaming of a fine day with his father. She says she's catching an early flight and will be in the City by 5:00 p.m., which is the precise moment I'm supposed to meet her in the park and hand him over. She'll file papers first thing Monday morning to terminate all visitation rights. File away, I say, because it won't work. No judge in town will totally exclude me from seeing my son once a month. And, who knows, maybe the judge we draw is a fan of cage fighting. She curses and I curse back and we finally get off the phone.

Looks like we've just begun to fight.

11.

The Sunday papers rage against cage fighting, with knee-jerk condemnations coming from all directions. The Internet burns with the story. A YouTube video of the attack on the referee has four million hits before noon, and Tadeo has instantly become the most famous cage fighter in the world, though he will never fight again. Slowly, the wounded are released from hospitals, and, fortunately, there were no serious injuries to the fans. Just a bunch of drunks throwing punches and launching chairs. Sean King remains in a coma, in serious condition. Crush is resting comfortably with a badly fractured jaw and a concussion.

Late in the afternoon, I am allowed to visit my client in one of the jail's attorney rooms. He's sitting on the other side of a thick metal screen when I walk in and take a seat. His face is cut and badly swollen from the fight, but that's the least of his problems. He is so subdued I wonder if he's been drugged. We chat for a moment.

"When can I get outta here?" he asks.

You'd better get used to it, I want to say. "Your first appearance is in the morning, in court. I'll be there. Nothing much will happen. They'll wait to see what happens with the referee. If he dies, then you're really up shit creek. If he recovers, they'll charge you with a bunch of stuff but it won't be murder. Maybe in a week or so we'll go back to court and request a reasonable bond. I can't guess what the judge will do. So, to answer your question, there's a chance you might bond out in a few days. There's an even better chance you'll stay in jail until a trial."

"How long will that take?"

"A trial?"

"Yes."

"Hard to say. Six months at the earliest; probably more like a year. The trial itself won't last very long because there won't be many witnesses. They'll just roll the video."

He looks down, as if he wants to cry. I love this kid but there's not much I can do for him, now or in six months. "Do you remember it?" I ask.

Slowly, he begins to nod. He says, "I just snapped. They cheated me out of a clear win. The ref made me fight his way, not mine. The ref kept getting in the way, you know, man, I just couldn't fight my fight. I mean, I didn't want to hurt the ref, but I just snapped. I was so angry, so destroyed when he raised that guy's hand. I kicked his ass, didn't I?"

"Crush or the referee?"

"Come on, man. Crush. I kicked his ass, right?"

"No, you did not. But you won the fight." I saw every second of the fight and I never felt as though the ref was in the way. As far as legal defenses go, I don't think much of this one: The ref held me back, cost me the match, so I caved in his face. It was justified.

"They took it away from me," he says.

"The referee is not a judge, Tadeo. The three judges did the scoring. You went after the wrong guy."

He picks at the stitches in his forehead and says, "I know, I know. I did wrong, Sebastian, but you gotta do something, okay?"

"You know I'll do everything possible."

"Will I serve some time?"

You're serving it now; get used to it. I've already played with the numbers. If Sean King dies, I'm thinking twenty years for second-degree murder, maybe fifteen for manslaughter. If he lives, three to five for aggravated assault. Since I'm not ready to share these thoughts, I punt by saying, "Let's worry about that later."

"Probably so, right?"

"Probably so."

There is a gap in the conversation as we hear doors clanging in the background. A jailer yells an obscenity. A tear emerges through Tadeo's swollen left eye and runs down his bruised cheek. "I can't believe it, man. I just can't believe it." His voice is soft and pained.

If you can't believe it, think about that poor ref and his family. "I need to run, Tadeo. I'll see you in the morning, in court."

"I gotta wear this in court?" he asks, tugging at his orange jumpsuit.

"Afraid so. It's just a first appearance."

12.

At 9:00 on Monday morning, I'm in a busy courtroom with a bunch of other defense lawyers and prosecutors. In one corner there is a collection of shady-looking men in orange jumpsuits, all handcuffed together and watched by armed bailiffs. These are the new arrestees, and this is their second stop on the judicial assembly line. The first stop being the jail. One by one their names are called, and after being uncuffed they saunter over to a spot in front of the bench, upon which sits a judge, one of twenty in our system who handles the preliminary matters. The judge asks them some questions, the most important being "Do you have a lawyer?" Very few of them do, and the judge then assigns them to the public defender's office. A rookie will pop up, stand beside his new client, and tell him not to say anything else. Dates will be set for return visits.

Tadeo Zapate, though, has a lawyer. They call his name and we meet in front of the bench. His face looks even worse. Most of the hushed conversations stop when the crowd realizes this is the guy everyone is talking about, the promising mixed martial arts fighter who is now the YouTube star.

"Are you Tadeo Zapate?" the judge asks with interest, the first time this morning he's seemed engaged.

"Yes, sir."

"And I assume Mr. Sebastian Rudd is your lawyer."

"Yes, sir."

An assistant prosecutor eases behind him.

The judge continues, "You are charged, at this point, with aggravated assault. Do you understand this?"

"Yes, sir."

"Mr. Rudd, have you explained to your client that the charges might change to something more serious?"

"Yes, sir, he understands."

"By the way, what is the latest on the referee?" he asks the assistant prosecutor, as if the guy were the treating physician.

"Last I heard, Mr. King's condition is still critical."

"Very well," His Honor says. "Let's meet back here in a week and see where things stand. Until then, Mr. Rudd, we won't discuss the matter of bail."

"Sure, Judge," I say.

We are dismissed. As Tadeo walks away, I whisper, "I'll see you at the jail tomorrow."

"Thanks," he says, then looks at the spectators and nods at his mother, who's sitting with an entire pack of crying relatives. She emigrated from El Salvador twenty-five years ago, has her green card, works a late shift in a cafeteria, and is raising a flock of children, grandchildren, and other assorted relatives. Tadeo and his cage skills were her ticket to a better life. Miguel holds her hand and whispers in Spanish. He's been chewed up by our judicial system a few times and knows the score.

I speak to them briefly, assure them I'm doing whatever can be done, then walk with them out of the courtroom and into a hallway where some reporters are waiting, two with cameras. This is what I live for.

13.

Quite the busy morning. While I'm in court with Tadeo, Judith does exactly as she promised and files a nasty motion to terminate all of my visitation rights, even the three hours I get on Christmas Eve and the two hours on my son's birthday. She claims I'm an unfit parent, a danger to his physical safety, and a "horrible influence" on the child's life. She demands an expedited hearing. Such theatrics. As if the kid were in danger.

Harry & Harry prepare a vicious response, and I file it Monday afternoon. Once again, we square off in her ongoing crusade to teach me valuable lessons. No judge will grant her demands, and she knows it. But she's doing it because she's angry and she thinks that if she drags me through the meat grinder once more I'll finally surrender and get out of their lives. I'm almost looking forward to the hearing.

First, though, we have another problem. On Wednesday, she calls my cell around noon and announces rudely, "We have a meeting at school this afternoon."

Oh really? This is maybe the second time I've been asked to

show up at the school and act like a parent. Until now, Judith has done a fine job of keeping me out of our son's business.

I ask, "Okay, what's up?"

"Starcher is in trouble. He got in a fight at school, punched another kid."

I am overwhelmed with fatherly pride and I almost laugh. But I bite my tongue and say, "Oh, gosh, what happened?" I want to add questions such as "Did he win?" "How many times did he punch him?" and "Was the other kid a third grader?" But I manage to control my excitement.

"That's what the meeting is all about. I'll see you in the principal's office at four."

"Four, today?"

"Yes," she says, bitchy and firm.

"Okay." I'll have to move a court appearance but it's no problem. I wouldn't miss this meeting for the world. My kid—a soft little boy who's never had a chance to be tough—punched somebody!

I smile all the way to the school. The principal has a big office with several chairs around a coffee table. We meet there, very casual. Her name is Doris—a frazzled veteran of at least forty years in public education. But she has an easy smile and a comforting voice. Who knows how many meetings like this she's suffered through. Judith and Ava are already there when I arrive. I nod at them without speaking. Judith is wearing a designer dress and is stunning. Ava, the former lingerie model, is wearing supertight leather pants and a tight blouse. She may have the brains of a gerbil but she still has a body that belongs on magazine covers. Both women look fabulous, and it's obvious, at least to me, that they spent some time dressing up for this occasion. But why?

Then Ms. Tarrant arrives, and things become clearer. She's

Starcher's teacher, a thirty-three-year-old knockout who got a divorce recently and, according to a source, is already back in the game. She has short blond hair, cut smartly, and large brown eyes that force everyone she meets to do at least one double take. Judith and Ava are no longer the hottest babes in the room. In fact, they're getting smoked. I stand and make a fuss over Ms. Tarrant, who enjoys the attention. Judith immediately goes into total-bitch mode—she's halfway there by nature—but Ava's eyes sort of linger when she looks at the teacher. Mine are lingering like crazy.

Doris gives us the basics: During recess yesterday afternoon, some second-grade boys were playing kickball on the playground. There were words, then a scuffle, then a boy named Brad pushed Starcher, who then smacked Brad on the mouth. It caused a slight cut, thus blood, thus it's a major incident. Not surprisingly, the boys clammed up when the teachers arrived and haven't said much.

I blurt out, "Sounds pretty harmless. Just boys being boys."

None of the four women agree, not that I expect them to. Ms. Tarrant says, "One of the boys told me that Brad was making fun of Starcher because his picture was in the newspaper."

"Who threw the first punch?" I ask, almost rudely.

They squirm and don't like the question. "Does that really matter?" Judith shoots back.

"Damn right it does."

Sensing trouble, Doris rushes in with "We have strict rules against fighting, Mr. Rudd, regardless of who starts the altercation. Our students are taught not to engage in this type of activity."

"I get that, but you can't expect a kid to get bullied without standing up for himself."

The word "bullied" is a hot one. With my kid now the victim, they're not sure how to respond. Ms. Tarrant says, "Well, I'm not sure he was being bullied."

"Is Brad a bad apple?" I ask the teacher.

"No, he certainly is not. I have a great group of kids this year."

"Sure you do. Including mine. These are little boys, okay? They can't hurt each other. So they push and shove on the playground. They are boys, dammit! Let them be boys. Don't punish them every time they disagree."

"We're teaching them lessons, Mr. Rudd," Doris says piously.

Judith snarls, "Have you talked to him about fighting?"

"Yes I have. I've told him that fighting is wrong, never start a fight, but if someone else happens to start one, then by all means protect himself. And what, exactly, is wrong with that?"

None of the four take a crack at answering this, so I shove on. "You'd better teach him now to stand up for himself, or he'll get bullied for the rest of his life. These are kids. They'll fight. They'll win some, lose some, but they'll outgrow it. Believe me, when a boy gets older and gets punched a few times, he loses his enthusiasm for fighting."

For the second time, I catch Ava glancing at Ms. Tarrant's legs. I'm glancing too; can't help it. They deserve a lot of attention. Doris is watching these mating rituals. She's seen it all before.

She says, "Brad's parents are quite upset."

I jump in with "Then I'll be happy to talk to them, to apologize and to have Starcher apologize too. How about that?"

"I'll handle this," Judith barks.

"Then why did you invite me to this little party? I'll tell you why. You want to make sure all blame is properly laid at my feet. Five days ago I took the kid to the cage fights; now he's brawling on the playground. Clear proof it's all my fault. You win. You wanted some witnesses. So here we are. Do you feel better now?"

This, of course, sucks the air out of the room. Judith's eyes glaze over with hatred and I can almost see steam coming out of her ears. Doris, the pro, rushes in with "Okay, okay. I like the idea of one of you having a chat with Brad's parents."

"One of the two of us, or one of the three of us?" I ask. What a smart-ass. "I'm sorry, but it gets kind of crowded."

Ava shoots daggers at me. I glance at the teacher's legs. What a ridiculous meeting.

Doris shows some spine by looking at me and saying, "I think you should do it. You're right; it's a boy thing. Call Brad's parents and apologize."

"Done."

"What's the punishment for Starcher?" Ava asks because Judith can't speak right now.

Doris says, "What do you think, Ms. Tarrant?"

"Well, there has to be a punishment."

I make matters worse by saying, "Don't tell me you're going to expel the kid."

Ms. Tarrant says, "No, he and Brad are friends and I think they've already moved on. What about a week with no recess?"

"Can he still have lunch?" I ask, just trying to clog the wheels of justice. I'm a lawyer; it's instinctive.

She smiles but ignores this. We hammer out an agreement and I'm the first one to leave. As I drive away from the parking lot, I realize I'm smiling. Starcher stood his ground!

Late that night, I e-mail Ms. Tarrant—Naomi is her first name—and thank her for doing such a fine job. Ten minutes later, she e-mails me back and says thanks. I fire right back and ask her to dinner. Twenty minutes later she informs me it's not a good idea to date parents of her kids. In other words, not now, maybe in the future.

It's Wednesday and raining. We've played Dirty Golf many times in bad weather, but Alan said no tonight; no more ruts in the fairways. Old Rico is closed for the evening. I'm wide awake, bored, worried about Tadeo and Doug Renfro, and I'm also fairly revved up at the slim prospects of chasing Ms. Tarrant. Sleep eludes me, again, so I grab an umbrella and hustle down to The Rack. At midnight, I'm losing ten bucks a game in nine ball to a kid who looks no more than fifteen. I asked him if he goes to school, to which he answered, "Occasionally."

Curly is watching us, and at one point whispers to me, "Never seen him before. Amazing." Mercifully, Curly closes the place at 1:00 a.m. The kid has picked my pockets for $90. I'll avoid him next time. At 2:00, I manage to close my eyes and fall asleep.

14.

Partner calls me at four. Sean King died of a cerebral hemorrhage. I make coffee and drink it in the dark while gazing down on the City, still and quiet at this hour. The moon is full and its light reflects off the tall buildings downtown.

What a tragedy. Tadeo Zapate will now spend at least the next decade or so behind bars. He's twenty-two, so he'll be too old to fight when he gets out. Too old for many things. I think about the money, but just for a minute. I invested $30,000 in the kid for a quarter share of his career earnings, which to date total about $80,000. Plus, I've picked up another $20,000 betting on him. So I'm slightly ahead on the cash side. I try not to think about his future earnings, which were going to be substantial. All that seems trivial now.

Instead, I think about his family, their hard life and the hope he gave them. He was their ticket out of the street life and the violence, to the middle class and beyond. Now they'll sink even deeper into poverty while he rots away in prison.

There is no defense, no credible legal strategy to save him. I've watched the video a hundred times now. The last flurry of blows to Sean King's face were absorbed while he was unconscious. It won't be difficult to find an expert who'll say those were the shots that did the fatal damage. But an expert will not be needed. This case is not going to trial. I'll serve my client well if I can somehow pressure the State to make us a decent offer. I just hope it's ten years and not thirty, but something tells me I'm dreaming. No prosecutor in this country would pass up the opportunity to nail such a high-profile murderer.

I force myself to think about Sean King, but I never knew the guy. I'm sure his family is devastated and all that, but my thoughts return to Tadeo.

At six I shower, get dressed, and head for the jail. I have to tell Tadeo that his life, as he knew it, is over.

15.

The following Monday, Tadeo Zapate and I appear in court again, though the mood is quite different. He's charged with murder now, and thanks to the Internet he's famous. It seems as though few people can resist the temptation of watching him kill Sean King with his bare hands.

As expected, the judge denies bail and they take Tadeo away. I've had two brief chats with the prosecutor and it looks like they're out for blood. Second-degree murder carries a max of thirty years. For a plea, they'll agree to twenty. Under our screwed-up parole system, he'll serve at least ten. I have yet to explain this to my client. He's still in denial, still in that fog where he's sorry it happened, can't explain it, but still believing that a good lawyer can pull some strings and get him off.

It's a sad day, but not a complete waste. In the large open hallway outside the courtroom, there is a crowd of reporters and they're waiting for me. There is no gag order yet, so I'm free to say all the ridiculous things that lawyers say long before the trials. My client is a good person who snapped when he got a raw deal. Now he is devastated by what happened. He cries in sympathy for the family of Sean King. He would give anything to have those few precious seconds back. We will mount a vigorous defense. Yes, of course, he hopes to fight again. He was helping his poor mother support her family and a house full of relatives.

And so on.

16.

With Harry & Harry churning out the paperwork, and with Judge Samson haranguing the City's lawyers whenever they get close to his courtroom, the civil action moved ahead at an unusually rapid pace.

We are in a race here, one that we will not win. I would love to try Doug Renfro's civil case in a packed courtroom before his criminal case is called. The problem is that we have a speedy-trial rule in criminal cases, but not in civil. In theory, a criminal case must be brought to trial or otherwise disposed of within 120 days of indictment, though this is routinely waived by the defendant's lawyer because more time is needed to prepare. There is no such rule in civil cases, which often drag on for years. In my perfect scenario, we would try the civil case first, get a huge verdict that would be front-page news and, more important, influence prospective jurors in the criminal case. The press can't get enough of the Renfro debacle, and I relish the chance to grill the cops on the witness stand for the benefit of the entire city.

If the criminal prosecution goes first, and if Doug Renfro is convicted, then the civil case will be much more difficult to win. As a witness, he'll be impeachable because of his conviction.

Judge Samson understands this and is trying to help. Less than three months after the botched SWAT raid, he orders all eight cops to appear in his chambers to be deposed by me. No judge,

federal or otherwise, would ever consider suffering through a single deposition; it would be far beneath his or her dignity. But to
set the mood and deliver the message to the cops and their lawyers that he is highly suspicious of them, Judge Samson orders
the depositions to be taken on his turf, with his law clerk and his
magistrate in the room.

It is a brutal marathon that pushes me to the limits. I begin
with Lieutenant Chip Sumerall, the leader of the SWAT team. I
elicit testimony regarding his experience, training, and partici-
pation in other home invasions. I am deliberately dull, tedious,
poker-faced. It's just a deposition, the purpose of which is to establish sworn testimony. Using maps, photos, and videos, we walk
through the Renfro affair for hours.

It takes six full days to depose the eight cops. But they're on
the record now, and they cannot change their stories at either the
criminal or the civil trials.

17.

The only time I spend in Domestic Relations Court is when
I'm dragged in to account for my sins. I wouldn't handle a divorce
or adoption at gunpoint. Judith, though, makes her living in the
gutter warfare of divorce trials and this is her turf. His Honor
today is one Stanley Leef, a cranky old veteran who lost interest
years ago. Judith represents herself, as do I. For the occasion she's
dragged in Ava, who sits as the lone spectator, in a skirt so short
you can see her name and address. I catch Judge Leef gazing at her,
enjoying the scenery.

Since we're both lawyers, and representing ourselves, Judge
Leef dispenses with the formalities and allows us to just sit and
talk, as if we're in arbitration. We are on the record, though, and
a stenographer is taking it all down.

Judith goes first, states the facts, and makes it sound as though I'm the worst parent in history because I took my son to the cage fights. Then, four days later, Starcher got in his first fight at school. Clear proof that I've turned him into a monster.

Judge Leef frowns as if this is just awful.

With as much drama as she can muster, Judith proclaims that all visitation rights should be terminated so the kid will never again be subjected to my influence. Judge Leef shoots me a quick glance that says, "Is she crazy?"

But we're not here for justice, we're here for a show. Judith is an angry mother and she's once again dragged me into court. My punishment is not the loss of visitation rights; rather, it's just the hassle of dealing with her. She will not be pushed around! She will protect her child at all costs!

From my seat, I tell my side of the story without embellishing a single word.

She produces a copy of the newspaper, with "her son" on the front page. What humiliation! He could have been seriously injured. Judge Leef is almost asleep.

She produces an expert, a child psychologist. Dr. Salabar, female of course, informs the court that she has interviewed Starcher, spent an entire hour with him, talked about the cage fights and the playground "brawl," and is now of the opinion that the carnage he witnessed while under my supervision had a detrimental effect on him and encouraged him to start a fight of his own. Judith manages to string this testimony out until Judge Leef is practically comatose.

On cross-examination, I ask, "Are you married?"

"Yes."

"Do you have a son or sons?"

"Two boys, yes."

"Did you ever take either son to boxing matches, wrestling matches, or cage fights?"

"No."

"Did either son ever get into a fight with another kid?"

"Well, I'm sure they did, but then I really can't say."

The fact that she won't answer the question speaks volumes. Judge Leef shakes his head.

"Did your boys ever get into a fight with one another?"

"I don't recall."

"You don't recall? Were you a loving mother who gave your sons all the attention possible?"

"I'd like to think so."

"So you were there for them?"

"As much as possible, yes."

"And you can't remember a single time when one of them got into a fight?"

"Well, no, not at this time."

"What about some other time? Strike that. Nothing further." I glance at the judge and he's frustrated. But things brighten up considerably when the next witness takes the stand. It's Naomi Tarrant, Starcher's teacher, and she's wearing a tight dress and stilettos. By the time she promises to tell the truth, old Judge Leef is wide awake. So am I.

Schoolteachers hate to get dragged into custody and visitation battles. Naomi is no exception, though she knows how to handle this situation. We've been swapping e-mails for a month now. She still won't agree to dinner, but I'm making progress. She testifies that Starcher had never shown any violent tendencies until a few days after his first trip to the cage fights. She describes the playground incident without referring to it as a fight or a brawl. Just a couple of boys who had a misunderstanding.

Judith calls her as a witness not to help in her search for the truth but to show Naomi, as well as everyone else, that she has the power to drag them into court and bully them.

On cross, I get Naomi to admit that, sooner or later, almost every normal boy she has ever taught has been involved in some type of scuffle on the playground. She's on and off the witness stand in fifteen minutes, and when Judge Leef dismisses her he looks a bit disappointed.

In closing, Judith repeats what's already been said and makes a strident plea to terminate all visitation rights.

Judge Leef stops her cold with "But the father is getting only thirty-six hours a month. That's not very much."

"Thank you," I say.

"That's enough," Judith scolds me.

"Sorry."

The judge looks at me and asks, "Mr. Rudd, will you agree to keep the child away from cage fighting, as well as boxing and wrestling matches?"

"Yes, I promise."

"And will you also agree to teach the child that fighting is a bad way to settle disputes?"

"Yes, I promise."

He glares at Judith and says, "Your petition is denied. Anything else?"

Judith hesitates for a second, then says, "Well, I'll just have to appeal."

"You have that right," he says as he taps his gavel. "This hearing is over."

18.

The criminal trial of Doug Renfro begins on a Monday morning, and the courtroom is packed with potential jurors. As they are processed and seated by the courtroom bailiffs, the lawyers meet in the chambers of the Honorable Ryan Ponder, a ten-year veteran of our circuit courts and one of our better presiding judges. As always on the first day of a significant trial, the mood is tense; everyone is on edge. The lawyers look as though they haven't slept all weekend.

We sit around a large table and cover some preliminary matters. As we wrap things up, Judge Ponder looks at me and says, "I want to get this straight, Mr. Rudd. The State is offering a deal whereby your client pleads guilty to a lesser charge, a ramped-up misdemeanor, and gets no jail time. He walks. And in return, he agrees to drop his civil suit against the City and all of the other defendants. Correct?"

"That's correct, sir."

"And he is saying no to this deal?"

"Correct."

"Let's get this on the record."

Doug Renfro is retrieved from a witness room and led into the judge's chambers. He is wearing a dark wool suit, white shirt, dark tie, and is dressed better than anyone in the room, with the possible exception of me. He stands tall, erect, and proud, an old soldier itching for a fight. It has been ten months since his home was invaded by the police, and though he has aged considerably, his wounds have healed and he carries himself with confidence.

Judge Ponder swears him to tell the truth. He says, "Now, Mr. Renfro, the State is offering you a deal, a plea agreement. It is in writing. Have you read it and discussed it with your lawyer?"

"I have, yes, sir."

"And you realize that if you take this plea agreement you will avoid this trial, walk out of here a free man, and never worry about going to prison?"

"Yes, I understand that. But I will not plead guilty to anything. The police broke into my home and killed my wife. They will not be charged and that is wrong. I'll take my chances with the jury." He glares at the prosecutor, gives him a look of disgust, and returns his gaze to Judge Ponder.

The prosecutor, a veteran named Chuck Finney, hides his face behind some paperwork. Finney is not a bad guy and does not want to be where he is now sitting. His problem is simple and obvious—an eager-beaver cop got wounded in a botched raid, and the law, in black and white, says the guy who shot him is guilty. It's a bad law written by clueless people, and now Finney is compelled to enforce it. He cannot simply drop the charges. The police union is breathing down his neck.

A word here about Max Mancini. Max is the City's chief prosecutor, appointed by the mayor and approved by the city council. He's loud, flamboyant, ambitious, a driven man who's going places, though it's not clear exactly where. He loves cameras as much as I do and will knock folks out of the way to get in front of one. He's crafty in the courtroom and boasts of a 99 percent conviction rate, same as every other prosecutor in America. Because he's the boss, he gets to manipulate the numbers, so he has real proof that his 99 percent is legitimate.

Normally, in a case as big as Doug Renfro's, with front-page coverage guaranteed and live-action shots morning, noon, and night, Max would be dressed in his finest and hogging the spotlight. However, this case is dangerous and Max knows it. Everybody knows it. The cops were wrong. The Renfros are victims. A guilty verdict seems unlikely, and if there's one thing Max Mancini cannot risk it's the wrong verdict.

So, he's hiding. Not a peep out of our chief prosecutor. I'm sure he's lurking around somewhere in the shadows, gawking at all the cameras and dying inside, but Max will not be seen during this trial. Instead, he dumped it on Chuck Finney.

19.

It takes three days to pick a jury, and it's clear that all twelve know a lot about the case. I have wrestled with the strategy of requesting a change of venue, but decided against it. There are a couple of reasons for this, one legitimate and the other based on pure ego. The first is that many people in this city are fed up with the cops and their brutal tactics. The second is that there are reporters and cameras everywhere, and this is my turf. Most important, though, my client prefers to be tried by a jury of his fellow citizens.

In a crowded courtroom, Judge Ponder says, "Ladies and gentlemen of the jury, we will now begin this trial with the opening statements. First, the State's attorney, Mr. Finney, then the defense, Mr. Rudd. I caution you that nothing you're about to hear is actually evidence. The evidence comes from only one source, and that's this witness chair right here. Mr. Finney."

The prosecutor rises solemnly from his seat at the table, a table filled with deputy prosecutors and useless assistants. It's a show of legal muscle, an attempt to impress the jury with the gravity of the case against Mr. Renfro. I have a different strategy. Doug and I sit alone, just the two of us. Two little guys facing the depthless resources of the government. The defense table seems almost deserted when compared to the army across the aisle. I live for this David versus Goliath image.

Chuck Finney is fiercely dull, and he begins with a grave "Ladies and gentlemen, this is a tragic case." No kidding, Chuck. Is that the best you can do?

Finney may not have his heart in this case, but he's not about to roll over. There are too many people watching, too much at stake. Now that the opening bell has sounded, the game is on. And the game is not about justice; from this point forward it's all about winning. He does a fair job of describing the dangers of police work, especially in this day and age of assault weapons, sophisticated criminals, drug gangs, and terrorists. Today's policemen are often targets, victims of extremely violent thugs who have no respect for authority. There's a war out there, a war on drugs, a war on terror, a war on pretty much everything, and our brave law enforcement officers have every right to arm themselves to the hilt. That's why the smart people we elect to make our laws decided six years ago to make it a crime for a person, yes even a homeowner, to fire upon our police when they are simply doing their jobs. That's why Doug Renfro is guilty as a matter of law. He fired upon our police, and he wounded Officer Scott Keestler, a veteran who was just doing his job.

Finney is striking the right chords and scoring some points here. A couple of the jurors glance disapprovingly at my client. After all, he did shoot a cop. But Finney is careful. The facts are not in his favor, regardless of what the law says. He is concise, to the point, and sits down after only ten minutes. A record for a prosecutor.

Judge Ponder says, "Mr. Rudd, for the defense."

As a criminal defense lawyer, I rarely have the facts in my favor. But when I do, I find it impossible to be subtle. Hit 'em fast and hard, and watch them scramble. I have believed since day one that I can win this case with the opening statement. I toss my legal pad on the podium and look at the jurors. Eye contact with every one of them.

I begin, "First they shot his dog Spike, a twelve-year-old yellow Lab who was fast asleep on his bed in the kitchen. What did Spike do to deserve getting killed? Nothing, he was just in the right place at the wrong time. Why would they kill Spike? They will attempt to answer this question with one of their standard lies. They will tell you that Spike threatened them, same as every other dog they kill when they invade private homes in the middle of the night. In the last five years, ladies and gentlemen, our gallant SWAT boys have killed at least thirty innocent dogs in this city, from old mutts to young puppies, all of whom were just minding their own business."

Behind me, Chuck Finney stands and says, "Objection, Your Honor. Relevancy. Not sure why the other SWAT maneuvers are relevant to this case."

I turn to the judge, and before he can rule I say, "Oh, it's relevant, Your Honor. Let's allow the jury to hear exactly how these raids go down. We will prove that these cops are trigger-happy and ready to shoot anything that moves."

Judge Ponder raises a hand and says, "That's enough, Mr. Rudd. I'll overrule the objection. It's just an opening statement and not evidence."

True, but the jurors have already heard me. I return to them and say, "Spike didn't have a chance. The SWAT team kicked in the front and back doors simultaneously, and eight heavily armed warrior cops raced into the Renfro home. By the time Spike could get to his feet and bark he was dead, blown away by three bullets from a semiautomatic handgun, the same kind used by Army Rangers. And the killing had just begun."

I pause and look at the jurors, some of whom are no doubt more distressed over the dead dog than anything else that happened that night.

"Eight cops, eight SWAT team members, all equipped with more gear and armor than any American soldier who fought in Vietnam or World War II. Bulletproof vests, night-vision goggles, highly sophisticated weapons, even black face paint to add a little drama. But why? Why were they there?" I'm pacing now, back and forth in front of the jury box. I glance at the spectators, the place is packed, and I see the chief of police in the front row, hat-

ing me. Their usual routine in any case involving the police is to
line up about two dozen uniformed cops on the front rows, where
they sit with folded arms and glare at the jurors. Judge Ponder,
though, would have none of it. I filed a motion to keep cops in
uniforms out of the courtroom, and he agreed. The eight SWAT
boys are being kept in witness rooms and missing the fun.

"This disaster began with the boy next door, a troubled kid
named Lance, nineteen years old and going nowhere. Lance was
rightfully unemployed but not altogether unproductive. He made
good money selling illegal narcotics, primarily the drug Ecstasy.
He was too smart to work the streets, so Lance used the Internet.
But not the Internet we know. Lance lived in the murky and forbidden world of the Dark Web, a place where Google and Yahoo
and the other great search engines do not go. Lance had been
buying and selling drugs on the Dark Web for two years when he
realized the Renfros had an unsecured wireless router. For a clever
boy like Lance it was easy to piggyback. For a year Lance bought
and sold Ecstasy, using the Renfros' wireless system, and of course
they didn't have a clue. This case, though, is not about drug trafficking, so don't be deceived. It's about a gargantuan screwup by
our police department. The state investigators were rounding up
online drug dealers and came across the Renfros' IP address. With
no other evidence, and no real investigation, they launched a sting.
They got two warrants: an arrest warrant for Doug Renfro, and a
search warrant for his home."

I pause here and get a drink of water. I have never felt such
stillness in a courtroom. All eyes are on me. All ears are listening. I return to the jury box and lean on the podium, as if I'm
having a friendly chat with my grandfather. "Now, back in the
old days and not too long ago, back when police work was done
by cops who knew their beat and knew how to handle criminals, back when the police knew they were police and not Navy

SEALs, back then, ladies and gentlemen, an arrest warrant would be served by a couple of officers who would drive over to Mr. Renfro's home, at a decent hour, ring his doorbell, step inside his house, and tell him he was under arrest. They would handcuff him and take him away, and do so with a great deal of professionalism. Another pair of officers would show up with the search warrant and get Mr. Renfro's computer. Within a couple of hours, the police would realize their mistake. They would apologize profusely to Mr. Renfro and take him home. Then they would solve their crime. Compare then with now. Now, at least in this city with its current leadership, the police launch surprise attacks on unsuspecting and law-abiding citizens in the middle of the night. And they shoot them, and their dogs, and when they realize they have the wrong house, they lie and cover up." Another long pause as I step behind the podium, glance at some notes I don't need, and return my gaze to the jurors. If any of them are breathing, I can't tell it. "Ladies and gentlemen, we have a bad law in this state that says that a homeowner, one like Doug Renfro, who fires upon an officer of the law, even if the cop is at the wrong house, is automatically guilty. So why bother with this trial? Why doesn't someone simply read the statute and tell Mr. Renfro to go to prison for the next forty years? Well, because there is no such thing as automatic guilt. That's why we have juries, and your job will be to decide if Doug Renfro knew what he was doing. Did he know the police were in his house? When he scrambled into the hallway and saw figures moving in the darkness, what was he thinking? I'll tell you. He was terrified. He was convinced some dangerous criminals had broken in and began shooting. And, most important, he did not know they were police officers. If he didn't know, then he cannot be found guilty. They couldn't be police officers, could they? Why would the cops come to his house when he'd done nothing wrong? Why would they show up at three in the morning, when everyone was sound asleep? Why didn't they knock on the door or ring the bell? Why did they kick in the front door, and the back? Why, why, why? Policemen don't behave in such an outrageous manner. Or do they?"

20.

The first witness is a big shot from the state police. Ruskin is his name, and he is put on the stand to begin the impossible task of justifying what the police were doing the night they raided the Renfros' home. With Finney serving up direct questions that have been so overly rehearsed they have no spontaneity, they plow through the "insidious" rise of drug trafficking on the Internet, the "distressing" rise in the number of teenagers who buy and sell there, and so on. I'm on my feet constantly with "Your Honor, I object on the grounds of relevancy. What does this testimony have to do with Doug Renfro?"

After Judge Ponder overrules me three times, he begins to get frustrated. Finney senses this and moves on. They walk through a tedious narrative in an attempt to explain how the state police set up an Internet scam to catch drug dealers. All in all, it was fairly successful. They caught about forty people in our state. Aren't they smart cops?

"Did you kill anybody else?" is my first question, fired from my seat as I jump into what will be a contentious cross-examination.

I ask Ruskin about the other arrests. Were SWAT teams used to serve warrants? Were there home invasions at three in the morning? Did anyone else lose a dog? Did you send in the tanks? Halfway through my cross-examination, I force him to admit what the world has known for months: They got the wrong house. His reluctance to admit it, though, damages his credibility.

In two hours I reduce Ruskin to a babbling fool, one who can't wait to get off the witness stand.

I am often a sanctimonious asshole when my clients are dead guilty. Give me an innocent man, though, and I reek of arrogance and superiority. I realize this and struggle mightily to give the impression, to the jury anyway, that I am actually likeable. I don't really care if they hate me, as long as they don't hate my client. But when representing a saint like Doug Renfro, it's imperative that I come across as zealous, but not offensive. Incredulous at the injustice, but also trustworthy.

Their next witness is Chip Sumerall, the leader of the invasion, a lieutenant on the force. He's brought in from a witness room and sworn to tell the truth. As always, he's wearing his uniform with as many patches and medals as possible. Full uniform and regalia and finery, but minus his service revolver and handcuffs. He's a cocky ass with a strut, thick arms, and a crew cut. We had words during his deposition and I glare at him as if he's already lying. Finney walks him through their narrative. They dwell on his extensive training and experience, his glorious record. They walk methodically through the time line of the Renfro episode. He passes the buck as best he can, saying more than once that he was just following orders.

I get a sense the entire courtroom is waiting for me to annihilate him on cross, and I struggle to control myself. I begin by commenting on his uniform, how nice and professional it is. How often does he wear it? What do some of the medals signify? Then I ask him to describe the uniform he was wearing the night he kicked in the door of the Renfro home. Layer by layer, article by article, weapon by weapon, from his steel-toed jackboots to his panzer-style combat helmet, we go through every bit of it. I ask him about his submachine gun, a Heckler & Koch MP5, designed for close combat and the finest in the world, he says proudly. I ask him if he used it that night and he says he did. I grill him on whether he fired the shots that killed Kitty Renfro, and he claims he doesn't know. It was dark and things happened fast. Bullets were flying; the police were "taking fire."

As I walk around the courtroom, I glance at Doug. His face is in his hands as he relives the nightmare. I glance at the jurors; some are in disbelief.

"You say it was dark, Officer. But you were outfitted with night-vision glasses, weren't you?"

"Yes." He's been well coached and keeps his answers as short as possible.

"And these are designed to allow officers to see in the dark, right?"

"Yes."

"Okay, then why couldn't you see in the dark?"

The answer is obvious; he squirms a bit, but he's a tough one. He tries to evade with "Well, again, it all happened so fast. Before I could focus, shots were fired and we just responded."

"And you couldn't see Kitty Renfro at the end of the hallway, thirty feet away, in her white pajamas?"

"I didn't see her, no."

I badger him relentlessly on what he saw or should have seen. When I've scored every point possible on this, I jump back to the issue of police procedure. Who authorized the SWAT mission? Who was in the room when the decision was made? Did he or anyone else have the common sense to say perhaps such a mission was not necessary? Why did you wait until three in the morning to go in, when it was dark? What led you to believe Doug Renfro was such a dangerous man? He starts to crack, to lose his cool. He looks to Finney for help but there's nothing he can do. He glances at the jury and sees nothing but suspicion.

I grind away and expose the idiocy of their procedures. We

talk about their training and their equipment. I even manage to bring the tank into the proceedings, and Judge Ponder allows me to show the jury an enlarged photo of it.

The real fun begins when I'm allowed to explore other botched raids. Sumerall has been suspended on two prior occasions for excessive force, and I walk him through those episodes. At times his face gets red. At other times he's sweating. Finally, at 6:00 p.m., after Sumerall has spent four grueling hours on the stand, Judge Ponder asks me if I'm almost finished.

"No, sir, just getting started," I say, real chipper, glaring at Sumerall. I'm so pumped I could go until midnight.

"Very well, then, we'll stand in recess until nine in the morning."

21.

At nine sharp on Friday morning, the jurors are led in and welcomed by Judge Ponder. Officer Sumerall is called and takes the stand again. Some of his cockiness is gone, but not all of it.

"Please continue your cross-examination, Mr. Rudd," Ponder says. With the assistance of a clerk, I unfold and mount a large diagram of the Renfro home, both first and second floors. I ask Sumerall, as the leader of this team, to enlighten us about how the eight men were selected. Why were they divided into two teams, one for the front door, one for the back? What was each man's role? What weapons did each cop have? Who made the decision not to ring the doorbell, but instead just go crashing in? How were the doors opened? Who opened them? Who were the first cops in? Who shot Spike, and why?

Sumerall cannot, or will not, answer most of my questions, and before long he's looking like an idiot. He was the commander, and proud of it, but on the stand he's not sure of a lot of details.

I hammer him for two hours and we take a break. Over a quick coffee, Doug tells me the jurors are skeptical and suspicious; a few seemed to be seething. "We got 'em," he says, but I caution him. Two of the jurors in particular worry me because they have ties to the police department, according to my old pal Nate Spurio. We met last night for a drink and he says the cops are leaning on numbers four and seven. I'll deal with it later.

I resist the urge to hound Sumerall for the entire day, something I do more often than I should. There is an art to cross-examination, and quitting while you're ahead is part of the skill. I haven't learned it yet because my instinct is to kick a brute like Sumerall repeatedly when he's already down.

Doug says, wisely, "I think you've done enough with this witness."

He's right, so I tell the judge I'm finished with Sumerall. The next witness is Scott Keestler, the cop who got shot, apparently by Doug Renfro. Finney takes him first on direct and tries his best to evoke some sympathy. The truth is—and I have all the medical reports—the bullet wound to his neck was only slightly more serious than superficial. In combat, he would have been given a couple of Band-Aids and sent back to the front. But the prosecution needs to score here, and Keestler sounds like he took a bullet between the eyes. They drag this out far too long, and we finally break for lunch.

When we're back in the courtroom, Finney says, "No more questions, Your Honor."

"Mr. Rudd."

At full volume, I pounce on Keestler with "Officer, did you murder Kitty Renfro?"

Talk about sucking the air out of a room. Finney stumbles to his feet, objecting. Judge Ponder says, "Mr. Rudd, if you—"

"We're talking about murder here, Judge, aren't we? Kitty

Renfro was unarmed when someone shot and killed her in her own home. That's murder."

Finney says loudly, "It is not. We have a statute on this point. Peace officers are not liable—"

"Maybe not liable," I interrupt. "But it's still murder." I wave my arms at the jury and demand, "What else do you call it?" Three or four actually nod affirmatively.

Judge Ponder says, "Please refrain from using the word 'murder,' Mr. Rudd."

I take a deep breath; so does everyone else. Keestler looks like a man facing a firing squad. I return to the podium, stare at him, and say politely, "Peace Officer Keestler, on the night of this SWAT raid, what were you wearing?"

"I'm sorry."

"What were you wearing, please? Tell the jury everything that was on your body."

He swallows hard, then begins clicking off the armor, weaponry, and so on. It's a long list. "Keep going," I say. He finishes with "Boxer shorts, T-shirt, white athletic socks."

"Thank you. Is that all?"

"Yes."

"Are you sure?"

"Yes."

"Absolutely certain?"

"Yes, I'm certain."

I stare at him as though he's a filthy liar, then I walk to the exhibit table and pick up a large color photograph of Keestler on a stretcher as he's being rushed into the ER. His face is clearly visible. Since the photo has already been introduced into evidence, I hand it to Keestler and ask, "That you?"

He looks at it, confused, says, "That's me."

The judge allows me to pass the photo to the jurors. They take their time, absorb the image, then I take it back. "Now, Peace Officer Keestler, looking at you in this photograph, what is this black stuff you're wearing on your face?"

He smiles, relieved. Aw shucks. "Oh that, that's just black camouflage paint."

"Also known as war paint?"

"I guess. It has several names."

"What's the purpose of war paint?"

"It's for camouflage purposes."

"So it's pretty important, huh?"

"Sure is, yes."

"It's necessary to insure the safety of the men on the ground, right?"

"Absolutely."

"How many of the eight peace officers in your SWAT team that night covered their faces with black war paint?"

"I didn't count."

"Did all of our peace officers wear black war paint that night?"

He knows the answer and he figures I do too. He says, "I'm really not sure."

I walk to my table and pick up a thick deposition. I make sure he sees it. "Now, Peace Officer Keestler—"

Finney stands and says, "Now, Your Honor, I'll object here. He keeps using the term 'peace officer.' I think that—"

"You used it first," Judge Ponder fires back. "You used it first. Overruled."

We eventually establish that four of the cops decorated themselves with black war paint, and by the time I move on Keestler looks as dumb as a teenager playing with crayons. It's time for some real fun. I say, "Now, Peace Officer Keestler, you play a lot of video games, right?"

Finney is back on his feet. "Objection, Your Honor. Relevancy."

"Overruled," His Honor says harshly without even looking at the prosecutor. Judge Ponder has become increasingly, and obviously, fed up with the police and their lies and tactics. We have all the momentum—a rarity for me—and I'm not sure how to handle it. Do I speed things along and get the case to the jury while they're on our side? Or do I plod along, scoring every possible point?

Scoring is so much fun, plus I have a hunch the jury is squarely on my side and enjoying this train wreck. "What are some of the video games you enjoy playing?"

He names a few—benign, almost kiddie-like games that make him sound like an overgrown fifth grader. He and Finney know what's coming and they're trying to soften the blow. In doing so, Keestler looks even worse.

"How old are you, Mr. Keestler?"

"Twenty-six," he says with a smile, finally an honest answer.

"And you're still playing video games?"

"Well, yes, sir."

"In fact, you've spent thousands of hours playing video games, right?"

"I guess."

"And one of your favorites is *Mortal Attack Three,* right?" I'm holding his deposition, a thick sworn statement in which I managed to hammer out the fact that he got hooked on video games when he was a kid and still loves them.

"I guess, yes," he says.

I wave his deposition like it's poison and say, "Well, haven't you already testified, in a sworn deposition, that you've been playing *Mortal Attack Three* for the past ten years?"

"Yes, sir."

I look at Judge Ponder and say, "Your Honor, I would like to show the jury a clip from *Mortal Attack Three.*"

Finney is turning flips. We've been arguing about this for a month, with Ponder withholding a ruling until this very moment. Finally, he says, "I'm intrigued. Let's take a look."

Finney tosses a legal pad on his table in total frustration. Ponder growls, "Enough of the theatrics, Mr. Finney. Take a seat!"

I rarely have the judge on my side and I'm not sure how to act.

The courtroom lights are dimmed while a screen drops from the ceiling. A tech guy has edited a five-minute clip of the video game. At my instruction, he cranks up the volume, and the jury is jolted by the sudden image of a bulky soldier kicking in a door as explosions rip through the background. An animal resembling a dog but with shining teeth and huge talons lunges forward and our hero guns him down. Villains appear in doors and windows, and they're all blown to hell and back. Bullets, the kind you can see, blast and ricochet. Body parts are ripped off. Blood is knee-deep. People scream and shoot and die with great drama, and after two minutes we've seen enough.

After five minutes, the entire courtroom needs a break. The screen goes blank and the lights come on. I glare at Keestler, who's still on the witness stand, and say, "All fun and games, right, Peace Officer Keestler?"

He does not respond. I watch him drown for a few seconds, then say, "And you also enjoy playing a game called *Home Invasion,* right?"

He shrugs, looks toward Finney for help, and finally grunts, "I guess."

Finney stands and says, "Judge, is this really relevant?" The judge is leaning on his elbows and ready for more. He says, "Oh, I think this is very relevant, Mr. Finney. Let's roll the tape."

The lights go down, and for three minutes we watch the same mindless mayhem and gore. If I caught Starcher playing this garbage, I'd lock him away in rehab. At one point, juror number six whispers loudly, "Good God!" I watch them as they stare at the screen, thoroughly disgusted.

When the videos are over, I force Keestler to admit that he also likes a game called *Crack House—Special Ops*. He admits the cops have a locker room in the basement of the police department. Courtesy of the taxpayers, it is equipped with a fifty-four-inch flat-screen television, and for fun the boys gather there between SWAT maneuvers and play video game tournaments. Over Finney's lame objections, I drag this out of Keestler, bit by bit. By now, he doesn't want to talk about it, and this makes matters worse for him and the prosecution. When I finish with him, he is destroyed and discredited.

As I sit down, I look at the gallery. The chief of police is gone, and for good.

Judge Ponder asks, "Who's your next witness, Mr. Finney?"

Finney has the hangdog look of a prosecutor who doesn't want to call any more witnesses. What he does want to do is catch the next train out of town. He looks at a notepad and says, "Officer Boyd." Boyd fired seven rounds that night. At the age of seventeen, he was convicted of a DUI but managed to get his record expunged later. Finney doesn't know about the DUI, but I do. At the age of twenty, Boyd received a dishonorable discharge from the Army. When he was twenty-four, his girlfriend called 911 and complained of domestic abuse. Things were swept under the rug; no charges stuck. Boyd is also the veteran of two other botched SWAT raids, and he's enthralled with the same video games that keep Keestler so occupied.

Getting Boyd on cross-examination could well be the highlight of my legal career.

Judge Ponder suddenly says, "We're going to recess until Monday morning at nine. I want to see the lawyers in my chambers."

22.

As soon as the door closes, Judge Ponder glares at Finney and growls, "Your case sucks. The wrong person is on trial."

Poor Finney knows it but cannot say so. In fact, at this moment he's unable to say anything at all. The judge hammers away. "Do you plan to put all eight of the SWAT team on the witness stand?"

"As of now, the answer is no," Finney manages to say.

I pounce with "Great, then I'll call them as adverse witnesses. I want all eight to face the jury." The judge looks at me fearfully. I have the absolute right to do this and they know it. Seconds pass as they try and imagine the nightmare of the other six toy soldiers facing the jury as I pound them like a madman.

His Honor looks at Finney and asks, "Have you thought about dismissing the charges?"

Of course not. Finney may be demoralized but he's still a prosecutor.

Normally, in a criminal trial the judge has the right to exclude the State's evidence and direct a verdict in favor of the defendant. This rarely happens. In this case, though, the statute declares that any person who fires upon a policeman who is entering his or her home, whether the cops have the correct address or the wrong one, is guilty of the attempted murder of an officer. It's a bad statute, poorly conceived and dreadfully written, but in Judge Ponder's opinion it does not afford him the option of dismissing the case.

We're headed for a final verdict.

23.

Over the weekend, one of the remaining six SWAT cops is suddenly hospitalized and cannot testify. One simply vanishes. It takes me a day and a half to annihilate the remaining four.

We're getting front-page coverage and the police department has never, ever looked so bad. I'm trying my best to savor this glorious moment because it's unlikely to happen again.

On the last day of testimony, I meet the Renfro family for an early breakfast. The topic is whether or not Doug should testify. His three adult children—Thomas, Fiona, and Susanna—are present. They have watched the entire trial and have no doubt our jury will not convict their father, regardless of what some lousy statute says.

I explain the worst-case scenario: Finney will get under his skin on cross-examination and try to irritate him. He'll make Doug admit that he fired five shots from his handgun and deliberately tried to kill the officers. The only way the State can win the case is for Doug to melt down on the stand, something we simply do not expect. The guy is solid, and he insists on testifying. At this point in any trial, the defendant has the right to testify, regardless of what his lawyer thinks. They press me on this. My instincts are the same as any criminal defense attorney: If the State has failed to prove its case, keep the client off the stand.

But Doug Renfro will not be denied.

24.

I begin by asking Doug about his military career. Fourteen years in uniform, proudly serving his country, without a blemish. Two tours in Vietnam, one Purple Heart, two weeks as a prisoner before being rescued. Half a dozen medals, an honorable discharge. A real soldier, not the dime-store variety.

A law-abiding citizen with only one speeding ticket on his record.

The contrasts are stark and speak for themselves.

On the night in question he and Kitty watched television until 10:00, then read for a few minutes until they turned off the lights. He kissed her good night, told her he loved her as always, and they fell asleep. They were jolted from their dreams when the assault began. The house shook, shots were fired. Doug scrambled for his pistol and told Kitty to call 911. In the frenzy that followed, he ran into the dark hallway and saw two shadows rising quickly from the stairwell. Voices were coming from downstairs. He hit the floor and began firing. He was immediately hit in the shoulder. No, he said emphatically, no one ever yelled out anything about the police. Kitty screamed and ran into the hallway and into a volley of bullets.

Doug breaks down when he describes the sounds of his wife being hit.

Half of the jurors are crying too.

25.

Finney wants no part of Doug Renfro. He attempts to prove that Doug deliberately fired upon the police, but Doug crushes him by saying over and over, "I didn't know they were cops. I thought they were criminals breaking into my house."

I call no other witnesses. I don't need them.

Finney walks through a halfhearted closing argument, during which he refuses to make eye contact with any of the jurors. When it's my turn, I recap the important facts and manage to control myself. It would be easy to flay the cops, to engage in unbridled overkill, but the jury has had enough.

Judge Ponder instructs the jurors as to the applicable law, then says it's time for them to retire and deliberate. But no one moves. What happens next borders on historic.

Juror number six is a man named Willie Grant. Slowly, he stands and says, "Judge, I've been elected as the foreman of this jury, and I have a question."

The judge, a jurist of great composure, is startled and looks wildly at Finney and me. The courtroom is again perfectly silent. Me, I'm not breathing. His Honor says, "Well, I'm not sure at this point. I have instructed the jury to retire and begin deliberations." The jurors have not moved.

Mr. Grant says, "We don't need to deliberate, Your Honor. We know what we're going to do."

"But I have repeatedly warned you against discussing the case," Ponder says sternly.

Unfazed, Mr. Grant replies, "We haven't discussed the case, but we have a verdict. There's nothing to discuss or deliberate. My question is, why is Mr. Renfro on trial and not the cops who killed his wife?"

There is an instant wave of gasping and chattering throughout the courtroom. Judge Ponder attempts to regain control by clearing his throat loudly and asking, "Is your verdict unanimous?"

"Damned right it is. We find Mr. Renfro not guilty, and we think these cops should be charged with murder."

"I'm going to ask the jurors to raise your hands if you agree with the not-guilty verdict."

Twelve hands shoot into the air.

I put my arm around Doug Renfro as he breaks down again.

PART FOUR

THE EXCHANGE

1.

I often disappear after a big trial, especially one that gets front-page coverage and plenty of airtime. It's not that I don't love the attention. I'm a lawyer; it's in my genes. But in the Renfro trial I humiliated the police department, embarrassed some cops, some really tough guys who are not accustomed to answering for their misdeeds. As they say, "The streets are hot right now," and it's time for a break. I load some clothes into the van, along with my golf clubs, some paperbacks, and half a case of small-batch bourbon, and ease out of town the day after the verdict. The weather is raw and windy, too cold for golf, so I head south like countless other snowbirds in search of the sun. I have learned through my meandering travels that almost every small town with a population above ten thousand has a public golf course. These are usually packed on weekends but not too crowded during the week. I play my way south, hitting at least one course per day, sometimes two, playing alone with no caddie and no scorecard, paying cash for inexpensive motel rooms, eating little, and sipping bourbon late at night while I read the latest James Lee Burke or Michael Connelly. If I had a pile of money, I could spend the rest of my life doing this.

But I don't, so I eventually return to the City, where my notoriety instantly catches up to me.

2.

About a year ago, a young woman named Jiliana Kemp was abducted as she was leaving a hospital after visiting a friend. Her car was found untouched on the third floor of a parking garage next to the hospital. Surveillance cameras caught her walking toward her car but lost her as she stepped out of range. The footage from all fourteen cameras was analyzed. It captured the license plates of every vehicle coming and going for a twenty-four-hour period, and revealed only one significant clue. An hour after Jiliana was seen walking to her car, a blue Ford SUV left the parking deck. The driver was a white male wearing a baseball cap and glasses. The SUV had stolen license plates from Iowa. During the night, the attendants saw nothing suspicious, and the one who took the ticket from the white male did not remember him. Forty vehicles had passed through the exit gate in the hour preceding the SUV's departure.

Detectives scoured every inch of the garage and found nothing. Her abductor made no demand for ransom. The search went from frantic to futile. An initial reward of $100,000 provoked no response. Two weeks later, the blue SUV was found abandoned in a state park a hundred miles away. It had been stolen a month earlier in Texas. Its license plates were from Pennsylvania, stolen of course.

The abductor was playing games. He had wiped the SUV clean; no prints, no hairs, no blood, nothing. His range, along with his planning, terrified the investigators. They were not chasing an ordinary criminal.

Adding to the urgency was the fact that Jiliana Kemp's father is one of the City's two assistant chiefs of police. Needless to say, the case was given the highest priority by the department. What was not made public at the time was that Jiliana was three months pregnant. As soon as she disappeared, her live-in boyfriend told her parents about the pregnancy. They kept this quiet as the police worked around the clock to find her.

Jiliana has not been heard from. Her body has not been found. She's probably dead, but when was she murdered? The worst possible scenario is also the most obvious: She wasn't killed immediately but was held captive until after she gave birth.

Nine months after her disappearance, as the reward money continued to pile up, a tip led the police to a pawnshop not far from my apartment building. A gold necklace with a small Greek coin had been pawned for $200. Jiliana's boyfriend identified the necklace as the one he'd given her the previous Christmas. In a full-court press, detectives worked furiously to establish a chain of possession. It led to another pawnshop, to another transaction, and finally to a suspect named Arch Swanger.

A thirty-one-year-old drifter with no apparent means of support, Swanger had a history of petty thievery and small-time drug dealing. He lived in a run-down trailer park with his mother, who was a drunk drawing disability checks. After a month of intense surveillance and scrutiny, Swanger was finally brought in for questioning. He was evasive and coy, and after two hours of fruitless interrogation clammed up and demanded a lawyer. With little hard evidence, the police let him go but continued to monitor his every movement. Still, he managed to slip away several times, but always returned home.

Last week, they picked him up again for questioning. He demanded a lawyer.

"Okay, who's your lawyer?" the detective asked.

"That guy named Rudd, Sebastian Rudd."

3.

The last thing I need is more trouble with the police. But, as we say in the trade, we don't always get to choose our clients. And every defendant, regardless of how despicable the person or his crime, is entitled to a lawyer. Most laymen don't understand this and don't care. I don't care either. This is my job. To be honest, I'm initially thrilled Swanger picked me, thrilled to be allowed to stick my nose smack in the middle of another sensational case.

This one, though, will haunt me forever. I'll curse the day I hustled over to Central to have my first chat with Arch Swanger.

The police department has more leaks than old plumbing, and by the time I arrive at Central word is out. A reporter with a cameraman catches me as I enter the building and demands to know if I represent Arch Swanger. I offer a rude "No comment" and keep walking. From that moment on, though, everyone in town knows I'm his lawyer. It's a perfect fit, right? A monstrous murderer and the rogue lawyer who'll defend anyone.

I've strolled through Central many times, and the place is always bustling with an urgent energy. Street cops in uniforms rush around, bantering crudely with those stuck behind desks. Detectives in cheap suits swagger through the halls, scowling as if they're pissed at the world. Frightened families sit on benches waiting for bad news. And there's always a lawyer huddled up with a cop in a tense negotiation, or hurrying to get to a client before he spills his guts.

Today, the air is especially heavy, the mood tense. I get more stares than usual when I walk through the front door. And why not? They've caught the killer; he's just down the hall. And here comes his lawyer to save him. Both should be grabbed and put on the rack.

Present too is the lingering rawness of the Renfro trial. It was only three weeks ago and cops have long memories. Some of these guys would like to take a nightstick and break a few of my bones, or worse.

They lead me through the maze to the interrogation rooms. Down the hall, smoking and looking into a one-way mirror, are two homicide detectives. One is Landy Reardon, the cop who called me with the news that, out of all the lawyers in the City, I had been chosen. Reardon is the best homicide detective in the department. He's nearing retirement now and the years have taken their toll. He's about sixty but looks ten years older, with thick white hair that goes untouched for the most part. He still smokes and has the jagged wrinkles as proof.

He sees me and nods. Come on over. The other detective disappears.

The good thing about Landy Reardon is that he is brutally honest and will not waste time on a case he can't prove. He digs hard for the evidence, but if it's not there, then it's not there. In thirty years, he's never charged the wrong murder suspect. But if Landy collars you for murder, the judge and jury will fall in line and you'll probably die in prison.

He's had the Jiliana Kemp case since the beginning. Four months ago, he had a mild heart attack and his doctor told him to retire. He found another doctor. I stand beside him and both of us look through the mirror. We do not say hello. He thinks all defense lawyers are scum and would never stoop to shake my hand.

Swanger is alone in the interrogation room. He's kicked back in his folding chair and has his feet on the table, totally bored with everything. "What's he said?" I ask.

"Nothing. Name, rank, and serial number, and after that he called for you. Said he saw your name in the newspaper."

"So he can read?"

"IQ of 130, I'd guess. He just looks stupid."

Indeed he does. Plump with a double chin; large brown freck-les from the neck up; head practically shaved but for a few waxed bristles, like the old butch crew cut from sixty years ago, pre-Beatles. To attract either attention or ridicule, he is wearing a pair of round-frame glasses, absurdly large and aqua blue in color.

"About those glasses," I say.

"Drugstore, cheap and fake. He doesn't need glasses but he fancies himself clever when it comes to disguises. Actually, he's pretty good. He's slipped our surveillance a few times in the past month but always comes home."

"What do you have on him?"

Landy exhales in fatigue and frustration. "Not much," he says, and I admire the guy's honesty. He's a brilliant cop and knows bet-ter than to level with me, but he inspires confidence.

"Enough for an indictment?"

"I wish. We're not even close to an arrest. Chief wants to hold him for a week or two. Crank up the pressure, you know, see if the guy'll break. But really to see if lightning will strike and we get lucky. Fat chance. We'll probably let him go again. Between me and you, Rudd, we ain't got much."

"Seems like you have plenty of suspicion."

Landy grunts and laughs. "We're good at that. Look at him, talk about suspicious. I'd give him ten years in solitary just based on the first impression."

"Maybe five," I say.

"Talk to him, and if you want, I'll show you the file tomorrow."

"Okay, I'm going in, but I've never met this guy and I'm not sure I'll be his lawyer. There's always the issue of getting paid and he doesn't look too prosperous. If he's indigent, PD takes over and I'm out of the picture."

"Have fun."

4.

Swanger takes his feet off the desk, stands, and we make our introductions. Firm handshake, eye contact, easy voice with no trace of concern. Playing it cool, I restrain myself from telling him to take off those damned glasses. If he likes 'em then I'm crazy about 'em.

"I saw you on TV," he says. "That cage fighter that killed the ref. Whatever happened to him?"

"The case is still pending, waiting for a trial. You go to cage fights?"

"No. I watch 'em on TV with my mum. I thought about getting into it a few years back."

I almost laugh. Even if he dropped thirty pounds and trained eight hours a day, this guy wouldn't last ten seconds in a cage. He'd probably faint in the dressing room. I sit at the table, empty-handed, and ask, "Now, what did you want to talk about?"

"That girl, man, you know the case. These guys think I'm involved in some way and they're hassling me. They've been on my ass for months now, always hiding in the shadows as if I don't know what's going on. This is the second time they've hauled me in here like something on television. You watch *Law & Order*? Well, these guys have watched way too much and they're really bad actors, know what I mean? That old one with the white hair, Reardon I think, he's the good guy, always just looking for the truth and trying to find ways to help me. Right. Then the skinny one, Barkley, he'll come in and start yelling. Back and forth. Good cop, bad cop, like I don't know the game. Ain't my first rodeo, pal."

"Your first murder charge, right?"

"Hang on, Superman. I ain't been charged yet."

"Okay, assuming you are charged with murder, I take it you want me to represent you."

"Well, gee, why else would I call you, Mr. Rudd? I'm not sure I need a lawyer right now but it damned sure feels like it."

"Understood. Are you employed?"

"Here and there. How much do you charge for a murder case?"

"Depends on how much a person can pay. A case like this, I'll need ten thousand up front and that'll just get us through the indictment phase. Once we're looking at a trial, then we get to the serious fee. If we can't agree, then you go elsewhere."

"Where's elsewhere?"

"Public defender's office. They handle virtually all murders."

"Figures. But what you're not factoring in here, Mr. Rudd, is all the publicity. Ain't too many cases as big as this one. Pretty girl, important family, and that thing with the baby. If she had a kid, then where is it, right? That'll drive the press crazy. So you gotta figure that this thing is front-page news, starting right about now. I've seen you on television. I know how much you love to bark and growl and strut in front of the cameras. This case will be a gold mine for my defense lawyer. Don't you agree, Mr. Rudd?"

He's hammering the nail on the head, but I can't admit this. I say, "I don't work for free, Mr. Swanger, regardless of the publicity. I have too many other clients."

"Of course you do. Big lawyer like you. I didn't call no rookie in here to save my ass. They're talking death penalty, man, and they mean it. I'll get the money, one way or the other. The question is, will you take my case?"

Usually, by this point in the first meeting, the accused has already denied the charges. I make a mental note that Swanger has not done so, has not ventured anywhere near the issue of his guilt or innocence. In fact, he seems to be welcoming an indictment, with a big trial to follow. I say, "Yes, I'll represent you, assuming we can come to terms on the money and assuming they actually indict you. I think they have a ways to go. In the meantime, don't say a word to the cops, any cop. Understood?"

"Got it, man. Can you get them to back off, stop the harassment?"

"I'll see what I can do." We shake hands again and I leave the room. Detective Reardon has not moved. He's watched our little meeting, and he's probably listened to it too, though that would be illegal. Standing next to him, in casual clothes, is Roy Kemp, father of the missing girl. He glares at me with unbridled hatred, as if the few minutes I just spent with their first and rather weak suspect is clear proof that I'm involved in his daughter's disappearance.

I have sympathy for the man and his family, but right now he wants to put a bullet in the back of my head.

Outside the building, more reporters have gathered. When they see me they start hopping and shoving. I brush by them with "No comment, no comment, no comment," as they lob their idiotic questions. One actually yells, "Mr. Rudd, did your client abduct Jiliana Kemp?" I want to stop, walk over to this clown, and ask him if he might possibly come up with a dumber question. But instead I push by them and hop in the van with Partner.

5.

At six o'clock, the anchormen scream the news that the police have a suspect in the Kemp case. They show footage of Arch Swanger being mobbed by reporters as he tries to leave Central not long after I did. According to sources, unnamed of course but undoubtedly from within the building, he's been interrogated by the police and will soon be arrested and charged with kidnapping and murder. To prove his guilt, he's hired Sebastian Rudd to defend him! They show me scowling at the cameras.

Finally, the City can breathe easier. The police have the killer. To relieve the enormous pressure on them, and to begin the process of poisoning public opinion, and to establish the presumption of guilt, they are manipulating the press, as always. A leak here and there and cameras show up to capture the face that everyone has been desperate to see. The "journalists" chase their tails, and Arch Swanger is as good as convicted.

Why bother with a trial?

If the cops can't convict with evidence, they use the media to convict with suspicion.

6.

I spend a lot of time in a building officially and affectionately known as the Old Courthouse. It's a grand old structure, built around the turn of the century, with soaring Gothic columns and high ceilings, wide marble hallways lined with busts and portraits of dead judges, winding staircases, and four levels of courtrooms and offices. It's usually crawling with people—lawyers doing their business, litigants searching for the right courtroom, families of criminal defendants wandering fearfully about, potential jurors clutching their summonses, and cops waiting to testify. There are five thousand lawyers in this city, and at times it seems as though every one of us is hustling around the Old Courthouse.

As I leave a hearing one morning, a man who looks vaguely familiar falls in beside me and says, "Hey, Rudd, got a minute?"

I don't like his looks, his tone, or his rudeness. What about "Mr. Rudd" to start with? I keep walking; so does he. "Have we met?" I ask.

"It doesn't matter. We have something to discuss."

I glance at him as we walk. Bad suit, maroon shirt, hideous tie, a couple of small scars on his face, the kind left behind by fists and beer bottles. "Oh really," I say as rudely as possible.

"Need to talk about Link."

My brain tells me to keep walking but my feet simply stop moving. My stomach does a long, nauseous flip as my heart races away. I stare at the thug and say, "Well, well, where is Link these days?"

It's been two months since his dramatic escape from death row and I haven't heard a word. Not that I would; however, I'm not completely surprised. Frightened, maybe, but not shocked. We move to the edge of the hallway for privacy. The thug says his name is Fango, and there's a 10 percent chance Fango is the name on his birth certificate.

In a corner, with my back to the wall so I can observe the foot traffic, we converse in voices that are low, our lips barely moving. Fango says, "Link's having a hard time of it, you know. Money's tight, real tight, because the cops are watching everybody even remotely connected to the businesses. They watch his son, his people, me, everybody. If I bought a plane ticket today for Miami, the cops would know about it. Suffocating, you know what I mean?"

Not really, but I just nod. He goes on, "Anyway, Link figures you owe him some money. He paid you a pile, got nothing in return, you really screwed him, you know, and now Link wants a refund."

I fake a laugh like this is just the funniest thing. And it is laughable—a client who loses wants his money back when the case is over. Fango, though, is not in a humorous mood.

"That's funny," I say. "And how much of a refund?"

"All of it. A hundred grand. Cash."

"I see. So all of the work I did was really for free, is that it, Fango?"

"Link would say that all of your work really sucked. Got him nowhere. He hired you because you're a hotshot gunslinger who was supposed to reverse his conviction and get him off. Didn't happen, of course, in fact he got slammed every which way. He thinks you did a lousy job, thus the refund."

"Link got slammed because he killed a judge. Oddly enough, when this happens, and it's quite rare, it really pisses off the other judges. I explained all this to Link before he hired me. I even put it in writing. I told him his case would be very difficult to win because of the overwhelming proof the State had. Sure he paid me in cash, but I put it on the books and sent Uncle Sam about a third of it. The rest of it was spent a long time ago. So, there's nothing left for Link. Sorry."

Partner approaches and I give him the nod. Fango sees him, recognizes him, says, "You got one pit bull, Rudd, Link still has a few more. You got thirty days to get the money together. I'll be back." He turns and deliberately brushes by Partner as he leaves. Partner could break his neck, but I gesture for him to be cool. No sense starting a fistfight in the middle of the Old Courthouse, though I've seen several here.

Most involved angry lawyers taking swings at each other.

7.

Not long after Tadeo got famous for killing a referee, I began receiving solicitations from doctors claiming to be expert witnesses, all wanting a part in the show. There were a total of four, all with medical degrees and impressive résumés, all with experience in courtrooms in front of juries. They had read about the case, seen the video, and, to varying degrees, all offered the same opinion; to wit, Tadeo was legally insane when he attacked Sean King in the ring. He did not understand right from wrong, nor did he appreciate the nature of what he was doing.

"Insanity" is a legal term, not a medical one.

I talked to all four, did some research, called other lawyers who'd used them, and settled upon a guy named Dr. Taslman, out of San Francisco. For $20,000, plus expenses, he is willing to testify on Tadeo's behalf and work his magic with the jury. Though he has yet to meet the defendant, he's already convinced he knows the truth.

The truth can be expensive, especially when it comes from expert witnesses. Our system is chock-full of "experts" who do little in the way of teaching, researching, or writing. Instead, they roam the country as hired guns testifying for fat fees. Pick an issue, a set of facts, a mysterious cause, an unexplained result, anything, really, and you can find a truckload of PhDs willing to testify with all sorts of wild theories. They advertise. They solicit. They chase cases. They hang around conventions where lawyers gather to drink and compare notes. They brag about "their verdicts."

Their losses are rarely mentioned.

They are occasionally discredited by nasty cross-examinations, in open court, but they stay in business because they are so often effective. In a criminal trial, an expert has to convince only one juror to hang things up and cause a mistrial. Hang it again on the retrial, and the State will usually throw in the towel.

I meet Tadeo in a visiting room at the jail, our usual spot, and discuss Dr. Taslman's possible role in his defense. The expert will testify that he, Tadeo, blacked out, went crazy, and has no recollection of what happened. Tadeo likes this new theory. Yes, come to think of it, he really was insane. I mention the fee and he says he's broke. I've already mentioned my fee, and he was even broker. Needless to say, I'll represent Tadeo Zapate simply because I love him. That, and the publicity.

It's the O. J. Simpson theory of legal fees: I'm not paying you; you're lucky to be here; go make a buck with your book.

Using Harry & Harry's paperwork, I file the proper notice
telling the court that we will be relying on an insanity defense.
Mr. Ace Prosecutor, Max Mancini, howls in response, as always.
Max is fully in control of the Zapate matter, primarily because of
the overwhelming proof of guilt, as well as the publicity. He's still
offering fifteen years for second-degree murder. I'm stuck on ten,
though I'm not sure my client would plead to that. As the weeks
have passed and Tadeo has become the beneficiary of hours of free
jailhouse legal advice, he has become even more rigid in his belief
that I can somehow pull the right strings and walk him out. He
wants one of those technicalities all of his cell mates know about.

Dr. Taslman comes to town and we have lunch. He's a retired
psychiatrist who never liked to teach or listen to patients. Legal
insanity has always fascinated him—the crime of passion, the irresistible impulse, the moment when the mind is so filled with emotion and hate that it commands the body to act violently and in a
way never contemplated. He prefers to do all the talking. It's his
way of convincing me how brilliant he is. I listen to his bullshit as
I try to analyze how a jury will react to him. He's likeable, intense,
smart, and a good conversationalist. Plus, he's from California,
two thousand miles away. All trial lawyers know that the greater
the distance an expert travels, the more credibility he has with the
jury.

I write him a check for half of his fee. The other half will be
due at trial.

He spends two hours evaluating Tadeo, and, surprise, surprise,
he is now certain the kid blacked out, went crazy, and does not
remember pummeling the referee.

So we now have a defense, shaky as it is. I'm not that encouraged because the State will haul in two or three experts, all at
least as credible as Taslman, and they will overwhelm us with
their brilliance. Tadeo will testify and do a credible job on direct,

perhaps even manage some tears, then he'll get chewed up by Mancini on cross-examination.

But the video doesn't lie. I'm still convinced the jurors will watch it over and over and see the truth. They will silently scoff at Taslman and laugh at Tadeo, and they will return a verdict of guilty. Guilty means twenty to thirty years. On the day of the trial, I'll probably get the prosecutor down to twelve to fifteen years.

How can I convince a headstrong twenty-two-year-old to plead guilty to fifteen years? Scare him with thirty? I doubt it. The great Tadeo Zapate has never scared easily.

8.

Today is Starcher's eighth birthday. The battered and abused court order that dictates the time I spend with my son clearly says that I get two hours with him on each of his birthdays.

Two hours is too much, according to his mother. She thinks one hour is plenty; actually, no time would be her preference. Shoving me out of his life completely is her goal, but I won't let that happen. I may be a pathetic father, but I am trying. And, there might come a day when the kid wants to spend time with me in order to get away from his quarreling mothers.

So I'm sitting at a McDonald's, waiting to begin my two hours. Judith eventually pulls up in her Jaguar, her lawyer car, and gets out with Starcher. She marches him inside, sees me, scowls as if she'd rather be anywhere else, and hands him over. "I'll be back at five o'clock," she hisses at me.

"It's already four-fifteen," I say, but she doesn't acknowledge me. She huffs away, and he takes a seat opposite me. I smile and say, "How's it going, bud?"

"Okay," he mumbles, almost afraid to speak to his father. I

cannot imagine the strict orders she hit him with during the drive over. Do not eat the food. Do not drink the drinks. Do not play on the playground. Wash your hands. Do not answer questions if "he" quizzes you about me or Ava or anything to do with our home. Do not have a good time.

It usually takes him a few minutes to shake off this drubbing before he can relax around me.

"Happy birthday," I say.

"Thanks."

"Mom tells me you're having a big party on Saturday. Lots of kids and cake and stuff like that. Should be fun."

"I guess," he says.

I wasn't invited to the party, of course. It's at his home, the place where he lives half his life with Judith and Ava. A place I've never seen.

"Are you hungry?"

He looks around. It's a McDonald's, a kid's paradise, where everything is carefully designed to make people crave the food that looks far more delicious on the walls than on the tables. He zeroes in on a large poster hawking a new ice cream float called the McGlacier. Looks pretty good. I say, "I think I'll try one of those. You?"

"Mom says I shouldn't eat anything here. Says it's all bad for me."

This is my time, not Judith's. I smile and lean forward as if we're now conspirators. "But Mom's not here, right? I won't tell, you won't tell. Just us boys, okay?"

He grins and says, "Okay."

From under the table I pull out a box that's covered in birthday wrapping and place it on the table. "This is for you, bud. Happy birthday. Go ahead and open it." He grabs it as I head toward the counter.

When I return with the floats, he's staring at a small backgammon board on the table. When I was a boy, my grandfather taught me to play checkers, then backgammon, then chess. I was fascinated with board games of all varieties. As a kid, I received board games for birthdays and Christmas. By the time I was ten, I had stacks of them in my room, a vast collection that I took meticulous care of. I seldom lost at any of the games. My favorite became backgammon, and I would pester my grandfather, my mother, my friends, anyone, really, to play. When I was twelve, I came in third place in a city tournament for kids. When I was eighteen, I was competing well in adult tournaments. In college, I played for money until the other students stopped gambling with me.

I'm hoping some of this might rub off on my son. It's becoming apparent that he will almost certainly look like me, walk like me, and talk like me. He's very bright, though I must admit he gets a lot of that from his mother. Judith and Ava are keeping him away from video games. After the Renfro trial, I am thrilled by this.

"What's this?" he asks, taking his McGlacier and looking at the board.

"It's called backgammon, a board game that's been around for centuries. I'm going to teach you how to play."

"Looks hard," he says as he takes a spoonful.

"It's not. I started playing it when I was eight years old. You'll catch on."

"All right," he says, ready for the challenge. I arrange the checkers and start with the basics.

9.

Partner parks our van in a crowded lot and walks into the mall. He'll enter a two-story restaurant that anchors one wing of the mall, and he'll find a window seat in a small bar area on the upper level. From there, he'll watch the van to see who else is watching the van.

At 4:00 p.m., Arch Swanger knocks on the sliding door. I open it. Welcome to my office. He takes a seat in a comfortable recliner and looks around. He smiles at the leather, the television, the stereo, the sofa, the refrigerator. "Pretty cool," he says. "Is this really your office?"

"It is."

"I figured a big shot like you would have a fancy office in one of those tall buildings downtown."

"I had one once, but it got firebombed. Now I prefer a moving target."

He stares at me for a second as if he's not sure I'm serious. The goofy blue glasses have been replaced by black readers that actually succeed in making him appear somewhat more intelligent. He's wearing a black felt driving cap that looks authentic. It's a nice look, an effective disguise. From ten feet away you wouldn't know it was the same guy. He says, "Really, your office was firebombed?"

"It was, about five years ago. Don't ask who because I don't know. It was either a drug dealer or some undercover cops. Personally, I think it was the narcs because the police showed little enthusiasm when it came to investigating the fire."

"You see, that's what I like about you, Mr. Rudd. Can I call you Sebastian?"

"I prefer Mr. Rudd, until I'm hired. After that, you can call me Sebastian."

"Okay, Mr. Rudd, I like it that the cops don't like you and you don't like them."

"I know a lot of the guys on the force and we get along fine," I say, fudging just a little. I like Nate Spurio and a couple of others. "Let's talk business. I've had a chat with the detective, our pal Landy Reardon, and they don't have much in the way of evidence. They're pretty sure you're the guy; they just can't prove it yet."

This would be the perfect time for him to deny his guilt. Something simple and thoroughly unoriginal like "They got the wrong guy" would be appropriate. Instead, he says, "I've had lawyers before, several of them, most appointed by the court, and I never felt like I could trust them, you know? But I feel like I can trust you, Mr. Rudd."

"Back to the deal, Arch. For a fee of $10,000 I'll represent you through the indictment stage. Once you're indicted, and facing a trial, my representation will end. At that point we'll sit down to discuss our future together."

"I don't have $10,000 and I think that's too much just to get to the indictment. I know how the system works."

He's not completely wrong about this. Ten grand for the initial skirmishes is a bit steep, but I always start on the high side. "I'm not going to negotiate, Arch. I'm a busy lawyer with a lot of clients."

From his shirt pocket he pulls out a folded check. "Here's five thousand, from my mother's account. It's the best we can do."

I unfold the check. Local bank. Five grand. Signed by Louise Powell. He says, "Powell was her third husband, dead. My parents divorced when I was a kid. Haven't seen my dear old dad in a long time."

Five grand keeps me in the game and in the news and it's not a bad fee for the first round or two. I refold the check, stick it in my shirt pocket, and pull out a contract for legal services. My cell phone is sitting on the small table in front of me. It vibrates. Partner's calling. "Excuse me a second. I gotta take this."

"It's your office."

Partner says, "You got two cops in a white Jeep fifty feet away, just pulled in and watching the van."

"Thanks. Keep me posted." I tell Swanger, "Your buddies picked up your tail. They know you're here and they know my van. Nothing wrong with a lawyer meeting with his client."

He shakes his head and says, "They follow me everywhere. You gotta help me."

I slowly walk him through the contract. When everything is clear, both of us sign it. For good measure I say, "I'm going straight to the bank. If the check doesn't clear, the contract is void. Understand?"

"You think I'd write a bad check?"

I can't help but smile. I reply, "Your mother wrote it. I don't take chances."

"She drinks too much but she's not a crook."

"I'm sorry, Arch. I didn't mean to imply that. It's just that I see my share of bad checks."

He waves me off and says, "Whatever."

We stare at the table for a minute or so, and I finally say, "Is there something you'd like to talk about, now that you have a lawyer?"

"You got a beer in that cute little fridge?"

I reach over, open the door, and pull out a can of beer. He pops the top and takes a long swig. He likes it, says with a laugh, "I guess this is the most expensive beer I've ever had."

"That's one way of looking at it. Keep in mind that no other lawyer would serve you a drink in his office."

"Got that right. You're the first." Another gulp. "So, Sebastian, it is Sebastian now, right, now that I've forked over the fee and we've signed a contract?"

"Sebastian works."

"Okay, Sebastian, in addition to some beer, what do I get for five thousand bucks?"

"Legal advice, for starters. And protection—the cops won't be tempted to drag you in and rough you up in one of their infamous ten-hour interrogations. It'll be hands off as they play it by the book. I have a relationship with Detective Reardon and I'll try to convince him that they don't have enough evidence to move forward. If they find any evidence, chances are I'll know about it."

He turns the can up, drains it, wipes his mouth with a sleeve. A thirsty frat boy could not have finished the beer any faster. It's another perfect moment for him to say something like "There is no evidence." Instead, he belches and says, "And if I'm arrested?"

"Then I'll be at the jail trying to get you out, which will be impossible. A charge of murder in this city means no bail. I'll file a bunch of motions and make some noise. I have friends at the newspaper and I'll leak the fact that the police have little in the way of evidence. I'll start intimidating the prosecutor."

"Doesn't sound like much for $5,000. Could I have another beer?"

I hesitate for a second and quickly decide that two will be his limit, at least in my office. I hand him another can and say, "I'll refund the money right now, Arch, if you're unhappy with our arrangement. As I've said, I'm a busy lawyer with a lot of clients. Five thousand bucks is not going to change my life."

He pops the top and takes a reasonable sip.

I ask, "You want the check back?"

"No."

"Then stop bitching about the fee."

He glares at me and for the first time I catch the cold, hollow stare of a killer. I've seen it before. He says, "They're gonna kill me, Sebastian. The cops can't prove anything, they can't find their man, and they're under a ton of pressure. They're afraid of me because if they arrest me then they have to deal with you, and since they have no evidence they don't want to go to trial. Imagine a not-guilty verdict after a huge trial. So, to sort of short-circuit everything, they're just gonna take me out and save everyone the trouble. I know this because they've told me. Not Detective Reardon. Not the big shots down at Central. But the cops on the street, some of those guys who follow me nonstop, twenty-four seven. They even watch the trailer when I'm asleep. They harass me, cuss me, threaten me. And I know they're gonna kill me, Sebastian. You know how rotten this department really is." He goes silent as he takes another drink.

"I doubt that," I say. "Sure, we have some bad apples, but I've never known them to rub out a murder suspect just because they couldn't nail him."

"I know a guy they killed, a drug dealer. Made it look like a botched delivery."

"I'm not going to argue about this."

"Here's the problem, Sebastian. If they put a bullet in my head, then they'll never find that girl's body."

My stomach flips but I remain stone-faced. It's customary for the accused to deny guilt. It's unheard of for him to admit to the crime, especially at such an early stage. I never ask criminal defendants if they're guilty; it's a waste of time and they lie anyway. I proceed carefully with "So you know where her body is?"

"Let me get this straight, Sebastian. You're now my lawyer and I can tell you anything, right? If I killed ten girls and hid their bodies and told you all about it, you couldn't repeat a word, right?"

"That's right."

"Never?"

"There's only one exception to the rule. If you tell me something in confidence, and I believe that it will endanger other people, then I am allowed to repeat it to the authorities. Other than that, I can never tell."

Satisfied, he smiles and takes a drink. "Relax, I didn't kill ten girls. And I'm not saying I killed Jiliana Kemp either, but I know where she's buried."

"Do you know who killed her?"

He pauses, says yes, then goes silent again. It's obvious he's not naming names. I reach into the fridge and get a beer for myself. We drink for a few minutes. He watches every move, as if he knows my heart is pounding away. Finally, I say, "Okay, I'm not asking for any information, but do you think it's important for someone, maybe me, to know where she is?"

"Yes, but I have to think about it. Maybe I'll tell you tomorrow. Maybe not."

My thoughts turn directly to the Kemp family and their unspeakable nightmare. At this moment I hate this guy and would love to see him locked up, or worse. Sipping a beer in my van like he's Joe Cool while the family suffers.

"When was she killed?" I asked, pushing it.

"I'm not sure. I didn't do it, I swear. But she did not give birth in captivity, if that's what you want to know. There was no baby sold on the black market."

"You know a lot, don't you?"

"I know too much and it's about to get me killed. I may have to disappear, you know?"

"Taking flight is a clear sign of guilt. It will be used against you in court. I wouldn't advise it."

"So you want me to stay here and take a bullet."

"The cops do not kill murder suspects, okay, Arch? Trust me on this."

He crushes his can and leaves it on the table. "I got nothing else to say right now, Sebastian. I'll see you later."

"You have my number."

He opens the door and gets out. Partner watches him as he glances around, looks for the cops, then enters the mall and disappears.

Partner and I drive straight to the bank. The check is no good. I call Arch for an hour and finally get him. He apologizes and promises the check will be good tomorrow. Something tells me I'd be a fool to believe him.

10.

It's 4:33 in the morning and my phone is ringing. I grab it and don't recognize the number. This is always trouble. "Hello," I say.

"Hey, Sebastian, it's me, Arch. Got a minute?"

Of course, Arch. Oddly enough, I'm not that busy in the middle of the night. I take a deep breath and say, "Sure, Arch, I have a minute. But it's four in the morning, so this better be good."

"I'm out of town, okay, officially on the run. I shook 'em off and slipped through their net, and I'm not coming back, so they'll never catch me."

"Big mistake, Arch. Better find yourself a new lawyer."

"You're my lawyer, Sebastian."

"The check is rubber, Arch. Remember what I said?"

"You still have it, run it through today. I swear it'll clear." His words are fast and clipped, and he sounds as though he'd been running. "Look, Sebastian, I want you to know where that girl is, okay? Just in case something happens to me. There are others involved, and I could easily end up on the short end of the stick, know what I mean?"

"Not really."

"I can't explain all of it, Sebastian. It's complicated. I got folks after me, cops as well as some guys who make cops look like Cub Scouts."

"Too bad, Arch. I can't help you."

"You ever see that billboard down the interstate, about an hour south of here, big bright sign in a cornfield, says, 'Vasectomy Reversals.' You ever see it, Sebastian?"

"I don't think so." Every reasonable thought and instinct tells me to cancel this call immediately. Just hang up, stupid. And never speak to him again. Physically, though, I freeze and cannot do it.

His voice is animated now, as if he's thoroughly enjoying this. "'Vasectomy Reversals by Dr. Woo. All insurance accepted. Call twenty-four hours a day. Toll-free number.' That's where she's buried, Sebastian, under that billboard, right next to a cornfield. My father had a vasectomy two years before I was born, not sure what went wrong and my mother was certainly perplexed. Maybe she was seeing someone on the side. So who's my daddy, right? I guess we'll never know. Anyway, I've always had this fascination with vasectomies. A snip here and a snip there, drive yourself home and shoot blanks for the rest of your life. Such a simple procedure but such dramatic results. You had the Big V, Sebastian?"

"No."

"Didn't think so. You're such a stud."

"So you buried her, is that what you're saying, Arch?"

"Ain't saying anything, Sebastian. Except good-bye and thanks for keeping this a secret. I'll check in later."

11.

I wrap myself in a blanket and sit outside on the small terrace. It's cold and dark and the streets far below are quiet and empty. In moments like these, I wonder why I became a criminal defense lawyer. Why have I chosen to spend my life trying to protect people who, for the most part, have done horrible things? I can justify it on the usual grounds, but at times like this my heart is not really in it. I think about architecture school, my second choice. But then, I know some architects and they have their own issues.

First scenario: Swanger is telling the truth. In that case, am I bound by ethics and duty to stay quiet? Hand in hand is the question, am I really his lawyer? No and yes. We signed a contract, but he breached the contract by paying with a bad check. No contract means no representation, but it's never that clear. I met with him on two occasions, and during both he considered me to be his lawyer. Both were clearly lawyer-client meetings. He asked for advice. I gave it. He followed most of it. He confided in me. When he told me about the body, he certainly thought he was talking to his lawyer.

Second scenario: Let's say I'm his lawyer, I never see him again, and I decide to tell the police what he told me. It would be a serious breach of client trust, probably enough to get me disbarred. But who will complain? If he's on the run, or dead, how much trouble can he cause me?

Third scenario: Plenty. If the body is where he says it is, and I tell the police, then Swanger will be hunted, found, tried, convicted, and given death. He would blame me, and he would be correct. My career would be over.

Fourth scenario: I cannot tell the police, under any circumstances. They don't know what I know, and I'm not about to tell them. I think about the Kemp family and their nightmare, but there's no way I can break a confidential relationship. With luck, the family will never know that I know.

Fifth scenario: Swanger is lying. He seemed too anxious to tell me. He's playing games and sucking me into some awful scheme that will only end badly. He knew the check would bounce. His poor mother has never seen $5,000 in her life, nor has he.

Sixth scenario: Swanger is not lying. I can leak the information to Nate Spurio, my mole deep in the department. The body will be found. Swanger will be caught and put on trial and I will be nowhere near the courthouse. If he killed the girl, I want him locked up.

I kick around several other scenarios and things get foggier, not clearer. At 5:30, I put on the coffee. While it brews I rack all fifteen balls and break with a rather soft shot. The neighbor next door has complained about the noise of clacking balls at weird hours, so I work on my finesse game. I run the table, sink the 8 ball in a corner, pour a cup of strong coffee, and run the table again. Another rack, and I leave the 4 ball an inch from the pocket. Thirty-three in a row. Not bad.

Vasectomy reversals?

12.

The police follow me, but halfheartedly. Partner says they're tailing me about half the time, that they got fired up when Swanger met me in the van, but that was over a week ago. Partner drops me off at Ken's Kars, a cheap secondhand lot in the Hispanic part of town. I've done some work for Ken, kept him out of jail, and he and I both know that our tag-teaming days are not over. He loves shady deals, the darker the better, and it's just a matter of time before a SWAT team shows up with another arrest warrant.

For twenty bucks cash, per day, Ken will "lease" me a serviceable car from his sad inventory, no questions asked. I do this occasionally when I think I'm being watched. My black Ford cargo van is quite easy to spot. The dented Subaru wagon Ken has selected for me, however, will never attract attention. I spend a few min-utes with him, swap some insults, and hit the road.

I weave through a run-down part of town, circling back here and there, with one eye on the mirror. I eventually find a bypass that takes me to the interstate, and when I'm sure there's no one following me, I head south. Fifty-two miles from the city limits, I pass Dr. Woo's sign on the other side of the road. As Swanger said, it's a large billboard at the edge of a cornfield. Next to the words "Vasectomy Reversals" is the large goofy face of Dr. Woo as he looks down upon the northbound traffic. I turn around at the next exit, drive four miles back to the sign, and park near it. Traffic roars by, the drafts from the big trucks almost lifting my little Subaru. Next to the shoulder there is a ditch covered with weeds and clogged with litter, and beyond the ditch there is a chain-link fence choked with vines. Beyond the fence is a gravel frontage road that borders the cornfield. The farmer who owns the place has carved out a narrow rectangle to lease to the sign company, and in the center of it there are four large metal poles that anchor the billboard. Around them are weeds, more litter, a few stray stalks of corn. Above them, Dr. Woo grins at the traffic as he hawks his skills.

He's the last guy I would trust with my testicles.

Though I have no experience, I suppose one could use dark-ness as cover, ease along the frontage road, dig a nice grave, drag a body over to it, refill the hole, scatter dirt and litter around, and cover it all up. Let a few months go by as the seasons change and the dirt settles.

And why would you pick a spot so close to an interstate high-way with twenty thousand cars a day? I have no idea, but I remind myself that I'm trying to understand the mind of a very sick per-son. Hiding in the open works all the time, I guess. And I'm sure that at 3:00 a.m. this place is fairly deserted.

I stare at the weeds under the sign and think about the Kemp family. And I curse the day I met Arch Swanger.

13.

Two days later, I'm waiting in a hallway in the Old Courthouse when I get a text from Detective Reardon. He says we need to talk, and soon. It's urgent. An hour later, Partner drops me off at Central and I hustle back to Reardon's cramped and suffocating office. No hellos, no handshake, no greeting of any kind, but then I don't expect any.

He grunts, "You got a minute?"

"I'm here," I say.

"Have a seat." There is only one place to sit—a leather bench covered with dust and files. I look at it and say, "That's okay. I'll just stand."

"Whatever. Do you know where Swanger is?"

"No, I have no idea. Thought you guys were bird-dogging him."

"We were, but he got away. No sign for over a week, nothing. Vanished." He falls into his wooden swivel chair and eventually gets both feet onto his desk. "Are you still his lawyer?"

"No. When he hired me he paid with a rubber check. Our contract is void."

A smirk, a fake smile. "Well, he thinks otherwise. This came in just after midnight, right here on my office phone." He reaches over and hits two buttons on his vintage answering machine. After the beep, Arch's voice begins: "This message is for Detective Landy Reardon. This is Arch Swanger calling. I'm on the road and I'm not coming back. You guys have hounded me for months and I'm tired of it. My poor mother is out of her mind because of your constant surveillance and abusive tactics. Please leave her alone.

She's completely innocent and so am I. You know damned well I didn't kill that girl, had nothing to do with it. I'd like to explain this to someone who's willing to listen, but if I come back you'll just bust my ass and throw me in jail. I got some good information, Reardon, and I'd like to talk to someone. I know where she is right now. How about that?"

There is a long pause. I look at Reardon and he says, "Hang on."

Arch coughs a couple of times, and when he resumes his voice is shaky, as though he's getting emotional: "Only three people know where she's buried, Reardon. Only three. Me, the guy who killed her, and my lawyer, Sebastian Rudd. I told Rudd because as a lawyer he can't tell anyone. Isn't that screwed up, Reardon? Why should a lawyer be able to keep such deadly secrets? I like Rudd, don't get me wrong. Hell, I hired him. And if by some lucky break you're able to find me, then I'll bring in Rudd to walk me." Another pause, then, "Gotta go, Reardon. Later."

I step over to the leather bench and sit on some files. Reardon turns off the answering machine and leans forward on his elbows. "It came in from a prepaid cell phone and we couldn't track it. We have no idea where he is."

I take a deep breath as I try to unscramble my thoughts. There is no strategic or commonsense reason for Swanger to tell the police that I know where the body is buried. Period! And the fact that he was so eager to tell me, and then blab it to the cops, makes me doubt him even more. He's a con, perhaps a serial killer, a psychopath who enjoys playing games and revels in the lying. But whatever he is, and whatever his motives, he has thrown me off a cliff and I'm free-falling.

The door suddenly opens and in walks Roy Kemp, assistant chief of police and father of the missing girl. He closes the door behind him and takes a step toward me. He's a tough guy, an ex-Marine with a square jaw and a grayish crew cut. His eyes are weary and red, evidence of the toll the last year has taken. His eyes also convey a hatred that makes my skin crawl. My collar is instantly wet.

Reardon gets to his feet, cracks his knuckles as if he's about to use his fists, and gives me a look that could kill, and probably will.

It's fatal to show weakness to a cop, or a prosecutor or judge, even a jury, but right now it is impossible to conjure up the slightest trace of confidence, let alone my usual cockiness.

Kemp gets right to the point with "Where is she, Rudd?"

I slowly get to my feet, raise both hands, and say, "I gotta think about this, okay? I'm caught off guard here. You guys had time to plan this ambush. Give me some time, okay?"

Kemp says, "I don't give a damn about your confidentiality and ethics and all that crap, Rudd. You have no idea what we're going through. It's been eleven months and eighteen days of sheer hell. My wife can't get out of bed. My whole family is falling apart. We're desperate, Rudd."

For all of his fearsomeness, Roy Kemp is a man in grievous pain, a father who's sleepwalking through his worst nightmare. He needs a body, a funeral, a permanent grave where he and his wife can kneel on the grass and properly mourn. The horror and uncertainty must be overwhelming.

He's blocking my narrow path to the door, and I'm wondering if he'll actually get physical.

I say, "Look, Chief, you're assuming that everything Arch Swanger says is the truth, and that could be a bad assumption."

"Do you know where my daughter is?"

"I know what Arch Swanger said, but I do not know if he's telling the truth. Frankly, I doubt it."

"Then tell us anyway. We'll go look."

"It's not that simple. I can't repeat what he said to me in confidence, you know that."

Kemp closes his eyes. I glance down and notice both his fists are clenched. Slowly, he relaxes them. I look at Reardon, who's glaring at me. I look back at Kemp, whose red eyes are open slightly. He's nodding, as if he's saying, "Okay, Rudd, we'll play it your way. But we'll get you."

Frankly, I'm on their side. I would love to spill my guts, help get the girl properly laid to rest, help track down Swanger, and watch with satisfaction as a jury nails him for murder. Sadly, though, that is not an option. I take a small step toward the door and say, "I'd like to leave now."

Kemp doesn't move, and somehow I manage to brush by him without provoking a fight. As I grab the doorknob I can almost feel a knife in my back, but I survive and make it to the hallway. I've never left Central in a bigger hurry.

14.

It's the third Friday of the month, time to see Judith for our mandatory two-drink meeting. Neither of us wants it, but neither is willing to surrender and quit. To do so would be to confess a weakness, something we both simply cannot do, not to each other anyway. We tell ourselves that we need to keep the lines of communication open because we share a son. That poor child.

This is our first drink since she dragged me into court in her futile effort to terminate all visitation rights. So, with that little brawl still hanging in the air, there will be an even thicker layer of tension. Frankly, I was hoping she would cancel. I could easily be provoked into a tongue-lashing.

I get to the bar early and find a booth. She arrives on time as always, but with a pleasant look on her face. Judith is not a pleasant person and doesn't smile much. Most lawyers battle stress, but most lawyers don't work in a firm with nine other women, all known to be ball-squeezing litigators looking for a fight. Her office is a pressure cooker, and I suspect her home life is not that much fun. The older Starcher gets, the more he talks about all the yelling between Judith and Ava. I, of course, pump the kid for all the dirt I can get.

"How was your week?" I ask, the standard opening.

"The same. Looks like you're on a roll. Another picture in the paper."

The waiter takes our orders, always the same: chardonnay for her, whiskey sour for me. Whatever pleasant thought she brought into the bar has now vanished.

"A bit premature," I say. "I don't represent the guy anymore. He couldn't handle the fee."

"Gee, think of all the publicity you'll miss."

"I'll find some more."

"I have no doubt about that."

"I'm not in the mood to swap insults. I get Starcher tomorrow for my thirty-six hours. Any problems with that?"

"What are your plans?"

"So I have to submit my plans to you for approval? When did the court order this?"

"Just curious, that's all. You need a drink."

We stare at the table for a few minutes, waiting for the alcohol. When it arrives, we grab the glasses. After the third gulp, I say, "My mother is in town. We'll take Starcher to the mall for the usual ritual whereby the noncustodial parent kills a few hours drinking coffee while the kid rides the carousel and bangs around the playground. Then we'll have bad pizza and bad ice cream in the food court and watch the clowns turn flips and pass out balloons. After that we'll drive down to the river and take a walk by the boats in the harbor. What else would you like to know?"

"You plan to keep him tomorrow night?"

"I get thirty-six hours, once a month. That's 9:00 a.m. tomorrow until 9:00 p.m. Sunday. Do the math. It's not that complicated."

The waiter pops in to ask how we're doing. I order another round, even though our glasses are not yet half-empty. Over the past year, I have almost managed to look forward to these brief meetings with Judith. We're both lawyers and occasionally we've found common ground. I once loved her, though I'm not so sure she felt the same. We share a child. I have entertained the fantasy that we could possibly develop a friendship, one that I need because I have so few friends. Right now, though, I can't stand the sight of her.

We drink in silence, two brooding ex-lovers who would really like to strangle one another. She breaks the tension with "What kind of person is Arch Swanger?"

We talk about him for a few minutes, then about the abduction and the nightmare the Kemp family is enduring. A lawyer she knows once handled a DUI for Jiliana's last boyfriend, which is supposed to somehow be enlightening.

The drinks are finished in thirty minutes, a record, and we part ways without even the obligatory peck on the cheek.

15.

It's a challenge each month to plan an activity that keeps Starcher entertained. He's already told me he's tired of the mall, the zoo, the fire station, miniature golf, and the children's theater. What he really wants to do is watch more cage fighting, but that's not going to happen. So, I buy him a boat.

We meet my mother at a place called the Landing, a contrived boathouse in the middle of City Park. She and I drink coffee while Starcher slurps his hot cocoa. My mother is worried about his upbringing. The kid has no table manners and never utters the words "sir," "ma'am," "please," and "thank you." I've pushed him on this and gotten nowhere.

The boat is a remote-controlled model racer with an engine that whines like a muffled chain saw. The pond is a large man-made circle of water with a gushing fountain in the center. It's a magnet for model boats of all varieties, and for all ages. Starcher and I fiddle with the remote controls for half an hour before everything makes sense. When he's comfortable, I turn him loose and take a seat next to my mother on a bench under a tree.

It's a beautiful day, with crisp light air and a brilliant blue sky. The park is crawling with people—families strolling about eating ice cream, new moms with massive strollers, young lovers rolling in the leaves. And no shortage of divorced fathers exercising their rights of visitation.

My mother and I chat about nothing of any importance as we watch her only grandson in the distance. She lives two hours away and does not get our local news. She's heard nothing of the Swanger affair and I'm not about to bring it up. She has a lot of opinions and does not approve my career. Her first husband, my father, was a lawyer who made a nice living in real estate. He died when I was ten. Her second husband made a fortune in rubber bullets and died at the age of sixty-two. She's been afraid to gamble on a third one.

I fetch us more coffee in paper cups and we resume our conversation. Starcher waves me over, and when I get there he hands me the controls and says he needs to go pee. The restroom is not far away, just on the other side of the pond in a building that houses the concession stands and park offices. I ask him if he needs help and he shoots me a dirty look. He is, after all, now eight years old and gaining confidence. I watch him as he walks to the building and enters the men's restroom. I stop the boat and wait.

There is a sudden commotion behind me, loud angry voices, then two gunshots crack through the air. People start screaming. About fifty yards away, a black teenager sprints across the park, leaps over a bench, darts between some saplings and into the woods, running as if his life is in danger. Evidently it is. Not far behind him is another young black male, angrier and with the gun. He fires it again, and people hit the ground. All around me, folks who were enjoying the day are now ducking, crawling, clutching children, and scurrying for their lives. It's a scene from television, something we've all witnessed before, and it takes a few seconds to realize that this is not fiction. That's a real gun!

I think about Starcher, but he's on the other side of the pond in the restroom, a good distance from the gunfire. As I duck and look wildly around, a man scampering away bumps into me, grunts "Sorry," and keeps moving.

When both the prey and the hunter are lost in the woods, I wait, afraid to move. Then, two more gunshots in the distance. If the second guy found the first guy, at least we didn't have to watch it. We pause, wait, then start to move again. My heart is racing as I stand and gawk at the thick trees along with everyone else. When it appears as though the danger has passed, I take a deep breath. People stare at each other, relieved but still stunned. Did we really just see what we just saw? Two policemen on bicycles fly around the corner and disappear into the woods. In the distance a siren can be heard.

I look at my mother, who's on the phone as if she missed it all. I look at the men's restroom; Starcher is still inside. I start walking that way, pausing to place the remote control on the bench beside my mother. Several men and boys have come and gone from the restroom.

"What was that?" she asks.

"Life in the big city," I say as I walk away.

Starcher is not in the restroom. I hurry outside and begin looking around. I grab my mother, tell her he's disappeared, and tell
her to check out the ladies' restroom. For several long minutes the
two of us scour the area, our fear mounting with each second. He's
not the kind of kid who would wander off. No, Starcher would
take a pee and head straight back to the pond to continue his boat
racing. My heart is pounding and I'm sweating.

The two bicycle cops emerge from the woods, without a suspect, and head our way. I stop them, tell them my son is missing,
and they immediately get on the radio. In my panic, I stop others
and ask them to help.

Two more bicycle cops arrive. The area around the Landing is
now a panic zone; everyone knows a kid is missing. The police are
trying to lock down the entire park, to keep anyone from leaving,
but there are a dozen points of entry and exit. Patrol cars arrive.
The urgent wail of sirens only adds to the alarm. I see a man in
a red sweater. I think I saw him enter the men's restroom. He
says yes, he was there, and he saw a kid at the urinal. Everything
seemed fine. No, he did not see the kid leave. I jog up and down
the sidewalks that weave through the park, asking everyone along
the way if they've seen an eight-year-old boy who seemed lost. He
was wearing jeans and a brown sweatshirt. No one has seen him.

As the seconds tick by, I try to calm myself. He has just wandered off. He has not been abducted. It doesn't work; I am in full
panic.

This is the awful story you read about but think it can never
happen to you.

16.

After half an hour my mother is ready to collapse. A medic sits
beside her on a park bench and tends to her. The police ask me to

stay with her too, but I cannot sit still. There are cops everywhere. God bless them.

A young man in a dark suit introduces himself as Lynn Colfax. He is the detective in the Missing Children Division, City Police. What kind of sick society needs an entire section of its police department dedicated to missing children?

He and I walk through the final moments. I stand exactly where I was standing when Starcher left for the restroom, less than a hundred feet away. I kept my eyes on him until he went inside, then I was jolted by the sound of gunfire. Step by step, thought by thought, we go through it all.

The men's restroom has only one door and no windows. It is inconceivable to me, and to Detective Colfax, that someone could grab an eight-year-old boy and physically remove him from the premises without being seen. But, at that moment, most of the people hanging around the Landing were either crouching behind benches or shrubs or flat on the ground as the bullets were fired. Other witnesses verify this. We estimate the diversion lasted fifteen, maybe twenty seconds. Plenty of time, I guess.

After an hour, I finally admit that Starcher has not simply wandered away. He has been taken.

17.

The best way to tell Judith is to make her see for herself. If something bad happens to our son, she will never forgive me, and she will always maintain that since I am such a lousy parent, am in fact thoroughly derelict in all areas of parental guidance, that his disappearance was and is completely my fault. Great, Judith. You win; I'm to blame.

It might help her to see the crime scene, especially with all the cops around.

I stare at my cell phone for a long time, then make the call. She answers with "What is it?"

I swallow hard and try to sound calm. "Judith, Starcher has disappeared. I'm at the Landing in City Park, with his grand-mother, and with the police. He disappeared about an hour ago. You need to get down here now."

She yells, "What?"

"You heard me. Starcher is missing. I think he's been abducted."

Again she yells, "What! How! Were you watching him?"

"Yes, as a matter of fact I was. We'll argue later. Just get down here."

Twenty-one minutes later, I see her racing along the side-walk, obviously a woman who's scared out of her mind. As she approaches the Landing and sees all the policemen, then me, then the yellow crime scene ribbon strung around the restrooms, she stops, throws a hand over her mouth, and breaks down. Lynn Col-fax and I walk over to her and try to calm her.

She grits her teeth and says, "What happened?"

She wipes her eyes as we go through it again. And again. She says nothing to me, as if I'm not a part of the drama. She won't even look at me. She grills Colfax until all questions have been asked. She takes complete charge of the family's side of things, even informs the detective that she is the custodial parent and all communication will be through her. Me, I'm viewed as nothing more than a negligent babysitter.

Judith has a photo of Starcher on her cell phone. Colfax e-mails this to his office. He says that posters will go up immediately. All alerts and warnings are already in play. Every policeman in the City is looking for Starcher.

18.

We eventually leave the Landing, though it is painful. I would prefer to sit here all afternoon and throughout the night, just waiting for my little boy to appear and ask, "Where's my boat?" It is the last place he saw his father. If he's just lost, then maybe he'll find his way back. We're sleepwalking through this, numb and stunned and telling ourselves that this is not really happening.

Lynn Colfax says he's been through this before, and the best move right now is for us to meet at Central, in his office, and talk about how to proceed. It's either an abduction, a disappearance, or a kidnapping, and all three pose different problems.

I take my mother to my apartment, where she is met by Partner. He'll take care of her for a few hours. She's blaming herself for not being more attentive, and she's griping because that bitch Judith wouldn't even acknowledge her presence. "Why did you ever marry that woman?" she asks. It wasn't by choice. Really, Mom? Can't we discuss this later?

Colfax has a neat desk and a calm, soothing presence. It means nothing to us—Judith and me. Ava, the third parent, is out of town. He begins by telling us a story about an abduction, one of the few with a happy ending. Most end badly, and I know this. I've read the summaries. With each passing hour, the chances of a good outcome get slimmer and slimmer.

He asks if there is anyone that we know of who might be a suspect? A relative, a neighbor, the pervert down the street, anyone? We shake our heads, no. I've already thought about Link Scanlon and I'm not ready to bring him into this. A kidnapping does not fit his profile. All he wants from me is $100,000 in cash, a refund, and I cannot believe he would resort to kidnapping my son for ransom. Link would prefer to break my right leg this week and my left leg the next.

Colfax says it's useful to immediately promise a reward for information. He says a good starting point is $50,000. Judith, the sole parent, says, "I can handle that." I doubt if she could stroke a check for that amount, but go, girl. "I'll split it," I say, as if we're playing cards.

To make an unbearable situation even worse, Judith's parents arrive and are escorted into the office. They grab their daughter and all three have a long cry. I stand against a wall, as far away as possible. They do not acknowledge my presence. Starcher lives with these grandparents about half the time, so they are very attached to him. I try to understand their grief, but I have loathed these people for so long I cannot stand the sight of them. When they settle down, they ask what happened and I tell them. Colfax helps me out with a few facts here and there. By the time we get through with the narrative, they are convinced everything was all my fault. Great—now we're getting somewhere.

I do not have to stay in the room. I excuse myself, leave the building, and return to the Landing. The police are still there, loitering around the boathouse, keeping people away from the men's restroom. I speak to them and express my gratitude; they are sympathetic. Partner arrives, says my mother has had two martinis and is somewhat subdued. He and I split up and roam the walkways of the park. The sun is setting; the shadows are getting longer. Partner brings me a flashlight, and we continue our search well into the night.

At 8:00 p.m. I call Judith to see how she's holding up. She's at home, with her parents, waiting by the phone. I offer to come over and sit, but she says no thanks. She has friends over and I wouldn't fit. I'm sure she's right about that.

I roam through the park for hours, shining my light at every bridge, culvert, tree, and pile of rocks. This is the worst day of my life, and when it ends, I sit on a bench at midnight and finally weep.

19.

Aided by whiskey and a pill, I manage to sleep for three hours on the sofa before waking in a pool of sweat. Wide awake now, and the nightmare only continues. I shower to kill time and check on my mother. She's had some pills and seems to be in a coma. At dawn Partner and I return to the park. There's nowhere else to go, really. What else am I supposed to do? Sit by the phone? It's in my pocket and it buzzes at 7:03. Lynn Colfax checks in to see how I'm doing. I tell him I'm at the park, still searching. He says they've had a few tips but nothing useful. Just some crackpots interested in the reward money. He asks if I've seen the Sunday morning newspaper. Yes, I have. Front page.

Partner brings some muffins and coffee, and we eat on a picnic table overlooking a pond that's used for skating in the winter. He asks, "Have you thought about Link?"

"Yes, I have, but I don't think it's him."

"Why not?"

"Not his kind of crime."

"You're probably right."

We return to the silence that defines our relationship, a quiet I have always appreciated. Now, though, I need someone to talk to. We finish eating and split up again. I cover the same paths and trails, look under the same footbridges, walk along the same creeks. I call Judith mid-morning, and her mother answers her cell phone. Judith is resting, and, no, they've heard nothing. Back at the Landing, the police have removed the crime scene tape and things have returned to normal. The place is bustling with people again, all apparently oblivious to yesterday's horror. I watch some boys race their boats around the pond. I stand where I stood yesterday when I saw Starcher for the last time. A dull pain rips through my gut and I'm forced to walk away.

At the rate I'm going, Starcher is the only child I'll ever produce. He was an accident, an unwanted child born in the midst of a raging war between his parents, but in spite of that he has blossomed into a beautiful boy. I haven't been much of a father, but then I've been shut out of his life. I never dreamed I could miss another human so much. But then, what parent can imagine a child being abducted?

Hours pass as I roam the park. I jump out of my skin when my phone rings, but it's only an acquaintance wanting to help. Late in the day, I sit on a park bench near a jogging trail. From out of nowhere, Detective Landy Reardon appears and sits beside me. He's wearing a suit under the standard black trench coat.

"What brings you here?" I ask, startled.

"I'm just the messenger, Rudd. Nothing more. Not involved, really. But your kid is okay."

I take a deep breath and lean forward, elbows on knees, thoroughly confused. I manage to grunt, "What?"

He stares straight ahead as if I'm not here. "Your kid's okay. What they want is an exchange."

"An exchange?"

"You got it. You tell me; I tell them. You tell me where the girl is buried, you get your kid back after they find her."

I don't know what to think or say. Praise God my kid is safe, but he's safe because the cops have snatched him and are holding him as bait! I tell myself I should be angry, furious, volcanic, but I am nothing but relieved. Starcher is okay!

"They? Them? You're talking about some of your own people, right?"

"Sort of. Look, Rudd, you gotta understand that Roy Kemp has pretty much checked out. They've put him on administrative leave for a month or so, but no one knows it. He's a mess, and he's out there acting on his own."

"But he has a lot of friends, right?"

"Oh yes. Kemp is highly regarded. He's a thirty-year man, you know, with a lot of contacts, a lot of pull."

"So this is an inside job. I don't believe it. And they've sent you to negotiate."

"I don't know where the kid is, I swear. And I don't like being where I am right now."

"That makes at least two of us. I guess I shouldn't be surprised. In fact, I should've known the cops were not above snatching kids."

"Back off, Rudd. You got a big mouth, you know that? Deal or no deal?"

"I'm supposed to tell you what Arch Swanger told me about the girl, right? Where she's buried. And let's say Swanger is telling the truth, you find the body, he gets busted for capital murder, and my career as a lawyer is over. My son is returned safely to his mother, and I get to spend a lot more time with him. In fact, I'll be a full-time dad."

"You're on the right track."

"And if I say no, what will happen to my kid? Am I supposed to believe that an assistant chief of police and his thugs will actually hurt a child as revenge?"

"I guess you gotta roll the dice, Rudd."

PART FIVE

U-HAUL LAW

1.

I fight the panic. I tell myself my son is safe, and I believe this. But the situation is so urgent that it is impossible to think rationally. Partner and I go to a coffee joint where we huddle in a corner. I walk through the various scenarios as he listens.

There is really no choice. The only important thing here is the safety and deliverance of my son; everything else fades in comparison. If I divulge the secret and lose my license to practice law, I'll survive. Hell, I might even prosper somewhere else, and I certainly won't be dealing with the likes of Arch Swanger again. This could be my ticket out of the profession, my one beautiful opportunity to walk away from the law and to search for real happiness.

I want that little boy in my arms.

Partner and I debate whether I should call Judith and bring her up to date. I decide not to, not now anyway. She will add nothing but stress and complications. And, much more important, she might let it slip to someone else that Kemp and associates have pulled an inside job. Reardon warned me to keep it quiet.

I call Judith anyway, just to check on her. Ava answers the phone and says Judith is in bed, medicated, and not doing well. The FBI just left the house. There is a swarm of reporters out in the street. Things are just awful. As if I don't know.

At 7:00 p.m. Sunday, I call Reardon and say we have a deal.

It takes an hour to get a search warrant. Obviously, the police have a friendly judge on standby. At 8:30, Partner and I leave the City, with one unmarked car in front of us and one behind, which is nothing unusual. By the time we get to Dr. Woo's sign, the police are there in force. Spotlights, two backhoes, at least two dozen men with shovels and sticks, and a canine squad of dogs in crates. I've told them everything I know, and they're examining the ground next to the rows of corn. State troopers guard the shoulder of the interstate, waving off any driver who might get curious.

Partner parks the van where they tell us to park, a hundred feet away from the sign and the action. We sit and watch and hope as the first few frantic moments slip away and the long hours begin. They methodically poke into every square inch of soil. They make a grid, comb through it, then make another one. The backhoes are not used. The dogs stay calm.

On the other side of the sign there are several unmarked black cars bunched together in the darkness. I'm sure Assistant Chief Kemp is waiting in one of them. I loathe him and would like to personally drill him between the eyes, but right now he's the man who can deliver my son.

And then I remember what he's been through: the horror, the fear, the waiting, the final resignation when he and his wife realized Jiliana was not coming home. Now he's sitting over there praying his men will find some bones, something for him to bury properly. That's the best he can expect—a skeleton. My expectations are far greater and certainly more realistic.

By midnight, I'm cursing Arch Swanger.

2.

As they work through the night, Partner and I take turns nodding off. We're starving and desperate for coffee, but we're not about to leave. At 5:20, Reardon calls my cell and says, "It's a dry run, Rudd, there's nothing here."

"I've told you everything I know, I swear."

"I believe you."

"Thank you."

"You can leave now. Get back on the interstate, head south to the Four Corners exit. I'll call you back in twenty minutes."

As we pull away, the searchers are packing up their gear. The dogs are still in their crates, resting. Arch Swanger is probably watching and laughing. We head south, and twenty minutes later Reardon calls again. He says, "You know that truck stop at Four Corners?"

"I think so."

"Park at the gas pumps but don't buy any gas. Walk inside, the restaurant is on the right, and at the far end, away from the counter, is a row of booths. Your kid will be there eating ice cream."

"Got it." I want so badly to say something as stupid as "Thanks," like I owe someone a debt of gratitude for kidnapping my child, not hurting him, and then giving him back. Truthfully, though, I am overcome with relief, joy, gratitude, anticipation, and a strange disbelief that this abduction just might end on a happy note. This never happens.

A minute later, my phone buzzes again. It's Reardon and he says, "Look, Rudd, there's nothing to be gained by pursuing this matter, asking a bunch of questions, running to the press, chasing cameras, you know, your typical routine. We'll take care of the press and leak it that you pulled off a dramatic rescue, after an anonymous phone call. Our kidnapping investigation will continue but will turn up nothing. Are we on the same page here, Rudd?"

"Yes, I'm with you." I'll agree to anything at this point.

"The story is that someone snatched your kid, got fed up with the brat because he probably acts a lot like you, and decided to ditch him at a truck stop. You got the story, Rudd?"

"Got it," I manage to spit out as I bite my tongue to keep from unloading every vile word in the book.

The truck stop is awash with lights and crowded with rigs stacked in neat rows. We park by the pumps and I walk quickly inside. Partner stays in the van to watch for anyone who might be watching us. The restaurant is busy with the breakfast crowd. The smell of thick grease hangs in the air. The counter is lined with beefy truckers devouring pancakes and sausages. I turn a corner, see the booths, pass one, two, three, and there in the fourth booth, all alone, is little Starcher Whitly, grinning from behind a large bowl of chocolate ice cream.

I kiss him on top of his head, tousle his hair, and sit across from him. "Are you okay?" I ask.

He shrugs and says, "Sure, I guess."

"Did anyone hurt you?"

He shakes his head. No.

"Tell me, Starcher. Did anyone do anything to hurt you?"

"No. They were very nice."

"And who is they? Who has been with you since you left the park on Saturday?"

"Nancy and Joe."

A waitress stops at the booth. I order some coffee and scrambled eggs. I ask her, "Who brought this kid in here?"

The waitress looks around, says, "I don't know. Some woman was here just a minute ago, said the kid wanted a bowl of ice cream. She must've left or something. I guess you're paying for the ice cream."

"Gladly. Do you have surveillance cameras?"

She nods at the window. "Out there, but not in here. Something the matter?"

"No. Thanks."

As soon as she leaves I ask Starcher, "Who brought you in here?"

"Nancy." He takes a bite of ice cream.

"Look, Starcher, I want you to put the spoon down for a moment, and I want you to tell me what happened when you went into the restroom at the park. You were racing your boat, you had to pee, and you walked to the restroom. Now, tell me what happened."

He slowly sticks the spoon into the ice cream and leaves it there. "Well, all of a sudden, this big man grabbed me. I thought he was a policeman because he was wearing a uniform."

"Did he have a gun?"

"I don't think so. He put me in a truck that was right behind the restroom. There was another man driving the truck and they drove away real fast. They said they were taking me to the hospital because something bad had happened to my grandmother. They said you would be at the hospital. So we drove and drove and then we were out of the City, way out in the country, and that's where they left me with Nancy and Joe. The men left, and Nancy said my grandmother was going to be okay, and that you would stop by real soon to get me."

"Okay. That was Saturday morning. What did you do the rest of Saturday, and all day yesterday, Sunday?"

"Well, we watched television, some old movies and stuff, and we played backgammon a lot."

"Backgammon?"

"Uh-huh. Nancy asked me what games I liked to play and I said backgammon. They didn't know what it was, so Joe went to the store and bought a backgammon board, a cheap one. I taught them how to play, and beat them too."

"So they were nice to you?"

"Real nice. They kept telling me you were at the hospital and couldn't leave."

Partner finally comes inside. He is relieved to see Starcher and gives the kid a pat on the head. I tell him to find the manager of the truck stop and locate the surveillance cameras; inform the manager that the FBI will want the footage, so take care of it.

My eggs arrive and I ask Starcher if he's hungry. No, he's not. He's been eating pizza and ice cream for the past two days. Anything he wanted.

3.

Since I've never been invited into Starcher's home, I decide that I will not take him there. I don't want the drama and theatrics. Half an hour from the City, I finally call Judith with the news that her son is safe. He's sitting on my lap as we ride up the interstate. She is almost too stunned to speak, so I give Starcher my phone. He says, "Hi, Mom," and I think she has a complete meltdown. I give them a few minutes, then take the phone back and explain that I got a call and was instructed to pick him up at the truck stop. No, he had not been harmed in any way, except maybe too much sugar.

The parking lot outside her office is still empty—it's only 7:30—and we wait in peace before the storm. The black Jaguar slides into the lot and brakes hard next to the van. I step out with Starcher as Judith gets out and lunges for the kid. She grabs him, bawling and clawing, and right behind are her parents and Ava. They take turns squeezing the kid; everybody's crying. I can't stand these people, so I walk over to Starcher, tousle his hair again, and say, "I'll see you later, bud."

He's being smothered and doesn't respond. I ask Judith to step aside for a moment, and when we're alone I say, "Can we meet here with the FBI later in the morning? There's more to the story."

"Tell me now," she hisses.

"I'll tell you when I want to tell you, and that's with the FBI listening. Okay?"

She hates it when she's not in control. She takes a deep breath, grits her teeth, and manages to say, "Sure."

I walk away, refuse to acknowledge her parents, and get in the van. As we drive away, I look at Starcher and wonder when I'll see him again.

4.

At 9:00 a.m., I'm in court for a preliminary hearing. By then, the news is out, courtesy of a leak by the police, that my son has been found and returned to his parents. The judge grants me a continuance and I hurry out of the courtroom. I have a handful of lawyer pals and several of them want to chat and offer congratulations. I'm just not in the mood.

Fango ambushes me in the hallway, just like he did three weeks ago. I keep walking and refuse to look at him. He falls in beside me and says, "Say, Rudd, Link is getting pretty anxious about the money. I told him about your kid and all, and, by the way, he sends his concerns."

"Tell Link to worry about his own problems," I snap as we march stride for stride.

"He is, and one of his problems just happens to be you and the money."

"Too bad," I say and walk even faster.

He labors to keep up with me, labors to think of something clever to say, and makes a big mistake with "You know, your kid just might not be that safe after all."

I wheel around and throw a tight right cross that lands perfectly on his chin. He walks into it and doesn't see it until it's too late. His head jerks so violently that I hear the crunching of bones somewhere, and in the first split second I think I've broken his neck.

But his neck is fine; he's been hit before, plenty of times, and has the scars to prove it.

Fango sprawls across the marble floor, and when he finally comes to rest he doesn't move. Out cold. A perfect knockout punch that I could never replicate. I'm tempted to kick him in the head a few times for good measure, but out of the corner of my eye I see a sudden movement. Another thug is moving toward me and he's reaching for a pocket and a weapon. Someone yells behind me.

The second thug goes down as hard as Fango when Partner whacks him over the head with a stainless steel baton he carries in his coat pocket. The baton is designed for just such occasions. When contracted it's about six inches long, but when whipped out properly it extends to eighteen inches and is equipped with a steel knob at its tip. It can easily crack a skull, is in fact designed to do so. I tell Partner to give it to me and disappear. A security guard runs over and looks at the two unconscious thugs. I hand him my bar association ID card and say, "Sebastian Rudd, Attorney-at-Law. These two goons just tried to jump me."

A crowd gathers. Fango wakes up first, mumbling and rubbing his jaw, then he tries to stand but can't find his feet. Finally, with the help of the security guard, he gets up, still wobbly, and wants to leave. A cop makes him sit on a nearby bench while an EMT tends to his buddy. Eventually, the second guy wakes up, with a very large knot on the back of his head. They ice it for a few minutes, then put him on the same bench with Fango. I stand close and glare at them. They glare right back. The EMT gives me an ice pack for my right hand.

Getting punched is nothing for these two and they're not about to press charges. That would require paperwork, a lot of questions, and no small amount of prying by the police. They work for Link Scanlon and they don't answer questions. Right now they can't wait to get out of the building and back on the streets, where they make the rules.

I tell the police that I, too, have no desire to press charges. As I walk away, I lean close to Fango and whisper, "Tell Link that if I hear one more word out of you, or him, I'm going to the FBI."

Fango sneers as if he might spit in my face.

5.

I suppose some days are meant to be spent with the FBI. I walk into the lobby of Judith's firm a few minutes after 11:00 a.m. The receptionist is smiling and chatting with a paralegal. They smile at me and gush with congratulations. I don't realize it immediately, but they think I'm some sort of hero. A lawyer sticks her head out of her office door and says congratulations. The mood is almost jubilant, and why not? Starcher has been rescued and is safely at home, where he belongs. We were all numb, shell-shocked, terrified, and waiting for the nightmare to become a tragedy. Instead, we got lucky.

Judith is in a large, well-appointed conference room with two FBI agents, Beatty and Agnew. Though my right hand is swollen and throbbing, I manage to shake their hands without any evidence of pain. I nod at Judith, say no to coffee, and ask how Starcher is doing. Just fine. Everything is swell.

Beatty, the talker, explains that Judith called the FBI late Saturday afternoon, but they had not officially entered the investigation. Agnew, the note taker, scribbles away and nods his head; whatever Beatty says is exactly true. The FBI does not get involved in kidnappings until the local police invite them in, or there is evidence that the victim has been moved across state lines. He prattles on for a while, smug with his importance. I let him go.

"Now," Beatty says, looking at me, "you wanted to meet?"

"Yes," I reply. "I know exactly who kidnapped Starcher, and I know why."

Agnew's pen stops in mid-stroke as everyone freezes. With her eyebrows arched, Judith says, "Do tell."

So I tell the story, all of it.

6.

The elation Judith felt upon our son's return dissipates halfway through my narrative. When it becomes apparent that the abduction was a direct result of another one of my notorious cases, her body language shifts dramatically and her mind starts racing away. Now, finally, she has clear proof that I am a danger to Starcher. She'll probably file papers this afternoon.

I avoid eye contact with her, but the vibes are strong enough to spike the tension in the room.

When I finish, Beatty seems stunned. Agnew has burned through an entire legal pad with his chicken scratch.

Beatty says, "Well, I guess there's a good reason the police didn't want us involved."

Agnew grunts his agreement. Judith asks, "How can you prove any of this?"

"I didn't say I could prove it. Proof will be difficult, if not impossible. There may be surveillance footage of Nancy at the truck stop, taking the kid in, but I bet she's disguised in some way. I doubt if Starcher could identify the guy who grabbed him at the park. I don't know. You have any suggestions?"

She says, "It seems pretty far-fetched, the theory that the police would abduct a child."

"So you don't believe me?" I fire back.

The truth is that she wants to believe me. She wants my story to be true; because then she can use it as evidence against me when she drags me back to court. She won't answer my question. "So what's next?" I ask Beatty.

"Wow. I'm not sure. We'll have a chat with our supervisor and go from there."

I say, "I have a meeting this afternoon with an investigator with the police. They'll seem concerned, ask a lot of questions, but it's going nowhere. They'll close the case by the end of the week and be happy with a good outcome."

Beatty asks, "And you want us to open an investigation?"

I look at Judith and say, "Perhaps we should talk about it first. I'm inclined to pursue Kemp. What about you?"

She says, "Let's talk."

Beatty and Agnew take their cue and stand to leave. We thank them and Judith walks them to the front door. When she returns to the conference room, she sits across from me and says, "I don't know what to do. I'm not thinking clearly right now."

"We can't allow the police to do this, Judith."

"I know, but don't you already have enough trouble with them? If Kemp is desperate enough to snatch a child, he might do anything. Now do you understand why I get nervous when Starcher is with you?"

I can't really argue with this.

"Do you think Swanger killed the girl?" she asks.

"Yes, and he's probably killed others."

"Great. Another lunatic out there gunning for you. You're a train wreck, Sebastian, and you're going to get someone hurt. I just hope it's not my child. We got lucky today, but maybe not tomorrow."

There's a knock on the door and Judith says, "Come in." The

receptionist tells her there is a reporter with a cameraman out front. Two more have called the office. "Get rid of them," she says, glaring at me. What a mess I've created.

We finally agree to do nothing for a few hours. I'll cancel the meeting with the police detective; the investigation is a sham anyway. As I leave I tell her I'm sorry, but she wants no part of an apology.

I sneak out a rear door.

7.

Reporters are looking for me, but I have had enough of the story. Others would like to find me: Link and his boys; Roy Kemp when he hears I'm talking to the FBI; perhaps even Arch Swanger, who's likely to phone in at any moment and ask why I sang to the police.

Partner takes me to Ken's Kars and I drive away in a dented Mazda with 200,000 miles on it. No lawyer, regardless of how impoverished, would be caught dead in such a vehicle. I know one who was leasing a Maserati when he was forced into bankruptcy.

I spend the rest of the day in my apartment, hiding and working on two cases. Around five o'clock, I call Judith to check on Starcher. He's fine, she says, and the reporters have gone away. I check the local news where the "dramatic rescue" is the lead story. They use some old footage of me walking into the police station and make it sound like I risked my life to save my son. The fools are swallowing all the bait the police give them. This too shall pass.

Because I've slept about six hours out of the last seventy-two, I finally collapse on the sofa and fall into a coma. Just after 10:00 p.m., my cell phone rings. I check the caller ID, then grab it. It's Naomi Tarrant, Starcher's teacher, the gorgeous young thing

I've been fantasizing about for months. I've asked her to dinner five times and have been hit with five noes. But, the rejections have been progressively softer. I have neither the talent nor the patience for the usual mating rituals—the stalking, the accidental encounters, the blind dates, the silly gifts, the awkward phone calls, the referrals from friends, the endless Internet chatting. Nor do I have the guts to go online and lie about myself to strange women. And, I fear I'm forever scorched and gun-shy from the Judith disaster. How can one human possess so much meanness?

Naomi wants to talk about Starcher, so we do. I assure her he was not harmed in any way. He'll never understand what really happened, and I doubt anyone will tell him. Frankly, he was pampered for about forty-five hours by two people he viewed as buddies. He'll be at school tomorrow and he needs no special attention. I'm sure his mother will arrive with a long list of demands and concerns, but that's his mother.

"What a bitch," Naomi says, dropping her guard for the first time. I'm surprised by this, but love it nonetheless. We spend a few minutes thoroughly trashing Judith and Ava, who we agree is an airhead, and I haven't had this much fun in years.

From left field she says, "Let's do dinner." Ah, the life of a hero. The power of celebrity. The reporters claim I risked my neck to save my son and women are throwing themselves at me.

We establish a few rules. The date has to be a big secret. The school does not expressly forbid its unmarried teachers dating unmarried parents, but it's certainly frowned on. And why ask for trouble? If Judith found out, she would probably file a complaint or a lawsuit or something from her bottomless bag of dirty tricks.

We meet in a dark, low-end Tex-Mex joint the following night. Her choice, not mine. Since no one speaks English no one will be listening. No one cares, especially me. Naomi is thirty-three years old and rebounding from a divorce. No kids, no discernible baggage. She begins by telling me all about Starcher's day at school. As expected, Judith brought him early and had some instructions. All went well; no one mentioned his little ordeal. Naomi and her classroom aide kept a close eye on him, and, as far as they could tell, nothing was said by his friends. He seemed perfectly normal and went about the day as if nothing had happened. Judith picked him up after school and grilled Naomi, but it was hardly out of the ordinary.

"How long were you married to her?" she asks in amazement.

"The paperwork says less than two years, but we could live together for only the first five months. It was unbearable. I tried to tough it out until the kid was born, but then I found out she was already seeing her latest girlfriend. I fled, he was born, and we've been fighting ever since. Getting married was a horrible mistake, but she was pregnant."

"I've never seen her smile."

"I think it happens about once a month."

The margaritas arrive in tall, salty mugs and we dive in. We briefly touch on her marriage, then move on to more pleasant matters. She's been dating, there are lots of calls, and I can understand why. She has soft, beautiful brown eyes that are hypnotic, even seductive. The kind of eyes you can gaze into for hours and wonder if they're real.

Me, I don't date much, don't have the time, too much work, and so on. The usual disclaimers. She seems fascinated by my work, the unpopular cases, the notoriety, some of the thugs I represent. We order enchiladas and I keep chatting away. I soon realize, though, that she follows the one rule of a great conversationalist: Keep the other person talking. So I push back and ask about her family, college, other jobs she's had.

I order a second margarita, she's half finished with her first, and we go back and forth with stories about our past. A platter of enchiladas arrives and she hardly notices. Judging by her figure, she has the appetite of a bird. I can't remember the last time I had sex, and the longer we talk the more I am consumed with that subject. By the time I finish both the food and the booze, I'm fighting the urge to lunge across the table.

But Naomi Tarrant is not impulsive. This will take time. It's Tuesday, so I ask her what she's doing Wednesday. No go.

"You know what I'd really like?" she asks.

What? Anything.

"This may seem a bit odd, but I'm really curious about mixed martial arts."

"Cage fights? You want to go to the cage fights?" I'm stunned.

"Is it safe?" she asks, and mentions the little episode involving the riot and Starcher's close call with disaster. Judith sued me again and Naomi got a subpoena to testify.

"If there's no brawl, it's pretty safe," I say. "Let's go." The truth is, at least half of the fanatics who show up at the fights and scream for blood are women.

We book a date for this coming Friday. I'm thrilled because there is another young fighter I need to evaluate. His manager has contacted me and needs some financial backing.

8.

Not surprisingly, Doug Renfro has not done well since his wife was murdered by one of our SWAT teams. The civil trial is two months away, and Doug is not looking forward to it. He's had his day in court and he's not ready for another one.

I meet him for lunch in an empty deli, and I'm startled by his appearance. He's lost a lot of weight, pounds that he needed. His face is gaunt and pale, and his eyes convey the pain and confusion of a defeated and lonely man.

He nibbles on a chip and says, "I've put the house on the market. I can't stay there, too many memories. I can see her in the kitchen. I can feel her sleeping in the bed next to me. I can hear her laughing on the phone. I can smell her body lotion. She's everywhere, Sebastian, and she's not going away. Worst of all, I can't help but relive those last few seconds, the gunfire and screams and the blood. I blame myself for so much of what went wrong. I often leave at midnight and go find a cheap motel where I pay sixty bucks and stare at the ceiling until sunrise."

"I'm sorry, Doug," I say. "It certainly wasn't your fault."

"I know. But I'm not rational. Plus I hate this damned city. Every time I see a cop or fireman or a garbage worker I start cursing the City and the fools who run it. I can no longer pay taxes to this government. So, I'm outta here."

"What about your family?"

"I'll see them whenever I need to. They have their own lives to live. I gotta take care of me this time, and that means I need a new start somewhere."

"Where are you going?"

"It changes every day, but right now it looks like New Zealand. As far away as I can get. I'll probably renounce my citizenship so I won't have to pay taxes here. I'm a bitter old man, Sebastian, and I have to get away."

"What about the civil trial?"

"I'm not going to trial. I want you to settle it as soon as you can. Hell, the City's liability is only a million. They'll pay that, won't they?"

"Yes, I assume. I haven't talked settlement with them, but they don't want to go to trial."

"Is there a way to get more than a million?"

"Maybe."

He slowly takes a sip of his tea and stares at me. "How?"

"I've got some dirt on the police department. Some crap that's pure filth. Extortion is what I'm thinking."

"I like it," he says with a smile, the first and only. "Can you move fast? I want to get outta here. I'm sick of this place."

"I'll see what I can do."

9.

When my cell phone buzzes after midnight, it's never a call I want to take. At 12:02 I pick it up and see that Partner wants to talk. "Hey, Boss," he says in a weak voice. "They tried to kill me."

"Are you okay?"

"Not really. I've got some burns but I'll be all right. I'm at the hospital, Catholic. We need to talk."

I strap a Glock 19 under my left armpit, put on a heavy coat and a brown fedora, and hustle down to the parking lot to retrieve my worn-out Mazda. Ten minutes later I enter the ER wing of the hospital and say hello to one Juke Sadler, one of the sleaziest lawyers in town. Juke roams the City's emergency rooms trolling for injured clients. Like a vulture, he loiters in the hallways watching for distraught relatives too panicked to think clearly. He's been known to have lunch and dinner in hospital cafeterias while passing out cards to those with broken bones. Last year he got in a fistfight with a tow truck driver who was hustling the family of a fresh car wreck victim. Both were arrested but only Juke got his photo in the newspaper. The bar association has been after him for years but he's too slick.

"Your man's down the hall," he says, pointing like one of those retired hospital volunteers in pink jackets. They actually caught him once wearing that jacket and posing as a greeter. They also caught him wearing a white collar and black jacket and pretending to be a priest. Juke is an unrepentant slimeball, but I admire the guy. He operates in the dark, murky waters of the law, where we have much in common.

Partner is in a gown, sitting on an exam table, his right arm covered in gauze. I take a look and say, "Okay, let's have it."

He was leaving an all-night chicken carryout restaurant with a snack for him and his mom. He got in the van, put it in reverse, and the damned thing blew up. A bomb, probably of the gasoline variety, probably stuck to the fuel tank and remotely detonated by someone sitting in a car nearby. Partner managed to scramble out and remembers hitting the pavement with his jacket on fire. He crawled away and watched the van turn into a fireball. Soon there were cops and firemen everywhere, a lot of excitement. He couldn't find his phone. A medic cut his jacket off and they loaded him into an ambulance. As they rolled him into the ER someone handed him his phone.

"Sorry, Boss," he says.

"Not exactly your fault. As you know, that van is heavily insured, for occasions just like this. We'll get a new one."

"I've been thinking about that," he says, grimacing.

"Oh really?"

"Yeah, Boss. Maybe we get something that's not quite so conspicuous, so easy to spot and follow. Know what I mean? Like, just the other day I was driving along the expressway and I got passed by a white cargo van owned by a flower delivery service. Standard white job, about the same size as ours, and I think to myself, 'That's the way to go. No one ever notices a white van with lettering and numbers painted on the sides.' And it's true. We got to blend in, Boss, not stand out in the crowd."

"And what exactly do we paint on the side of our new van?"

"I don't know, something fictitious. Pete's Parcel. Fred's Flowers. Mike's Masonry. Doesn't really matter, just something to go with the flow."

"I'm not sure my clients would appreciate a generic white van with a fake name painted all over it. My clients are very discerning."

He laughs at this. The last client to step into my van was Arch Swanger, a likely serial killer. A young doctor suddenly appears and steps between us without a word. He examines the bandages and finally asks Partner how he feels. "I wanna go home," he says. "I'm not staying overnight."

This is fine with the doctor. He loads Partner down with bandages, gives him some samples of painkillers, and disappears. A nurse has the discharge instructions and paperwork. Partner puts on his unburned pants, socks, and shoes and walks out with a cheap blanket wrapped around his upper body. We leave the hospital and drive to the fried chicken restaurant.

It's almost 2:00 a.m. and a police cruiser is still parked near the crime scene. Strands of bright yellow tape surround the van, which is nothing but a smoldering, blackened frame. "Stay here," I say to Partner and get out of the car. By the time I walk forty feet and stop at the yellow tape, a cop is coming toward me.

"That's far enough, pal," he says. "This is a crime scene."

"What happened?" I ask.

"Can't say. It's under investigation. You need to back away."

"I'm not touching anything."

"I said back away, okay?"

I pull a business card out of my shirt pocket and hand it to him. "I own the van, okay? It was a gasoline bomb stuck to the gas tank. Attempted murder. Please ask your investigator to call me later this morning."

He looks at the card but is unable to put together a response.

I return to the car and sit in silence for a few minutes. "Want some chicken?" I finally ask.

"No. Not much of an appetite now."

"I think I'd like some coffee. You?"

"Sure."

I get out of the car again and walk into the restaurant. There are no customers, the place is dead, and the obvious question is, why does a chicken place stay open twenty-four seven? But that's a question for someone else. A black girl with steel in both nostrils is loitering by the cash register. "Two coffees please," I say. "No cream."

This pisses her off but she starts moving anyway. "Two forty," she says as she grabs a pot, one that probably hasn't been touched in hours. As she sets the two cups on the counter, I say, "That van out there belongs to me."

"Well, I guess you need a new van," she retorts with a sassy smile. How clever.

"Looks like it. Did you see it blow up?"

"Naw, didn't see it, but I heard it."

"And I'm betting that you or one of your co-workers ran outside with a cell phone and caught it all on video, right?"

She's nodding smugly. Yes.

"Did you give it to the police?"

A grin. "Naw, don't do nothing to help no PO-lice."

"I'll give you a hundred bucks if you'll e-mail me the video, and I won't tell a soul."

She whips her phone out of her jeans pocket and says, "Gimme your address and the cash."

We do the deal. On the way out I ask, "Any surveillance cameras outside?"

"Naw. PO-lice already asked about that. Man who owns this place is too cheap."

In the car, Partner and I stare at my cell phone and watch the video, which is nothing more than the fireball he's already described. At least two fire trucks answered the call and it took a while to douse the flames. The video runs for fourteen minutes and, while entertaining because it is my van, it reveals nothing useful. When the screen goes blank Partner asks, "Okay, who did it?"

I reply, "I'm sure it's Link. We punched out two of his thugs on Monday. Tit for tat. We're playing hardball now."

"You think Link's in the country?"

"I doubt it. That would be too risky. I'll bet he's close by, though, Mexico or the Caribbean, someplace just out of reach but someplace that's easy to get to and from."

I start the engine and we drive away. I'm impressed with how much Partner has talked tonight. The excitement of getting blown up has loosened his tongue. I can tell he's in pain but he would never admit it.

"You got a plan?" he asks.

"Yes. I want you to find Miguel Zapate, Tadeo's brother. Now that the promising MMA career is over, I'm sure Miguel is devoting all his time to peddling drugs. I want you to explain to Miguel that I need some protection; that I'm representing his little brother on a murder rap for free, completely pro bono because I love the kid and he can't afford to pay me; and that I'm getting squeezed by some thugs who work for Link Scanlon. Fango is one, though I've never known his real name."

"They call him Tubby. Tubby Fango, but his real name is Danny."

"Impressive. Who's the other one, the one you plunked with your little baton?"

"Goes by Razor, Razor Robilio, real name is Arthur."

"Tubby and Razor," I say, shaking my head. "When did you take care of this bit of research?"

"After the altercation on Monday, I decided to snoop a little. Wasn't that hard, really."

"Nice work. So give the names to Miguel and tell him that he needs to contact these boys and tell them to back off. Miguel and his boys are running coke, something Link had control of thirty years ago. It's unlikely Tubby and Razor have crossed paths with Miguel, but you never know. There are always strange connections down in the sewers. Please make it clear to Miguel that I don't want anyone hurt; just some intimidation. Got it?"

"Got it, Boss."

We're in the projects. The streets are dark and empty. However, if I stepped out of my car at this moment and showed my white face, I would immediately attract some unpleasant types. I made that mistake once before, but, thankfully, I had Partner with me. I pull to the curb outside his building and say, "I assume Miss Luella is waiting."

He nods and says, "I called her, told her it was just a scratch. She'll be all right."

"You want me to come in?"

"No, Boss. It's pushing three. Go get some sleep."

"Call me if you need anything."

"You got it, Boss. Are we shopping for a new van tomorrow?"

"Not yet. I have to deal with the cops and my insurance company."

"I need some wheels. Mind if I start looking online?"

"Go right ahead. And take care."

"You got it, Boss."

10.

Since I cannot, at this moment, stand the thought of being in her presence, and she certainly prefers to avoid looking at me, Judith and I decide to hash things out over the phone. We begin somewhat pleasantly with the latest update on our son. He's doing well, no damage, no desire to really talk about last weekend. With that out of the way, we get down to business.

Judith has decided that she does not want to pursue an FBI investigation into Roy Kemp and the kidnapping. She has her reasons and they are solid. Life is good. Starcher is fine. If Kemp and company are desperate enough to snatch a kid in return for information, then who knows what else they might do. Let's leave them alone. Besides, proving Kemp was involved seems impossible. Can we really trust the FBI to go after a high-ranking law enforcement official? Plus, her trial calendar is packed. She doesn't want the distraction. Why should we complicate our already stressful lives?

Judith is a fighter, a tough gal who backs down from nothing. She's also a conniving tactician who avoids the dangers of unintended consequences. If we push an investigation into Kemp, we have no idea what might happen next. And since we're dealing with a tough guy who's not thinking clearly, it's smart to assume retaliation is likely.

To her surprise, I do not argue. We reach an agreement, a rare occurrence in our relationship.

11.

Our mayor is a three-term guy with the imposing name of L. Woodrow Sullivan III. To the public and the voters, he's simply Woody, a smiling, backslapping, friendly sort who'll promise anything for a vote. In private, though, he's an abrasive, sour prick who drinks too much and is fed up with his job. He can't walk away, though, because he has no place to go. He's up for reelection next year and it appears as though he has no friends. Right now his approval rating is around 15 percent, low enough to force any proud politician to quit in disgrace, but Woody's fought back before. He'd rather do anything than suffer through the meeting we're about to have.

The third man in the room is the city attorney, Moss Korgan, a classmate of mine in law school. We despised each other back then and things have not improved. He edited the law review and was headed for a gilded career in a fancy corporate law firm, one that imploded and left him scrambling for lesser work.

Woody and Moss. Sounds like an ad for hunting gear.

We meet in the mayor's office, a splendid room on the top floor of City Hall, with tall windows and views in three directions. A secretary pours coffee from an old silver pot as we take our places around a small conference table in one corner. We struggle through the obligatory chitchat and make ourselves smile and act relaxed.

Through discovery in the civil trial, I have let it be known that I intend to subpoena both of these guys to the witness stand. This fact hangs over the table like a dark cloud and makes professional politeness almost impossible.

Woody brusquely says, "We're here to talk about a settlement, right?"

"Yes," I say, and remove some papers from my briefcase. "I have a proposal, one that is rather lengthy. My client, Doug Renfro, prefers to settle all claims and get on with his life, what's left of it."

"I'm listening," Woody says rudely.

"Thank you. First, the eight city cops who murdered Kitty Renfro must be fired. They have been on administrative leave since the murder, and—"

"Do you have to use the word 'murder'?" Woody interrupts.

"They haven't been convicted of anything," Moss adds.

"We're not in a courtroom, okay, and if I want to use the word 'murder,' then I'll use it. Frankly, there is no other word in the English language adequate enough to describe what your SWAT boys did. It was murder. It's embarrassing that these thugs have not been terminated and that they're still getting their full salaries. They have to go. That's number one. Number two, the chief has to go with them. He's an incompetent jerk who should not have been hired in the first place. He oversees a corrupt department. He's an idiot, and if you don't believe me, then ask your voters. According to the last poll, at least 80 percent of the people in this city want him fired."

They nod gravely but cannot make eye contact. Everything I've said has been said on the front page of the *Chronicle*. The city council passed a no-confidence vote by three to one against the chief. But the mayor won't fire him.

The reasons are simple and complicated. If the eight warrior cops and their chief are terminated before the civil trial, they would likely become hostile witnesses against the City. It's best if they remain united in their defense against the Renfro lawsuit.

I continue, "Once the lawsuit is settled you can finally terminate them, right?"

Moss says, "Need I remind you that our liability is capped at $1 million?"

"No, you need not. I'm very aware of that. We'll take the million as a settlement, and you immediately fire the eight cops and the chief."

"Deal!" Woody practically yells across the table as he slaps it with a palm. "Deal! What else do you want?"

Even though the City is on the hook for a measly million bucks, these guys are terrified of another trial. During the first one, I exposed in dramatic detail the gross malfeasance of our police department, and the *Chronicle* broadcast it on the front page for a week. The mayor, the police chief, the city attorney, and the council members were in bunkers. The last thing they want is another high-profile trial in which I humiliate the City.

"Oh, I want a lot more, Mayor," I say. Both look at me with blank faces. Slowly, fear begins to form in their eyes. "I'm sure you remember the story of my little boy getting kidnapped last Saturday. Pretty frightening stuff but a good ending and all that happy horseshit. What you don't know is that he was kidnapped by members of your police department."

Woody's tough-guy facade melts as his face droops and turns pale. Moss, a former Marine, is proud of his perfect posture, but right now he can't keep his shoulders from sagging. He exhales as the mayor sticks a fingernail between his teeth. Their eyes meet briefly; identical looks of terror.

With a bit of drama, I drop a document on the table, just out of their reach. I say, "This is a ten-page affidavit, signed by me, in which I describe, under oath, the kidnapping, an abduction orchestrated by Assistant Chief of Police Roy Kemp, in an effort to coerce me to divulge the location of his missing daughter's body. Arch Swanger was never my client, contrary to what you've read and what you believe, but he did tell me where the body was supposedly buried. When I refused to pass along this information to the cops, my son was kidnapped. I caved, told Detective Reardon what I knew, and a full-scale dig took place at the location last Sunday night. They found nothing; the body was not there. Kemp then released my son. Now he wants me to forget all about it, but that's not going to happen. I'm working with the FBI. You think you have problems with the Renfro case, just wait until the City finds out how rotten your police department really is."

"Can you prove this?" Moss says with a dry throat.

I tap the affidavit and reply, "It's all right here. There is surveillance footage from the truck stop where I found my son. He has been able to identify one of his abductors, a cop. The FBI is hot on the trail and chasing leads."

This is not entirely true, of course, but how could they know? As in any war, the truth is the first casualty. I remove another document from my briefcase and place it next to the affidavit. "And this is a rough draft of a lawsuit I plan to file against the City for the kidnapping. Kemp, as you know, is on administrative leave, still on your payroll, still an employee. I'll sue him, the department, and the City for a crime that will be front page from coast to coast."

"You want Kemp fired too?" Moss asks.

"I don't care if Kemp stays or goes. He's a decent chap and a good cop. He's also a desperate father who's going through hell. I can give him a break."

"Mighty nice of you," Woody mumbles.

"What's this got to do with the settlement?" Moss asks.

"Everything. I'll bury the lawsuit and forget about it, get on with my life, and keep a closer eye on my kid. But I want another million bucks for Renfro."

The mayor rubs his eyes with his knuckles as Moss sags even lower. They are overwhelmed and for one long minute cannot piece together enough words to respond. Finally, Woody mumbles a rather pathetic "Holy shit."

"This is extortion," Moss says.

"It certainly is, but right now extortion is a few notches down the pole. At the top is murder, followed by kidnapping. You don't want to start a pissing contest with me."

The mayor manages to stiffen his spine and say, "And how are we supposed to find another million bucks to pass along to you and Mr. Renfro without someone leaking it to the press?"

"Oh, you've moved money around before, Mayor. You've

been caught a couple of times, got embarrassed with the scandals, but you know the game."

"I did nothing wrong."

"I'm not a reporter, so knock it off. Your budget this year is 600 million. You have rainy-day funds, discretionary funds, slush funds, reserves for this and for that. You can figure it out. The best route may be to deal with the city council in executive session, pass a resolution to reach a confidential settlement with Renfro, and handle the money offshore."

Woody laughs but not because of anything humorous. "So you think we can trust the city council to keep this quiet?"

"That's your problem, not mine. My job is to get a fair settlement for my client. Two million is not fair, but we'll take it."

Moss gets to his feet, looking dizzy. He paces to a window and stares out at nothing. He stretches his back and paces around the room. Woody seems to grasp the reality that the sky is falling and asks, "Okay, Rudd, how much time do we have?"

"Not much," I reply.

Moss says, "We need some time to investigate this, Sebastian. You come in here, drop a bomb like this, and expect us to believe everything. There are a lot of moving parts here."

"Indeed, but an investigation will only cause leaks. And where will it take you? You're going to call in Kemp and ask him if he kidnapped my son? Gee, I wonder what he'll say. You can dig for months looking for the truth and you won't find it. And, I'm not in the mood to wait." I slide the affidavit and the lawsuit across the table in Woody's direction. I stand and grab my briefcase. "Here's the deal. Today is Friday. You have the weekend. I'll be here at ten Monday morning to wrap things up. If you boys can't figure it out, I go straight to the *Chronicle* with that little pile of papers. Imagine the story, the damage. Headlines on cable around the clock."

Woody is pale again. He says lamely, "I'm in Washington Monday."

"Then cancel. Get a bad case of the flu. Ten Monday, gentlemen," I say as I open the door.

12.

Naomi is not too impressed with my rented Mazda. As we make our way downtown toward the auditorium, I explain what happened to my other vehicle. She is shocked that there are bad guys loose in the City who would attach an explosive device to my van to intimidate me and kill Partner. She wants to know how soon the police will catch these guys and bring them to justice. She doesn't understand when I explain that (1) the police have no real interest in catching them because I am who I am and (2) the police can't catch them because these guys don't leave behind clues.

She asks if she's safe in my company. When I tell her I have a gun strapped to my torso and wedged just under my left armpit, she takes a deep breath and gazes out the window. Sure, we're safe, I promise her.

In an effort at full disclosure, I tell her about my last office and the firebombing. No, the police have not solved that crime either, primarily because they were probably involved in the act. Either them or some drug dealers.

"No wonder you struggle with women," she observes. And she's right. Most of them get spooked early in the game and gravitate toward safer men. Naomi, though, has a gleam in her eye and seems to enjoy the threat of danger. After all, the cage fights were her idea.

I've pulled strings and our seats are ringside, third row back. I buy two tall beers and we settle in to watch the crowd. Unlike the theater or cinema, or the opera or symphony, or even a basketball game, the fans arrive in a rowdy mood, many of them already half-drunk. It's another nice crowd, probably three to four thousand, and I marvel at the speed with which the sport has gained popularity. I also think of Tadeo, a talented kid now sitting in jail when he should be at the top of tonight's card. His trial is just around the corner and he still expects me to pull a miracle and walk him out, a free man. For Naomi, I recount, in great graphic detail, the night not too long ago when Tadeo attacked the referee and this entire place turned into a riot. Starcher thought it was cool and wants to return for more fun.

She thinks that's a bad idea.

A trainer recognizes me and stops by for a chat. His kid is a 150-pounder who fights in the second match and has not lost in his last six. As he talks he can't keep his eyes off Naomi. Because she's a knockout and dressed fashionably, she's getting plenty of looks.

The trainer thinks his kid has a future and they need some backing. Since I'm viewed as a big-shot lawyer with plenty of cash, at least in this world, I'm a player who can make a career. I tell the guy we can talk later. Let me watch the kid for a couple of fights and then we'll meet. The trainer asks about Tadeo and shakes his head sadly. What a waste.

When the place is packed, the lights go down and the crowd becomes frantic. The first two fighters enter the cage and introductions are made.

"You know these guys?" Naomi asks excitedly.

"Yes, just a couple of brawlers, not much talent. Street fighters really."

The bell sounds, the brawl is on, and my hot little schoolteacher sits on the edge of her seat and starts yelling.

13.

At midnight we're in a pizza dive, tucked into a narrow booth and sitting very close together. There has been some touching and hand-holding and there seems to be a mutual attraction. I certainly hope it's mutual. She nibbles on a slice of pepperoni and prattles on about the main event, a heavyweight blood-fest that ended with a vicious choke hold. The loser stayed on the mat for a long time. Eventually, she gets around to the kidnapping and wants to know how much I know. I explain that the FBI is digging and I can't say anything.

Was there a ransom demand? I can't say. A suspect? Not that I know of. What was he doing at that truck stop? Eating ice cream. I'd like to give her the details but it's too early; maybe later, when everything is settled.

As we drive back to her place, she says, "It might be difficult to have a relationship as long as you're wearing a gun."

"Okay. I can lose it. But it will always be close by."

"I'm not sure I like that."

Nothing else is said until I park outside her condo. "I had a great time," she says.

"So did I." I walk her to the door of her condo and ask, "So when can I see you again?"

She pecks me on the cheek and says, "Seven tomorrow night. Right here. There's a movie I want to see."

14.

Partner picks me up in another rental, a shiny new U-Haul cargo van with "$19.95 a Day—Unlimited Mileage" splashed on both sides in bright green and orange paint. I look at it for a minute or so before finally getting in. "Nice," I say.

"I thought you'd like it," he says, grinning. His bandages are hidden under his clothing; there's no evidence of his wounds. He's too tough to admit soreness or pain.

"I guess we'd better get used to it," I say. "The insurance company is dragging its feet. Plus it'll take a month to get a new one customized." We're moving through downtown traffic, just a couple of delivery boys with a van full of furniture. He stops in front of City Hall and parks illegally. A U-Haul van with such vivid colors is bound to attract a swarm of traffic cops.

"I chatted with Miguel," he says.

"And how did that go?" I ask, my hand on the door handle.

"Okay. I just explained things, said you were getting squeezed by some tough guys and needed a little protection. He said he could take care of it, said it was the least he and the guys could do for you and all that happy crap. I emphasized that no one gets hurt, just a friendly hello to Tubby and Razor so they'd get the message."

"What do you think?"

"It'll probably work. Link's gang is pretty thin these days, for obvious reasons. Most of his muscle is gone. I doubt if his boys want to mix it up with a drug gang."

"We'll see. Back in thirty minutes," I say as I get out.

Woody canceled his trip to Washington and is waiting in his office with Moss. Both look as though they've had a bad weekend. It's Monday and my goal is to ruin the rest of their week. There are no handshakes, no forced pleasantries, not even the offer of coffee.

I jack up the tension with "Okay, boys, do we have a deal? Yes or no? I want an answer now, and if I get the wrong answer I'll leave this building and walk down the street to the *Chronicle*. Verdoliak, your favorite reporter, is waiting at his desk."

Woody stares at the floor and says, "Deal."

Moss slides across a document and says, "This is a confidential settlement agreement. The insurance company will pay the first million now. The City will kick in half a million this fiscal year, same for next. We have a litigation reserve fund we can manipulate, but we need to split the two payments between this year and next. It's the best we can do."

"That'll work," I say. "And when will the chief and the SWAT boys get the ax?"

"Tomorrow morning," Moss says. "And that's not in this agreement."

"Then I won't sign the agreement until they are terminated. Why wait? What is so difficult about getting rid of these guys? Hell, the whole city wants them canned."

"So do we," the mayor says. "Believe me, we want them out of the picture. Just trust us on this, Rudd."

I roll my eyes at the word "trust." I pick up the agreement and read it slowly. A phone buzzes on the mayor's imposing desk but he ignores it. When I finish reading, I drop it on the table and say, "Not one word of apology. My client's wife is murdered, he gets shot, then he gets dragged through a criminal trial, faces prison, goes through hell and back, and not one word of apology. No deal."

Woody utters a bitter "Shit!" and jumps to his feet. Moss rubs his eyes as if he might start crying. Seconds pass, then a full minute, with nothing said. Finally, I glare at the mayor and say, "Why can't you man up and do what's right? Why can't you call one of your press conferences, just like you do for every other minor crisis, and start with an apology to the Renfro family? Announce a settlement in the civil case. Explain that after a thorough investigation it's now clear that the SWAT team disregarded all rules of procedure and safety and that the eight cops are being terminated, immediately. And their boss goes with them."

"I don't really need your advice when it comes to doing my job," Woody says, but it's a lame response.

"Maybe you do," I say. I'm tempted to storm out again, but I don't want to lose the money.

"Okay, okay," Moss says. "We'll redraft it and throw in some language addressing the family."

"Thank you," I say. "I'll be back tomorrow, after the press conference."

15.

I meet Doug Renfro for lunch in a coffee shop near his home. I explain the settlement, and he is thrilled to be getting two million. My contracted fee is 25 percent, but I'll cut it to only 10 percent. He is surprised by this and, at first, wants to argue. I'd like to give him all the money, but I do have some overhead. After I split with Harry & Harry, I'll net around $120,000, which is low for the time I've spent on the case, but still a decent fee.

As he takes a sip of coffee, his hand starts shaking and his eyes suddenly water. He sets the cup down and pinches the bridge of his nose. "I just want Kitty," he says, lips quivering.

"I'm sorry, Doug," I say. What else?

"Why did they do it? Why? It was so senseless. Kicking in the doors, guns blazing like idiots, the wrong house. Why, Sebastian?"

All I can do is shake my head.

"I'm outta here, I'll tell you that right now. Gone. I hate this city and the clowns who run it, and I gotta tell you, Sebastian, with these eight cops now out of work and pissed off and looking for trouble, I don't feel safe. You shouldn't either, you know?"

"I know, Doug. Believe me, I think about it all the time. But then, I've pissed them off before. I'm not one of their favorites."

"You're a helluva lawyer, Sebastian. I had my doubts at first. The way you came on so strong while I was still in the hospital. I kept thinking, 'Who is this guy?' I had other lawyers try and hustle the case, you know? Some real clowns poking around the hospital. But I ran them off. Glad I did. You were great at trial, Sebastian. Magnificent."

"Okay, okay. Thanks, Doug, but that's enough."

"Fifteen percent, okay? I want you to take 15 percent. Please."

"If you insist."

"I do. My house sold yesterday, nice profit. We'll close in two weeks. I think I'm going to Spain."

"Last week it was New Zealand."

"It's a big world. I might go everywhere, live on a train for a year or so. See it all. Just wish Kitty could be with me. That girl loved to travel."

"We should get the money soon. I'll see you in a few days and divvy it up."

16.

I watch the press conference in my apartment. At some point in the last few hours, Mayor Woody has made the calculated decision that groveling might get him more votes than stonewalling. He stands behind a podium, and for the first time in recent history there is no one behind him. Not a soul. He's all alone: no city councilman hamming it up for the cameras; no wall of thick-necked uniformed officers; no grim-faced lawyer frowning as if in hemorrhoidal agony.

He explains to the small group of reporters that the City has settled its legal claims with the Renfro family. There will be no civil trial; the nightmare is over. Terms confidential, of course. His deepest apologies to the family for what happened. Mistakes were made, obviously (though none by him), and he has made the decision to act decisively and bring this tragedy to a close. The chief of police is fired, as of now. He is ultimately responsible for the actions of his officers. All eight members of the SWAT team are also terminated. Their actions cannot be tolerated. Procedures will be reviewed. And so on.

He wraps it up nicely with another apology, and at times looks and sounds as though he's ready to cry. Not a bad acting job for Woody and it might even win him some votes. But any fool can read the polls.

Gutsy move, Woody.

Now, as if my life is not already complicated enough, there are eight more ex-cops loose on the streets mumbling my name and looking for some type of revenge.

The money arrives soon enough and Doug and I do our business. The last time I see him he's getting into a taxi headed for the airport. He said he's still not sure where he's going, but he'll figure it out when he gets there. He said he might stare at the departure board and throw a dart.

I'm hit with a twinge of envy.

17.

Tadeo insists that I stop by the jail for a visit at least once a week, and I really don't mind. Most visits include a conversation relating to his upcoming trial and others that have nothing to do with anything but surviving in jail. There is no gym or place to exercise—he'll have those in prison but we don't talk about this—and he is frustrated in his efforts to stay in shape. He's doing a thousand sit-ups and push-ups each day and looks fit to me. The food is terrible and he says he's losing weight, which of course leads to a discussion about his preferred fighting weight once he gets out. The longer he stays in jail and the more free legal advice he gets from his cell mates back there, the more delusional he becomes. He's convinced he can charm a jury, blame it all on a quick bout of insanity, and walk. I explain, again, that the trial will be hard to win because the jury will see the video at least five times.

He's also begun to doubt my belief in him, and on two occasions he's mentioned the involvement of another lawyer. This won't happen because he'll have to pay a fat fee to someone else, but it's still irritating. He's beginning to act like a lot of criminal defendants, especially those from the street. He doesn't trust the system, including me because I'm white and part of the power structure. He's convinced he's innocent and wrongly locked up. He knows he can sway a jury if given the chance. And I, as his lawyer, need only to work a few tricks in the courtroom and, just like on television, he'll be a free man. I don't argue with him but I do try and keep things realistic.

After half an hour I say good-bye and am relieved to be away from him. As I work my way through the jail, Detective Reardon appears out of nowhere and almost bumps into me. "Say, Rudd, just the man I'm looking for."

I've never seen him at the jail before. This encounter is not accidental. "Oh, yeah, what's up?"

"Got a minute?" he says, pointing to a corner away from the other lawyers and jailers.

"Sure." I don't really want to spend time with Reardon, but he's here for a purpose. I'm sure he wants to drive home the point that our suspended assistant chief of police, Roy Kemp, continues to be deeply concerned about keeping the kidnapping just between us boys. When we're alone, he says, "Say, Rudd, I hear you got in a scrape with a couple of Link Scanlon's thugs in the courthouse last week. Witnesses say you poleaxed both of them, knocked 'em cold. Too bad you didn't put a bullet between their eyes. Wish I coulda seen it. Hard to believe you got the balls to slug it out with a couple of leg breakers."

"Your point?"

"I figure Link sent word to you that he wants something, probably money. We know about where he is; we just can't get to him. We think he's broke and so he sends a coupla goons to put the squeeze on you. For some reason you don't want to be squeezed. They push, you coldcock them in broad daylight outside a courtroom. I like it."

"Your point?"

"Do you know these two guys? I mean, their names?"

Something tells me to play dumb. "One is called Tubby, no last name. Don't know the other. Got time for a question?"

"Oh sure."

"You're Homicide. Why, exactly, are you concerned with Link and his thugs and me having some fun with them?"

"Because I'm Homicide." He whips open a file and shows me an eight-by-ten color photo of two dead bodies in some sort of trash heap. They're lying facedown, with their wrists tied tightly behind them. The backs of their necks are caked with dried blood. "Found these two stiffs in the city landfill, wrapped in an old piece of shag carpet. The bulldozer shoved it down a small embankment and Tubby and Razor rolled out. Tubby is Danny Fango, on the right there. Razor, on the left, is Arthur Robilio." He shuffles the deck and pulls out another eight-by-ten. The two bodies have been rearranged and are lying faceup, side by bloody side. The black boot of a cop is in the picture, next to the mangled head of good old Tubby. Their throats have been cut wide and deep.

Reardon says, "Each got two slugs back of the head. That plus a switchblade from ear to ear. Does it every time. So far, clean killings, no prints, ballistics, forensics. Probably a common gang thing, no big loss to society, know what I mean?"

My stomach flips as acid fills my throat. There is a strong urge to vomit, along with a light-headedness that could mean a quick faint. I turn away from the photos, shake my head in disgust, and tell myself to try, if humanly possible, to act unconcerned. I manage to shrug and say, "So what, Reardon? You think I rubbed these guys out because they jumped me in the courthouse?"

"I don't know what I'm thinking right now, but I got these two Boy Scouts on the slab and nobody knows nothing. As far as I know, you were the last person to get in a fight with them. You seem to enjoy operating down in the gutter. Maybe you got some friends down there. One thing leads to another."

"You can't even sell that to yourself, Reardon. Weak as water. Go accuse somebody else because you're wasting time with me. I don't kill. I just defend killers."

"Same thing if you ask me. I'll keep digging."

He leaves and I find a toilet. I lock the stall door, sit on the lid, and ask myself if it's possible.

18.

We park the U-Haul in a slot at a hot-dog drive-in and order sodas from a cutie on skates. Neither of us has an appetite. She brings the drinks and Partner rolls up the window, by hand, the old-fashioned way. He takes a long sip, and staring straight ahead says, "No way, Boss. I made myself real clear. Scare 'em but don't touch 'em. Nobody gets hurt."

"They're not in pain," I say.

"But, Boss, you gotta understand how things work in the gutter. Say Miguel and his boys track down Tubby and Razor and manage to create a confrontation. They make threats, but let's say Tubby and Razor are not bothered by threats. Hell, they've been making 'em for thirty years. They don't appreciate the intrusion and let it be known. Miguel has to stand his ground. Words get heated, more threats are made, and at some point things get outta hand. Takes just one punch to start a brawl and before long somebody pulls a gun or a knife."

"I want you to talk to Miguel."

"Why? He'll never admit it, Boss. Never."

I sip through the straw and force down the beverage. Everything seems to be locked up—from throat to bowels. After a long gap, I say, "We're assuming it's Miguel. It could be someone else. Tubby and Razor have spent a career breaking arms, maybe they pushed the wrong guy this time."

Partner nods and manages a weak "Could be."

19.

I'm awake at 3:37 a.m. when my cell phone begins vibrating. Slowly, I pick it up. Caller unknown, the worst kind. With great reluctance I say, "Hello."

I'd recognize the voice anywhere. "This Rudd?" he asks.

"It is. Who's calling?"

"Your old client Swanger, Arch Swanger."

"I was hoping I'd never hear from you again."

"I don't miss you either, but we gotta talk. Since you can't be trusted and don't hesitate to sacrifice your clients, I'm assuming your phone is tapped and the cops are listening."

"Nope."

"You're a liar, Rudd."

"Fine, hang up and don't call me back."

"Not that simple. We gotta talk. That girl is alive, Rudd, and bad things are going on."

"I don't care."

"There's an all-night pharmacy at the corner of Preston and Fifteenth. Buy some shaving cream. Behind a can of Gillette Menthol you'll find a small black phone, prepaid. Take it but don't get caught shoplifting. Call the number on the screen. It's me. I'll wait thirty minutes, then I'm leaving town. Got it, Rudd?"

"No, I'm not playing this time, Swanger."

"The girl is alive, Rudd, and you can bring her back. Just like you rescued your kid, now you can be the real hero. If not, she'll be dead in a year. It's all you, buddy."

"Why should I believe you, Swanger?"

"Because I know the truth. I may not always tell the truth, but I know what's going on with the Kemp girl. It ain't pretty. Come on, Rudd, play along. Don't call your thug and don't use that goofy U-Haul van. Seriously? What kind of lawyer are you?"

The line goes dead and I lie on my back and stare at the ceiling. If Arch Swanger is on the run, and I know for a fact that he is because he's number one on our cops' most wanted list, Link Scanlon being number two, then how in the world could he know that I'm buzzing around town these days in a rented van? And how could he purchase and hide a prepaid cell phone?

Twenty minutes later I park in front of the pharmacy and wait until two winos move away from the front door. This is a sketchy part of town and it's not clear why this company, a national chain, would select this neighborhood for an all-night drugstore. I walk inside and see no one except for the clerk, who's flipping through a tabloid. I find the shaving cream and the phone, which I quickly stick into a pocket. I pay for the shaving cream, and as I drive away I punch in the number.

Swanger answers with "Just keep driving. Hit the interstate and go north."

"To where, Swanger?"

"To me. I want to look you in the eyes and ask you why you told the cops where I buried the girl."

"Maybe I don't want to talk about it."

"You will."

"Why did you lie, Swanger?"

"It was just a test to see if you can be trusted. Obviously you cannot. I want to know why."

"And I want to know why you can't leave me alone."

"Because I need a lawyer, Rudd, plain and simple. What am I supposed to do? Take the elevator up to the fortieth floor and confide in a guy in a black suit who charges a thousand bucks an hour? Or maybe call one of those bozos you see on the billboards begging for bankruptcies and car wrecks? I need a real guy from the streets, Rudd, a real slimeball who knows how to play dirty. Right now you're the man."

"No I'm not."

"Take the White Bluff exit off the interstate and go east for two miles. There's an all-night burger joint currently advertising a double-patty melt with real Velveeta cheese. Yum-yum. I'll watch you go in and take a seat. I'll make sure you're alone and nobody's following you. When I walk in you won't recognize me at first."

"I'll be packing some heat, Swanger, permit and all, and I know how to use it. Nothing funny, okay?"

"No need for that, I swear."

"Swear all you want to, but I don't believe a word you say."

"Makes two of us."

20.

There is a lack of ventilation and the air is thick with the smell of greasy burgers and fries. I buy a coffee and sit at a table in the center for ten minutes as two drunk teenagers in a booth giggle and talk with their mouths full. In a far corner an obese, elderly couple gorge themselves as if they'll never see food again. Part of this joint's marketing brilliance is that the entire menu is half price from midnight to 6:00 a.m. That and the Velveeta.

A man in a brown UPS uniform enters and does not look around. He buys a soft drink and some fries and is suddenly seated across from me. Behind round frameless glasses I finally recognize Swanger's eyes. "Glad you could make it," he says, barely audible.

"A real pleasure," I say. "Cute uniform."

"It works. Here's what's happening, Rudd. Jiliana Kemp is very much alive but I'm sure she wishes she were dead. She had her baby a few months back. They sold it for fifty thousand bucks, on the high end. The range, I'm told, is twenty-five to fifty, for a little Caucasian thing from good stock. The darker ones go cheaper."

"Who is they?"

"We'll get to it in a minute. Right now she's working long hours as a stripper and hooker in a sex club a thousand miles away. She's basically a slave, owned by some nasty types who've got her hooked on heroin. That's why she can't leave and that's why she'll do whatever she's told. Don't suppose you've ever dealt with human trafficking?"

"No."

"Don't ask how I got involved. A long sad story."

"I really don't care, Swanger. I'd like to help the girl but I'm not sticking my nose into it. You said you needed a lawyer."

He picks up a single fry and examines it as if looking for poison, then slowly puts it into his mouth. He glares at me from behind the fake lenses, and finally says, "She'll work the clubs for a bit, then they'll decide to breed her again. They pass her around, you know, and when she gets pregnant they'll get her off the drugs and lock her away. The baby's gotta be healthy, you know. She's one of eight or ten girls on their payroll, mostly white but a few brown ones, all from this country."

"All abducted?"

"Of course. You don't think they volunteered?"

"I don't know what to think." I hope he's lying but something tells me he's not. Either way, the story is so repulsive I can only shake my head. I can't help but see the images of Roy Kemp and his wife on the news pleading for a safe return of their daughter.

"Real tragic," I say. "But I'm losing patience here, Swanger. First, I can't believe anything you say. Second, you said you needed a lawyer."

"Why did you tell the cops where she was buried?"

"Because they kidnapped my son and forced me to cough up what you'd told me."

He likes this story and can't hold back a smile. "Really? The cops kidnapped your son?"

"They did. I caved, told them, they raced out to the site, wasted an entire night digging, and when it became apparent you were lying, they released my kid."

He crams three fries into his mouth and chomps like he's working an entire pack of bubble gum. "I was in the woods, watching, laughing my ass off at those clowns. I was also cussing you for telling my secret."

"You're a sicko, Swanger. Why am I here?"

"Because I need money, Rudd. It ain't easy living on the run like this. You wouldn't believe some of the shit I have to do to generate cash and I'm sick of it. There's about 150 grand in reward money sitting in a pot somewhere in the police department. I figure if I can get the girl back to her family, then I should get some of the money."

I don't know why I'm shocked by this. Nothing this idiot says should surprise me. I take a deep breath and say, "Allow me to make some sense of this. You kidnapped the girl a year ago. The good people of our city donated their cash for a reward fund. Now you, the kidnapper, would like to return the girl, and for this act of great humanity you think you should get some of the reward money, the same money now being held to solve the crime you committed. Right, Swanger?"

"I got no problem with that. It works on all fronts. They get the girl; I get the cash."

"More of a ransom deal, I think."

"Call it what you like. I don't care. I just gotta have some cash, Rudd, and I figure a lawyer like you can make it happen."

I jump to my feet and say, "What you need is a bullet, Swanger."

"Where you going?"

"Home. And if you call me again I'll call the cops."

"I'm sure you will."

Our volume has increased and the drunk teenagers are staring at us. I walk away and manage to get outside before he catches me and grabs my shoulder. "You think I'm lying about the girl, don't you, Rudd?"

I quickly grab the Glock 19 from the holster under my left armpit and grip it with my right hand. I back away as he freezes, staring at the pistol. I say, "I don't know if you're lying and I don't care. You're a sick puppy, Swanger, and I'm sure you'll die an awful death. Now leave me alone."

He relaxes and smiles. "You ever hear of a town called Lamont, Missouri? No reason to, really. Podunk place of a thousand people, an hour north of Columbia. Three nights ago a twenty-year-old girl, first name of Heather, disappeared. The whole town's in a panic, everybody's in on the search, stomping through the woods and looking under bushes. No sign whatsoever. She's all right, I mean at least she's alive. She's living in the same warehouse with Jiliana Kemp, west-central Chicago, getting the same abuse. Check it out online, Rudd, the Columbia paper ran a small story this morning. Just another girl, this one five hundred miles away, but these guys are hard-core traffickers."

I grip the pistol even tighter and resist the urge to raise it shoulder high and put a couple into his skull.

PART SIX

THE PLEA

1.

Jury selection in the trial of Tadeo Zapate begins on Monday. It will be a circus because the press is giddy with anticipation and the courthouse is buzzing. The YouTube video of Tadeo laying waste to the referee Sean King has over sixty million hits. Our fearless *Action News!* heroes show it repeatedly during the evening and morning broadcasts. Same video, same drivel, same grim shaking of heads as if it just can't be believed. It seems as though everyone has an opinion and few of them favor my client. On three occasions I have asked the court for a change of venue, and all three requests have been quickly rejected. Two hundred prospective jurors have been summoned for Monday, and it will be fascinating to see how many claim to have no knowledge of the case.

Right now, though, it's Friday, around midnight, and I'm lying naked under the sheets with Ms. Naomi Tarrant close by. She is sleeping, purring in long deep breaths, dead to the world. Our second session began around ten, after pizza and beer, and though it lasted for less than half an hour it was nonetheless thrilling and utterly exhausting. We both admit that we've been a bit on the inactive side, and we're having a grand time catching up. I have no idea where this nascent relationship might be headed, and I'm always overcautious—a result no doubt of the permanent damage inflicted by Judith—but as of right now I adore this girl and would like to see her as often as possible, naked or otherwise.

I wish I could sleep like that. She's in a coma and I'm lying here wide awake, not aroused—that would be normal—but thinking of so many things other than sex. The trial Monday; Swanger and his tale about the Kemp girl; the bloody bodies of Tubby and Razor, rolled up in old cheap carpet and dumped in the landfill, probably by Miguel Zapate and his gang of drug dealers. I think of Detective Reardon and almost shudder at the idea that he and others in the police department suspect, either slightly or strongly, that I had something to do with the murders of Link's thugs. I wonder if Link has decided to leave me alone, now that I can snap my fingers and get people whacked.

So many thoughts, so many problems. I'm tempted to ease out of bed and go find some booze, then I remember that Naomi doesn't keep the stuff in her apartment. She's a light drinker and a healthy eater, and she does yoga four days a week to keep things superbly toned. I don't want to wake her, so I lie still and stare at her back, at the smooth perfect skin that rises and falls over her shoulder blades and lifts again to form the cutest bottom I've ever seen. She's thirty-three years old, recently divorced from a creep she wasted seven years with, childless and seemingly unconcerned by it. She doesn't talk much about her past but I know she has suffered greatly. Her first love was her college boyfriend who was killed by a drunk driver a month before their wedding date. With moist eyes, she told me she could never love another man that much.

I'm not really looking for love.

I cannot shake the thoughts of Jiliana Kemp. She is or was a beautiful girl, like my companion here, and there is a good chance that she is alive and living a life that is indescribable. Arch Swanger is a psychopath, and probably a sociopath, and he would rather lie than tell the truth about anything. But he wasn't lying about young Heather Farris, late of the village of Lamont, Missouri, a twenty-year-old dropout who was working the graveyard shift at a convenience store when she vanished with no clues. They're still combing the woods and bringing in bloodhounds and offering rewards but nothing has worked so far. How did Swanger know about her? It's possible he caught an early news report, but that's not likely. I went online immediately, found her story, and began following it in the Columbia newspaper. Lamont is over five hundred miles away from here, and, sadly, she's just another missing girl from a small town. Heather has not made the national news.

What if Swanger is telling the truth? That Jiliana Kemp and Heather Farris are two girls out of a dozen who've been kidnapped by a sex-trafficking ring and forced to strip, screw, and breed while they live on heroin? The fact that I know this, or at least suspect it, makes me feel like an accomplice. I am not Swanger's lawyer and I made that very clear. Indeed, I felt a real rush of adrenaline when I gripped my Glock and thought about putting him out of his misery. There are no ethical constraints binding me to silence and confidentiality with this scumbag. And even if there were, I would be inclined to ignore them if doing so might save some girls.

I stopped worrying about ethics a long time ago. In my world, my enemies are ruthless. If I make nice, I get crushed.

It is now 1:00 a.m. and I'm even wider awake. Naomi rolls over and flings a leg in my direction. I gently stroke her thigh—how can flesh be so smooth—and she whimpers as if somewhere in her deep sleep she likes the touching. I manage to get still and close my eyes.

My last thought is of Jiliana Kemp, living in our generation's version of slavery.

2.

Partner and I spend most of Saturday in the basement of the law offices of Harry & Harry, poring over juror questionnaires and ponderous reports put together by Cliff, a jury consultant, who, so far, has billed me $30,000. The tally for Tadeo's defense is just under $70,000, all from my pocket of course, and it will continue to climb. He and I have not discussed the payment of fees because it's a waste of time. He's broke, and Miguel and the rest of the drug gang have little interest in my compensation. They figure I made enough money from Tadeo's brief career. I assume they also think that in the rules of the streets the removal of Tubby and Razor is worth a bundle. Tit for tat. We're all even.

Cliff is of the opinion that the defense of Tadeo Zapate has quite a mountain to climb. He and his firm have done their usual work of (1) polling a thousand registered voters in this metropolitan area and asking hypothetical questions; (2) hurriedly researching the backgrounds of all two hundred prospective jurors; and (3) reviewing every news report that mentions the ugly incident in which Sean King was beaten. From the poll, an astonishing 31 percent of those questioned know a little or a lot about the case, and the vast majority of these favor conviction. Eighteen percent have seen the video. In the garden-variety murder case, regardless of how sensational, finding 10 percent who are aware of it is unusual.

Unlike most consultants, Cliff is known for his bluntness. That's why I use him. His bottom line: "Chances of an acquittal are slim. Chances of a conviction are high. Cut a deal; negotiate a plea bargain. Run for the hills."

When I first read his report, I called him immediately and said, "Come on, Cliff, I'm paying you all this money and your best advice is to run for the hills?"

He's a real smart-ass and his reply was "No, actually, I'd sprint for the hills. Your client is toast and the jury will throw the book at him."

Cliff will be in the courtroom Monday watching and taking notes. As much as I love the cameras and the attention, I'm not looking forward to it.

3.

At 4:00 p.m., Partner and I climb into my sparkling-new customized Ford cargo van, complete with all the usual finery I need for such a splendid mobile office, and head for the university. At Partner's suggestion, I agreed to tone it down, to move away from conspicuous black to more of a soft bronze exterior color. Painted on both sides, in small block letters, are the words "Smith Contractors," another nice touch Partner really wanted. He's convinced that we will now blend in with the world and be harder to spot by the police, Link, my own clients, and all the other bad guys, real and potential, lurking out there.

He drops me off in front of the university's aquatic center and leaves in search of a suitable parking place. I drift inside, hear the echoing voices, find the pool, and send a text message to Moss Korgan. Swarms of small, skinny kids are heavily involved in a swim meet. The bleachers are half-packed with noisy parents. A breaststroke race is under way and little girls splash and kick in all eight lanes of the fifty-meter pool.

Moss replies, "Right side, third section, top row."

I look and see no one, but I'm sure he's watching. I'm wearing a leather jacket with my long hair under the collar, along with jeans and a blue-and-orange Mets cap. This is really not my crowd and I don't expect to be recognized, but I rarely take chances. Just last week Partner and I were having a sandwich in a café when a jerk walked over and informed me that, in his opinion, my little cage fighter should rot in jail for the rest of his life. I thanked him and asked him to please leave us alone. He called me a crook. Partner stood and the guy got lost.

As I climb the steps I get a nose full of the smell of chlorine. Starcher once mentioned swimming, but one of his mothers told him the sport was too dangerous because of all the chemicals they put in the water. I'm surprised they don't keep the kid in a bubble.

I sit alone for a moment, far away from anyone else, and watch the action in the pool. The parents yell and the noise gets louder and louder until it suddenly stops and the race is over. The kids pull themselves out of the water as their mothers wait with towels and advice. From here, they appear to be about ten years old.

Moss rises from a group of parents across the pool and slowly walks around it. He climbs the bleachers in front of me and eventually takes a seat, about three feet away. His body language says it all—he hates where he is and would rather be talking to a serial killer. "This better be good, Rudd," he says without looking at me.

"And hello to you too, Moss. Which one is your kid?" Stupid question; there are about a thousand of them down there crawling around the pool.

"That one," he says with a slight nod. What a smart-ass, but then I asked for it. "She's a twelve-year-old freestyler. Won't get wet for another thirty minutes. Can we get on with this?"

"I have another deal for you, and it's even more complicated than the last one."

"That's what you said. I almost hung up, Rudd, until you mentioned the Kemp girl. Let's have it."

"Swanger tracked me down again. We met. He claims to know where she is, that she went full term with the pregnancy, the baby got sold by some traffickers who feed her heroin in exchange for all manner of sexual activities."

"Swanger is a proven liar."

"He certainly is but some of what he says is true."

"Why did he contact you?"

"He says he needs help and, not surprisingly, he needs money. There's a chance he'll contact me again, and if he does I can possibly put the police on his trail. That trail might lead to Jiliana Kemp, or not. There's no way to know, but right now the police have nothing else."

"So you're sacrificing your client again."

"He's not my client. I made that clear to him. He may think of me as his lawyer, but it's a waste of time to analyze what Arch Swanger might be thinking."

A loud buzzer goes off and eight boys plunge into the water. Instantly, the parents start yelling, as if the kids can hear them. Other than "Swim faster!" what can you scream at a splashing kid in the heat of a race? We watch them until they make the turn. Moss says, "And what do you want from us?"

"I go to trial Monday with my cage fighter. I want a better deal. I want a five-year plea bargain with a guarantee that he serves his time in the county penal farm. It's a softer place. There's a nice gym. The kid can stay in shape, serve about eighteen months, get paroled when he's, say, twenty-four, and still have a future in the ring. Otherwise, he'll serve fifteen and come out a hardened street thug with only one thing on his mind—more crime."

He's already rolling his eyes. He exhales in disbelief, as if everything I've just said is a complete joke. He shakes his head; I must be an idiot.

Finally, with great effort, he manages to say, "We have no control over the prosecutor. You know that."

"Mancini was appointed by the mayor and confirmed by the city council, same as you. Our interim police chief was appointed by the mayor and confirmed by the city council. Same for Roy

Kemp, who's still on leave. Can't we find a way to work together here?"

"Mancini won't listen to Woody. He hates him."

"Everybody hates Woody, and he hates everybody right back. Somehow he's survived three terms. Here's how you sell it to Woody. Are you listening?"

He has yet to look at me, but now he turns and glares. He looks back at the pool and crosses his arms over his chest, my signal to spill it.

"Okay, play along, Moss, help me walk through this. Let's assume I can lead the cops to Swanger, assume further that Swanger can lead the cops to Jiliana Kemp. Somewhere in west-central Chicago, by the way. Assume they rescue the girl, and guess what? Our beloved mayor, the Honorable L. Woodrow Sullivan III, gets to hold the first press conference. Imagine that scene, Moss. You know how Woody loves a press conference. It will be his finest moment. Woody in a dark suit, all smiles, a row of cops behind him, all grim-faced but happy because the girl has been saved. Woody makes the announcement as if he personally found her and pulled off the miracle. An hour later we get our first glimpse of the happy Kemp family reunited, with Woody, of course, wedging himself into the photo as only he can do. What a moment!"

Moss softens a bit as he absorbs this visual. It rattles around his brain. He wants to dismiss it and tell me to go to hell, but it's simply too rich. Creativity fails him, as usual, so he simply says, "You're crazy, Rudd."

No surprise. I press on with "Since we're grasping for the truth here, and making bold assumptions, let's say that Swanger is not lying. If so, Jiliana is one of many girls snatched from their families and sold into bondage. Almost all are white American girls. If their ring is busted and the traffickers are caught, then the story echoes from coast to coast. Woody gets more than his share of the credit; certainly enough to shine in this town."

"Mancini will never go along."

"Then fire Mancini. On the spot. Call him on the carpet and force his resignation. The mayor has that power under our version of democracy. Replace him with one of those little ass-kissing bureaucrats. There are only a hundred of them."

"I think there are fifteen," he says.

"Sorry. So out of fifteen assistant city prosecutors, I'm sure you and Woody can find one with a bit of ambition, one who'll do what you tell him or her to do in exchange for the big office. Come on, Moss, this is not that complicated."

He leans forward, deep in thought, elbows on knees. The noise fades. The crowd goes quiet as one race ends and the next one starts to get organized. Thankfully, I've never been to a swim meet, but it appears as if this ordeal goes on for hours. I thank Starcher's mothers and their fear of chlorine.

He needs some help, so I prod on. "Woody has the power, Moss. He can make this happen."

"Why does it have to be a deal? Why can't you just do the right thing and cooperate with the police? If you believe Swanger, and if he's really not your client, then help out the cops here. Hell, you're talking about an innocent young woman."

"Because I don't work that way," I say, though I've lost sleep trying to answer his question. "I have a client to represent, one who's guilty, as most are, and I'm desperate for ways to help him. I don't get clients who have the potential to make a lot of money, legally, but this kid is different. He could lift himself and his rather large and growing family out of the ghetto."

"A ghetto here is better than where they came from," he blurts, and immediately wishes he hadn't said it.

Wisely, and uncharacteristically, I let it pass.

We watch a group of taller boys limber up and stretch nervously at the start. I say, "There's something else."

"Oh, a multipart deal. What a surprise."

"About a month ago, the cops found a couple of bodies at the landfill. Two thugs who worked for Link Scanlon. For some reason, I'm a suspect. Don't know how serious things are, but I'd rather not deal with it."

"I thought Link was your client."

"He was, but let's say that when he vanished he was less than pleased with my services. He sent the two thugs to squeeze some money out of me."

"Who whacked them?"

"I don't know but it wasn't me. Seriously, you think I'd run the risk?"

"Probably."

I snort a cheap laugh. "No way. These guys are career goons with lots of enemies. Whoever whacked them comes from a long list of folks who wanted to."

"So, let me get this straight. First, you want the mayor to force Mancini to lighten up on your cage fighter so he can plead to a sweet deal and protect his career. Second, you want the mayor to lean on the police department to look elsewhere for whoever rubbed out Link's boys. And, third, what was third?"

"The best part. Swanger."

"Oh right. And in return for the mayor putting his neck on the block, you might be able to help the police find Swanger, who just might be telling the truth and who just might be able to lead them to the girl. That right, Rudd?"

"That covers it."

"What a crock of shit."

I watch him as he walks down the aisle in the bleachers and

circles around the far end of the pool. On the other side, he walks up four rows and returns to his seat beside his wife. From far away, I stare at him for a long time, and he never casts even the slightest glance in my direction.

4.

C, for Catfish Cave. It's a few miles east of town in a dingy suburb, a bedroom community of tract houses built sixty years ago with materials designed to last fifty years. The restaurant offers bargain buffets of fish and vegetables, all now battered and fried to hell and back but previously frozen for months, even years. For only ten bucks, the customers can graze and gorge for hours without limits. They heap their platters as if they're starving, and wash it all down with gallons of sugary tea. For some reason alcohol is served but people do not come here for the booze. Tucked away in a dark, neglected corner is an empty bar, and it is here that I occasionally meet Nate Spurio.

The last time we met it was B for a bagel shop. The time before it was A, for an Arby's roast beef joint in another suburb. Nate's career hit a dead end a decade ago. He can't be fired, and, evidently, he can't be promoted. But if by some chance he was spotted having an off-duty drink with me, he would find himself directing traffic in front of an elementary school. He's too honest for police work in this town.

His boss is a Captain Truitt, a decent guy who's very close to Roy Kemp. If I want to deliver a message to Kemp, the path begins here over a couple of drinks. I lay it all on the table. Nate is surprised that I hold even the faintest hope that Jiliana Kemp is still alive. I assure him that I don't know what to believe and believing anything Swanger says is probably a mistake. But, what is there to lose? He certainly knows something, which is a lot more than our investigators can say. The more we talk and drink, the more Nate is convinced that the police department and its union can pressure both the mayor and Max Mancini. Our former chief of police was an idiot who allowed our force to become what it is, but Roy Kemp is still held in high regard by his brothers. Saving his daughter is worth a reduced plea bargain for every defendant now sitting in jail.

I repeatedly caution Nate that finding her is against the odds. First, I'm not sure I can find Swanger, or that he'll want to see me again. The last time we met I almost shot him. I have the prepaid cell phone but haven't used it since our last meeting. If it doesn't work, or if he doesn't answer it, then we're out of luck. And if I meet him and the police are able to follow him, what are the odds that he'll lead them to the strip club in west-central Chicago? Pretty slim, I think.

Nate has the emotional range of a monk but he can't hide his excitement. When we leave the bar he says he's headed to Truitt's house. There, they'll talk off the record, and he expects Truitt to immediately inform Roy Kemp that a possible deal is brewing. It's a long shot, but when it's your daughter you'll try anything. I urge him to hustle up; the trial starts tomorrow.

5.

Late Sunday night, Partner and I go to the city jail for the last pretrial meeting with our client. After half an hour of sniping with the jailers, I'm finally allowed to see Tadeo.

The kid frightens me. During his time in jail, he has absorbed a lot of free advice from his new pals, and he's also convinced himself that he's famous. Because of the video, he gets a lot of mail, almost all of it from admirers. He thinks he's about to walk away from the trial a free man, beloved by many and ready to continue his brilliant career. I've tried to bring him back to reality and convince him that the people writing him letters are not necessarily the same type of people who'll be sitting in the jury box. The letter writers are from the fringe; several have even proposed marriage. The jurors will be registered voters from our community, few of whom have any fondness for cage fighting.

As always, I pass along the latest plea offer of fifteen years for second-degree murder. He laughs with a cocky smirk, same as before. He doesn't ask for my advice and I don't offer it. He's turned down fifteen years so many times it's not worth discussing. Wisely, he has followed my advice and shaved and trimmed his hair. I've brought along a secondhand navy suit, with a white shirt and tie, an outfit his mother found at Goodwill. On his neck below his left ear is a tattoo of some baffling origin, and it will be partially visible above his collar. Since most of my clients have tattoos I deal with this issue all the time. It's best to keep them away from the jurors. In Tadeo's case, though, our jurors will be treated to his astonishing display of ink when they see the video.

Evidently, when a guy makes the decision to become a cage fighter, his first stop on the way to the gym is the tattoo parlor.

There's a gap between us that's been growing for some time. He thinks he'll walk. I think he'll go to prison. He sees my doubts of a successful outcome as not only a lack of confidence in him but also in my own ability in the courtroom. What's really bothersome is his insistence on testifying. He truly believes he can take the stand and con the jury into believing (1) the fight was stolen from him by Sean King, and (2) he snapped, attacked, blacked out, and went temporarily insane, and (3) now feels real bad about it. After he explains everything to the jury, he wants to make a dramatic, emotional apology to the King family. Then all will be well and the jury will rush back with the proper verdict.

I have attempted to describe the rough treatment he'll get when

I turn him over to Max Mancini for a bit of cross-examination. But, as usual, he has no appreciation for what happens in the heat of a trial. Hell, I'm not always sure what's about to happen.

None of my warnings register with Tadeo. He tasted enough glory in the cage to know what's out there. Money, fame, adulation, women, a big house for his mother and family. It will all be his soon enough.

6.

It's impossible to sleep the night before a jury trial opens. My brain is in a state of hyped-up overdrive as I struggle to remember and organize details, facts, things to do. My stomach roils with anxiety and my nerves are frayed and popping. I know it's important to rest and appear fresh and relaxed before the jury, but the truth is I'll look the same as always—tired, stressed, eyes bloodshot. I sip coffee just before dawn and, as usual, ask myself why I do this. Why do I subject myself to such unpleasantness? I have a distant cousin who's a great neurosurgeon in Boston, and I often think about him at moments like this. I suppose his world is quite tense as he cuts into the brain, with so much at stake. How does he handle it physically? The nerves, the butterflies, yes even diarrhea and nausea? We rarely speak, so I've never inquired. I remind myself that he does his job without an audience, and if he makes a mistake he simply buries it. I try not to remind myself that he makes a million bucks a year.

In many ways, a trial lawyer is like an actor onstage. His lines are not always scripted, and that makes his job harder. He has to react, to be quick on his feet and with his tongue, to know when to attack and when to shut up, when to lead and when to follow, when to flash anger and when to be cool. Through it all, he has to convince and persuade because nothing matters but the jury's final vote.

I eventually forget about sleep and go to the pool table. I rack the balls and break them gently. I run the table and drop the 8 ball into a side pocket.

I have a collection of brown suits and I carefully select one for opening day. I wear brown not because I like the color but because no one else does. Lawyers, as well as bankers and executives and politicians, all believe that dress suits should be either navy or dark gray. Shirts are either white or light blue; ties, some variety of red. I never wear those colors. Instead of black shoes, today I'll wear ostrich-skin cowboy boots. They don't really match my brown suit but who cares? With my ensemble laid out on the bed, I take a long shower. In my bathrobe, I pace around the den, delivering at low volume another version of my opening statement. I break another rack, miss the first three shots, and lay down my cue stick.

7.

The courtroom is packed by 9:00 a.m., the appointed hour for all two hundred potential jurors to show up and get processed. And, since capacity is only two hundred, there is gridlock when a horde of spectators and a few dozen reporters also show up and jockey for position.

Max Mancini struts about in his finest navy suit and sparkling black wingtips, flashing smiles at the clerks and assistants. With all these people watching, he's even nice to me. We huddle and chat importantly as the bailiffs deal with the throng.

"Still fifteen years?" I ask.

"You got it," he says, smiling and looking at the audience. Obviously, between Moss and Spurio, the word has not yet made

its way to Max's ears. Or maybe it has. Maybe Max was told to
cut a deal and get a plea, and maybe Max did what I would expect
him to do: told Woody and Moss and Kemp and everybody else to
go to hell. This is his show, a big moment in his career. Just look
at all those folks out there admiring him. And all those reporters!

Presiding this week is the Honorable Janet Fabineau, quietly
known among the lawyers as Go Slow Fabineau. She's a young
judge, still a bit on the green side, but maturing nicely on the
bench. She's afraid to make mistakes, so she's very deliberate. And
slow. She talks slow, thinks slow, rules slow, and she insists that the
lawyers and witnesses speak clearly at all times. She pretends this
is for the benefit of the court reporter who must take down every
word, but we suspect it's really because Her Honor also absorbs
things . . . real slow.

Her clerk appears and says the judge wants to see the lawyers
in chambers. We file in and take seats around an old worktable,
me on one side, Mancini and his flunky on the other. Janet sits at
one end, eating slices of apple from a plastic bowl. They say she's
always fussing over her latest diet and her latest trainer, but I've
noticed no progress on the reduction front. Mercifully, she does
not offer us any of her food.

"Any more pretrial motions?" she asks as she looks at me.
Chomp, chomp.

Mancini shakes his head no. I do the same and add, for reasons
that are solely antagonistic, "Wouldn't do any good." I've filed
dozens and they've all been overruled.

She absorbs this cheap shot, swallows hard, takes a sip of what
looks like early morning urine, and says, "Any chance of a plea
bargain?"

Mancini says, "We're still offering fifteen years on a second
degree."

I say, "And my client still says no. Sorry."

"Not a bad offer," she says, slinging a cheap shot back at me. "What would the defendant take?"

"I don't know, Your Honor. At this point, I'm not sure he's willing to plead guilty to anything. Things might change after a day or two of trial, but right now he's looking forward to his day in court."

"Very well. We can certainly accommodate him."

We talk about this and that and kill time while the bailiffs process the jurors and get things organized. Finally, at 10:30, the clerk says the courtroom is ready. The lawyers leave and take their places. I sit next to Tadeo, who looks a bit awkward all dressed up. We whisper and I assure him things are going swell, just as I expected, so far anyway. Behind us, the prospective jurors stare at the back of his head and wonder what awful crime he has committed.

When instructed, we all rise in deference to the court, as Judge Fabineau enters, her bulky figure nicely camouflaged by the long black robe. Because so much of their dreary work is done without an audience, judges love crowded courtrooms. They are the supreme rulers over everything in sight and they like to be appreciated. Some tend to grandstand, and I'm curious to see how Janet conducts herself with so many watching. She welcomes everyone to the proceedings, explains why we're all here, rambles on a bit too long, and finally asks Tadeo to stand and face the crowd. He does so, smiles as I instructed him to do, then sits down. Janet introduces Mancini and me. I simply stand and nod. He stands and grins and sort of opens his arms as if welcoming the people into his domain. His phoniness is hard to stomach.

The jurors have now been numbered and Fabineau asks those holding 101 through 198 to leave the courtroom and take a break. Call the clerk at 1:00 p.m. and see if you're needed. Half of them file out, some in a hurry, some actually smiling at their luck. On one side of the courtroom, the bailiffs place the remaining prospects in rows of ten, and we get our first look at the likely jurors. This drags on for an hour and Tadeo whispers that he's bored. I ask him if he prefers staying in jail. No, he does not.

The pool is purged of those over the age of sixty-five and those with doctors' excuses. The ninety-two we are now staring at are ready to be examined. Fabineau breaks for lunch and we're told to be back at 2:00 p.m. Tadeo asks if there's any chance of a proper lunch in a nice restaurant. I smile and say no. He's headed back to the jail.

As I huddle with Cliff, the jury consultant, a uniformed bailiff approaches and asks, "Are you Mr. Rudd?"

I nod and he hands me some papers. Domestic Relations Court. A summons for an emergency hearing to terminate all parental rights. I curse under my breath, walk to the jury box, and take a seat. That bitch Judith has waited until this moment to further complicate matters. I read on and my shoulders begin to sag. Yesterday, Sunday, was my day to spend with Starcher; twelve hours, from 8:00 a.m. to 8:00 p.m., a modified, verbal agreement between Judith and me. Being preoccupied with the trial, I of course forgot about this and stiffed my kid. In Judith's twisted way of thinking, this is clear proof that I'm an unfit father and should be completely banished from my son's life. She demands an emergency hearing as if Starcher is in imminent danger, and if one is granted it will be the fourth in the past three years. She's 0 for 3! And she's perfectly willing to go 0 for 4 to prove something. What, I don't know.

I buy a once-frozen Fresh! Sandwich out of a machine and stroll down to Domestic Relations. Machine food is often underrated. Carla, a deputy clerk I once hit on, pulls the file and we look it over, our heads just inches apart. When I hit on her about two years ago she was "in a relationship," whatever the hell that means. What it really meant was that she had no interest in me. I took it in stride. I've had my balls busted so many times I'm surprised when a woman says, "Maybe." Anyway, Carla must be out of her relationship because she's all smiles and come-ons, which is not that unusual among the army of deputy clerks and secretaries and receptionists who clog these offices and hallways. A single straight male lawyer with a little cash and a nice suit gets plenty of looks from the unmarried ladies, and from some of the married ones as well. If I played the game, had the time and interest, I could run these gals into the ground. Carla, though, has chubbed up considerably in recent months and is not looking nearly as good as before.

She says, "Judge Stanley Leef."

"Same one as last time," I reply. "I'm surprised he's still alive."

"Looks like your ex is a tough one."

"That's a huge understatement."

"She's in here from time to time. Not very friendly."

I thank her, and as I'm leaving she says, "Call me sometime."

I want to say, "Well, if you'll hit the gym for about six months, then I'll take a look and consider it." Instead, and because I'm such a gentleman, I say, "Sure."

Judge Stanley Leef stiff-armed Judith in her last effort to strip me of parental rights. He had no patience with her and ruled on the spot in my favor. The fact that she rolled the dice with this latest filing and got stuck with Leef again says a lot about her integrity, and her naïveté. In my world, if the case is critical—and what could be more drastic than cutting off a respectable father's right to see his child—all measures must be taken to insure a fair hearing before the proper judge. This might require the filing of a motion to ask an unwanted judge to step aside. It might require a complaint with the State Board of Judicial Ethics. My preferred method, though, is simply a cash bribe to the right clerk.

Judith would never consider any of these tactics. Thus, she's stuck with Leef again. I remind myself that this is not about winning or losing, not about this judge or that one. It's nothing but abuse of the court system to harass a former spouse. She has no worries about legal fees. She has no fears of retribution. She roams this section of the Old Courthouse every day, so this is her turf.

I find a bench and read her petition as I finish my sandwich.

8.

For the afternoon session, we move our chairs to the other side of our tables and stare directly at the jurors. And they stare at us as if we're aliens. Under Fabineau's selection scheme—and every trial judge is given great leeway in devising methods to pick juries—those with numbers one through forty are seated in the first four rows, and from there we'll likely find our final twelve. So, we zero in on them as Her Honor rambles on about the civic importance of jury service.

Of the first forty, there are twenty-five whites, eight blacks, five Hispanics, one young lady from Vietnam, and another one from India. Twenty-two females, eighteen males. Thanks to Cliff and his team, I know their names, addresses, vocations, marital situations, church memberships, and histories of litigation, unpaid debts, and criminal convictions, if any. For most of them, I have photographs of their homes or apartments.

Picking the right ones will be tricky. Carved in stone is the belief that you want all the black jurors you can get in a criminal trial, because blacks have more sympathy for the accused and a greater distrust of the police and prosecutors. Not so today. The victim, Sean King, was a nice young black man with a good job, a wife, and three clean-cut kids. For a few bucks on the side, he refereed boxing matches and cage fights.

When Fabineau finally gets around to the matters at hand, she asks how many in the pool are familiar with the facts surrounding the death of Sean King. Out of the ninety-two, about a quarter of the hands go up, an enormous percentage. She asks them all to stand so we can jot down their names. I glance at Mancini and shake my head. Such a response is unheard of and, in my opinion, clear proof that the trial should be moved. But Mancini just keeps smiling. I write down twenty-two names.

To prevent further contamination, Judge Fabineau decides to take each of the twenty-two and quiz them individually. We return to her chambers and gather around the same table. Juror number three is brought in. Her name is Liza Parnell and she sells tickets for a regional airline. Married, two kids, age thirty-four, husband sells cement. Mancini and I are all charm as we attempt to curry favor with this potential juror. Her Honor takes charge and starts questioning. Neither Liza nor her husband is an MMA fan, in fact she calls the sport disgusting, but she remembers the riot. It was all over the news and she saw the video of Tadeo pounding away. She and her husband discussed the incident. They even prayed at church for the recovery of Sean King, and were saddened by his death. She would have a difficult time keeping an open mind. The more she is quizzed, the more she realizes how firmly she believes Tadeo is guilty. "He killed him," she says.

Mancini asks a few of the same questions. I take my turn but do not waste time. Liza will get the boot soon enough. For now, though, she is instructed to return to her seat on row one and not say a word.

Juror number eleven is the mother of two teenage boys, both of whom love cage fighting and have spent hours discussing Tadeo and Sean King. She hasn't watched the video, though her boys begged her to. She does, however, know all about the case and admits to having plenty of preconceived notions. Mancini and I politely poke and prod but get nothing. She, too, will be excused.

The afternoon grinds on as we work through the twenty-two jurors, all of whom, it turns out, know far more than they should. A couple claim they can set aside their initial opinions and decide the case with open minds. I doubt this, but then I am the defense lawyer. Late in the day, after we have finished with the twenty-two, I renew my motion for a change of venue. Armed with fresh and irrefutable evidence, I argue that we've just seen clear proof that too many people in this city know far too much about the case.

Go Slow listens and acts as though she believes me, which I think she does. "I'll overrule your motion for now, Mr. Rudd. Let's proceed and see what tomorrow brings."

9.

After court, Partner drives me to the warehouse where Harry & Harry conduct their operations. I meet with Harry Gross and we review Judith's latest petition. He'll prepare a response, one similar to the other three already on file, and I'll sign and file it tomorrow.

Partner and I go to the basement, where Cliff and his team are already at work. From the first four rows of the pool, numbers one through forty, nine people were quizzed privately during the afternoon session. I expect all nine to be excused for cause, or for good reason. Each side has four challenges, four automatic hooks that can be used for no reason whatsoever. That's a total of eight. There is no limit on the number who can be excused for cause. The trick, the skill, the art, is reading the jurors and trying to determine which to challenge. I get only four strikes, same as the prosecution, and one mistake can be fatal. Not only do I decide whom to keep and whom to strike, but I also play chess with Mancini. Whom will he get rid of? Certainly the Hispanics.

I do not expect an acquittal, so I'm angling for a hung jury. I have to find the one or two jurors who might show some sympathy.

For hours, over bad carryout sushi and bottles of green tea, we dissect each potential juror.

10.

There are no phone calls in the middle of the night; nothing from Arch Swanger, nor Nate Spurio. Not a word from Moss Korgan. Evidently, my brilliant offer of a deal didn't get very far. As the sun rises, I'm at my computer responding to e-mails. I decide to send one to Judith. It reads, "Why can't you stop the war? You've lost so many battles and you'll lose this one. The only thing you'll prove is how ridiculously stubborn you are. Think about Starcher, not yourself." The response will be predictably harsh and well crafted.

Partner drops me off in a strip mall out in the suburbs. The only store open is a bagel shop where smoking is illegally permitted. The owner is an old Greek who's dying of lung cancer. His nephew has rank at City Hall and health inspectors don't bother the place. It features strong coffee, real yogurt, decent bagels, and a layer of rich, blue cigarette smoke that's a throwback to the days not long ago when it was common to eat in a restaurant while inhaling the fumes and vapors of those close by. Nowadays, it's still hard to believe we tolerated that. Nate Spurio goes through two packs a day and loves this place. I take a deep breath out front, fill my lungs with clear air, walk inside, and see Nate at a table, coffee and newspaper in front of him, a fresh Salem screwed into the corner of his mouth. He waves at a chair and puts the paper away. "You want coffee?" he asks.

"No thanks. I've had enough."

"How are things going?"

"You mean life in general or the Zapate trial?"

He grunts, tries to smile. "Since when do we talk about life in general?"

"Good point. Nothing from Mancini. If he's in on the deal, he damned sure doesn't act like it. Still offering fifteen years."

"They're working on him, but, as you know, he's a prick who's going places. Right now he's onstage and that means a lot to him."

"So Roy Kemp is hammering away?"

"You could say that. He's tightening every screw he can find. He's desperate—can't say I blame him. And he hates you because he thinks you're withholding information."

"Gee, I'm sorry. Tell him I hate him too because he kidnapped my kid, but nothing personal. If he'll get to the mayor, who can then get to Mancini, we might have us a deal."

"It's in the works, okay. Things are moving."

"Well, things need to move faster. We're picking a jury and based on what I've seen and heard so far my guy is in deep trouble."

"That's what I hear."

"Thanks. We'll probably start calling witnesses tomorrow and there aren't many of them. This could be over by Friday. We need to cut the deal quickly. Five years, county penal farm, early parole. Got it, Nate? Does everybody up the food chain understand the terms of the deal?"

"Plain as day. It's not that complicated."

"Then tell them to make it happen. My guy is about to get slammed by this jury."

He pulls on the cigarette, fills his lungs, asks, "Are you around tonight?"

"You think I'm leaving town?"

"We should probably talk."

"Sure, but now I gotta run. I have this trial today and we're out here beating the bushes looking for some jurors to bribe."

"I didn't hear a word, and I'm certainly not surprised."

"See you, Nate."

"A real pleasure."

"And you really should stop smoking."

"Just take care of yourself, okay. You got your own problems."

11.

Go Slow is late for court, which, on the one hand, is not that unusual because she is a judge and the party doesn't start until she arrives. On the other hand, though, this is a high-water mark for her career and you'd think she would arrive early and savor the moment. But I learned a long time ago not to waste time analyzing why judges do the things they do.

Everyone has been waiting for at least an hour, with no word on what's causing the delay, when her courtroom deputy snaps to attention and calls us to order. Her Honor sweeps onto the bench as if she's already terribly burdened and tells everybody to sit down. No apology, no explanation. She launches into some introductory remarks, not a single word of which is even remotely original, and when she runs out of gas she says, "Mr. Mancini, you may examine the panel for the State."

Max is quickly on his feet, strutting along the mahogany railing that separates us from the spectators. With ninety-two jurors on one side, and at least that many reporters and spectators on the other, the courtroom is again packed. They're even leaning against the rear wall. Max rarely has such an audience. He begins with a dreadful, sappy monologue about how honored he feels to just be in the courtroom representing the good people of our city. He feels a burden. He feels an honor. He feels an obligation. He feels a lot of things, and within a few minutes I notice some of the jurors start to frown and look at him as if to say, "Is this guy serious?"

After he's talked about himself for too long, I slowly stand, look at Her Honor, and say, "Judge, can we please get on with this?"

She says, "Mr. Mancini, do you have some questions for the pool?"

He replies, "Of course, Your Honor. I didn't realize we were in such a hurry."

"Oh, there's no hurry, but I really don't want to waste time." This, from a judge who was an hour late.

Max begins with textbook questions about prior jury service, and experiences with the criminal justice system, and prejudices against the police and law enforcement. By and large, it's a waste of time because people rarely reveal their true feelings in such a setting. It does, however, give us plenty of time to study the jurors. Tadeo is taking pages of notes, at my direction. I'm scribbling too, but I'm primarily watching body language. Cliff and his associate are on the pews across the aisle, watching everything. By now, I feel as though I've known these people, especially the first forty, for years.

Max wants to know if any of them have ever been sued. A standard question but not a great one. This is, after all, a criminal matter, not a civil one. Out of the ninety-two, about fifteen admit to being sued at some point in their past. I'll bet there are at least another fifteen who are not admitting it. This is, after all, America. What honest citizen has never been sued? Max seems thrilled with this response, as if he's really found fertile dirt to dig in. He asks if their experiences within the court system would in any way affect their ability to deliberate in this case.

Naw, Max. Everybody loves to get sued. And we do so without the slightest resentment toward the system. But he flails away with follow-up questions that go nowhere.

For nothing but spite, I stand and say, "Your Honor, could you remind Mr. Mancini that this is a criminal case, not a civil one?"

"I know that!" Max growls at me and we exchange nasty looks. "I know what I'm doing."

"Move along, Mr. Mancini," Her Honor says. "And please keep your seat, Mr. Rudd."

Max fights his anger and lets it pass. Changing gears, he wades into a sensitive matter. Has anyone in your immediate family ever been convicted of a violent crime? He apologizes for intruding into such a private matter, but he has no choice. Please forgive him. From the rear, juror number eighty-one slowly raises a hand.

Mrs. Emma Huffinghouse. White, age fifty-six, a freight company dispatcher. Her twenty-seven-year-old son is serving twelve years for a drug-fueled home invasion. As soon as Max sees her hand he throws up his and pleads, "I don't want the details, please. I know this is a very private matter and very hurtful, I'm sure. My question is this: Was your experience with the criminal justice system satisfactory or unsatisfactory?"

Seriously, Max? We're not filling out a survey for consumer satisfaction.

Mrs. Huffinghouse stands slowly and says, "I think my son was treated fairly by the system."

Max almost leaps over the bar to run hug her. Bless you, dear, bless you. What an endorsement for the forces of good! Too bad, Max, she's useless. We won't get close to number eighty-one.

Juror number forty-seven raises his hand, stands, says his brother spent time in jail for aggravated assault, and, unlike Mrs. Huffinghouse, he, Mark Wattburg, was not favorably impressed with the criminal process.

But Max thanks him profusely anyway. Anybody else? No more hands. There are three others, and I suppose I know it but Max doesn't. This confirms that my research is better than his. It also alerts me to the fact that these three are not altogether forthcoming.

Max moves on as the morning drags. He steps into another delicate minefield, that of victimhood. Have any of you been the victim of a violent crime? You, your family members, close friends? Several hands go up and Max does a nice job of eliciting information that's useful, for a change.

At noon, Her Honor, no doubt exhausted by two hours on the bench and probably craving apple slices, announces a ninety-minute break. Tadeo wants to stay in the courtroom for lunch. I make a pleasant request to his handler, who agrees, to our surprise. Partner hustles down the street to a deli and returns with sandwiches and chips.

As we eat, we talk softly, keeping our voices low so the deputies and bailiffs cannot hear us. There is no one else in the courtroom. The gravity of the setting and surroundings has settled in and Tadeo has lost some of his cockiness. He's absorbed the unforgiving stares from those who might be called upon to judge him. He no longer believes that they are his peers. Softly, he says, "I get the feeling they don't like me."

Such a perceptive young man.

12.

Max finishes up around three and hands off to me. By now, I know more than enough about these people and I'm ready for the selection. However, this is my first chance to speak directly to the pool, and it's an opportunity to lay the groundwork for what every lawyer hopes will become some level of trust. I watched their faces and I know many of them found Max to be obsequious, even a bit goofy. I have an abundance of flaws and bad habits, but fawning is not part of my act. I don't thank them for being there—they were summoned, they have no choice. I don't pretend that we're doing something great and they're a part of it. I don't brag on our judicial system.

Instead, I talk in broad terms about the presumption of innocence. I urge them to ask themselves if they haven't already decided that my client is guilty of something or else he wouldn't be here. Don't raise your hand, just nod along with me if you think he's guilty. It's human nature. It's the way our society and culture work these days. There's a crime, an arrest, we see the suspect on television, and we're relieved that the police have caught their man. Presto, just like that. Crime solved. Guilty party in custody. These days we never, never stop and say, "Wait, he's presumed to be innocent and he's entitled to a fair trial." We rush to judgment.

"Questions, Mr. Rudd?" Go Slow squawks into her microphone.

I ignore her, point to Tadeo, and ask if they can truthfully say that, at this moment, they believe he's completely innocent.

Of course, there is no response because no prospective juror will ever say she's made up her mind already.

I move on to the burden of proof and discuss it until Max has had enough. He stands, arms open wide in complete frustration, and says, "Your Honor, he's not quizzing the panel. He's giving a law school lecture."

"Agreed. Either ask your questions or sit down, Mr. Rudd," Go Slow says, rather rudely.

"Thank you," I reply like the smart-ass I really am. I look at the first three rows and say, "Tadeo doesn't have to testify, doesn't have to call any witnesses. Why? Because the burden of proving him guilty lies with the prosecution. Now, let's say he doesn't take the stand. Will that matter to you? Will you tend to think he's hiding something?"

I use this all the time and rarely get a response. Today, though, juror number seventeen wants to say something. Bobby Morris, age thirty-six, white, a stonemason. He raises his hand and I nod at him. He says, "If I'm on the jury, then I think he should testify. I want to hear from the defendant."

"Thank you, Mr. Morris," I reply warmly. "Anybody else?" With the ice broken, several others raise their hands and I gently ask follow-up questions. As I had hoped, it becomes a discussion as more and more lose their inhibitions. I'm easy to talk to, a nice guy, a straight shooter with a sense of humor.

When I'm finished, Her Honor informs us we will pick the jury before we go home and gives us fifteen minutes to look at our notes.

13.

The e-mail from Judith reads, "Starcher is still upset. You are such a pathetic father. See you in court."

I'm tempted to fire something back, but why bother? Partner and I are driving away from the courthouse. It's dark, after 7:00 p.m., and it's been a hard day. We stop at a bar for a beer and a sandwich.

Nine whites, one black, one Hispanic, one Vietnamese. With their names and faces so fresh I have to talk about them. Partner, as always, listens dutifully with little comment. He has been in the courtroom for most of the past two days and he likes the jury.

I stop at two beers, though I really want several more. At nine o'clock, Partner drops me off at an Arby's, and I fiddle with a soft drink for fifteen minutes waiting on Nate. He finally arrives, orders some onion rings, apologizes for being tardy. "How's the trial going?" he asks.

"Got a jury late this afternoon. Opening statements in the morning, then Mancini starts calling witnesses. Should go pretty fast. We got a deal?"

He shovels in a large, crusty ring and chews fiercely while looking around. The place is empty. He swallows hard, says, "Yep. Woody met with Mancini two hours ago and fired him. He replaced him with a flunky who was planning to move for a mistrial first thing in the morning. Mancini backed down and agreed to play along. He wants to meet with you and the judge at 8:30 tomorrow."

"The judge?"

"You got it. Seems Woody and Janet Fabineau have some mutual dealings, friends, whatever, and Woody insisted on putting her in the loop. She's good to go. She'll take the plea, approve the bargain, sentence your boy to five years at the penal farm, recommend early release. Just like you said, Rudd."

"Marvelous. And Link's thugs?"

"That investigation is going nowhere. Forget about it." He sucks on his straw and selects another onion ring. "Now, Rudd, the fun part."

"The last time I saw Swanger, the meeting was arranged through a prepaid cell phone he left behind for me in a pharmacy. I still have the phone. It's right outside in my van. I haven't used it since, so I don't know if it'll work. But if I get Swanger on the phone I'll try to set up a meeting. I'll have to give him some cash."

"How much?"

"Fifty grand, unmarked. He's not stupid."

"Fifty grand?"

"That's about a third of the reward money. I'm assuming he'll grab it because he's broke. Anything less might cause problems. Last year you guys cashed in forfeited assets to the tune of four million bucks, all retained by the department, pursuant to our brilliant state law. The money's there, Nate, and Roy Kemp would spend anything for the chance to see his daughter again."

"Okay, okay. I'll pass it along. That's all I can do."

I leave him with his onion rings and hurry to the van. As Partner drives away, I open the cheap phone and call the number. Nothing. An hour later, I call again. And again. Nothing.

14.

Aided by exhaustion, the two beers, and a couple of whiskey sours, I fall asleep with the television on. I wake up in my recliner, still wearing a suit but no tie, socks but no shoes. My cell phone is ringing; caller ID says "Unknown." It's 1:40 a.m. I take a chance and say hello.

"You looking for me?" Swanger asks.

"Yes, as a matter of fact," I say, collapsing the footrest and bolting to my feet. Things are foggy and my brain needs blood. "Where are you?"

"Dumb question. Any more stupidity and I'm hanging up."

"Look, Arch, there could be a deal in the works. That is if you're telling the truth, which, frankly, no one involved believes you're capable of."

"I didn't call to get insulted."

"Of course not. You called because you want money. I think I can broker a deal, act as the middleman, without a fee of course. I'm not your lawyer, so I won't be sending you a bill."

"Very funny. You're not my lawyer because you can't be trusted, Rudd."

"Okay, next time you snatch a girl, hire somebody else. You want the money or not, Arch? I really don't care."

There is a brief pause as he thinks about how much he needs cash. Finally, "How much?"

"Twenty-five thousand now to tell us where the girl is. If they find her, then twenty-five more."

"That's only a third of the reward money. You taking the rest?"

"Not a dime. As I said, I'm getting nothing, and that's the very reason I'm asking myself what the hell I'm doing in the middle of all this."

Another pause as he contemplates a counteroffer. "I don't like the deal, Rudd. I'll never see the other twenty-five."

And we'll never see the girl, I think but don't say. "Look, Arch, you're getting twenty-five thousand bucks from the very people who would shoot you on sight. That's a lot more than you made last year with honest work."

"I don't believe in honest work. Neither do you. That's why you're a lawyer."

"Ha-ha. You're clever. You want a deal, Swanger? If not, I'm butting out. I got more important things on my mind these days."

"Fifty grand, Rudd. Cash. Fifty grand and I'll tell you and you alone where the girl is right now. If this is a setup or if I smell a cop anywhere around, I'll bolt, make a call, and the girl will be gone for good. Understand?"

"I got it. I'm not sure about the money, but all I can do is pass this along to my contact."

"Work fast, Rudd, my patience is running thin."

"Oh, you'll find the time if the money's on the table. Who are you kidding, Swanger?"

The line goes dead. So much for a good night's sleep.

15.

Three hours later, I stop at an all-night convenience store and buy a bottle of water. Outside, I'm approached by a cop in plain clothes who grunts, "You Rudd?" Since I am, he hands me a brown paper grocery bag with a cigar box inside. "Fifty grand," he says. "All in hundreds."

"That'll do," I say. What am I supposed to say? "Thanks"?

I leave the City, alone. During my last conversation with Swanger, about an hour ago, he instructed me to ditch my "thug" and do the driving myself. He also told me to forget the fancy new van and drive something else. I explained that, at the moment, I had nothing else and didn't have time to run get a rental. The van will have to do.

I try not to dwell on the fact that this guy is watching me. He knew the moment Partner and I began buzzing around in a U-Haul van. Now he knows I have new wheels. It's astonishing that he's in the City enough to know these things, yet still undiscovered by the police. I suspect he'll finally disappear when he gets the money, which will not be a bad thing.

As instructed, I call him as I leave the City on the southern bypass of the interstate. His directions are precise: "Go sixteen miles south to exit 184, take Route 63 east to the town of Jobes." As I drive, I remind myself that I have this trial that's supposed to kick off in just a few hours, or is it? If Judge Fabineau is really in the loop, what does that mean for the rest of the day?

I have no idea how much surveillance is tracking me right now, but I'm sure it is substantial. I didn't ask questions, didn't have time to, but I know Roy Kemp and his team have called in all the bloodhounds. There are two mikes in my van and a tracking device inside the rear bumper. I've allowed them to listen to my cell phone, but just for the next few hours. I'll bet they already have people closing in on the town of Jobes. A helicopter or two in the air above me would not be a surprise. I'm not frightened—Swanger has no reason to harm me—but my nerves are jumping nonetheless.

The money is unmarked and cannot be traced. The police don't care if they get it back; they just want the girl. They're also assuming Swanger is smart enough to spot anything fishy.

Jobes is a small town of three thousand. When I pass a Shell station on the edge of town, I call Swanger, as instructed. He says, "Stay on the line. Turn left just past the car wash." I turn left onto a dark, paved street with a few old houses on both sides. He says, "You swear you got fifty grand, Rudd?"

"I do."

"Take a right and go over the railroad tracks." I do as I'm told, and he says, "Now turn right onto that first street. It has no name. Stop at the first stop sign and wait."

When I stop, a figure suddenly appears from the darkness and yanks the passenger door handle. I press the button to unlock it and Swanger jumps inside. He points left, says, "Go that way and take your time. We're headed back to the interstate."

"Great to see you again, Arch." He's wearing a black do-rag that covers his eyebrows and ears. Everything else is black too, from the bandanna around his neck to his combat boots. I almost ask him where he parked, but why bother?

"Where's the money?" he demands.

I nod over my shoulder and he grabs the bag. He opens the cigar box, and with a small key-chain light counts the money. He looks up, says, "Take a right," then keeps counting. As we are leaving the town, he takes a deep, satisfied breath, and offers me a goofy grin. "All here," he says.

"You doubt me?"

"Damned right I doubt you, Rudd." He points to the Shell station and says, "You want a beer?"

"No. I don't normally drink beer at five-thirty in the morning."

"It's the best time. Pull in."

He goes inside without the money. He takes his time, selects a bag of chips to go with his six-pack, and strolls back to the van as if he has no concerns whatsoever. When we're moving again, he rips off a can and pops the top. He slurps it and opens the chips.

"Where are we going, Arch?" I ask with no small amount of irritation.

"Get on the interstate and head south. This van still smells new, you know that, Rudd? I think I liked the old one better." He crunches a mouthful of chips and washes it all down with a gulp of beer.

"Too bad. Don't spill any crumbs, okay? Partner gets really pissed off if he finds crumbs in the van."

"That your thug?"

"You know who it is." We're on Route 63, still dark and deserted. No sign of sunrise. I keep glancing around thinking I'll see some of the surveillance, but of course they're too good for that. They're back there, or up there, or waiting at the interstate. Then again, what do I know about such things? I'm a lawyer.

He pulls a small phone out of his shirt pocket and holds it up for me to see. He says, "Know one thing, Rudd. If I see a cop, smell a cop, or hear a cop, all I do is push this button on this phone, and somewhere, far away, bad things happen. You understand?"

"Got it. Now, where, Arch? That's the first thing. Where, when, how? You have the money; now you owe us the story. Where is the girl and how do we get her?"

He drains the first can, smacks his lips, reloads another mouthful of chips, and for a few miles it seems as though he has gone mute. Then he opens another beer. At the intersection, he says, "Go south."

Traffic in the northbound lane is busy as the early commuters head for the City. The southbound, though, is practically deserted. I look at him and want to slap the smirk off his face. "Arch?"

He takes another drink and sits taller. "They've taken the girls from Chicago to Atlanta. They move around a lot, every four or five months. They'll work a town pretty hard, but then after a while people start talking, the cops start sniffing around, and so they disappear, set up shop somewhere else. It's hard to keep secrets when you're offering pretty young women at good prices."

"If you say so. Is Jiliana Kemp still alive?"

"Oh yes. Very much so. She's quite active, not like she has a choice."

"And she's in Atlanta?"

"The Atlanta area."

"It's a big city, Arch, and we don't have time to play games. If you have an address, then give it to me. That's the deal."

He takes a deep breath and another long drink. "They're in a big strip mall where there's traffic, lots of cars and people come and go. Atlas Physical Therapy is the name of the company, but it's nothing but an upper-end brothel. No number in the phone book. Therapists on call. Appointments only, no walk-ins. Every customer has to be referred by another customer, and they—the head therapists—know who they're dealing with. So if you're a customer, you park in the lot, maybe step into the Baskin-Robbins for an ice cream, stroll along the sidewalk, then duck into Atlas. A guy wearing a white lab coat says hello and acts real nice, but under the coat is a loaded piece. He pretends to be a therapist, and he does in fact know a lot about broken bones. He takes your money, say $300 cash, and leads you back to some rooms. He points to one, you walk in, and there's a small bed and a girl who's young and pretty and almost naked. You get twenty minutes with her. You leave through another door and no one knows you've had your therapy. The girls work all afternoon—they get the mornings off because they're up late—then they load 'em up and take 'em to the strip clubs where they dance and do their routines. At midnight, they take 'em home, to a fairly nice apartment complex where they're locked down for the night."

"Who is they?"

"They are the traffickers, some extremely nasty guys. A gang, a ring, a cartel, a disciplined band of criminals, most with ties to eastern Europe, but some local boys as well. They abuse the girls, keep them terrified and confused and hooked on heroin. Most people in this country don't believe there's sex trafficking in their cities, but it's there. It's everywhere. They, the traffickers, prey on runaways, homeless kids, girls from bad families looking for escape. It's a sick business, Rudd. Really sick."

I start to rebuke him and curse him, remind him of his rather important role in a business he seems to detest, but it would serve no purpose. Instead, I go along with him. "How many girls now?"

"It's hard to say. They split 'em up, move 'em around. A few have disappeared for good."

I don't really want to pursue this. Only a creep involved in the business would know so much about it.

He points and says, "Turn around at this exit and go back north."

"Where are we going, Arch?"

"I'll show you. Just hang on."

"Okay. Now about that address."

"Here's what I would do if I were the cops," he says with a sudden voice of authority. "I'd watch the place, Atlas, and I'd nab a john when he comes out, fresh from therapy. He's probably a local insurance agent who's not getting any at home and he's taken a shine to one of the girls—you can actually ask for your favorite but the request is nonbinding; they got their rules—or maybe he's a local ambulance chaser like you, Rudd, just another sleazy lawyer who's hitting on everything but not scoring much, and for three hundred bucks he gets his therapy."

"Anyway."

"Anyway, they grab the guy, scare the living shit out of him, and within minutes he's singing like a choirboy. He tells them everything, especially the layout of the interior. They make him cry, then let him go. They, the cops, already have a warrant. They surround the place with one of those SWAT squads, and it goes down beautifully. The girls are rescued. The traffickers are caught red-handed, and if the cops do it right they can flip one of them instantly. If he sings, he'll implicate the entire ring. There could be hundreds of girls and dozens of goons. Could be huge, Rudd, all because of you and me."

"Yeah, we're a real team, Swanger."

I take the exit ramp, cross over the interstate, and reenter it headed north. All the eyes watching my van must be wondering what the hell. My passenger pops another top, his third. The chips are gone and I'm sure there are crumbs left behind. I push it to seventy miles an hour and say, "The address, Arch."

"It's in the suburb of Vista View, about ten miles due west of downtown Atlanta. The strip mall is called West Ivy. Atlas Physical Therapy is next door to Sunny Boy Cleaners. The girls will get there around 1:00 p.m."

"And Jiliana Kemp is one of them?"

"I've already answered that, Rudd. You think I'd tell you all this if she wasn't there. But the cops better go in quick. These people can roll up and move in a matter of minutes."

I have what I want, so I go quiet. For some reason I say, "Can

I have a beer?" For a second he looks irritated, as if he needs all six himself, but then he smiles and hands one over.

16.

A few miles down the road, and after a long, pleasant stretch of silence, Swanger nods and says, "There it is. Dr. Woo and his billboard for vasectomy reversals. Brings back memories, right, Rudd?"

"I spent a long night there, watching them dig. Why'd you do that, Arch?"

"Why do I do anything, Rudd? Why did I grab that girl? And mistreat her? And sell her? She's not the first, you know?"

"I really don't care at this point. I just hope she's the last."

He shakes his head and says with some sadness, "No way. Pull over here on the shoulder."

I hit the brakes and the van rolls to a stop under the bright lights from Dr. Woo. Swanger grabs the sackful of money, leaves the beer behind, and yanks the door handle. He says, "Tell those dumb-ass cops they'll never find me." He jumps out, slams the door, and bounces down the shoulder into some tall grass, over a fence, and under the billboard. The last image is Swanger ducking low between the thick posts, scrambling fast, and making tracks, then disappearing into the tall corn.

To be safe, I drive half a mile down the interstate, pull off again, and call the cops. They've listened to every word spoken in the van for the past hour, so there's little for me to say. I do stress that it would be a mistake to try and corner Swanger until the raid takes place in Atlanta. They seem to agree. I see no activity in and around the cornfield by the billboard.

As I'm driving back to the City, my cell phone buzzes. Max Mancini. I say, "Good morning."

"I just spoke with Judge Fabineau. Seems as if she's been stricken with severe food poisoning. No court today."

"Gee, that's awful."

"I knew you'd be disappointed. Get some sleep and we'll talk later."

"Okay. Am I supposed to check in with you?"

"Yes. And, Rudd, nice work."

"We'll see."

I pick up Partner at his apartment and we settle in for a long breakfast at a waffle place. I recount the adventures of the past seven hours, and he, typically, listens without a word. I need to lie down and try to sleep, but I'm too wired. I try to kill time around the courthouse, but I'm so preoccupied with the raid in Atlanta I can think of nothing else.

Normally, I would be frantically preparing for Tadeo's trial, but now I doubt it will take place. I've kept my end of the bargain, and regardless of what happens to Jiliana Kemp, we should have a deal. A nice little plea bargain that will allow my client to fight again, and soon. But I trust no one I'm dealing with at the moment. If the raid produces nothing, it would not be a surprise if the mayor, Max Mancini, Moss Korgan, Go Slow Fabineau, and the police brass all get together in a room and decide, "Screw Rudd and his client! Let's go to trial."

17.

By 2:00 p.m. eastern time the parking lot of the West Ivy Shopping Center is crawling with federal agents, all dressed in a wide variety of casual garb and driving nondescript vehicles. Those with more substantial weapons are hiding in unmarked vans.

The unlucky john is a forty-one-year-old car salesman named

Ben Brown. Husband, father of four, nice home not far away. After therapy, he leaves Atlas through an unmarked door, makes it to his vehicle, a demo, and is allowed to drive half a mile before being pulled over by a local cop. Ben's first words are to the effect that he damned well wasn't speeding, but when a black SUV wheels to a stop in front of him he suspects deeper trouble. He is introduced to two FBI agents and led to the rear seat of their vehicle. He is placed under arrest for soliciting prostitution and told he will probably be indicted for all manner of federal offenses at a later date. Atlas, he is informed, is part of an interstate sex ring; thus the federal charges. Ben's life flashes before his eyes and he's barely able to hold back tears. He tells the agents he has a wife and four kids. They are not sympathetic. He's facing years in jail.

The agents, however, are willing to deal. If he tells them everything, they will allow him to hop in his car and drive away, a free man. On the one hand, something tells Ben to clam up and demand an attorney. On the other, he wants to trust them and save his skin.

He starts talking. This is his fourth or fifth visit to Atlas. He usually had a different girl; that's what he likes about the place, the variety. Three hundred bucks a pop. No paperwork, of course not. He was recommended by a friend at the car dealership. Everything is kept very quiet. Yes, he has vouched for two other buddies. Recommendations are required; security seems tight; confidentiality ensured. Inside, there is a small reception area where he always meets the same man, Travis, who wears a white lab coat, tries to look the part. Through a door there are six to eight rooms, all about the same—small bed, small chair, naked girl. Things go quick. It's sort of like a drive-through sex shop, in and out, unlike one time in Vegas where the girl hung around and they ate chocolates and drank champagne.

No smiles from the FBI. "Any other men there?"

Yes, maybe, seems like there was one other guy one time. Everything's real clean and efficient, except the walls are pretty thin and it's not unusual to hear some rather graphic sounds from other therapy sessions. The girls? Well, of course there is a Tiffany and a Brittany and an Amber, but who knows what the real names are.

Ben is told to go and sin no more. He speeds away, eager to run tell his buddies to stay away from Atlas.

The raid happens moments later. With all doors blocked by heavily armed agents, there is no time to even think about resistance or escape. Three men are handcuffed and hauled away. Six girls, including Jiliana Kemp, are rescued and taken into protective custody. Just before 3:00 p.m., she calls her parents, sobbing hysterically. She had been abducted thirteen months earlier. And, she had given birth in captivity. She has no idea what happened to her baby.

Under enormous pressure, one of the three men, an American, takes the bait and starts singing. Names pour forth, then addresses, then everything else he can think of. As the hours pass, the web grows rapidly. FBI offices in a dozen cities put everything else on hold.

One of Mayor Woody's banker buddies has a corporate jet and the guy is eager to send it. By 7:00 p.m. on a day when she would normally be ending another nightmare at Atlas and preparing for a night of stripping and table dancing, Jiliana Kemp is suddenly flying home. A flight attendant takes care of her and will later say she cried all the way.

18.

Once again, Arch Swanger slips through the net. There is no sign of him after he disappears into the cornfield. The police think they could have caught him then and there, but since they were ordered to wait until after the raid, they somehow lost him. It's apparent that he has an accomplice. From the point where I picked him up at the stop sign in Jobes, it's about forty miles to Dr. Woo's sign beside the interstate. Someone had to be driving a getaway car.

I doubt I've heard the last of him.

19.

After dark, Partner and I drive to the jail to deliver the great news to Tadeo. He is being offered the deal of all deals—a light sentence, an easier prison, a guarantee of early parole for good behavior. With some luck, he'll be back in the ring in two years, his career bolstered by the ex-con aura and that famous YouTube video. I have to admit I'm getting excited thinking about his comeback.

With great satisfaction, I lay it all on the table. Or most of it. I spare him the details of the Swanger adventure, and instead place emphasis on my prowess as a negotiator and much-feared trial lawyer.

Tadeo is not impressed. He says no. No!

I attempt to explain that he cannot simply say no. He's facing a decade or more in a tough prison, and now I'm delivering a deal so fantastic that the presiding judge can't believe it. Wake up, man! No.

I am stunned, incredulous.

He sits with his arms crossed over his chest, such an arrogant little punk, and says no over and over. No deal. He will not plead guilty under any circumstances. He has seen his jurors, and, after a few doubts, he is once again confident they will not convict him. He will insist on taking the stand and telling his side of the story. He is cocky, hardheaded, and irritated by my desire to see him plead guilty. I keep my cool and go back to the basics—the charges, the evidence, the video, the shakiness of our expert testimony, the composition of the jury, the bloodbath that awaits him on cross-examination, the likelihood of ten or more years in prison, everything. Nothing registers. He's an innocent man who sort of accidentally killed a referee with nothing but his hands, and he can explain it all to the jury. He'll walk out a free man, and when he does, well, then it'll be payback time. He'll find a new manager and a new lawyer. He accuses me of being disloyal. This makes me angry and I tell him he's being stupid. I ask him whom he's listening to back there in the cell block. Things go from bad to worse, and after an hour I storm out of the room.

I thought I might sleep tonight, but it looks like I'll go through the usual pretrial insomnia.

20.

At 5:00 on Thursday morning, I'm drinking strong coffee and reading the *Chronicle* online. It's all about the rescue of Jiliana Kemp. The largest photo on page one is just what I envisioned: Mayor Woody at the podium in all his glory, with Roy Kemp beside him, a wall of blue behind them. Jiliana is not in the photo, though there is a slightly smaller one of her getting off the jet at the airport. Baseball cap, big sunglasses, collar turned up, you can't tell much but she looks reasonably good. She is resting at home with her family and friends, it says. The sex-trafficking story runs for pages, and the FBI operation is obviously still in progress. Arrests are being made across the country. So far, about twenty-five girls have been rescued. There was a shooting in Denver but no serious injuries.

Thankfully, there's not a word about Jiliana's heroin addiction, or about the lost baby. One nightmare is over; others continue. I suppose I should take some measure of quiet satisfaction in having had a hand in this, but I don't. I bartered information to benefit a client. That's all. Now that client has gone stupid and I get nothing out of the deal.

I wait until 7:00 a.m. to send a text message to both Max Mancini and Judge Fabineau. It reads, "After extensive discussions, my client refuses to accept the plea agreement now being offered by the prosecution. I have strongly advised him to accept it, to no avail. It appears as though the trial must go on, pending the health of the judge. Sorry. SR."

Mancini responds, "Let's tee it up. See u soon." He, of course, is thrilled because he's back on center stage. Evidently, Judge Fabineau has made a quick recovery. She texts, "Ok, the show must go on. We'll meet in chambers at 8:30. I'll inform my bailiff."

21.

The players assemble in the courtroom as if nothing happened yesterday, or at least nothing that would in any way affect the trial. A few of us know—me, the prosecutor, the judge, Partner—but no one else knows, nor should they. I whisper to Tadeo. He has not changed his mind; he can win this trial.

We retire to the judge's chambers for our early morning update. To cover my ass, I inform her and Max that I want to put my client on the record, so there will be no doubt in the years to come about his refusal to take a plea. A bailiff brings him in, no cuffs, no restraints. He's smiling and being very polite. He's put under oath and says he has a clear mind and knows what's going on. Fabineau asks Mancini to recite the terms of the plea agreement: five years for a guilty plea to manslaughter. Her Honor says that she cannot promise any particular prison facility, but is of the opinion that Mr. Zapate would do quite well just down the road at the county penal farm. Only six miles away; his mother can visit frequently. Furthermore, she does not control parole, but as the sentencing judge she has the authority to recommend an early release.

Does he understand all of this? He says he does, and goes on to say that he ain't pleading guilty to anything.

I state that I have advised him to take the deal. He says yes, he understands my advice, but he's not taking it. We go off the record and the court reporter shuts down. Judge Fabineau folds her fingers together like a veteran kindergarten teacher, and in a painfully deliberate manner tells Tadeo that she has never seen such a good deal for any defendant charged with the death of another person. In other words, boy, you're a fool to refuse this deal.

He doesn't budge.

Next, Max explains that he, as a career prosecutor, has never offered a plea deal as lenient as this one. It's extraordinary, really. Eighteen months or so in the pen, full access to the weight room, and there are excellent facilities at the penal farm, and you'll be back in the cage before you know it.

Tadeo just shakes his head.

22.

The jurors file in and glance around expectantly, nervously. There is an air of excitement in the courtroom as this drama is about to unfold, but I feel nothing but the usual thick knot in my stomach. The first day is always the hardest. As the hours pass, we'll settle into a routine and the butterflies will slowly dissipate. At the moment, though, I'd like to go vomit. An old trial lawyer once told me that if the day came when I walked into a courtroom and faced a jury without fear, then it was time to quit.

Max rises purposefully and walks to a spot in front of the jury box. He offers his standard welcoming smile and says good morning. Sorry about the delay yesterday. Again, his name is Max Mancini, chief prosecutor for the City.

This is a grave matter because it involves the loss of life. Sean King was a fine man with a loving family, a hardworking guy trying to earn a few bucks on the side as a referee. There is no dispute as to the cause of death, or who killed him. The defendant, sitting right over there, will try and confuse you, try and convince you that the law makes exceptions for people who temporarily, or permanently, lose their minds.

Baloney. He rambles on a bit without notes, and I've known for some time that Max gets in trouble when he goes off script. The more skilled courtroom advocates convey the impression that they are speaking extemporaneously, while in truth they have spent hours memorizing and rehearsing. Max is not one of those, but he's not as bad as most prosecutors. He does a very smart thing by promising the jurors that they will soon see the now famous video. He makes them wait. He could, even at this initial stage of the trial, show the video. Go Slow has already said so. But he teases them with it. Nice move.

His opening statement is not long because his case is ironclad. Impulsively, I stand and tell Her Honor that I will reserve my opening statement until the beginning of our defense, an option under our rules. Max bounces forth and calls as his first witness the widow, Mrs. Beverly King. She's a nice-looking lady, dressed for church, and terrified of the witness chair. Max walks her through the standard sympathy ritual and within minutes she's in tears. Though such testimony has nothing at all to do with guilt or innocence, it is always allowed to hammer home the fact that the deceased is indeed dead and that he or she left behind loved ones. Sean was a faithful partner, devoted father, hard worker, breadwinner, loving son to his dear mother. Between sobs we get the picture, and, as always, it is dramatic. The jurors swallow it whole and a few glare at Tadeo. I've yelled at him not to look at the jurors, but instead sit attentively at the table and scribble nonstop on a legal pad. Do not shake your head. Do not show any reaction or emotion. At any given time, at least two members of the jury are looking at you.

I do not cross-examine Mrs. King. She is excused and returns to her seat next to her three children in the front row. It's a lovely family, on display for everyone, but especially the jurors.

The next witness is the medical examiner, a forensic pathologist named Dr. Glover, a veteran of these battles. Because my career has involved a number of grisly murder cases, Dr. Glover and I have tangled before in front of juries. Indeed, in this very courtroom. He conducted an autopsy on Sean King the day after he died and has photos to prove it. A month ago Mancini and I almost came to blows over the autopsy photos. Normally, they are not admitted because their gruesomeness is so prejudicial. However, Max convinced Go Slow that three of the milder ones are probative. The first is of Sean lying on the slab, naked but for a white towel over his midsection. The second is a close-up of his face with the camera directly above him. The third is of his shaved head, turned to the right to reveal considerable swelling from several incisions. The twenty or so photos wisely excluded by Go Slow are so graphic that no sane trial judge would allow the jury to see them: sawing off the top of the skull; tight photos of the damaged brain; and the last one of the brain sitting alone on a lab table.

The ones deemed admissible are projected on a tall, wide screen. Mancini walks the doctor through each one. The cause of death was blunt-force trauma inflicted by repeated blows to the upper face. How many blows? Well, we have the video to show us. This is another smart move by Max—to introduce the footage with the medical expert on the stand. The lights go dim, and on the large screen we get to relive the tragedy: the two fighters in the center of the ring, both confident of victory; Sean King raises the right hand of Crush, who seems surprised; Tadeo's shoulders slump in disbelief, then suddenly he hits Crush from the side, a real sucker punch; before Sean King can react, Tadeo lands a hard right to his nose, then a left; Sean King falls back and lands against the wire cage, where he sits, slumped over, defenseless, out cold; and Tadeo springs on him like an animal, pounding away.

"Twenty-two blows to the head," Dr. Glover tells the jurors, who are mesmerized by the violence. They're watching a perfectly healthy man get beaten to death.

And my idiot client thinks he'll walk.

The video ends when Norberto rushes into the ring and grabs Tadeo. At that point, Sean King's chin is on his chest and his face is nothing but blood. Crush is out cold. Chaos ensues as others scramble into the picture. As the riot breaks out, the screen goes black.

Doctors tried everything to relieve the intense swelling of Sean King's brain, but nothing worked. He died five days later without regaining consciousness. An image of a CT scan takes the place of the video, and Dr. Glover talks about cerebral contusions. Another image, and he talks about hemorrhaging within the hemispheres. Another reveals a large subdural hematoma. The witness has been discussing autopsies and causes of death with juries for many years, and he knows how to testify. He takes his time, explains things, and tries to avoid esoteric words and phrases. This must be one of his easier cases because of the video. The victim was perfectly healthy when he walked into the cage. He left on a stretcher and the world knows why.

Arguing with a true expert in front of a jury is always tricky business. More often than not, the lawyer loses both the fight and his credibility. Because of the facts in this case, I have very little credibility to begin with. I'm not willing to lose any more. I stand and politely say, "No questions."

When I sit down, Tadeo hisses at me, "What're you doing, man? You gotta go after these dudes."

"Knock it off, okay?" I say through gritted teeth. I'm really tired of his arrogance and he's obviously distrustful of me. I doubt if things will improve.

23.

As we break for an afternoon recess, I get a text message from Miguel Zapate. I've seen him in the courtroom throughout the morning, one of several relatives and friends clustered in the back row, watching intently but from as far away as possible. We meet in the hallway and stroll outside. Norberto, the former manager of Team Zapate, joins us. Partner follows at a distance. I make sure they understand that Tadeo is refusing a very good plea bargain. He could be out in eighteen months and fighting again.

But they have a better deal. Juror number ten is Esteban Suarez, age thirty-eight, a truck driver for a food supply company. Fifteen years ago he emigrated legally from Mexico. Miguel says he has a friend who knows him.

I hide my surprise as we wade into treacherous waters. We turn down a narrow one-way street with all sunlight blocked by tall buildings. "How does your friend know him?" I ask.

Miguel is a street punk, a low-end drug runner for a gang that is heavily involved with cocaine smuggling but not heavily involved with its profits. In the murky chain of distribution, Miguel and his boys are stuck in the middle with no room to grow. This is where Tadeo was when we met less than two years ago.

Miguel shrugs and says, "My friend knows lots of people."

"I'm sure he does. And when did your friend meet Mr. Suarez? Within the past twenty-four hours?"

"It doesn't matter. What matters is the fact that we can deal with Suarez, and he's not that expensive."

"Bribing a juror can land you in the same pen with Tadeo."

"Senor, please. For ten grand Suarez hangs the jury, maybe even gets an acquittal."

I stop walking and stare at this small-time thug. What does he know about acquittals? "If you think that jury is going to let your brother walk, then you're crazy, Miguel. Ain't going to happen."

"Okay, then we hang it. You said yourself that if they hang once, then hang twice, then the prosecutor will dismiss everything."

I start walking again, slowly because I'm not sure where we're headed. Partner trails fifty yards behind. I say, "Fine, go bribe a juror, but I'm not getting involved."

"Okay, senor, give me the cash and I'll get it done."

"Oh, I see. You need the money."

"Yes, senor. We don't have that kind of cash."

"I don't either, especially not after representing your brother. I've forked over thirty grand for a jury consultant and twenty for a shrink, plus twenty more for other expenses. Keep in mind, Miguel, in my business I'm supposed to get paid by the client, cash fees for representation. And the client also covers all expenses. It's not the other way around."

"Is that why you're not fighting?"

I stop again and glare at him. "You have no idea what you're talking about, Miguel. I'm doing the best I can with the facts I have. You guys are under some misguided notion that I can fit your brother into a big, mysterious loophole in the law and walk him out of there a free man. Guess what? It ain't going to happen, Miguel. Tell that to your hardheaded brother."

"We need ten thousand, Rudd. And now."

"Too bad. I don't have it."

"We want a new lawyer."

"Too late."

24.

D is for donut. After another sleepless night I meet Nate Spurio at a bakery near the university. For breakfast he's having two honey-glazed filled with jelly, and black coffee. I'm not hungry, so I choke down the coffee. After a few minutes of small talk, I say, "Look, Nate, I'm pretty busy these days. What's on your mind?"

"The trial, huh?"

"Yes."

"I hear you're getting hammered."

"It's pretty ugly in there. You called. What's up?"

"Not much. I've been asked to pass along some kind words from Roy Kemp and family. They took the girl off to rehab someplace. She's a mess, obviously, but at least she's safe and with her family. I mean, look, Rudd, these people thought she was dead. Now they got her back. They'll do whatever it takes to make her whole again. And, they might have a lead on the baby. This thing is still unfolding all over the country. More arrests last night, more girls taken into custody. They got a tip related to the baby-selling angle and they're all over it."

I nod, take a sip, say, "That's good."

"Yes it is. And Roy Kemp wants you to know that he and his family are very grateful to you for getting the girl back and making all this happen."

"He kidnapped my child."

"Come on, Rudd."

"His daughter was kidnapped, so he must know how it feels. I don't care how grateful he is. He's lucky I called off the FBI or he might be sitting in jail."

"Come on, Rudd. Let it go. There's a happy ending here, thanks to you."

"I deserve nothing and I want no part of it. Tell Mr. Kemp to kiss my ass."

"Will do. They got a lead on Swanger. Last night, a tip from a bartender in Racine, Wisconsin."

"Great. Can we meet in a week or so and have a beer? I'm rather preoccupied right now."

"Sure."

25.

I huddle with Partner and Cliff in the hallway before the trial resumes Friday morning. At this point Cliff's job is to sit in various places among the spectators and watch the jurors. His reaction to yesterday is not surprising: The jurors have no sympathy for Tadeo and they've made up their minds. Grab the plea deal if it's still on the table, he keeps saying. I tell him about my conversation with Miguel the day before. Cliff's response: "Well, if you can bribe one you'd better do it quick."

As the jury files in, I steal a look at Esteban Suarez. I planned to just glance at him quickly, as I normally do during trials. However, he's gawking at me as if he expects me to hand over an envelope. What a goofball. There is little doubt, though, that someone has made contact with him. There's also little doubt that he can't be trusted. Is he already counting his money?

Judge Fabineau says good morning and welcomes everyone back to her courtroom. She goes through the standard routine of quizzing the jurors about any unauthorized contact with sinister people hoping to sway them. I glance back at Suarez. He's staring at me. I'm sure others are noticing this.

Mr. Mancini stands and announces, "Your Honor, the State rests. We may have additional witnesses for rebuttal, but for now we'll rest."

This is not surprising because Max gave me a heads-up. He's called only two witnesses because that's all he needs. Again, the video says it all, and Max is wise to let it speak for itself. He's clearly established the cause of death and he's certainly nailed the perpetrator.

I walk to the jury box, look at everyone but Suarez, and begin by stating the obvious. My client killed Sean King. There was no premeditation, no planning. He hit him twenty-two times. And Tadeo doesn't remember it. In the fifteen or so minutes before he attacked Sean King, Tadeo Zapate was struck in the face and head a total of thirty-seven times by Crush, also known as Bo Fraley. Thirty-seven times. He wasn't knocked out, but he was mentally impaired. He remembers little past the second round, when Crush landed a knee to his jaw. We will show you, the jury, the entire fight, count the thirty-seven blows to the head, and prove to you that Tadeo did not know what he was doing when he attacked the referee.

I am brief because there's just not much I can say. I thank them and leave the podium.

My first witness is Oscar Moreno, Tadeo's trainer and the man who first saw his potential as a sixteen-year-old boxer. Oscar is about my age, older than Tadeo's gang, and he's been around the block. He hangs out in a gym for Hispanic kids and offers to train the more talented ones. He also happens to have a clean record, a real asset when calling witnesses to the stand. Past criminal convictions always come back to bite you. Juries are tough on felons under oath.

With Oscar, I lay the groundwork for the events leading up to the fight. It's an effort to appeal to the jury's sense of compassion. Tadeo is a poor kid from a poor family whose only real chance in life so far has been inside the cage. We finally get around to the fight and the courtroom lights go down. The first time through, we watch the fight without interruption. In the semidarkness, I watch the jurors. The women are turned off by the sport's brutality. The men are thoroughly engrossed. During the rerun, I stop the tape each time Tadeo takes a shot in the face. The truth is that most of these were not that damaging and Crush scored only minor points with them. But to jurors who don't know any better, a punch to the face, especially one blown out of proportion by Oscar and me, becomes a near-lethal blow. Slowly, methodically, I count them. When they are displayed in such exaggerated manner, one can easily ask how in the world Tadeo stayed on his feet. With 1:20 to go in the second round, Crush is able to yank Tadeo's head down and bang it into his right knee. It's a nasty shot all right, but one that hardly fazed Tadeo. Now, though, Oscar and I make it look like the cause of permanent brain damage.

I stop the video after the end of the second round, and through carefully rehearsed questions and answers I elicit from Oscar his impressions of his fighter between rounds. The kid's eyes were glazed over. He could only grunt, not speak. He was unresponsive to questions fired at him by Norberto and Oscar. He, Oscar, thought about waving the ref over and stopping the fight.

I would put Norberto on the stand to verify these lies, but he has two felony convictions and would be humiliated by Mancini.

Left unsaid in this testimony is the fact that I was also in the corner. I was wearing my bright yellow "Tadeo Zapate" jacket and trying to act as though I was somehow needed. I have explained this to Max and Go Slow and assured them that I saw and heard nothing crucial. I was just a spectator; thus I cannot be considered a witness. Max and Go Slow know I'm here out of love and not money.

We watch the third round and count more blows to Tadeo's head. Oscar testifies that when the fight was over Tadeo thought he had one more round. He was out of it, barely conscious but still on his feet. After he attacked Sean King and was pulled off by Norberto and others, he was like an enraged animal, unsure of where he was or why he was being restrained. Thirty minutes later, as he was changing in the dressing room while the police watched and waited, he began to come around. He wanted to know what the cops were doing there. He asked who won the fight.

All in all, not a bad job of creating some doubt. However, even a casual viewing of all three rounds clearly shows a fight that was fairly even. Tadeo dished out as much damage as he absorbed.

Mancini gets nowhere on cross. Oscar sticks to the facts he has created. He was there, in the corner, talking to his fighter, and if he says the kid took too many shots to the head, so be it. Max can't prove otherwise.

Next I call our expert, Dr. Taslman, the retired psychiatrist who now works as a professional witness. He wears a black suit, crisp white shirt, tiny red bow tie, and with his horn-rimmed glasses and long, flowing gray hair he looks incredibly smart. I slowly walk him through his qualifications and tender him as an expert in the field of forensic psychiatry. Max has no objections.

I then ask Dr. Taslman to explain, in layman's terms, the legal concept of volitional insanity, the standard adopted by our state a decade ago. He smiles at me, then looks at the jurors in much the same way an old professor would enjoy chatting with his adoring students. He says, "Volitional insanity means simply that a person who is mentally healthy does something wrong, and at the time he knows it's wrong, but at that moment he is so mentally unbalanced, or deranged, he cannot prevent himself from doing it anyway. He knows it's wrong, but he cannot control himself and thereby commits the crime."

He has watched the fight many times, and the video of its aftermath. He has spent a few hours with Tadeo. During their first meeting, Tadeo told him he did not remember the attack on Sean King. Indeed, he remembered virtually nothing after the second round. However, during a later session, Tadeo seemed to recollect certain things that happened. For example, he said he remembered the smug look on Crush's face as his arm was raised in victory. He remembered the crowd screaming its disapproval of the decision. He remembered his brother Miguel yelling something. But he remembered nothing to do with the assault on the referee. Regardless, though, of what he remembered, he was blinded by emotion and had no choice but to attack. He had been robbed and the nearest official was Sean King.

Yes, in Dr. Taslman's opinion, Tadeo was so deranged he could not stop himself. Yes, he was legally insane, and therefore unaccountable for his actions.

And there is another, quite unusual factor in play here that makes the case unique. Tadeo was in a cage designed for fighting. He had just spent nine long minutes trading punches with another fighter. He makes his living punching people. To him, at that crucial moment, it was okay to settle the matter with more punches. Put in context, and in the environment of that instant, he felt as if he had no choice but to do what he did.

When I'm finished with Taslman, we break for lunch.

26.

I stop by Domestic Relations to check the court file. As expected, old Judge Leef has denied Judith's request for an emergency hearing, and has scheduled the matter four weeks from now. His order also states that regular visitation will continue unchanged. Take that, sweetheart.

Cliff, Partner, and I walk a few blocks to a diner and hide in a booth for a quick sandwich. The morning's testimony could not have gone better for Tadeo. All three of us are surprised at how well Oscar did on the stand, and how believable he was in telling the jurors that Tadeo had been knocked out, but was still standing. Few fight fans would believe that, but there are none on our jury. For $20,000, I expected Dr. Taslman to perform admirably, and he did. Cliff says the jurors are thinking now, with some doubt firmly planted. However, an acquittal is impossible. A hung jury is still our only chance. And it could be a long afternoon as Mancini goes after our expert.

Back in court, Max begins by asking, "Dr. Taslman, at what moment did the defendant become legally insane?"

"There is not always a clear beginning and ending. Obviously, Mr. Zapate became furious over the judges' decision awarding the fight to his opponent."

"So, before that moment, was he insane by your definition?"

"It's not clear. There is a strong likelihood that Mr. Zapate had been mentally impaired during the last few minutes of the fight. This is a very unusual situation, and it's not possible to know how clearly he was thinking before the decision was announced. It's pretty obvious, though, that he snapped quickly."

"How long was he legally insane?"

"I don't think it's possible to say."

"Okay, under your definition, when the defendant whirled around and struck Sean King with the first punch, was that an assault?"

"Yes."

"And punishable by some standard?"

"Yes."

"And excusable, in your opinion, because of your definition of legal insanity?"

"Yes."

"You've seen the video many times. It's clear that Sean King made no effort to defend himself once he fell to the deck and was sitting against the cage, right?"

"That appears to be the case."

"Do you need to see it again?"

"No, not at this time."

"So, after only two punches, Sean King is down and out, unable to protect himself, right?"

"That appears to be the case, yes."

"Ten punches later, his face is bleeding and basically pulverized. He cannot protect himself. The defendant has hit him twelve times around the eyes and forehead. Now, at that point, Doctor, was the defendant still legally insane?"

"He could not control himself, so the answer is yes."

Mancini looks at the judge and says, "Okay. I want to run the video again in slow motion." The lights are dimmed yet again, and everyone stares at the large screen. Max runs it in super slow-mo and announces loudly as each punch lands, "One! Two! He's down now. Three! Four! Five!"

I glance at the jurors. They may be tired of this footage but they're still captivated by it.

Max stops with blow number twelve and asks, "Now, Doctor, you're telling this jury that they're looking at a man who knows he's doing wrong, violating the law, but cannot physically or mentally stop himself. Is that right?" Max's tone is one of incredulity and mockery, and it's effective. What we're watching is a slaughter by one pissed-off fighter. Not a man driven insane.

"That's correct," Dr. Taslman says, not yielding an inch.

Thirteen, fourteen, fifteen, Max counts them off slowly and stops at twenty. Max calls out, "Now, at this point, Doc, is he still insane?"

"He is, yes."

Twenty-one, twenty-two, and bodies land on Tadeo as Norberto finally dives on and stops the carnage. Max asks, "How about now, Doc, they've pulled him off and the attack is over? At what point does the boy return to sanity?"

"It's hard to say."

"A minute later? An hour later?"

"It's hard to say."

"It's hard to say because you don't know, right? In your opinion, legal sanity is like a switch that flips on and off, rather conveniently for the defendant, right?"

"That's not what I said."

Max pushes a button and the screen disappears. The lights are brightened as everyone takes a breath. Max whispers to an assistant and picks up another legal pad covered with notes. He shuffles to the podium, glares at the witness, and asks, "What if he hit him thirty times, Dr. Taslman? You'd still diagnose him as legally insane?"

"Under the same set of facts, yes."

"Oh, we're talking about the same facts. Nothing has changed. What about forty times? Forty blows to the head of a man who's clearly unconscious. Still legally insane, Doc?"

"Yes."

"This defendant showed no signs of stopping after only twenty-two. What if he landed a hundred shots to the head, Doc? Still legally insane in your book?"

Taslman earns his money with "The greater number of punches is clearer evidence of a deranged mind."

27.

It's Friday afternoon and there's no way we can finish the trial today. Like most judges, Go Slow likes to jump-start the weekend. She warns the jurors about unauthorized contact and recesses early. As the jurors file out, Esteban Suarez glances my way one more time. It's as if he's still looking for the envelope. Bizarre.

I spend a few minutes with Tadeo and recap the week. He still insists on taking the stand, and I tell him that will probably happen Monday morning. I promise to stop by the jail on Sunday and go through his testimony. I repeat my warning that it's never a good idea for the accused to testify. He's taken away in handcuffs. I spend a few minutes with his mother and family and answer their questions. I'm still pessimistic but I try to hide it.

Miguel follows me out of the courtroom and down a long hallway. When no one is listening, he says, "Suarez is waiting. Contact confirmed. He'll take the money."

"Ten grand?" I ask, just to make sure.

"Sí, senor."

"Then go for it, Miguel, but just leave me out of it. I'm not bribing a juror."

"I guess then, senor, that I need a loan."

"Forget it. I don't make loans to clients, and I don't make loans that'll never be repaid. You're on your own, pal."

"But we took care of those two thugs for you."

I stop and glare at him. This is the first time he's mentioned Link's boys—Tubby and Razor. Slowly, I say, "For the record, Miguel, I know nothing about those two. If you whacked 'em, you did it on your own."

He's smiling and shaking his head. "No, senor, we did it as a favor for you." He nods to Partner in the distance. "He asked. We delivered. Now we need the favor returned."

I take a deep breath and stare at a huge stained-glass window the taxpayers paid for a century earlier. He has a point. Two dead thugs are worth more than ten grand, at least in the currency of the street. The breakdown comes with the communication. I didn't request two dead thugs. But now that I benefit from their demise, am I obligated to return the favor?

Suarez is probably wearing a wire and maybe even a camera. If the money can be traced to me, then I'm disbarred and headed for prison. I've had close calls before, and I prefer life on the outside. I swallow hard and say, "Sorry, Miguel, but I will not be involved."

I turn and he grabs my arm. I shake him off as Partner approaches. Miguel says, "You'll be sorry, senor."

"Is that a threat?"

"No. A promise."

28.

There are fights tonight, but I've seen enough bloodshed for one week. I need to find another sport, and at the moment it happens to be chasing the most lovely Naomi Tarrant. Since we're still meeting on the sly, or at least afraid of being seen by someone who might recognize her as a teacher, we are visiting dark bars and low-end restaurants. Tonight we go to a new place, a Thai restaurant east of town, far away from the school where Naomi teaches Starcher. We are confident we will not be seen by anyone we know.

Not quite. Naomi sees her first, and since she can't believe it, she asks me to verify. It's not easy because we don't want to get caught. The restaurant is sufficiently dark and it has a series of meandering nooks and alcoves. It's a great place to hide and have a meal without seeing many people. As Naomi returns from the ladies' room, she sees three booths in the rear of a dining room. Seated in one of them, side by side and deep in conversation, are Judith and another woman. Not Ava, the current partner, but someone else. A curtain of beads is partially closed at the booth and blocking some of the view, but she is certain it's Judith. Common sense would say that the two women, if only friends or associates or colleagues, would be sitting across the table from each other. But these two women are shoulder to shoulder and lost in another world, according to Naomi.

I sneak around to the men's room, duck behind some fake potted plants on a shelf, and see what I desperately want to see. I hustle back to the table and confirm it all with Naomi.

I consider leaving and avoiding an embarrassing situation. We don't want Judith to see us, and I'm absolutely certain she doesn't want us to see her.

I consider sending Naomi to the car, then crashing Judith's little rendezvous. How cool it would be to watch her melt and start lying. I'll ask about Ava, send my regards.

I consider Starcher and what this might mean in the war being waged by his biological parents. His mothers aren't legally married so I suppose it's okay for one or both to see other women, though I seriously doubt they have an open relationship. How am I supposed to know the rules? But if Ava finds out, there will be even more warfare, more grief for the kid. And more ammunition for me.

I consider calling Partner and getting him to follow Judith, maybe take some photos.

As I consider all of this and sip a whiskey sour, Judith appears from around the corner and walks straight to our table. In the distance I see her friend leave hurriedly through the front door, one last furtive, tell-all glance over her shoulder. Judith, in full-bitch mode, says, "Well, well, didn't expect to see you here."

I'm not about to allow her to intimidate Naomi, who's temporarily stricken. I say, "Didn't expect to see you either. Here alone?"

"Yes," she says. "Just picking up some takeout."

"Oh really. Then who's the girl?"

"What girl?"

"The girl in the booth. Short sandy hair, buzzed on one side in the current fad. The girl who just broke her neck getting out of the front door. Does Ava know about her?"

"Oh, that girl. She's just a friend. Does the school allow its teachers to date its parents?"

"It's frowned upon but not prohibited," Naomi says coolly.

"Does Ava allow you to date other people?" I ask.

"Wasn't a date. She's just a friend."

"Then why did you just lie about her? Why did you lie about the takeout?"

She ignores me and glares at Naomi. "I guess I should report this to the school."

"Go ahead," I say. "I'll report it to Ava. Is she keeping Starcher while you're out fooling around?"

"I'm not fooling around and my son is none of your business right now. You blew it last weekend."

A little Thai guy in a suit eases over and with a big smile asks, "Everything okay here?"

"Yes, she's just leaving," I say. I look at Judith. "Please. We're trying to order."

"See you in court," she hisses and turns on her heels. I watch her leave and she does not take any food with her. The little Thai guy slides away, still smiling. We drain our drinks and eventually look at the menus.

After a few minutes, I say, "Our secret is safe. She won't say anything to the school because she knows I'll call Ava."

"You'd really do that?"

"In the blink of an eye. This is a war, Naomi, and there are no rules, no thoughts of fighting fair."

"Do you want custody of Starcher?"

"No. I'm not a good enough father. But I do want to remain relevant in his life. Who knows? One day he and I might be friends."

We spend the night at her place and sleep late Saturday morning. We're both exhausted. We awake to the sounds of heavy rain and decide to fix omelets and eat in bed.

29.

The last witness for the defense is the defendant himself. Before he is called on Monday morning, I hand the judge and the prosecutor a letter I've written to Tadeo Zapate. Its purpose is to inform him in writing that he is testifying against the advice of his attorney. I grilled him for two hours the day before, and he thinks he's ready.

He swears to tell the truth, smiles nervously at the jury, and immediately learns the frightful lesson that the view from the witness stand is quite intimidating. Everyone is gawking and waiting to hear what he might possibly say in his defense. A court reporter will record every word. The judge is scowling down, as if she's ready for a quick reprimand. The prosecutor is eager to pounce. His mother far away in the back row looks terribly worried. He takes a deep breath.

I walk him through his background—family, education, employment, lack of criminal record, boxing career, and his success in mixed martial arts. The jury, along with everyone else in the courtroom, is sick of the video, so I won't show it. Sticking to our script, we talk about the fight and he does an adequate job of describing what it was like getting hit so many times. He and I know that Crush did not land many serious blows, but no one on the jury understands this. He tells the jury he doesn't remember the end of the fight, but can recollect a fuzzy image of his opponent raising his arms in a victory that he didn't deserve. Yes, he snapped, though he can't really recall everything. He was overwhelmed by a sense of injustice. His career was gone, stolen. He vaguely remembers the referee raising Crush's arm, then everything went black. The next thing he remembered, he was in the dressing room, and two cops were watching him. He asked the cops who won the fight, and one of them said, "Which fight?" They put handcuffs on him and explained he was under arrest for aggravated assault. He was baffled by this, couldn't believe what was happening. At the jail, another cop told him Sean King was in critical condition. He, Tadeo, began crying.

Even today, he still can't believe it. His voice cracks a bit and he wipes something from his left eye. He's not a very good actor.

As I sit down, Mancini bounces to his feet and calls out the first question: "So, Mr. Zapate, how many times have you gone insane?" It's a brilliant opening, a great line delivered with just enough sarcasm.

He proceeds to make a fool out of Tadeo. When was the first time you went insane? How long did it last? Anybody get hurt the first time? Do you always black out when you go insane? Have you seen a doctor for your insanity? *No!* Why not! Since you attacked Sean King, have you been evaluated by a doctor, one not connected to this trial? Does insanity run in your family?

After thirty minutes of this assault, the word "insanity" means nothing. It's a joke.

Tadeo works hard to stay cool, but he can't help himself. Mancini is practically laughing at him. The jurors seem amused.

Max asks about his record as an amateur boxer. Twenty-four wins, seven losses. Max says, "Now, correct me if I'm wrong, but five years ago when you were seventeen and fighting in the Golden Gloves district tournament, you lost a split decision to a man named Corliss Beane. That right?"

"Yes."

"Very tough fight, right?"

"Yes."

"Were you upset by the decision?"

"I didn't like it, thought it was wrong, thought I won the fight."

"Did you go insane?"

"No."

"Did you black out?"

"No."

"Did you in any way voice your frustration with the decision?"

"I don't think so."

"Well, do you remember it or did you lose your memory again?"

"I remember it."

"While you were still in the ring, did you hit anybody?"

Tadeo shoots me a guilty look that betrays him, but says, "No."

Mancini takes a deep breath, shakes his head as if he hates to do what he's about to do, and says, "Your Honor, I have another bit of video that I think might help us here. It's the end of the fight five years ago with Corliss Beane."

I stand and say, "Your Honor, I know nothing about this. It was not disclosed to me."

Max is ready because he's been planning this ambush for weeks. He says, with great confidence, "Your Honor, it wasn't disclosed because that was not required. The State is not offering the video as proof of this defendant's guilt; therefore, under our

Rule 92F, there's no disclosure. Rather, the State is offering the video to challenge the credibility of this witness."

"Could I at least see it first before the jury sees it?" I ask, slowly.

"That sounds reasonable," Go Slow responds. "Let's take a fifteen-minute recess."

In chambers, we watch the video: Tadeo and Corliss Beane in the center of the ring with the ref, who raises Beane's right hand in victory; Tadeo yanks away from the ref, walks to his corner, yelling something in an angry fit; he stomps around the ring, becoming more unhinged with each second; he walks to the ropes, screams at the judges, and inadvertently bumps into Corliss Beane, who's minding his own business and savoring the win; others are in the ring and someone starts pushing; the ref steps between the two fighters and Tadeo shoves him; the ref, a big guy, shoves back; for a second it looks as though the ring is on the verge of chaos, but someone grabs Tadeo and pulls him away, kicking and screaming.

Again, the camera doesn't lie. Tadeo looks like a sore loser, a hothead, a brat, a dangerous man who doesn't care if he starts a brawl.

Go Slow says, "Looks relevant to me."

30.

I watch the jurors as they watch the video. Several shake their heads. When it's over, the lights come up, and Max gleefully returns to the mock-insanity crap and hammers away. Tadeo's credibility is thoroughly trashed. I cannot resurrect him on redirect.

The defense rests. Mancini calls his first rebuttal witness, a shrink named Wafer. He works for the state mental health department and has credentials that cannot be questioned. He went to colleges in this state and has our accent. He is not the brilliant expert from afar like Taslman, but he's quite effective. He's watched the videos, all of them, and he's spent six hours with the defendant, more time than Taslman.

I haggle with Wafer until noon but score little. As we are breaking for lunch, Mancini grabs me and asks, "Can I talk to your client?"

"About what?"

"The deal, man."

"Sure."

We step to the defense table where Tadeo is sitting. Max leans down and says in a low voice, "Look, dude, I'm still offering five years, which means eighteen months. Manslaughter. If you say no, you really are insane because you're about to get twenty years."

Tadeo seems to ignore him. He just smiles, shakes his head no.

He's even more confident now because Miguel has found the cash and delivered the envelope to Suarez. This, I will learn only after it's too late.

31.

After lunch we meet in chambers, where Go Slow has on display a plastic plate covered with sliced carrots and celery, as if we're interrupting her meal. I suspect it's all for show. She asks, "Mr. Rudd, what about the plea bargain? I understand the deal is still on the table."

I shrug and say, "Yes, Judge, I have discussed it with my client, as has Mr. Mancini. The kid won't budge."

She says, "Okay, we're off the record here. Now that I've seen the evidence, I'm leaning toward a longer sentence, something like twenty years. I didn't buy the insanity stuff, neither did the jury. It was a vicious attack and he knew exactly what he was doing. I think twenty years is appropriate."

"May I pass this along to my client? Off the record, of course?"

"Please do." She drowns some celery in table salt, looks at Mancini, and asks, "What's next?"

Max says, "I have just one more witness, Dr. Levondowski, but I'm not sure we need him. What do you think, Judge?"

Go Slow bites the end of a stalk. "Your call, but I think the jury is ready." Chomp, chomp. "Mr. Rudd?"

"You're asking me?"

"Oh why not?" Max says. "Put yourself in my shoes and make the call."

"Well, Levondowski is just going to repeat what Wafer said. I've crossed him before and he's okay, but I think Wafer is a far better witness. I'd leave it at that."

Max says, "I think you're right. We'll rest."

United, a real team.

During Max's closing argument, I keep glancing at Esteban Suarez, who seems to be thoroughly captivated by his feet. He's withdrawn into a cocoon and appears to hear nothing. Something has changed with this guy, and for a second I wonder if Miguel has managed to get to him. If not with cash, then with threats, intimidation. Maybe he's promised a few pounds of cocaine.

Max does a nice job of recapping the case. Mercifully, he does not show that damned video again. He drives home the undeniable point that Tadeo might not have planned his deadly assault on Sean King, but he clearly intended to inflict severe physical injury. He didn't intend to kill the referee, but in fact he did. He could have thrown one punch, or two, and stopped. Guilty of assault but no major crime. But no! Twenty-two vicious shots to the head of a man who could not defend himself. Twenty-two blows delivered by a highly trained fighter whose admitted goal was to see every opponent leave the ring on a stretcher. Well, he achieved his goal. Sean King left on a stretcher and never woke up.

Max fights off the natural prosecutorial tendency to beat the drum too long. He's got the jury and he can sense it. I think everybody senses it, perhaps with the exception of my client.

I begin by saying that Tadeo Zapate is not a murderer. He's lived on the streets, seen his share of violence, even lost a brother to senseless gang wars. He's seen it all and wants no part of it. That's why his record is spotless: no history of violence outside the ring. I pace back and forth in front of the jury box, looking at each juror, trying to connect. Suarez looks like he wants to crawl into a hole.

I play for sympathy and touch slightly on the issue of insanity. I ask the jury for a not-guilty verdict, or, in the alternative, manslaughter. When I return to the defense table, Tadeo has moved his chair as far away from mine as possible.

Judge Fabineau instructs the jurors, and they retire at 3:00 p.m.

The waiting begins. I ask a bailiff if Tadeo can visit with his family in the courtroom while the jury is out. He confers with his colleagues and then reluctantly agrees. Tadeo steps through the bar and takes a seat on the front bench. His mother, a sister, and some nieces and nephews gather around him and everybody has a good cry. Mrs. Zapate has not physically touched her son in many months and she can't keep her hands off him.

I leave the courtroom, find Partner, and head for a coffee bar down the street.

32.

At 5:15, the jurors file back into the courtroom, and there is not a single smile among them. The foreman hands the verdict to a bailiff, who hands it to the judge. She reads it, very slowly, and asks the defendant to please stand. I stand with him. She clears her throat and reads, "We, the jury, find the defendant guilty of second-degree murder in the death of Sean King."

Tadeo utters a soft groan and drops his head. Someone in the Zapate clan gasps from the back row. We sit down as the judge polls the jurors. One by one, all guilty, unanimous. She congratulates them on a fine job, tells them their checks for jury duty will be in the mail, and dismisses them. When they're gone, she sets deadlines for posttrial motions and such, and gives a date a month from now for sentencing. I scribble this down and ignore my client. He ignores me right back as he wipes his eyes. Bailiffs surround him and slap on handcuffs. He leaves without a word.

As the courtroom thins out, the Zapate family makes a slow exit. Miguel has his arm around his mother, who is distraught. Once they're outside in the hallway, and within clear view of some reporters and TV cameras, three cops in suits grab Miguel and tell him he's under arrest.

Obstruction of justice, bribery, and jury tampering. Suarez was indeed wearing a wire.

33.

Since I lost, I avoid the reporters. My phone is buzzing, so I turn it off. Partner and I go to a dark bar to lick our wounds. I knock back almost an entire pint of ale before either of us speaks. He starts with "Say, Boss, how close did you come to bribing Suarez?"

"I thought about it."

"I know you did. I could tell."

"But something wasn't right. Plus, Mancini was playing it straight, not cheating. When the good guys start cheating, then I have no choice. But Mancini didn't have to. We tried a clean case, which is unusual."

I finish the pint and order another. Partner has had two sips of his. Miss Luella frowns on drinking and will say something if she smells it.

"What happens to Miguel?" he asks.

"Looks like he'll be spending time with his brother."

"You gonna defend him?"

"Hell no. I'm sick of the Zapate boys."

"You think he'll sing about Link's thugs?"

"I doubt it. He's in enough trouble as it is. A couple of murders won't help him much."

We order a basket of fries and call it dinner.

After we leave the bar, I keep the van and drop Partner off at his apartment. It's Monday and Naomi is busy grading tests. "Make sure Starcher gets an A," I tell her. "Always," she says. I need to be loved but she can't play tonight. I finally go home, and the place feels cold and lonely. I change into jeans and walk down to The Rack, where I drink beer, smoke a cigar, and shoot eight ball for two hours, all alone. At ten I check my phone. Every Zapate in town is looking for me: mother, an aunt, a sister, and Tadeo and Miguel from jail. Seems they need me now. I'm fed up with these people, but I know they're not going away.

Two reporters are calling. Mancini wants to have a drink. Why, I have no idea.

And there is a voice mail from Arch Swanger. Condolences on the big loss. How in hell?

I need to leave town. At midnight, I load the van with some clothes, the golf clubs, and half a case of small-batch bourbon. I flip a coin, head north, and last for two hours before I almost fall asleep. I stop at a budget motel and pay forty bucks for one night. I'll be on a golf course, somewhere, by noon, all alone.

This time I'm not sure I'm going back.

ROGUE
LAWYER

QUESTIONS FOR DISCUSSION

1. Sebastian claims to defend certain clients because "he hates injustice." However, multiple times throughout the novel, Sebastian has a chance to do the "right thing" and help other people, but he doesn't due to his obligations as an attorney. How does Sebastian's hatred of injustice get hampered by attorney-client privilege and his obligations to his clients? Do you agree with some of his choices?

2. How did the first-person narration from Sebastian's point of view impact your opinion of Sebastian? Did you trust him? Would you trust him more or less if the story came from a different point of view?

3. Organized crime plays a role in the ultimate outcome of the novel. Sebastian mentions two mobsters that he has represented: Link Scanlon and Dewey Knutt. What are the differences in these two clients for Sebastian? Would you represent either of these men?

4. Several times throughout the novel Sebastian claims he doesn't work for free. However, he represents Arch Swanger for free after his check doesn't clear and he represents Tadeo Zapate for free because he cares for him and also receives favors from his cousins. Are working for free and working in exchange for favors the same thing?

5. More than once throughout the novel Sebastian has to deal with police misconduct. During these instances of misconduct, Sebastian normally has to resort to something shady or illegal in order to defeat this police misconduct. What's the difference between the police's misconduct and Sebastian's? Do you think Sebastian's perception changes after Kemp and his men kidnap Sebastian's son?

6. Judith refers to Sebastian as a "pathetic father" more than once. Sebastian even says to Naomi that "he's not a good enough father" to have sole custody. However, when Starcher is kidnapped, Sebastian is willing to do whatever it takes to get him back safely. Did your perception of Sebastian as a father change after seeing what he did and what he was willing to do to get Starcher back? Do you think, given the dangerous nature of his work, that he should be involved in Starcher's life at all?

7. How are power and publicity linked throughout the novel?

8. We're introduced to many lawyers in this book (Max, Judith, Huver, Sebastian). Most of them are inclined to play dirty or circumvent the law to try to get what they want throughout the book. Is it possible to stay completely clean as a lawyer in this book as Max appears to be?

9. How does the novel define injustice? Do you agree? Do you think it's impossible to avoid injustice entirely in a lawyer's line of work?

10. Sebastian goes the extra mile for his clients. Were you surprised that he used the cops kidnapping his son as leverage in the settlement talks for Doug Renfro? Would you have done

the same thing? Would you have been okay with letting the cops that kidnapped your child walk away unscathed?

11. Given the things he's willing to do for his clients and how hard he fights for them, were you surprised by Sebastian's actions during Tadeo's trial at the end, especially when Tadeo was somebody he claimed to care about?

12. At the end of the novel, were you surprised that Sebastian wouldn't bribe Suarez? Given some of the ways in which he "cheats" throughout the novel, why do you think Sebastian drew the line at jury tampering?

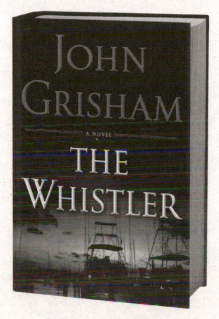